Greenwich Secrets

Greenwich Secrets

Claudette Rothman
Gerald L. Jones

To order additional copies of this book, contact:
Xlibris Corporation
1-888-795-4274
www.Xlibris.com
Orders@Xlibris.com
76177

Contents

Introduction

Greenwich, Connecticut, is a town well-known to the rest of America as a place where the average household income exceeds the national average by a hefty amount; in fact it has one of the highest per capita income levels in the nation and probably the world. But when one visits this town of just over sixty thousand residents it is surprising how commonplace and ordinary it appears. The main street is called Greenwich Avenue; and on it one can find delis, shoe shops, and pharmacies, nothing to suggest the affluence found within its borders. But when in Greenwich it is quite possible that the woman standing next to you in the CVS drugstore might be the former Shahess of Iran or a member of the Trump family.

The wealthy citizens of Greenwich are a people of excess: they drink too much, they eat too much, they drive their Bentleys too fast, and finally, they screw too much and with too many partners. It is all a matter of not just having money but using it to buy whatever they want and buy it in abundance. Thousand-dollar-an-ounce caviar is good only until a neighbor buys fifteen-hundred-dollar-an-ounce caviar. The family Mercedes-Benz becomes passé when a business partner buys a Rolls-Royce. And one's beloved spouse ceases to excite one when a younger, more amply built stranger shows one some special attention.

Everything in Greenwich is up for grabs to the highest bidder, and the bids get pretty high when interested parties count their bank accounts in the billions. That is not to say that Greenwich is totally different from anywhere else in America. Every place has its standard of pleasure and excess, but none compare with the excess in this small village of high rollers, nor can the price tag attached to the pleasures elsewhere match those here. For the moneyed people of Greenwich the town is their home base, but the world is their playground. There is an old saying, "You never should defecate where you eat," and the Greenwich blue bloods live by that rule. Well, almost all of them do; those that don't often end up in the headlines sooner or later.

There also are the working people of Greenwich who make a living by dirtying their hands, but even they give off an air of superiority not found in most municipalities. It is as if they are saying, "We may be workers, but our bosses are far superior to your bosses." Greenwich is funny that way. Not too many years ago the name was pronounced Green-witch, but the citizenry found such usage very pedestrian and adopted the English pronunciation. Remnants of the old name can be found in such quaint affectations as witch-shaped weather vanes appropriately painted green. But when a person and even a town comes of age and into its own, childish ways must be left behind; and since the financial boon days of the 1980s, this town has taken itself seriously—very seriously.

With great wealth comes many things—luxury cars, club memberships, and all the other accoutrements of money. But there are things which do not automatically come with riches, things like morality, a conscience, and most of all class. In an ordinary town anywhere across America there are people of all classes who have problems and make mistakes; some are minor and some not. Either way they end up making the local papers, or at the very least the rounds of the local gossip circuit. Dirty laundry is part of human nature, and likewise it is human nature for others to capitalize on it. One would expect such an axiom to hold true in any place and at any time, but in the apt words of the devil in *Porgy and Bess*, "That ain't necessarily so."

Where you find great wealth you will also find an equal amount of wrongdoing, be it monetary, sexual, or whatever your preference might be. But in this place, however, the dirty laundry stays hidden, quietly stashed away or more often ignored thanks to a healthy bit of cash applied adeptly to the right sources. Anyone can be bought, if the price is right, but the cost of silence is much cheaper than you might suspect, and in a place like Greenwich there is always enough cash floating about to keep lips sealed and ears closed. Every place that people gather to live together has its share of secrets, as does Greenwich, but its secrets are somewhat larger and juicier than most. One might even say they can be almost unique, but it could definitely be said that Greenwich secrets, if not unique, are at the very least quite distinct.

As is true in any civilized nation there are some secrets which by law need to be revealed, judged, and punished if necessary. Such a secret would, of course, be murder. When someone engages in the practice of murder, it is in their best interest that the said murder be kept eternally in the shadows. So it is in Greenwich where murder is rare, and the few that happen usually go unsolved for many years because of the nearly impenetrable veil of silence, which is a requisite part of the ways of the rich and famous.

9

One case in point being the Martha Moxley case where the brutal murder of a wealthy teenage girl remained unsolved for decades, until the somewhat unorthodox investigation of a novelist brought a conclusion to the case, albeit a guilty verdict which some still question.

The story of Elizabeth Dawson of Greenwich, Connecticut, is a story in which one woman's curiosity and sense of justice tore off the covering of paid silence and revealed a case in which murder, adultery, and conspiracy would rock the staid and rarified atmosphere of one of America's most pampered communities. The mayhem reached to the highest and most refined levels of society. Ms. Dawson is no stranger to luxury and wealth, but she is from the stock which earned their wealth and carried with them the sensibilities and values of the hardworking and honest people from which she came.

A woman with resources, a sense of purpose, and the means to pursue that which interests her is a deadly combination for the wrongdoer who happens to fall into the environs of her interest. Such was the case with a media-ignored murder case just across the border from the refined precincts of Greenwich—a murder meant to look like a random act of senseless violence in a town located on the "wrong side of the tracks." But to the keen eye and inquisitive intellect of our heroine, there was much more to the story, much more detail lying beneath the layers of old money freely spent to bury the truth. Sex, betrayal, corruption, and murder are a toxic mix which, no matter how deeply buried, will eventually boil up to the surface and, with a little digging, can turn into a geyser mightier than Old Faithful.

There are times when very ordinary people rise to very extraordinary circumstances, and this is such a situation. Elizabeth Dawson was an exceptional person in her

10

element. She was a keen businesswoman, an exemplary mother, and a generous leader of society; but crime and criminal investigation were not her forte. Yet she rose to the occasion and, as you will see, took on a case which the police, by neglect or design, had relegated to the cold case file. Most murder mysteries revolve around two central figures—the murderer and the investigator. This story will be not different as together we follow the intrepid Ms. Dawson, as she comes up against a very odd case and, in spite of the disadvantage of being a civilian in police matters, takes on a powerful man and his family who have the influence and cash flow to lead the police, the media, and the people down the garden path.

It is a story which could have happened in Bakersfield, California; Gainesville, Florida; Plano, Texas; or Bloomington, Indiana, but it did not happen in any of those places. It took place in a swanky, self-satisfied small town which believes it is situated on the very top of the world. There are no moral judgments being made here; only observations about attitudes and practices which complicate getting to the truth of a matter, especially when the matter in question is one which the "right" people do not want the truth to be exposed. Having huge amounts of money and an elitist outlook on life does not constitute being a bad person or using one's money for evil purposes, but one must admit that doing wrong and covering up the wrongdoing becomes exponentially easier with the application of cold hard cash. And it cannot be stressed forcefully enough that the Greenwich evildoers in question had such an abundance of filthy lucre as to make any search for justice a daunting task for even the most professional of detectives, let alone a private citizen armed simply with her laptop and a nose for news.

Chapter One

Murder as a Faux Pas

Did you ever have one of those days? You know the type. A day when you wake up praying for some kind of distraction or diversion from the bullshit which life throws at you. Well, that is exactly what Elizabeth Dawson was trying to find when she decided to try her hand at Internet blogging. Elizabeth and her husband, Joseph, were residents of the Connecticut enclave of the affluent known as Greenwich. And they were very much a part of the affluence—so much so that six months after the Bernie Madoff Ponzi scheme scandal they were still licking their financial wounds and trying to get their minds off their losses from the fiasco. The loss of millions of dollars is no small irritant; and Elizabeth, known to the locals as Lizzy, was ripe for a nonsensical hobby to distract her from the financial maelstrom surrounding her life.

To really get to know Lizzy you have to take a look at where and how she lives. Let's start with her place of residence. Greenwich is the sort of place well insulated from the humdrum of the poverty, the need, and the hard work most of us know as part of everyday life. It is a real-world Shangri-la of plenty tucked between the ethnically diverse and financially hard-pressed towns of Port Chester, New York, and Bridgeport, Connecticut. It is a tailored bed of roses between patches of ragweed on life's highway. Lizzy and Joe liked living among those roses, and the prospect of wreck and ruin was a very unnerving one. So Lizzy began a mental inventory of activities which would distract her and amuse her and might actually allow her to find some lighthearted fulfillment. The tried-and-true Greenwich distractions such as the garden club or the slightly more exotic mushroom picking club were too tired and staid for the contemporarily minded Lizzy. In fact it may have been the trendy appeal of the Internet which sparked the idea of blogging into Lizzy's mind.

Once settled in on the idea of creating a blog, Lizzy decided upon a spicy name for the blog and hit upon the title "GreenwichSecrets.com." Then she began to explore the aspects of what she could do with it, beyond distraction and amusement. There might actually be some social relevance buried beneath the gossip and chatter of the "normal" blog scene. It was this desire to do some good while having a bit of fun that caused Lizzy to stumble upon a story that would come to consume her intellect and her free time. In an effort to find interesting and appealing content, most bloggers scour the news organs to find items for inclusion in their sites. For every premium item one expects to wade through hundreds of examples of inanity and irrelevance. But like lightning, a prime story strikes in a flash; and if not caught by a practiced lens, it can be gone equally quickly.

To the untrained eye of an amateur blogger such a story will in all probability be lost, but Lizzy felt something deep and strong go off in her being when she caught sight of this story. The photo of an attractive young man caught her attention and might have been clicked past were it not for two details in the headline. The first being the bold word "MURDER" and the other being the location of said murder, Port Chester, New York. A handsome blond man killed just over on the wrong side of the tracks in the neighboring town. Those details seemed enough to warrant a closer look. Lizzy held no great promise for this news item—probably just a businessman mugged and killed in the seedy nearby town. While Greenwich averaged a murder every ten years or so, Port Chester was quite another story, but their high crime rate rarely spilled over the nearby state and town lines.

No place on earth is without its share of sleaze, but people in this burg like to tell themselves that they are different. This is the kind of place where people don't fuck, they copulate; like the time the local Catholic priest copulated with dozens of preteen boys. That was one of the messier little episodes in town history. Embarrassing episodes make life interesting, even a bit dangerous, but murder is another matter altogether. Murder is a dirty business, too dirty and sordid to be tolerated in this place, and among this august body of citizens. Murder is bad news anywhere, but here it is more than tragic; it is a social faux pas.

This particular murder had a twist to it. The victim may have been found in the streets of Port Chester, but there was a Greenwich connection, in fact a rather major one. Beyond the headline and the pretty picture there was more than a hint of scandal. There seemed to be a link, a romantic link, between the dead man and a member of a prominent Greenwich family, the family of J. Richard Randolph, a major player in the financial district in Manhattan and a pillar of Greenwich society.

They say a trained news reporter can smell a story across a city, but it did not take a nose for news to catch the smell coming from *this* story. Lizzy raised an eyebrow and ironically gave a little sniff at the air as she hit the print button and started her way down a trail leading to God knows where. A bit of casual amusement was about to obliterate thoughts of Ponzi schemes, market downturns, and dwindling assets. There was no way to know where she was going with this, but Lizzy knew that often the best part of travel was the going and not necessarily the arriving.

Lizzy was not the typical rich matron. In fact at a young and fit forty years of age, she was the farthest thing from what people think of as a matron. She and Joe had taken a modest newlywed nest egg and through wise and lucky investments, and some hard work, turned it into a respectable fortune. Their $10,000,000 mansion sat on a tranquil patch of backcountry property complete with a shallow pond and shady trees reminiscent of a Louisiana bayou. Theirs was a stately home with a dignity that befitted old money. But for all of its grace and charm it was a beehive of activity thanks to the bustling lives of Lizzy and Joe and their two sons, Troy and Scott. Despite two teenage sons the house was an immaculate sanctuary for the family, the kind of place that would put Martha Stewart to shame. Their home was many things, but it was the last place one would look for an Internet detective, well, any kind of detective for that matter.

Life for Lizzy and her immediate and extended family seemed very normal and almost carefree, save for the effects of the worldwide recession which loomed large over their futures. But that was, in fact, the very reason that she reached out to find a way to forget the situation and focus on something new and different.

16

Lizzy's personal life was always a whirlwind of family and social commitments, but things had slowed down a bit since the financial downturn had cooled her personal business. She had studied interior design at a prestigious northeastern college and for a time enjoyed a sizable client base of billionaires, politicians, professional athletes, and entertainment figures.

Unfortunately when money is tight, if that phrase can be applied to billionaires, one of the first household budget items to be sacrificed is redecorating. As hard as it is to accept, these are times when the one-year-old $10,000 divan will just have to make due for another year or, God forbid, two! If times were not good for the stock market, then they were even worse for the field of interior design. Even more disturbing was the recent relocations of several of her clients—household downsizing one might call it. Not to mention those who had lost everything and could no longer be found in town. With fewer and fewer houses to redesign, Lizzy found herself devoting more and more time to her blogging, filling page after page with news items of merit; but her mind constantly returned to this mysterious story of death and, perhaps, intrigue just over the border in New York State.

Lizzy sat in a chaise overlooking the pond one warm afternoon, her Mac Notebook in, appropriately enough, her lap as she let her mind wander over the facts she had gathered from the blog news item. She tried to piece together the circumstances and the connections which were beginning to meld from her study of the obvious information before her and the pertinent bits of detail which she had gathered through her research and a bit of old-fashioned social gossip. What was emerging was a picture of a fairly normal, if broken, family and a stranger who came in contact with them by a none-too-unusual series of events. She glanced at her pad filled with scribbled notes and came across the word "normalcy" followed by a question mark just above a column of facts concerning the Randolph family.

She chuckled to herself as she said the word out loud. Normalcy. What exactly did that word mean? She knew the dictionary definition, and she even recalled that it was a term invented by Warren Harding in the presidential campaign of 1920. At the moment it sounded rather political and very artificial, especially when applied to a family. How normal was any family? Was the Randolph family "normal"? Or for that matter could she honestly say that her family was normal? Didn't popular culture now tell us that all families are to one extent or another dysfunctional? How dysfunctional might the Randolphs be? And dysfunctional in what ways? The annoying clatter of a gaggle of Canada geese landing in the pond roused her from her musings on families, and she headed back to the house to start dinner for her "normal" family.

Joe and Lizzy enjoyed a quiet dinner, chatting pleasantly over glasses of a delightful Chablis while Troy and Scott ate in the den in front of the television. How much more normal could a family be? Although not openly discussed the nagging question of family gnawed at the back of Lizzy's mind. After a quick cleanup of the dinner dishes assisted by Joe, and a quick peck on the cheek and playful pat on the bottom, Lizzy headed for the library. Off to check the day's e-mails, hoping for responses to some subtle questions she had floated to local friends concerning the Randolph family. She was not disappointed when she heard the familiar male voice resound from her computer: "You've got mail." She sighed contently as she settled into the comfy leather desk chair and prepared to sort the juicy from the mundane e-mails filling her computer screen. This looked to be a rewarding evening of reading.

Lizzy's semi-reclined posture sprang to rigid attention as she opened an e-mail which bore the subject line "Randolph Hedge Fund—Trouble in Paradise?" The e-mail was from a friend and client who happened to belong to the Bentley Cove Club, an elite local yacht club where Richard and Suzette Randolph held membership. Mixed with the elation of a possible revelation in "the Case," as Lizzy now mentally called it, was a sinking feeling of dread. Joe had placed a fairly large portion of their assets in the Randolph Fund, and a wave of financial unease swept through Lizzy as she read the contents of the e-mail. Would this news add to the worry which she was trying so hard to escape from? Was more of their way of life in jeopardy than she had suspected? The comments in the e-mail were vague and concluded with a request for a luncheon date where matters could be discussed more discreetly. Lizzy placed a finger lightly over the delete key as thoughts ran through her mind of ending her blog and retreating to membership in the garden club. Would continuing with the Case bring more unpleasant, even disastrous, news for her life?

From nowhere a feeling of resolve and courage entered Lizzy's soul as she hit the reply button and began to type a response to the e-mail. With fingers that still trembled ever so slightly she composed a message agreeing to a luncheon date the following Thursday at the Barcelona restaurant, a Spanish eatery which was one of her favorites. If she was going to hear bad news, at the very least she would hear it while eating a gourmet meal, a nice paella perhaps, and sipping an icy sangria. Damn it! There had to be some pleasure left for her even if that pleasure might be fleeting! Reading more e-mails became

suddenly tedious, and she noticed that her comfy desk
chair now seemed too hard and cold. She managed to
delete a few dozen pieces of junk mail before she decided
to give up for the evening and call it an early night. Until
she knew more she would put on a brave face; there was
no need to worry Joe just yet. It might all turn out to be
nothing, and if it was indeed more bad news, it could
wait . . . at least until next Thursday.

The next few days were very difficult for Lizzy. She
tried to remain cheerful and unaffected by the financial
sword of Damocles hanging over her head, but her mood
had soured, and her temper became acute. Spending
more and more time pond-side with her laptop she
aroused the notice of her husband and sons, but they
gave her space in an attempt to ride out this rare episode
of ill humor. Lizzy's mind was not idle even during this
time of agitation and angst. She began to jot notes on
her leather-bound pad concerning the Randolphs. They
were former clients, who had hired her to redecorate their
home just last year, but they had never hit it off with
each other, and the relationship remained on a purely
professional level. Suzette Randolph was by far the more
congenial half of the middle-aged couple. Richard, who
was known as Jack, a shortened form of his actual first
name of Jonathan, was a haughty and barely civil man of
forty-seven years of age.

A few years ago the Randolphs had been the first
family of Greenwich. Jack had served a single term as
the town's first selectman, a New England municipal
office roughly equivalent to the office of mayor elsewhere.
His foray into politics consisted of a single term because
he held the public in such disdain that it disgusted him
to be called their "public servant." The most notable
event of his staunchly Republican administration was a

distasteful episode regarding the town's magnificent park and beach, known as Todd's Point. A group of wealthy Greenwich ladies had been forcibly escorted off the beach where they had planned to convene a weekly exercise group. The official reason given by the first selectman's spokesperson for the police action was said to be the lack of a permit. However, all levels of town society knew that the real reason was the fact that the ladies were wealthy African Americans. Jack's feeling toward African Americans was the town government's worst-kept secret. Lizzy remembered engaging in polite conversation with Jack when measuring his den and home office for remodeling. The pleasantries turned to politics which the progressive Lizzy knew would be trying at best. The early presidential primaries had just been completed, and Lizzy was an early and strong supporter of the young senator from Illinois, Barack Obama. Jack was a fiery supporter of Fred Thompson, a die-hard right-winger from Tennessee.

Lizzy was not surprised at Jack's dislike for the African American Obama, but she was taken aback by Jack's comment, "It's a goddamned shame the way these primaries are going, only old Freddy Thompson can stop that buck from Illinois." The crude and decidedly antiquated racial epithet gave Lizzy a very real physical pang in her stomach. Gritting her teeth she decided at that moment what style she would choose for the Randolph interiors—antebellum plantation. She knew that such a choice would be seen as sheer and utter sarcasm, but at that point she would have preferred to lose this job and these clients. Several days later when she presented sketches of her ideas to Jack and Suzette she was appalled to find that Jack, rather ironically, adored the idea and approved the plans over Suzette's timid objections. She had pegged Jack better than she had ever imagined. She smiled to herself as she pictured Jack bedecked in a Colonel Sanders white suit replete with black string tie and almost laughed out loud when the thought entered her mind that he might just have such a suit!

It was difficult to imagine that a man such as Jack could also be a major player in the world of high finance. For all his regressive tendencies the man had a mind for investments and had compiled an enormous and highly regarded hedge fund which ran a not-too-distant second to the now-defunct Madoff Fund. Lizzy wondered if the Randolph Fund would make as loud a noise if it came tumbling down as had done the now-infamous Madoff Fund. For her family's sake she hoped that that day would never come. Why the hell had she and Joe trusted their money to this man? Oh yes, now she remembered. It was the huge profits that the fund had brought in for them. Even good people can be tempted by the lure of quick and easy profit margins. Money wasn't everything to Lizzy. She loved her family, friends, and life; but the mansion, Mercedes, Porsche, club memberships, and other comforts had become a solid part of their lives and a part which they would be hard-pressed to relinquish without a fight. Past mistakes may have been made, but now was a time to banish the past and move on. And at this very moment it was time to start digging for information again.

Rereading several revelatory e-mails Lizzy remembered that Jack and Suzette had actually divorced last summer, oddly enough continuing to live in separate parts of their extensive estate along with their son and daughter. There was something to be said for old-fashioned civility which allowed a couple to part so amicably and remain associated even if only for the sake of the children, as it is often said. So how were these two individuals connected to the death of a forty-two-year-old man from Jackson Hole, Wyoming? There were lots of holes in the Internet news stories regarding the Case. A simple mention that the victim was a resort owner and had recently visited the Randolphs prior to his death was too open-ended. Why had he visited the Randolphs? Was the reason business, or was it social? Did he come to see Jack, or was it Suzette? How long before his death had he stood in the plantation-style rooms of the Randolph house? The details added up less and less the more times that Lizzy read the articles. Had Randolph money greased the palms of local news agents in order to keep the details scarce and vague? Lizzy tore out the several pages on which she had jotted notes, paper clipped them together, and slipped them into the side pocket of her folder. She scribbled a title on a fresh piece of yellow legal paper which read, "The questions to be answered." And finding answers was exactly what she planned to do between now and her Thursday luncheon.

Midmorning the following day Lizzy was busily dialing up several friends and former clients with ties to the Randolphs. Most of the conversations were casual chitchat about soccer mom subjects: how were the kids doing in school, wasn't last Saturday's lacrosse game exciting, and then, subtly, how are the Randolphs doing these days? Such a pity about their breakup. The bait resulted in some major strikes, and like the fishing fan she was, Lizzy reeled in a respectable catch of new and exciting information. It is always amazing how the right allusions in a chat can result in a complete turn of direction and subject matter. Talk of lacrosse scores can quickly turn into whispered comments about lives, loves, and even tawdry circumstances given the right impetus. It was in the tawdry arena where Lizzy gleaned the most helpful information that morning. Dirt was beginning to emerge about the divorce of Jack and Suzette and the domestic expediency which kept them living in the same house, but very little about the murder victim could be found. Lizzy spoke the three details she knew about him aloud to no one in particular: William Pierce, forty-two years of age, owner of several resorts in the western states. William, God rest his soul, deserved more than the standard "name, rank, and serial number"; but where would she find his story?

Looking over the more gritty information about the Randolph divorce brought Lizzy's mind back to thoughts of her family. The revelations about Jack and Suzette's rocky relationship and the resulting divorce made Lizzy feel better about her family. She and Joe had enjoyed twenty-two years of marriage. Having married at eighteen years old she had often worried that she had been too immature to have entered wedlock so young, but the years had proven those worries futile. In twenty-two years there had been fights and even a few nights when one of them had spent the night at a local motel, but they always ended up in each other's arms within days of even the most heated blowout. Lizzy decided that a good portion of their stability as husband and wife rested in the fact that while they loved each other very deeply, they also profoundly liked each other. It sounded trite to claim that one's spouse was also one's best friend, but she could honestly not think of a single person's company that she enjoyed more than Joe's. She felt fairly confident that Joe felt the same way—sometimes things like that need never be said because they were so clearly evident.

With the first good mood she had felt in several days Lizzy lazily walked in from the pond and dropped her computer and notepad on the desk in her office. Glancing over at the phone she noticed that the red indicator light showed that there were messages awaiting her attention. Caller ID told her that there were seven calls to be reviewed, and the first was from Lucy Provence, the family attorney. Lucy was a Yale-trained lawyer with a high powered clientele throughout the tri-state region. This call had been made from her home over on North Street, not from her Greenwich Avenue or Manhattan, Fifth Avenue, offices, an indication that this was probably a friendly personal call. Lucy had been a friend for quite some time now, going back to her studies at law school, and a time when her name was Lucia Maria Provenzano. Italians are a very prevalent population in the southern tier of New England, but high-priced lawyers tend to have English or, in this case, French surnames, and Lucy was a very high-priced lawyer. The decision to change her name and ethnic identity came late in law school when one of her professors asked her, "Am I correct in assuming, Ms. Provenzano, that you plan to practice criminal law?" The quite obvious underlying meaning of the question was, of course, an allusion to her becoming a Mafia legal mouthpiece. The papers requesting a legal name changed were filed in the courts two days later.

Lucy's call was not the anticipated friendly conversation Lizzy had looked forward to when she dialed the phone. Lucy was friendly enough, but after a moment she turned serious.

"Look, kiddo, I have heard some buzz at the Greenwich office that you have been playing Miss Marple regarding the Pierce case, and that is making some townsfolk a bit nervous."

Lucy had just confirmed that the Case was more than most people would admit it was; there was something much deeper. Lizzy knew she had struck pay dirt because trivial matters do not unnerve the staid people of this town. Something was rotten in the state of Greenwich, to paraphrase Shakespeare! She could tell from the familiar use of "kiddo" that Lucy was reaching out as a concerned friend to warn her that she was treading in some precarious waters. She felt a tinge of affirmation in being taken seriously enough to be warned about something. She also took pleasure in the reference to Agatha Christie's character of Miss Marple. If she was to be the new Miss Marple, then she would be just as persistent and thorough as the fictional detective and shameless snoop!

By the time Lucy hung up her phone she had managed to feed Lizzy a surprising large number of leads and opened several new avenues of information which needed to be explored. For someone who had called to warn her to back off her investigation (that is what Lizzy mentally now called her activities with the Case), Lucy had actually greatly piqued Lizzy's curiosity and encouraged her to move ahead with her work. The thought occurred to her that for some unknown reason, perhaps Lucy was trying to build her interest and increase her desire to look into this matter. Might it be even that the people behind the "buzz" wanted to see Lizzy dig deeper. She came to the conclusion that this investigation was turning out to be very stimulating to her intellect and tickled her pink on a very personal level. She might just consider doing this for a living if she could get licensed. But then again, all the enjoyment might be lost if it became a job, and possibly a dangerous job. After all no one had ever called her before to warn her off an activity. Beyond being a distraction, this was beginning to be fun!

One of the things which Lucy had casually mentioned was the fact that the Randolph divorce was not as friendly and smooth as it appeared. Lucy was not a divorce attorney, but lawyers tend to drink in packs, and after-court cocktail sessions could be very rich in asides and gossip. Somewhere along the line, Lucy had had a talk with Suzette's attorney, Marcia Abernathy, a ruthless hellion in and out of the courtroom who rarely took on a male client. She was a feminist before all other calling, and she was in what seemed to be a personal vendetta to clean out every wealthy man in Greenwich via their estranged spouses and the Connecticut divorce laws. She was also a Liberal Democrat who detested First Selectman Randolph, so when Suzette parked her pretty derriere on one of the office visitor chairs a very wolfish smile spread across Abernathy's face. All that was missing was a single glistening drop of blood at the corner of her mouth to realize a full-blown werewolf pose. She did not like Jack; and suddenly a weapon, a very powerful weapon against him, just fell into her hands in the guise of Jack's distraught wife.

Lizzy did not dare probe Lucy for details on the Randolph divorce; a cunning attorney would be put off by an amateur's attempt to pump her for information. So Lizzy just asked her directly for details. Lucy's responses were helpful, but Lizzy knew that in the cards she was dealt there were aces missing—aces which were probably tucked securely in her attorney friend's vest pocket. Obviously Lucy was giving her enough, but not too much of the story. This cat-and-mouse game was beginning to annoy Lizzy, and she felt like a character on the television series *The X-Files*. In the show it took nine years to answer a single question at the heart of the story. She was damned if she was going to allow herself to be teased and enticed by tidbits of information handed out in a fashion designed to lead her by the nose to a destination someone else had devised. If one well ran dry, there were plenty of others in town which were full; and she knew how to dip the ladle and come up with what she needed, one way or another.

It took a bit of effort for Lizzy to shake the anger she was feeling at being played with by Lucy's information game, but it was best to count Lucy as an ally and not allow her to become an adversary in reality or even in perception. She felt distinctly like a person fed a delicious meal only to have it taken away before she had finished. The sense of being somehow cheated lingered, but pettiness would not be an asset in this venture, so Lizzy put it aside and reached for her notepad and a pen. The time had come to sit and inventory the details of the Case and from whence they came. Pages were filling up and patterns were emerging, but the Bill Pierce column was still empty save for three bits of information—the same three as she had had at the beginning.

Thursday had finally arrived; a surprisingly bright, cheerful, and confident Lizzy rolled out of bed at eight o'clock. After a quick shower, and a healthy breakfast of whole grain cereal and skim milk, she felt like a prizefighter who was in his prime and itching for a bout. Her steps as she walked to her office were strong and deliberate. She was ready to take on the revelations of later in the day, but just now she felt a great desire to immerse herself in the e-mails she was sure would be waiting for her. The e-mail account showed that seventeen e-mails had arrived since yesterday; many were late-night communiqués in response to her calls and letters of the past few days. It struck her that most of the subject lines were blank or had very innocuous titles, and that made her grin broadly. She knew that dirt never announced itself with a flourish. The vaguer the titles the more sensitive information they probably contained. Her plan was to open all of them quickly, sort them by relevance, and then wade through each with a keen eye. She never realized that plan because the very first one she opened was too provocative to click away from.

She opened the third e-mail first. It was from Suzanne Delany, a close-by neighbor of the Randolphs, if living nearly a mile from the Randolph house could be called "close-by." Suzanne was a close confidante of Lizzy's which seemed quite appropriate since she was also her younger sister. Suzanne had married a Chelsea actor/waiter named Scott some fifteen years ago, to the chagrin of her parents and family. But Scott had proven them all wrong when two years after their marriage he had landed an impressive role on a major network soap opera. In the following years, that role had developed into several costarring parts in major motion pictures and most recently a dramatic project in which he was the headliner. When good fortune strikes, it sometimes rolls in like a tidal wave, and it seemed that Suzanne and Scott were riding that wave to fame and fortune. They now owned a clothing line and a men's cologne named Delany. The fortune kept coming and was well spent on a huge home and not one but two Rolls-Royce automobiles. (One never refers to a Rolls as a car, you know.) Suzanne had wanted a new Silver Shadow, while Scott opted for a 1960s antique Silver Ghost.

Any news that Suzanne had to share would be revealing, but also suspect. Though Suzanne was beautiful and wealthy, she also had been diagnosed with bipolar disorder and, depending on her faithfulness in taking her medication, might not be relating information which could be deemed totally trustworthy. As she read the e-mail Lizzy could tell that, at least for the moment, Suzanne's state of mind was good. The e-mail started with her characteristic nickname for Lizzy, Big Sis, which in and of itself was a good sign. Lizzy read on, "I did as you asked and made some notes about the Randolphs. To my surprise once I got started I managed to fill up a few sheets about things I have heard, things I have heard about, and rumors which have circulated around the club and the neighborhood." Most of the information was fairly common knowledge, but there were tidbits which were not commonly known about the situation at the Randolph estate. It seemed to answer one of Lizzy's questions about Bill Pierce; he had most definitely been visiting with Suzette; and the visits were many and entailed days and even, on occasion, a week or more at a time.

As she read on Lizzy suddenly shouted an uncharacteristic exclamation of "holy shit" as she came to the words "I don't know if you knew, but talk is that Suzette is three months pregnant." Again very uncharacteristically, Lizzy pumped the air and said, "Yes! Now we are getting somewhere!" Suzette's pregnancy and Pierce's visits might be totally unrelated, but statistically what were the chances of that? She reached over to her notepad and pulled out the sheet concerning Bill Pierce; tentatively and in pencil she wrote, "Possible father of Suzette's unborn child." It might be a stretch to come to such a conclusion, but it was more likely true than not. A woman living in a large house with her ex-husband and entertaining a good-looking man for weekends and more is likely to have engaged in sex with him, at least a normal woman anyway. If you risk scandal by sharing your home with a man over extended periods, why wouldn't you also have him share your bed? It was common sense.

As if by divine providence, to back up Lizzy's theory, she read on to discover that the social opinion of most of the Randolphs' friends and associates was that Jack and Suzette had not had sex in some five or six years. Lizzy now remembered that during her work for the Randolphs she was a bit surprised to see that they each had their own bedroom, and those bedrooms were on different floors of the same wing. It had struck her as odd at the time, but odd and rich are nearly synonyms in many cases when dealing with such people. Turning to the many notes on the Randolphs she began to scribble furiously, adding details to their profile in what was becoming a case file. As she reached for a third clean sheet on her pad the antique mantel clock chimed a single time. Looking up she realized that she had better head to the Barcelona to be prompt for her one thirty luncheon since it was a twenty-minute winding ride from the backcountry to downtown Greenwich, and it would not do to be late for this important tête-à-tête.

Finding a parking spot a few feet away from the entrance Lizzy noticed her luncheon date standing next to her white BMW with a mildly agitated look on her face. As she approached Jenny Stuart, the author of the mysterious e-mail about the possibility of trouble with the Randolph Fund, Jenny's mouth uplifted into a quite pleasant smile; and as greetings were exchanged, a suggestion was made that they eat elsewhere. Lizzy's heart sank a bit, the visions of paella and sangria dissolving abruptly from her mind. When Jenny suggested the Greenwich Avenue Diner, Lizzy could not stop herself from asking why such a dramatic change of venue and menu? The answer sent a small tingle down Lizzy's spine.

"I love Barcelona too, but I think it best we go somewhere that we are less likely to run into people from our social circle, if you will forgive that snobby term," said

31

Jenny quietly. In an equally quiet tone, she added, "I'd rather not be overheard, if you know what I mean."

Sliding into a vinyl booth which squealed loudly as Lizzy's leather belt made contact with it, she half grunted and half sighed at the prospect of the possible combination of bad news and greasy food. To add insult to injury she noticed that her menu had stains from a former patron's chili long ago spilled on it. "Hmmm," she intoned as she scanned the list of entrées for something that she might actually enjoy. In the end she ordered a simple bacon lettuce and tomato sandwich, light on the mayo. Now that that chore was completed she hoped that Jenny would get down to business quickly and avoid small talk. She was not disappointed when Jenny began to speak as the waiter left their table.

"I am sure that you are aware of this, but the Securities and Exchange Commission is looking into the Randolph Fund," were the first words out of Jenny's mouth. Lizzy had to contain herself not to shout "Oh shit!" once again today. Regardless of what else might be said in this secretive little meeting, the worst of the worst had just been dropped on her.

Trying not to show her personal disappointment Lizzy excused herself and headed off to the ladies' room at the back of the diner. Makeup or not, this called for a splash of cold water on her face, as cold a splash as she could get out of the slightly rusty faucet before her. It did not solve anything, but the shock of icy water on her delicate face gave her a grasp on her composure and the clear-headedness to go back to the table and hear what Paul Harvey used to call "the rest of the story." Lizzy needed to know how accurate this information was since no one else had even hinted at this situation. Sadly, she discovered that Jenny and her husband had lost a sizable amount of money in the Madoff scandal, forcing Jenny to return to the workforce to help make ends meet. The job she had landed was as a legal secretary in the offices of Jack Randolph's attorneys. Lizzy felt as if she needed another splash of icy water but decided to forgo that pleasure to shorten the length of time that she must endure the bad news in its entirety.

Seeing the color drain from Lizzy's face, Jenny knew that her news had struck a nerve. In the hopes of alleviating some of Lizzy's obvious discomfort she added, "I thought for sure you would have had at least a hint of the situation. After all your sister and her husband stand to lose everything since they invested so heavily in the fund."

Now, it really was time for something stronger than cold water, so she hailed the waiter and asked for the strongest drink in the house adding, "And make it neat and make it a double!" After nibbling on a BLT of fatty bacon, wilted lettuce, and too much mayo, Lizzy begged off any further discussion and asked if they could get together in a day or two to finish their talk. Jenny knew that her news had bowled Lizzy over and quickly agreed to stop over at the Dawson house midmorning on Saturday. As they drove back to the Barcelona, Lizzy silently cursed the fact that she had left her car there and now had to endure another five to ten minutes with Jenny in her Beamer. She did not blame Jenny for her sudden depressed mood, but she just did not want to see her face any longer for today.

Driving home Lizzy turned up the air-conditioning and the radio in a vain attempt to find a bit of comfort. Pouring herself a rather full glass of Merlot she brought the rim to her lips. Stopping short of her first sip she threw the goblet to the floor as through gritted teeth she cursed alcohol as a false refuge and then cursed herself saying, "Why the fuck am I taking this out on our good Waterford?" After all, if the money was gone so would be the Waterford, the country club, and the house in time. And now she realized that it would all be gone for Suzanne and Scott as well. Knowing that fact brought tears to her eyes; they rolled down her face like rivulets after a spring shower. Lizzy was a strong woman, and it was much easier for her to cry over her sister's misfortunes than her own, and a good cry was exactly what she needed at this particular moment.

After nearly thirty minutes of shedding tears over the disastrous news she had just received, the old tried-and-true Lizzy returned as she dried her eyes, walked over to the bathroom and applied a few drops of Visine to each eye, straightened her smart jacket, and practically marched across the house to the den. Mumbling to herself she scanned the rows of DVD sets on the massive bookshelves and with a loud "aha" pulled a boxed set out of its place with a smile. "Miss Marple never cries, and if I am Greenwich's Miss Marple, then neither will Lizzy Dawson," she said as she placed a disc into her player and watched the screen come to life with the opening titles of *Murder Ahoy. A little diversion would be helpful right about now,* she thought; and although she would never have admitted it, in the back of her mind she hoped that she might pick up some pointers from the film. It was a silly thought, but a bit of silliness would feel good to her after this trying afternoon.

Sometimes people can be such sticklers about very unimportant matters, thought Lizzy as she watched her movie. This absurd murder mystery comedy was a perfect example. It was based on Agatha Christie's character of Miss Marple, but the writers had tailored it to the wonderful elderly British actress Margaret Rutherford.

The elements were the same as a Christie novel, but it was infused with humor, and Miss Marple imbued with quirky idiosyncrasies which endeared her to viewers far beyond the more serious and staid Marple who flowed directly from Christie's pen.

Early in the film Marple marches into the town tailor shop and leaves a short time later dressed in a uniform which appears to be that of a female officer in the Royal Navy. Her actual role in the story is that of a trustee on the board of a small private naval cadet training school; nothing military and nothing official, and yet there she was parading around dressed like an admiral. The silliness of the situation amused Lizzy and made her think of her own British heritage and the magnificent uniforms which her father, Gordon Winthrop-Beasley, wore as the colonial governor of the Caribbean Islands of Saint Vincent and the Grenadines. Her dad had been born in London to a prominent political family and had entered the Royal Diplomatic Corps after Oxford. During a posting at the United Nations in New York City he had met and fallen in love with Lizzy's mother, Rebecca. Shortly after their marriage the happy couple learned that Gordon was to be named a royal governor, by no less an official than Queen Elizabeth herself. When Rebecca was about to give birth to a baby a year later, they flew from their villa on Mustique to the Queen Victoria Hospital in Kingstown, the capital of Saint Vincent. The child being a beautiful girl, there was little question that the child would share the Christian name of the glorious monarch.

After ninety minutes of amusement and reminiscences Lizzy felt surprisingly better than she ever expected to on that dismal afternoon. She decided then and there not to bring this horrible news up to Joe. He must be aware of the situation since he kept a close eye on their investments. If it was truly a crucial situation he would surely bring it up to her. She was in no way a naive and dim-witted wife who delegated all fiscal responsibilities to her husband. Quite to the contrary they had divided responsibilities between themselves for differing aspects of their investments. He looked after the direct stock investments and she tended the real estate holdings. Each kept the other informed on general detail. Likewise, they totally trusted each other to deal with the countless minor details of their interests. She knew that if Joe thought the situation was truly serious he would have had a talk with her weeks ago. They had weathered the losses from the Madoff Fund, and they would weather these as well, together as always.

With a newfound peace of mind Lizzy threw herself back into the Case. Bit by bit details were coming to light about the mysterious victim, Bill Pierce. Among the bad news which Jenny had shared was a detail which had been overlooked by the press in their coverage of what they were referring to as the "possible suicide" of Pierce, the fact that he was the owner of several dude ranch style resorts in the western states. The largest of them was the Brandywine Ranch in Jackson Hole. Lizzy decided on a two-pronged course of action to learn more about Pierce's holdings. First, she did a routine Google search which yielded the Web site of the Brandywine, and then she added a new page to her blog which concentrated on Bill's role as owner of the ranch. She hoped that a search by interested Net surfers would lead them to the page, and once there, they would leave comments which would contain more information directly from Jackson Hole locals. These would be the kind of people who actually knew the ranch and might even be personal friends of its late owner.

The article on the Brandywine had to be concise, open ended with enough loose ends to elicit comments which would fill in some of the blanks which bedeviled Lizzy's growing profile of Bill and the circumstances of his death. The thought occurred to her that she, Joe, and the boys had not had a vacation in over a year; and a few days at a ranch resort might just do them all some good. Horseback riding, skiing in the Rockies, and a little hiking would be relaxing for Joe, Troy, and Scott. Some investigative snooping would certainly be a mother lode of information for the Case. The Brandywine Ranch was not yet heavily associated with the Pierce matter in the public mind, so for all her family and friends would know, it would simply be a pleasure trip intended to blow off some steam. She smiled to herself at the cleverness of this plan and placated her conscience by telling herself that she would not be lying to Joe, since for him and the boys it would, indeed, just be a nice, relaxing getaway.

Over dinner Lizzy mentioned her idea for the trip to Joe and the boys. She was delighted to hear all of them jump at the suggestion. Joe suggested that they could do a day or two of fishing in mountain streams in addition to skiing and the more Wild West aspects of the ranch. Lizzy already was thinking about doing some fishing, but not of the sort that Joe had in mind. To be on the safe side Lizzy suggested that they plan and book the entire trip online, telling Joe how much they could save by doing the reservations and bookings through one of the discount online travel services. Her real intention was to avoid the local travel agents who might discuss this trip with other Greenwich clients. Brandywine was not common knowledge to the townsfolk, but one could not be too careful with this parcel of information. The Brandywine had scarcely been mentioned in any news item reported thus far, and it had remained well hidden while in plain sight. No one seemed to regard it as an important item in the story, and Lizzy wondered if she might be making too much of it. But then again, how could a man's livelihood not be an integral part of his life and perhaps his untimely death?

By the end of church services the next morning and after a family brunch with a number of church friends, Lizzy was to realize that being careful might be something she had overlooked with regard to the safety of herself and her family. Ethan Rivers was a family friend whom the Dawsons had met at their parish church, the Anglican Church of the Atonement, which was just two miles from their home. Lizzy's British heritage attracted her to the quaint church when she learned that it used the 1662 prayer book of the Church of England. The sound of the exalted Elizabethan English prayers carried her back to a different time and place in her life, a time past, but very fondly remembered. Such a church often attracts the kind of person that would be called eccentric in polite social circles and downright odd by persons of lesser breeding. Rivers fit the eccentric label extremely well. He owned a local real estate firm and prided himself on not quite fitting into the twenty-first century. Custom suits tailored in the Edwardian style were just one of his many charming affectations, but in one regard he was a modern man—he adored the Internet and had a blog of his own entitled "Floating Down the Rivers." Lizzy vaguely remembered that Ethan's blog had made mention of the Pierce murder several weeks ago, but she found that he had deleted every reference to the matter just a few days after he had posted them. Curiosity was getting the best of Lizzy in church that morning, as she noted that Ethan was sitting just two pews ahead of her. During the coffee hour following the service she asked him to join them for brunch. He readily accepted.

Brunch was a pleasant affair of omelets and an assortment of waffles, pancakes, and crepes followed by hot gourmet coffee and warm conversation. Father Richard Redanz, the pastor of Atonement, joined the group after overseeing the coffee-hour cleanup at the church hall. Arriving just a few minutes late his inclusion turned the conversation to church matters for most of the actual meal. Lizzy liked Redanz very much, and like the rhythmic cadence of the old English prayers, his words were delivered in a gentle Oxford accent which belied his strongly Germanic surname. As the conversation broke up into small chats among small groups (brunch having expanded into a group of eleven), Lizzy managed to engage Ethan in an exchange about the latest trends on the Internet. Subtly she mentioned his blog and inquired if he had any late-breaking news for his update the following morning. Using those topics as a springboard, she broached the subject of the Pierce situation.

Ethan, usually a good-natured and somewhat blustery sort, suddenly changed his mood and the tone of his voice as he responded to Lizzy's comment.

"Well, that is a matter that I am loath to address, but since it is among friends I will tell you the entire bizarre story," Ethan said. After taking a long draft of his Earl Grey tea, he continued, "Never in my life have I had a threat of physical violence made against me."

His statement was not entirely true, however. Having been eccentric even at an early age he was often the target of jeers and minor acts of violence throughout his primary and secondary school years in the private schools of Greenwich.

His small and probably unconscious lie aside, he looked truly disturbed as he said, "I withdrew the story after a blatant threat was made against my person and my property!"

Lizzy's eyebrows arched in amazement at the obvious seriousness with which Rivers was telling his story. Threats being made over a blog story? Just how perilous was the pursuit of the truth in the Case? She cleared her thoughts to concentrate on Ethan's words as he went on, "The same night as I posted the blog story the phone rang just past eleven thirty. I picked up the receiver with my usual greeting of 'Rivers here!' only to be met by total silence. As I started to take the phone from my ear, I heard a muffled man's voice tell me to drop the Pierce matter unless I wished to lose my good health to an untimely accident and my business to a chance fire caused by old and frayed wiring in the walls."

Abruptly, Ethan placed his teacup down, wiped his moist forehead, and excused himself, explaining that he had just recalled an early afternoon showing for a wealthy client at the other end of town. He was up and gone before Lizzy could even wish him a good afternoon. At the time Lizzy could not have predicted that Ethan had had any inkling of who had made the threatening phone call, but in a telephone exchange that evening from a calmer Rivers he would tell her that he was sure that the call had been prompted by Jack Randolph. He had not recognized the caller's voice and was quite sure it would not have been Randolph personally, but a chance meeting with Randolph outside his office some days later convinced him of Jack's involvement. Jack had greeted him in a more friendly way than usual, had asked about his health for no apparent reason, and feigned concern over what he observed as the beginnings of a head cold in Ethan. But the piece de resistance was Jack's parting words: "When I was first selectman I should have reformed the fire codes in this town; an old building like yours could probably use some rewiring. That is something to consider, Rivers. Something to seriously consider."

For the second time since beginning to work on the Case, Lizzy had thoughts of clearing all case information from her laptop and using all her paper notes as kindling to start a nice fire in the office fireplace. This entire matter might be a bit more than she had bargained for when it all first began just a few weeks ago. She knew that embarrassing personal information could make a person irate, but would they become murderously enflamed? With a gentle tap with the heel of her palm on her forehead Lizzy said out loud, "Murderously enflamed enough to kill Bill Pierce!" She had answered her own question, and although she did not enjoy the prospect of actual physical danger, she knew that she enjoyed some advantages which Ethan had not. Randolph, among other things, was a sexist; and he would never take a female blogger as seriously as a male. Besides, he would more than likely write off Lizzy's comments as "ladies' gossip," if he had even bothered to read them at all. *I think I have dodged that bullet,* thought Lizzy but added a grimace when she considered her choice of metaphor to describe the situation.

Monday was a dull day, and Lizzy decided not to check her blog for comments but rather to devote her day to the mundane aspects of being a businesswoman, wife, and mother. A parent-teacher conference was going on today at the Dunbar School, and she had appointments at 11:00 and 11:30 a.m. with Troy's and Scott's teachers respectively. She knew that each conference would last no more than the allotted thirty minutes slated for

41

them. Troy was about to graduate from Dunbar and was a top honors student; there would be no shocks or disappointments from his instructors. Scott, while not an honors student, was never a source of any problems academically or behaviorally. The conferences went smashingly. The only surprise was the fact that Lizzy thought it would be impossible for her to be prouder of the boys than she already was. The conference reports proved her wrong. This called for a celebration, and the boys would be treated to a special lunch at any restaurant which they chose. To Lizzy's mild disapproval they chose the McDonald's over on the Post Road in the borough of Old Greenwich. Lizzy was not a snob, but she disliked the choice of eateries because of the coarse language of the Post Road clientele. The boys enjoyed the finer things of life, but their choice of friends and female interests tended to be from the public high school, which was close enough to that particular McDonald's to ensure that they would run into friends there.

As expected, Troy and Scott ran into friends and excused themselves from Mom's company to sit in a corner with their comrades. Lizzy sighed to think that twice in a short period her hopes for an elegant and delicious lunch had been derailed. She ordered her Big Mac meal and selected a quiet table by the window. She might have to eat at McDonald's; but she could at the very least avoid the city workers, who, as usual, were liberally peppering their conversation with the words "fuck" and "cocksucker." She was no prude, but she did have standards. Gingerly unwrapping a side order of chicken tenders Lizzy happened to glance out the large window beside her and noticed a black Mercedes convertible with specialty Connecticut license plates reading "Suzz E." Plates which she recognized as belonging to none other than Suzette

Randolph. A Randolph at McDonald's seemed as likely as seeing the Bush family car parked at an abortion clinic. She made a quick and discreet scan of the interior of the McDonald's to see if Suzette might actually be slumming for lunch. No Suzette was present. A second look out the window revealed a midnight blue Beamer sedan pulling out of the parking slip next to Suzette's Mercedes. Even with just a glimpse she knew that the female figure in that car was Suzette, and she was casually draping herself across the shoulder of a handsome dark-haired man who appeared to be in his late twenties at most.

Lizzy giggled to herself in delight at the sight. She blushed slightly as her grand aunt Joan popped into her mind. Joan was her mother's aunt and was a very perky eighty-four years of age. Among family members she had the nickname of Rona, after the celebrity gossip Rona Barrett, because of her stellar ability to uncover and convey gossip at lightning speed. Lizzy wondered if she had inherited the "gossip gene" from dear old Aunty Jo, and at the moment she actually hoped she had, since it would come in very handy in this endeavor of hers. Taking a page out of Joan's playbook, Lizzy acted quickly and grabbed a pen from her purse to jot down the license number from the departing Beamer. A good friend at the state police headquarters might be persuaded to run the number and reveal the identity of the car's owner.

"Damn it!" Lizzy blurted out as she hung up the phone later that afternoon. Charlie Mazur, her contact at the state police, was on vacation and not due back in his Hartford office until the seventeenth, two weeks from now. A lieutenant drew a full month of vacation each year, and it appeared Charlie was taking it all at once. How she hated detours when she was making such good progress with the investigation! Taking out her Rolodex she quickly looked for other police contacts which she had. When you buy and sell homes as a business you come into contact with the police quite often. It is always a good idea to check out a property for a past history of criminal activity, so you get to know policemen, and usually the inquiries end up with a high-ranked officer. Reading each name aloud from the Rolodex, she discarded most of them as being too local to ask them for such a delicate favor. Finally she hit upon a friend in the New York City Police. She could run the plates for any car in the nation, and she was far enough away not to be familiar with the Greenwich goings-on. She also rarely questioned the motives for such a favor.

Lizzy dialed the number to the office of the chief of detectives at the NYPD and after several transfers heard the cheerful voice of her friend Bernice. Lizzy cut to the chase and made her request to Bernice. The response she received was equally blunt: "No problem, call me back in half an hour, and I'll give you the name. Talk to you then." Now that was the kind of no-nonsense response she liked! The intervening thirty minutes were spent reading and tidying her notes, but the chime of the mantel clock reminded her that she had forgotten to make dinner. A call to Papa John's Pizza and a quick order of three pepperoni pies solved that problem. She knew that Joe and the boys would be elated to feast on pizza as their tastes often differed from the healthy meals that she preferred to serve. They liked their pizzas, and she gained some time to work on the Case. Everyone would be happy; this would definitely be a win-win situation.

Reveling in a sense of coming out on top of the situation Lizzy realized that forty-five minutes had passed since she called Bernice, and at a quarter to five she would be pushing the envelope in getting back to her. New York Police offices close promptly at five o'clock, and the higher the rank, the quicker officers fled from their offices; she dialed and, with a sigh of relief, heard Bernice say without greeting, "John Finelli, Pickwick Lane, Greenwich, Connecticut. Can I hit the road now, Lizzy?" Seventeen years as a cop before working her way up to assistant deputy chief gave Bernice an abrupt and terse manner which at the moment pleased Lizzy greatly. With an equally terse "Thanks, Bee, say hello to Mort," Lizzy ended the phone call as she gripped the Post-it pad on which she had written the information. Maybe she was more like a new Sam Spade than Miss Marple: tough, fearless, and to the point. That thought appealed to Lizzy as she said, "Play it again, Sam," mixing up two of Humphrey Bogart's memorable roles.

A clamor of feet coming down the hallway steps alerted Lizzy to the fact that Troy and Scott had a number of friends over for the evening. She hit a memory key on the phone and asked the person on the other end, "Has my order for three pepperoni pizzas left yet? No? Good, let's make that six pies and make the other three sausage and mushroom. Thanks." Another problem solved in short order; she was on a roll tonight, and she liked the feeling. Suzette and this Finelli person could wait until tomorrow; this was going to be a family night. Dinner that evening was another mark in the winning column. Everyone ate out on the deck and watched TV on the portable flat-screen TV set up outside for the occasion. The boys' guests were the usual male buddies, but tonight there were several girls included, and it became obvious as the evening progressed that the two prettiest girls were quite fond of Troy and Scott. It was equally obvious that those feelings were mutual. The entire evening made Lizzy feel almost giddy with the thought that, while her family might have their problems, they were a happy and normal group. As she and Joe watched the DVD that the kids had rented their positions had turned into a cuddle, and that too felt good to Lizzy. In fact it felt very good.

While the kids had all raided the soda bin in their double refrigerator, Joe and Lizzy decided on a rich red Chianti with their pizza. After the kids had left, the Chianti was followed by two sizable servings of Drambuie liqueur, a favorite of Bonnie Prince Charlie, who was, according to Lizzy's father, a distant relative on the Scottish side of the family. The liqueur gave Lizzy a warm and dreamy feeling and aroused thoughts of romance, which she soon learned were on Joe's mind as well. What followed was a night of kissing, caressing, and gentle lovemaking which ended hours later with the couple spooning like young lovers, with Joe still inside of her. As she nodded off to sleep, Lizzy felt as if this were their first time together: so romantic, so gentle and so peaceful. She did not have a care in the world except the man she loved and who had once again proved to her that he loved her just as deeply. Her conscious mind was in a state of euphoria, and she knew that the alcohol played no part in that feeling. She was in love, and unlike so many women, it was with her own husband.

The conscious mind is our reality. Better put, it is the reality which we perceive. What we feel is genuine, but the human mind sometimes separates the many thoughts in our minds from the reality of the moment. For Lizzy all the Suzettes, Pierces, and Randolphs were neatly tucked into her subconscious as she fell into a deep sleep that night. But the subconscious has a way of spilling over and emerging in our dreams, and that night Lizzy had quite a dream. It was something which would wake her early the next morning with a troubled feeling and with a new and greater purpose to her work

46

with her blog investigations. In her dream she had met Bill Pierce in the bar of a western-style hotel, and they had talked for what seemed like hours. None of what the dream man was telling her had anything directly to do with the story she was piecing together. There was talk about Suzette and Jack Randolph, but for the most part, the conversation revolved around an infatuation he had for another woman and how Suzette had somehow damaged the relationship he had hoped to build with this unnamed woman. Lizzy was a fairly religious woman, and dream reading was akin to superstition and horoscopes in her mind, but she felt something deep inside her telling her that this was something more.

In a way Lizzy was glad that the dream had aroused her so early. Today she was going to go over some specs on a house which she planned to buy, renovate, and resell. She needed some time to examine the house papers which she had ignored for nearly two weeks and find as businesslike a suit to wear as she owned. The seller was one of Greenwich's more dour financial magnates, and he would expect as professional an attitude from the prospective buyer as he presented to her. Sanford Wainwright owned dozens of estates in the backcountry of Greenwich. He only lived in one, but he liked to station family and close business associates in grand homes at his expense, not out of generosity but for the control which such "kindness" gave him over them. People showed no rebellion or disloyalty to the man who provided them with palatial digs. That is the kind of logic only a man capable of owning over half a dozen Greenwich estates could have, but Wainwright believed it like the gospel.

Among the real estate holdings of Sanford Wainwright were a number of smaller homes which he could not bring himself to call estates. For no apparent reason he would tire of a home, or perhaps find it useless after evicting a nephew or company vice president. He put them on the market quietly; and Lizzy, being friends with one of his many personal assistants, usually caught wind of them before the majority of realty investors in town. This property was an eight-bedroom house which Wainwright playfully called a cottage. It sat at the end of one of the common backcountry private roads which peppered the highly affluent northern regions of Greenwich. Lizzy used her GPS to locate the best route to the house and typed in the location on, heaven help us, Wainwright Road. The pleasant female voice of the GPS said in its monotone way, "Location not found," to the annoyance of the now time-pressed Lizzy. In a fit of anger she struck the screen of the GPS and muttered, "GPS must stand for Goddamned Piece of Shit." Rustling through a pile of maps in her glove box she found the laminated book of maps for backcountry Greenwich. It was a rare volume produced by the local realty council for the use of their agents. People were not encouraged to take pleasure rides in the backcountry. In fact there was a local joke regarding the discouragement of the practice, "If you decide to take a ride in the backcountry, don't bother to pack a lunch. It will be provided by the Greenwich Police."

Lizzy found the page on which the Wainwright Cottage should be located, and despite examining it three times, she was confounded to find nothing even mildly associated with a Wainwright Road. She decided to give it a go one more time and concentrated on landmarks which she knew were on the way to the house. From Round Hill Church she traced the main road north until she spotted a familiarly named road. Pickwick Road sprang out at her, and if that were not enough of a shock, she realized that "Pickwick Road" changed names at the point where it ceased to be a public thoroughfare and became a private road. Pickwick Road changed names to the elusive Wainwright Road about half its length to the east of the main street.

Shock and elation had to be put on the back burner for the moment, Wainwright was waiting, and the distance between him and Lizzy was not decreasing any as she sat in her driveway stunned by the coincidence which had just fallen directly into her lap. She pushed the speed limit and prayed that the Greenwich constabulary was off at the town doughnut shop at the moment. Her luck held as she pulled into the driveway and saw Wainwright being let out of his late-model Bentley by a liveried chauffeur. Wainwright turned out to be quite a charming man, insisting that Lizzy call him by what seemed the overly familiar nickname of Sandy. Their discussion of the sale of the house went smoothly; and Lizzy was amazed that at the first mention of price, her newfound friend said, "I have overpriced this cottage and would not even consider letting you pay the asking price. What do you say we reduce it by 10 percent?" Was he truly such a nice man, or was there more to him than met the eye? Despite her suspicions, her gut told her that he was genuine.

After the talk of house sales had ended Wainwright insisted that Lizzy join him for a quick bite at a nearby café nestled along one of the backcountry's charming, and yet annoying, roundabouts. The café was French and the food was excellent, finally, a rewarding lunch after so many disappointments. Lizzy rallied enough courage to ask Sandy why he wished to sell such a nice house and at such a reasonable price. His smile at the question surprised her, and his honest explanation which followed equally took her aback. It seemed that Sandy had stationed his lovely eighteen-year-old granddaughter in the house just over a year ago. The granddaughter had made serious noises about buying an apartment in Manhattan's Greenwich Village to pursue a career as an artist, rather than enter a college and study a reputable subject like business or law. The backcountry house and a new Porsche had convinced her to say put in Greenwich town rather than village and to promise, after a one-year hiatus from school, to return to studies at a proper college somewhere reasonably close to Greenwich—perhaps Grandpa's alma mater of Yale in New Haven.

There was the reason in a nutshell. So where was the granddaughter, and why was the house vacant and up for sale? As if reading Lizzy's mind, Wainwright continued, "My granddaughter lives in Greenwich Village now and has started studies at the School of Visual Arts. I bought her a two-bedroom condominium in the East Village and even bought a permanent parking spot for her car nearby." The expression on Lizzy's face must have been evident because Wainwright chuckled and explained, "I would much rather that she live in Manhattan and study art than live in that house and carry on with one of the neighbor boys, who has been showing, in my opinion, improper attention to her. I may be an old man, but I can see what is good for a young woman these days. And playing house, especially in my house, with a ne'er-do-well Italian is beyond the pale!"

Lizzy was amused at the emphasis and pronunciation which Sandy placed on the word "Italian." Stressing the "I" in Italian made him sound for a fleeting moment like Archie Bunker, but she could tell that his feelings if bigoted were sincere.

Continuing with his story Wainwright actually addressed his seemingly anti-Italian comments, excusing them with the statement, "Now don't get me wrong, Elizabeth, I do not dislike Italians in general, but this family is just not the sort that anyone would like their granddaughter becoming involved with. I would prefer not to think of my own kinswoman as a gun moll."

His words conjured up images of 1920s Chicago rather than present-day Greenwich, but his intentions were understandable. There were criminal elements even in this fair community and even in its most rarified areas. How serious could this fling between the Wainwright girl and her Italian beau have really been? Lizzy wondered if this could be the grist for a steamy romance novel in which the purebred WASP girl would succumb to the charms of yet another Italian stallion.

Lizzy tried to reassure Sandy that his paternal concerns were not misplaced and asked if he was quite sure that the boy was actually part of a family connected to organized crime. She had hoped that maybe Sandy had misjudged the boy and his family and, even if it meant losing the purchase of the house, that she could play peacemaker and reunite a pair of star-crossed lovers.

Wainwright could sense the sentimentality creeping into Lizzy's eyes and became more direct as he slightly raised his voice and said, "When a family owns a large cartage firm and the patriarch of the family has the nickname Skinny Boy tucked between his Christian and surnames, I would presume they were part of organized crime. And Matthew may be a handsome, charming, and intelligent boy; but he is also heir to, what one might call, the family business. Forgive me, but I would prefer that my sweet child not become the first lady of the Finelli brothers' refuse empire!"

Were this a scene from a cartoon, Lizzy's eyes would have distended at least a foot from their sockets. She felt as if a dark room had just been lighted with a bank of floodlights.

Chapter Two

All the News That Fits

As a young woman Lizzy once attended a presidential campaign rally at which Eugene McCarthy spoke. It was a grand affair, and the hall was filled to capacity with exuberant and excited people. The next day she picked up a local newspaper and looked for an article covering the events at the rally. Near the bottom of page 3 there was a small article with a photo entitled "McCarthy Rally Attracts a Lackluster Crowd of Local Students." The photo showed a nearly empty hall populated by people who appeared to be milling about with nothing to do. Lizzy was appalled to read the article's claim that only a few of the town's more radical college students had shown up to hear McCarthy and that they were none too impressed by his speech. The reality was quite the opposite of the paper's telling of the event. In fact a clock in the photo showed that the picture was taken some five hours prior to the arrival of Senator McCarthy and even before the folding chairs in the hall had been set up. That was the last time Lizzy ever believed anything she heard in the press again.

That early lesson of the frequent dishonesty of the press served Lizzy well over the years. Since those early years she had seen stories reported from a purely biased viewpoint which made it evident that the press sometimes created the news instead of objectively reporting it. The most recent case which still angered her was the hack job the Connecticut media had done on Ned Lamont, the winner of the Connecticut Democratic senatorial primary. The right-wing incumbent Joe Lieberman was smashed in the primary by antiwar voters like Lizzy and Joe, and yet the state media organs had decided that should Lieberman run as an independent candidate, they would do everything in their power to get him elected. And that was exactly what they did. Lizzy knew she harbored resentment against the press, but she tried to remain objective as she reviewed the media coverage of the William Pierce story.

Lizzy's objectivity was tried almost from the first moment when she realized that the premier story quite clearly stated that the Port Chester Police had classified the matter as a probable suicide. The print, television, and Internet media had all given the distinct impression that there was little or no doubt that Bill Pierce had taken his own life in his car parked just a few blocks from the state border. "Merciful God, how these bastards lie," whispered Lizzy as she read and reread the reports from the day following the recovery of Bill's body. Even the headlines were blatant in their disregard for the truth. "Unidentified out-of-state man found dead near Port Chester line," read the very first report printed in the *Port Chester Vanguard*. Did no one else see that it was impossible to know that

53

the man was from out of state if he was unidentified? She remembered an old insult which might be applied to people who accepted this drivel and asked herself, "Were they blind or were they just stupid?"

If the coverage of the *Vanguard* upset her, then the utter lack of serious coverage by the snooty *Greenwich Time* made her boil with rage. The *Time*'s initial coverage was three days after the discovery of the body and consisted of a two-line comment in the "Police Blotter" section of the paper. It read, "Male body found near town line in Port Chester. Case ruled suicide by PC police." It seemed ironic that most of the crime reported in the *Greenwich Time* was from other nearby towns. A joke had been made sometime back that the Greenwich Police were primarily occupied by two crimes—jaywalkers and people wearing clashing ensembles. She knew that there was a grain of truth to that joke and, while being grateful that crime was so slow, rued the fact that the low crime rate made crime and danger somewhat of a non-issue to Greenwich townsfolk. She remembered with a sad smile how the town's first female first selectman, Leila King, had sent out an armored SWAT team to the town hall on September 11, 2001, because she believed that terrorists would soon be overrunning the town with her being the prime target. When there was crime in town it was minor for the most part, but the thrill of a major incident could easily fan hysteria among these people.

A week after Bill was found there had been one article in the weekly *Greenwich Patriot* that pretty much summed up all that would ever be printed about the matter. It said simply that a Wyoming businessman, aged forty-two, had been found in his rent-a-car in Port Chester; his name William Pierce, his occupation hotelier, and his last known local stay had been with friends in

Greenwich. The only new information was a reference to the classification of his death being changed from suicide to probable murder. The only mention of the incident by the television media was a thirty-second story on Channel 68 WCTI-TV the Hartford Fox Affiliate, and that coverage identically echoed the brief details reported by the *Port Chester Vanguard*. Within a week of the first story the media coverage abruptly ended.

Through her political and charity work over the years Lizzy had made a number of friends in the local media. The press knew that if there was an elegant soiree or a charity ball in town Lizzy would be a part of it, so they often contacted her for details on the event, becoming friendly with her to ensure her availability for future comments. Lizzy sometimes used those friendships to reverse the tables and used them as sources for information on any number of subjects that piqued her interest. She worked those contacts hard for information on the Case, but to her chagrin they were very closed mouth on this subject. Early on she decided that Bill's Greenwich contacts must be high placed to rate the contrived apathy which the press was showing to the story. The "right people" did not have to bribe the media to squash a story; they simply threatened to pull advertisements from the papers or turn mum when their input was required as background for articles. Lizzy knew that there were things just as valuable as money in cases like these, and the elite of Greenwich knew exactly how to use them when the situation warranted it.

When the regular media failed her, Lizzy knew where to go for information; it was as close as her ever-present laptop. If you regard the Internet as a gold mine, then Lizzy was no haphazard old prospector, she was a veritable strip miner. If there were facts to be found she would uncover them, and for the past two months she had been hard at

55

work digging for the information she knew was there. She thanked God for the "gossip gene" which she shared with Great-Aunt Joan. With the Wainwright deal well on its way to fruition she padded her way barefoot to her office and settled into her office chair which once again felt cozy and inviting. She popped open her well-used laptop and brought up her blog going straight to the comment forum on the Case. The results brought a beaming smile to her face as she counted well over fifty comments under her last posting. She had baited the hook, and the fish were biting. Now to reel them in.

The diversity of the comments was gratifying to Lizzy as she noticed that more than a few were from blog readers in Wyoming. Evidently the gloss over of Bill's death had riled a fair number of his hometown friends and even, if the comment identifications could be trusted, several of his relatives. She noted that several of the comments were lengthy, but she decided to read them in chronological order, instead of jumping directly to the meatier ones as she was tempted to do. She knew that in blogging one comment drew out the next, and they flowed in order, so the best place to begin was the beginning. The first comment expressed a wish that everyone would drop the entire matter and let Bill rest in peace. *A reasonable comment from a grieving friend,* she thought as she scrolled down to the next comment. As she read the following one Lizzy could see that not everyone thought that dropping the subject was reasonable at all. The gist of the second writer was a blunt opinion that Bill could only rest in peace when his killer was brought to justice, which made her retract her initial thought on the matter. Justice was exactly what Bill needed to be at peace.

After reading the first page of comments Lizzy now had a better idea of who William Pierce was and how he had lived his life. He had owned the Brandywine Ranch as she already had learned; but it was the flagship of three resorts which were located in Nevada, Colorado, and, of course, Wyoming. The Jackson Hole ranch was the largest and the most popular with out-of-state tourists. It is a kind of western fantasy where a visitor could act like a cowboy during the day and enjoy a luxurious five-star hotel, restaurant, and nightclub after their Wild West playtime was over. Bill had worked for the resort, when it had been called the Silver Star Ranch, as an assistant desk manager; but somehow after one year of employment he had managed to purchase the place as well as its two sister ranches in nearby states. Even the bloggers were at a loss to explain the sudden rise to ownership which had occurred some ten years ago. "Hmmm," slipped from her lips as Lizzy read on. "A regular rags-to-riches story," she added as an afterthought. Either this had been a Horatio Alger story or there was much more to Bill's early life than met the eye.

The evening sped by uneventfully in the Dawson household; the boys were out on dates, Joe was in the den watching the History Channel, and Lizzy was in front of the laptop screen reading page after page of blogger input until eyestrain caused her to beg off further research. This seemed like a good time to sit on the patio and sip a cool glass of wine. The stars were exceptionally bright tonight; and the quiet, if it could be called that, was broken only by the croaking of frogs in the pond and the occasional baying of the neighborhood dogs at the ivory-colored moon. This had been a productive day all told. She had worked with the cleaning lady all morning, having the kind-hearted soul that she did. Lizzy had employed a somewhat dim-witted woman to clean her house and had made it a practice to assist her in finding dirt and

57

removing it. Left to her own devices the cleaning lady was known to spend an entire morning dusting and realigning toiletry bottles in each of the bathrooms. Lizzy genuinely liked the woman and did whatever was necessary to keep her, as long as the house was properly cleaned. She had always been like that—someone who honestly cared about other people. Maybe that was why she had been devoting so much time to giving Bill Pierce some justice, even if it was posthumously.

The following day her calendar was clear, so Lizzy resumed her research among the now-growing number of blog comments. Around noon she decided it was time for a quick lunch break and headed for the kitchen. As she peered into the well-stocked refrigerator a thought occurred to her: Joe was out for the entire day and the boys were at school, so why fix lunch? A nice meal out would feel good right about now, and she had an odd taste for chicken tenders, and what better to satisfy that craving than the McDonald's over in Old Greenwich? She was amused at herself by the contrived combination of her appetite for food and her appetite for some snooping. She grabbed her canvas tote bag, filled it with her paperwork, and jumped in the car.

The McDonald's was quite full with the usual lunchtime patrons, but Lizzy managed to occupy the same seat as she had when taking the boys out the other day. Scanning the interior first she was satisfied that Suzette was nowhere to be found. Actually that did not surprise her since she doubted that Suzette ever actually ate here. McDonald's was a perfect rendezvous spot where no one would ever expect to find her, but Suzette's taste in cuisine would hardly be satisfied by a Big Mac. Lizzy herself seemed very disinterested in her meal as she turned her gaze to the sprawling parking lot. Her eyes widened as she craned her neck to take a look at the farthest reaches of the lot. Sure enough there was the Mercedes with the telltale license plates. The midnight blue Beamer was nowhere to be seen, but a pattern had been established, and that was contenting enough for Lizzy to dive into her chicken tenders with relish.

The rest of her meal was spent divided between munching on her food and reading over her notes. Lizzy thought to herself that this lunch had been a very productive one. Little did she know that it was about to become the most productive lunch hour of her life. Feeling happy and full, Lizzy decided that she could use some fresh air and a bit of exercise, so she headed to Todd's Point Park for a brisk trot through the nature preserve. She loved the serenity of the setting while resenting the exclusivity which the town practiced regarding its use. She recalled the humorous story of how one of her friends had thwarted the security at the park several years ago. Her friend, Reverend Jeremy Collins, had been giving a friend a tour of Greenwich when he decided to make a visit to Todd's Point. As they pulled up to the guard post at the entrance to the park a teenaged park worker leaned out of the booth and informed them that the park was closed to non-Greenwich residents. Collins leaned over from the passenger seat and said in his best imitation of an Irish brogue, "I'm so sorry, lad, me friend here was telling me about the glories of this preserve; and since I happened to be the president of Ireland, I was hoping you might make an exception for me visit." The teenager stepped back, stood at attention as he saluted, and said, "President of Ireland! Sure, dude! You can go in!" The fact that the president of Ireland at the time was a woman was lost on the boy, but it showed that even the most sacred of Greenwich sanctuaries could be breached by a cunning-enough outsider.

And here she was at the very guard booth from her recollections, and here too was a Greenwich security guard scanning the beach permit affixed to Lizzy's car. With a quick nod he opened the gate, and paradise was hers. Many visitors drove the circumference of the park through its winding and secluded lanes, but Lizzy wanted to get some exercise, so she parked her car and set off on a pathway. Lizzy loved to do a fast-paced trot for the cardiovascular benefits, and even though the high stepping gait and pumping arm motion looked quite silly to her, she knew that this routine was designed for the maximum good. Off she trotted down her favorite pathway which was usually free of cars and the occasional cyclist. About halfway down the five-mile pathway she noticed the bumper of a parked car which was otherwise obscured by the brush on a side path that was not much more than two ruts in the dirt. She might have ignored the car entirely except for a hint of midnight blue near the bumper and a slight motion to the car and the branches which made contact with it. *There is no way this is what I think it is,* thought Lizzy as her curiosity got the best of her, and she crept slowly down the rough lane.

As she took cover in the spreading branches of a mulberry bush, Lizzy realized that by sheer chance she had found the dark blue Beamer belonging to the infamous Finellis, and the motion of the car seemed very close in rhythm to the timing of animated lovemaking. Venturing a few steps closer she peeked into the car. At this angle it was obvious that the passenger seat was totally reclined, and someone was lying on top of another person. Lizzy backed away when she realized how close she had come to the Beamer, but even at this angle she could see the firm, smooth cheeks of a well-toned male posterior moving up and down to the accompaniment

60

of low female moans. The Beamer, plus the Mercedes parked at McDonald's, plus the scene played out a few days ago equaled Suzette and the young Matthew Finelli carrying on an illicit affair under the town's usually acute social radar. Suzette was in her forties and Matthew in his early twenties, which made for juicy gossip by itself; but when Suzette's connection to Bill Pierce was added to the equation, the results were explosive.

Lizzy fished her cell phone out of her pocket and used its camera feature to capture the situation for future reference. Dropping the trotting posture for a quick-paced jog, Lizzy headed back to the car where she quickly jotted down details of today's discovery in her notes. This had been another exceptional day for the investigation. Lizzy had found yet another major piece of this sordid jigsaw puzzle, and some of those pieces were beginning to fit together at long last. This was another tidbit which could be alluded to discreetly on her blog with heaven knows what results. Now might be a good time to return to the newspapers, but not the crime pages, rather, the social news to see what had been going on with the Randolphs since their extremely cordial divorce. It was one odd thing for a couple to share a house after a divorce, but would Jack Randolph tolerate Suzette's affairs, if, in fact, he was aware of them?

The social pages were rather mute regarding the divorce of Jack and Suzette. That was to be expected, but their pictures were ubiquitous in the photos of private parties and town social events. With a keen eye and a magnifying glass Lizzy examined the many news photos of Suzette over the past six months and noticed a telltale change in Suzette's figure. The revealing gowns were replaced about two months ago by more draping and fully tailored dresses, but on the most recent occasions the skimpy

61

and elegant ensembles had returned with a vengeance. Had Suzette "taken care" of her pregnancy? If she had, there would be no trace of the procedure. In fact, chances were that an abortion had been performed somewhere out of state or even at a clinic in France or Switzerland. One could never have enough distance between oneself and such a socially embarrassing and personal option. Lizzy stopped a moment and considered that perhaps the media was not as useless as she had concluded; maybe she had neglected to use it to its fullest. When dealing with people of wealth and power their every move was grist for the media mill and could be found if sought in the proper places, and the society pages could be a very rich field of information.

The afternoon was grey and wet as Lizzy decided to build a small fire in the office fireplace. It had been an extremely productive day thus far. The purchase agreement on the Wainwright house had been signed, and a report from the assessor's office placed a value on the new acquisition which exceeded the buying price by nearly $100,000. Only in a town like this could a hundred thousand be an acceptable loss to rid oneself of a less-than-pleasant memory. It made no sense to Lizzy, but she was on the gainful side of the deal, and she was not about to complain. Once the paperwork had been copied and filed she sat down to a cup of herbal tea and her laptop. A cursory glance at the headlines revealed that this was a slow news day. No mention of President Obama or the North Korean missile crisis was to be found in the headlines; just prattle about some problem which Madonna was having with yet another overseas adoption.

The phone rang, and Lizzy engaged in a half-hour conversation with the potential buyers of her house on

Mountainview Terrace. Only in Greenwich could a tiny road up a gentle hill be named Mountainview. The town fathers had had a gift for hyperbole when they named the "newer" town streets over a hundred years ago. The town itself and the central downtown area dated back some three hundred sixty years, but the past hundred years had seen the community expand into the woods and pastures surrounding the original town footprint. The house on Mountainview was located in an area which had grown greatly from the mid-1950s to the present. New homes were interspersed between nineteenth-century Cape Cods and carpenter Gothic farmhouses. Lizzy and Joe had bought one of the dilapidated farmhouses two years ago and within a week of purchase had bulldozed it down. It had not been worth renovating and was quickly becoming the type of house that seemed out of place among the finer houses rising around it. The spot on which the farmhouse had stood was now occupied by what the locals were currently calling a McMansion. Lizzy disliked the term but readily admitted that their contracting company was one of Greenwich's top purveyors of said McMansions.

This deal was two years in the making, and Lizzy was delighted that a sale seemed just around the corner. After hanging up the phone she hit a familiar speed dial button and soon heard a crisp voice say, "Rivers here!" Ethan Rivers had been the realtor who had found the clients interested in the Mountainview house, and for that Lizzy was most grateful. The house had stood complete and unsold for over a year and was beginning to become a considerable drain on the Dawsons' exchequer. Ethan had found a charming young couple with a double trust fund who needed a suitable residence in which to live and entertain the host of other trust fund babies who made up their social circle. Mountainview was a stone's throw from several of the best local clubs, but it had one disadvantage. There was not a school anywhere near the premises. That fact did not seem to bother the young buyers; with unlimited cash, youth, and a cadre of exciting friends, children were the last thing on their minds.

Ethan Rivers had sold the couple on the rock-solid constitution of the house, a point which greatly amused Lizzy. She knew that the marble veneer of the columns and the stone facing on the house were but a fraction of an inch of façade covering sheets of plywood and pine timbers. There was nothing wrong with the construction. Lizzy and Joe had supervised the construction and made certain that it not only met building codes but exceeded them. Yet like so many things in life it was disappointing to think that the castlelike façade covered a timber house not too far advanced from the farmhouse which it replaced. The buying price of the farmhouse had been $750,000. The cost of demolition and construction of the new house had been $500,000. With odds and ends the total cost had been nearly $1,500,000. Lizzy smiled broadly at the accepted selling price of $3,025,000. Even after Ethan's commission and legal fees the Dawsons would be bringing home a tidy profit. Should the Randolph Fund collapse, Lizzy knew that the Dawson family lifestyle would survive, and that made her feel quite good about herself.

After the lengthy conversation about commissions, points, and mortgages ended, Lizzy and Ethan turned to small talk and, of course, friendly gossip.

"Elizabeth, old girl, how is the blog coming along? I dare say you have bigger stones than I to continue with that Pierce story. Egad! I still give a little shiver when I think about my experience with it!" intoned Rivers in his best Victorian vocabulary.

Lizzy prodded Ethan to say more about the Case. She knew full well that blog aside Ethan was a man with many business and social contacts which fed him a constant stream of information about people and things in town.

"Good gravy old girl, I am sure that by now you are aware that Suzette has chosen to murder her unborn child. What a bloody nasty business and how grateful Tiffany would be to bear such a gift," Ethan reported in an accent which was growing very tiresome to Lizzy's ear.

Were he not such a good friend, fellow Atonement member, and wonderful source, she would be tempted to tell him to grow up and act like a normal human being. Lizzy, however, was too kind to be so very mean.

Before Lizzy could question the identity of the Tiffany person whom he had mentioned, Ethan excused himself from the conversation with a quick "Ta ta, old girl," and he was gone. Besides his Masterpiece Theater affectations Lizzy felt very annoyed by his flighty and abrupt manners in ending conversation, or as he might put it "taking his leave." Who, in heaven's name, was Tiffany; and why would she be grateful to carry Suzette's baby? Maybe what Tiffany would prefer was to carry a baby by a specific father, thus envying Suzette. Who was the logical candidate for the baby's father? Who else but Bill Pierce! Without fully realizing it Lizzy had just laid her hands on a major piece of the puzzle. Now all she needed to do was fit it into the framework she had already been assembling.

With the mysterious Tiffany on her mind, Lizzy turned her attention to her blog which now had a page count of nine, each filled with comments from across the country. Starting at the latest comment she read backward until she came upon a comment 5 from the bottom.

It was identified as coming from Bill's brother Timothy Pierce, and what it said shocked and elated Lizzy, "I curse the day that Bill met that horrible family from Connecticut. I will never understand what he saw in that woman. A married woman with husband and kids in tow doesn't strike me as the kind of person Bill was looking for at all. For all her beauty, I guess Tiffany was too young and too poor to suit his tastes. I know he loved Tiffany, but Bill never took her seriously as a potential wife. I wish he had; then maybe he'd still be here in Jackson Hole alive and well."

Lizzy took a sip of her lemonade and thought how mundane a drink to have while reading such a thrilling revelation, but lemonade would have to do for now. There was no way she would interrupt her research at this moment.

Searching her bookmarks Lizzy highlighted the Brandywine Ranch site, and after a moment the sight of the now-familiar ranch entered her screen. Clicking on the "Staff" heading in the site's toolbar she scanned the list of ranch officials. Sure enough, there was the name Tiffany Gould listed under the heading of "Hostesses." Clicking on the name she discovered a small photo and a blurb which described Tiffany as the evening hostess of the Broken Arrow dining room, the resort's elegant restaurant. What the blurb did not say was amply said by the accompanying photograph. Tiffany was a beautiful young girl with flowing dark hair, alabaster skin, and deep luxurious brown eyes, eyes so dark that one could hardly distinguish the iris from the pupil. *Oh my, this girl is gorgeous,* thought Lizzy as she tried in vain to enlarge the tiny picture. Where the media had failed her, a little old-fashioned gossip and the Internet had delivered.

Fishing out her Visa card from her wallet, Lizzy typed in the URL of a discount travel service into the address bar of her screen. Now was the time to book some tickets to Jackson Hole and make reservations at the Brandywine Ranch. She knew that Joe would not be happy to have the suggested trip booked without his consultation, and an early departure date would add to his discomfort at the idea, but the excuse could be made that Priceline had offered the best deal for booking with the least advanced departure. She kept in mind that the boys' school term would be ending on the Friday of next week, so her window of availability was satisfyingly close. Making the arrangements for the airline tickets, rent-a-car, and transport to Kennedy Airport went quickly and smoothly. When price was not really an issue a deal could be struck in less than twenty minutes. Four tickets on WestAm airlines with a stopover in Chicago ten days from today, a rent-a-car waiting at the Jackson Hole Airport, and a limo reserved from Greenwich to Kennedy were all arranged through the online travel service. William Shatner would have been proud of her!

Lizzy was reveling in a sense of self-contentment when a thought struck her. What if there were no rooms available at the Brandywine Ranch on the dates she had selected for their trip? She reopened the Brandywine site and located the reservations telephone number. She would rather make these arrangements with a live operator, avoiding any possible glitch with the online system. A lively and twangy voice answered at the Brandywine, "Brandywine Ranch Reservations, this is Pam, how may I assist you?" Lizzy made her request for accommodations for four, two adults and two teens for a seven-day stay. After a moment of silence broken only by the sound of typing on a keyboard, Pam returned and said, "I'm afraid that the only rooms we have available for four on those dates are in our Chief Seattle Suite which consists of three bedrooms, two sitting rooms, and a den. The cost of which is $800 a night at the tourist season rate." With an audible groan Lizzy read off the numbers from her credit card and reserved the suite. Any savings made with the discount travel service had just been consumed by the exorbitant room rate. This trip had better pay hefty dividends in information at this price.

At dinner that night Lizzy broke the news to the family. As expected Troy and Scott greeted the news with shouts and high fives. Joe on the other hand sat for a moment stony-faced. When he did speak he slowly and deliberately said, "Ten days from today. Kind of short notice, if you ask me." Before she could given him a sheepish excuse, his face broke into a smile, and he added, "That sounds great to me! We could use a rest, and maybe you can take a break from this story of yours." With a guilty little grin Lizzy simply said, "You can say that again." To use that unfortunate metaphor again, Lizzy had dodged another bullet, this time a domestic one.

The following ten days, nine not counting that evening, were hectic ones. Many details needed to be handled, including the possibility that legal papers might be ready for signatures on several tentative deals which were in the offing. The boys insisted that they must have new outfits for the week out west. After all Greenwich beach attire would not do for a couple of young cowpokes. Joe volunteered to take the boys out to a clothing store he located on the Internet which sold just the kind of duds that they were looking for, so that was one chore that Lizzy could cross off her list. On the way back from shopping at Colorado Roy's Emporium of Clothes, Joe stopped by the

Tack Shop just up the road from the house. The cowboy hats at Colorado Roy's reeked of New York urban cowboys, so Joe decided to splurge and buy the entire family proper wide-brim hats at the Tack Shop. He knew he would be dropping somewhere in the neighborhood of a thousand dollars for four adult-sized hats at Greenwich's snootiest riding shop, but this was the first family vacation in a number of years, and he wanted to do it right. Luckily he was as yet unaware of how much a week in the Chief Seattle Suite was going to dent the family account; but sometimes, at least in the short term, ignorance can definitely be bliss.

Lizzy had tried very hard to budget her time while working so hard to be ready for a week's absence from home and business life. She had judged periods of time needed for the many chores ahead, but she had one unexpected matter that arose which required more time than she currently had at her disposal. Her blog was exploding with information. New comments were piling up, and she felt sure that she must have struck a nerve with her latest posting because the volume of response had more than tripled in the past few days. To her family it began to appear as if Lizzy had grown a new appendage at the end of her right arm. Slung from her right shoulder and held tightly with her right hand was her trusty laptop. What had been a daily routine of simply checking e-mails and blog comments was beginning to become an obsession. Even the marital bed had been invaded by the shiny silver notebook. Lizzy had taken up the habit of sleeping with her laptop next to her, to keep herself busy on the many occasions when she would awaken in the middle of the night.

Joe had not objected to the practice of having the laptop share the bed with him and his wife. It seemed like a quaint little quirk and was totally harmless, but as time wore on he would often find himself awakened by the clicking of the keys as Lizzy returned e-mails and posted more material on her blog. It also occurred to him that all the activity centered predominantly around the Pierce story. A small tinge of jealousy sometimes ran across Joe's mind when he considered how much time his wife was spending researching about a very young and handsome man-about-town; but his jealousy turned to embarrassment when he remembered that Bill Pierce was a young, handsome, and very dead man-about-town. As if his flirtations with jealousy were not enough, he also found annoyance that the laptop occupied a share of his bed which just happened to be located between himself and his lovely wife.

Each time Lizzy read the new comments on her blog she felt as if fate were paving her way to Wyoming with a trail of clues and information which would allow her to zero in on facts while she was checking out the scene and people at the Brandywine Ranch. This trip would take her as close to Bill Pierce's life as she would ever get. The man was dead, but the patterns and associations of his life were freshly interrupted at the ranch. She thought about the dream she had in which Bill had spoken about someone in his life who was his true love. She also wondered if the ranch's bar would look like the room she had been in during the dream. There were many things to ponder, and providence or fate was on her mind tonight. The problem was that Lizzy did not believe in fate and, thinking about her dream, wondered if some other force might be guiding and helping her along the way.

Lizzy realized long ago that the term "media" had two different meanings. The first meaning was that of the formal press, be it newspaper, television, radio, and even the Internet. The second definition was much broader and considerably older than the electronic news which we consume. The second kind of media was conversation, just plain old conversation, not all that different from the town crier of the past. People conveyed news by word of mouth from the dawn of humanity. If the formal media would not provide her with what she needed, then she would reach out to a greater extent to friends and neighbors. Her first unscheduled stop this afternoon would be a quick visit to Father Redanz. She would kill two birds with one stone with this appointment. She had been meaning to speak to him about her dream to see what he thought about it and the fact that so many details had fallen into her lap by sheer coincidence, and she also knew that as a local clergyman he heard a lot about what was going on around town. If the conversation were thoughtfully directed, he would gladly tell what he knew, as long as it was not under the seal of the confessional.

Calling ahead, Lizzy managed to secure about an hour with the good padre, and away she went reviewing her questions as she drove. The rectory of Church of the Atonement was a simple affair just off the center of town, and she knew she could slip into the miniparking area in front of the house. Father Redanz was already outside watering some of the flowers in the garden he was so very proud of. Looking up from his gardening he greeted Lizzy with a warm and charming "Good day, my dear lady." Richard Redanz was a man of nearly fifty years of age, tall and portly with a majestic air about him, an air which somewhat carried over to his personality. He could be a very charming individual, but he could also come across haughty and arrogant. Lizzy was grateful that he seemed to be in one of his best personable moods at the moment. One of the things Lizzy liked about him was his attention to women; some even thought he was a bit of a flirt, especially husbands who did not appreciate being mildly ignored as he fawned over their wives. Lizzy found that extra attention very endearing, as did most of his female parishioners.

After the usual casual words of greeting Lizzy got down to business. She related the entire content of her dream about Bill Pierce, down to the tiniest detail of decor and dress. Being a professional interior designer was a great help at remembering design details, and Lizzy felt sure that she could have easily reproduced the bar from her dream given enough space and time.

Following her description of the dream, Lizzy told her pastor, "I have had a string of very lucky coincidences which, added to this dream, make me wonder if there isn't a higher purpose to this whole matter and maybe I am getting a little divine assistance with it."

The response which Redanz gave her was not a very satisfying one. He told her, "Now, Elizabeth, you and I both know that dreams are the products of overflow from our conscious minds. They are a release by which we can explore areas of our minds which we restrain while awake. Yes, they do have meaning, but it is the meaning which our own minds assign them as a message to us."

Reaching for a volume from one of his many bookshelves, Lizzy noticed the title, *A Freudian Interpretation of Dreams*; but before he cracked the book open he located a second volume which was a similar book, but authored by Jung.

Oh brother, thought Lizzy. This was not at all the kind of reaction which she had expected. Trying to avoid a long lecture on dreams, she quickly changed the subject to the feeling about the coincidences and the guidance she felt in her endeavor. This time she was not too disappointed in Redanz's answer.

"Elizabeth, we are all guided in one way or another by God, the Holy Spirit is active in every human life, and that certainly includes yours. But none of us is able to determine what and where that guidance is, not even me." He quickly added, "And also remember that there are other forces in the world which try to guide us as well, forces which may or may not be personal, but which steer us in the wrong direction in many ways."

He gave an example, "Do you recall that book which was written about the Martha Moxley incident? I cannot judge; but I would venture to guess that part of the motivation, guidance if you will, of that author was as much a dislike for the Kennedy family and the desire for a best seller, as it was for a sense of justice."

Greed and possibly hatred could be strong motivators, but Lizzy knew that the Case was different. The motivation here was a search for justice. And she knew that motivation alone could not create these amazing coincidences.

When the conversation finally turned to news about town, the mood lightened considerably. Father Redanz was a popular figure in Greenwich, having been a rector there for over twenty years. He knew people, and he socialized with town figures and their own clergy. One item which surprised Lizzy was the news that after their divorce Jack and Suzette also parted company religiously. Jack remained at the prestigious Saint Saviour Episcopal Church in the center of town, while Suzette had become a member of the very trendy Evangelical Church of Round Hill. Round Hill Church was the "in spot" to worship for the younger and nouveau riche set. In the great easing of social structures of the last generation, some people, especially the young, came to realize that money is money.

73

The only people who really disapprove of the new rich are the old money people, and their ways were quickly passing away. Suzette had chosen to attend a place filled with rich, young, and often available millionaires. It just seemed the natural thing for her to do.

Rumor had it that Suzette, while happy with her new church home, was looking for yet another church to belong to and for good reason. After one Sunday service a small boy had pulled open the door of a large Porsche SUV, mistaking it for his family's vehicle. Much to his shock, there in the reclined front seat were Suzette and one of the church's handsome young singles. While the couple was still essentially dressed the boy easily caught sight of the man entering Suzette as she bounced up and down on his lap wildly. Evidently the sex had been so intense that the couple had not noticed the opening of the door and continued until the boy let out a horrified shout. The experience might have been a turn-on for a boy of twelve or more years, but to a child of seven the sight of adult sex was quite traumatizing.

Details had been spread around town, mostly by the boy's parents, who also decided not to call the police under two conditions: first, that the amorous couple both leave the church and, second, that they jointly pay for an extended regime of counseling sessions for the youth. An agreement was drafted and signed on the next day. The pastor of the church discreetly asked the members of the Greenwich clergy circle, at their next meeting, to help him relocate his two exiles, not giving any details but implying what everyone in the room suspected from the start of his comments.

As she sat listening, Lizzy felt a pang of revulsion. Suzette had amassed a string of lovers, including Bill Pierce, which probably stretched back more than a few years and was very much current with the inclusion of young Matthew Finelli. Lizzy knew that there isn't a woman or man who hasn't considered cheating on their spouse at some point in their marriage, but Suzette now appeared to be the town tramp, albeit a very wealthy and still influential tramp. Father Redanz proved to be a good source of information as he added many other small tidbits of information revolving around the Case and the private lives of Greenwich's former first couple. For all the stately manners and Ivy League educations of these people, it was becoming quite apparent that all levels of society have their dirty laundry, and Lizzy was peering directly into it at its basest. In the South it is said that poor people have roaches while the rich have palmetto bugs, a difference of semantics, not reality. They all have things in common, even if the similarities don't always meet the eye.

Feeling somewhat disappointed in at least the spiritual side of her conversation with Father Redanz, Lizzy pulled out of the rectory driveway and ran down her mental checklist of things which needed to be done for the upcoming trip. There were plenty of errands to be run and preparations to be made; but she knew that she, Joe, and the boys would rise to the occasion and be ready when it was time to head to the airport. The more time which passed in her investigation of the Case, the more Lizzy realized how much hard work she was putting into it. Her multi-tiered life was beginning to take a toll on her, and she was starting to feel some wear and tear physically. Lizzy and Joe were health conscious. Part of their exercise regime was a nice long walk after dinner and before bed, but lately the walks had begun to tire Lizzy. The thought struck her that the idea of a vacation right now might be just what the doctor ordered.

In preparation for her investigation in Jackson Hole, Lizzy decided that a more in-depth perusal of the Wyoming newspapers might uncover some clues that would prove of help when she was actually on the scene. Jackson Hole is a fairly small and very affluent community; in fact one might envision it as Greenwich with a cowboy hat. Much like Greenwich the local papers were small affairs with many pages devoted to society news and community events. Hard news was not a big priority with the town editors. The Pierce case had been somewhat of an exception since this was a hometown boy who had done well with his life, only to lose it in an untimely and mysterious death. Lizzy did not expect to find very much new from reading the Wyoming press, but she did catch a detail which had eluded her in the past. William Pierce was not a native of Jackson Hole, or even Wyoming. He had been born in Ohio and in a town that rang a bell with Lizzy.

The *Jackson Hole Republican-Sun* newspaper mentioned that while Bill was a beloved member of the local community, replete with snakeskin boots and a ten-gallon Stetson cowboy hat, he had been born and raised in Lakewood, Ohio, very coincidentally, as Lizzy would later discover, the birthplace and childhood home of Suzette Benoit Randolph. Another report in a regional newspaper was a long article which contained vignettes of Bill's life from reminiscences of friends and acquaintances, which proved to be quite informative. One story sprang out at Lizzy in part because it reconfirmed earlier stories of Bill's sudden and unexplained rise from assistant desk manager of the ranch to the position of sole owner within a year of his arrival. That fact made her begin to wonder just how long Bill had lived in Wyoming and from what source he had managed to raise the money to buy the resort.

Bill Pierce had been a man of mystery even before his death on the East Coast. Lizzy thought to herself that she had come upon an enigma, an enigma of the same sort that she pondered about sites she had seen while driving through the outer boroughs of New York City: young men in impoverished neighborhoods "chilling" in brand-new BMW and Mercedes convertibles. These boys lived in subsidized projects and tumbled-down houses in the Bronx and Brooklyn, and yet there they were in $75,000 cars. Something just did not add up. The frustration which she felt over not being able to understand those situations returned to her as she wondered how a middle-management person could buy his employer's business after working there for just one year. Things about Bill often did not add up, and this was one of those things, one of the largest of those things.

It was obvious from the Wyoming news coverage that Bill Pierce had been a well-liked businessman and a beloved part of his community. Mention was made often of his generosity in the community and the active part he personally played in making life more pleasant for his fellow inhabitants of Jackson Hole. He was a sponsor of a number of children's sports teams, as well as the boys and girls' club in town. Words shared by the local Baptist pastor seemed to indicate that Bill also was active, at least to some degree, in the Hardin Street Baptist Church of Jackson Hole. He was a man of many parts. The problem for Lizzy was that she could not as yet see how these many parts were joined together to form this handsome and interesting man. She planned to find out soon enough after her plane landed at Jackson Hole Airport.

After spending half the night reading Wyoming news stories about Bill Pierce's murder and the future of the Brandywine Ranch, Lizzy decided to sleep in the following morning. She had the next few days scheduled out and was sure that everything would be in order for the trip. Around ten the following morning the door chimes from the front door sounded, and a half-asleep Lizzy stumbled to the door to find Emily Engelby on her doorstep. Emily was a neighbor from down the road and a casual acquaintance of the Dawson family. Her two daughters attended the same school as Lizzy's sons, and one of them had even dated Troy. Emily was a tall and beautiful woman who had done a good bit of modeling before she married Gerald Engelby, a prominent Broadway theatrical producer. She also was one of the African American ladies who had been ushered off the beach at Todd's Point by the forces of First Selectman Randolph sometime ago. Having been a popular model often compared to Imam and being married to a white husband well-known in the entertainment field, she was not accustomed to racial prejudice. The beach incident had left her with a permanent distrust of the lofty Greenwich society and a sincere dislike for Jack Randolph.

Lizzy wondered what the unexpected visit from Emily might be about as she invited her in and offered her some coffee. Emily accepted the offer; and as the two sat, preparing to talk, she came very quickly to the point.

"Lizzy, I know that your blog has been investigating the Pierce murder. You seem to be pointing to the Randolphs, so I thought something I have heard might be helpful to you. I have been told by my husband that a backer of his newest play is the uncle of a young woman who works at the Brandywine Ranch and is carrying William Pierce's baby." Before Lizzy could react Emily added, "And she is the reason Bill and Suzette called off their engagement."

Lizzy's head began to swim as she ingested this startling new information. She had known about the affair between Bill and Suzette and the fact that this affair may have broken up the Randolph marriage. This was the first rumor that she had heard about an engagement, let alone one that had been broken.

Lizzy was about to engage in a little old-fashioned information pumping when Emily told her, "Liz, anything and everything I know is yours for the asking. I want to see that bigoted bastard on Randolph Hill come tumbling down, and I mean all the way down."

Here was an excellent source of dirt which like so many others had dropped right into Lizzy's lap, another reason to believe that something, somewhere was giving her a bit of unexplained assistance in the Case. Lizzy excused herself and went to her office to fetch her trusty leather notebook and pen to do this interview in a calm professional manner. Details needed to be catalogued and recorded because one never knew where a clue might lead. Lizzy was not about to treat this as a matter of gossip and rumor anymore. She knew that she had evolved from a person gathering gossip and having a bit of fun to a serious combination of journalist and investigator.

Not wasting any time Lizzy launched into a series of questions which she hoped would progress to questions and answers she had not yet anticipated. Emily was a rich source of inside information, and Lizzy intended to gather as much information as she could from Emily before heading off to her trip to Jackson Hole. The more details she carried with her, the better she would be able to build on them at the ranch. Lizzy's mind was beginning to function like that of a detective, and she was well aware of the transition taking place in her. As much as she loved her work as an interior designer, she found herself wishing that she had attended John Jay College of Criminal Justice instead of the Fashion Institute of Technology. There was so much information coming in that she sometimes felt a bit overwhelmed by trying to sort and categorize it all in a logical and chronologically correct manner. She was now working with a cooperative source and one who was aware of where her line of questioning was leading, but what would it be like to subtly question people who were not aware of what she was doing and might be hesitant to part freely with very personal information? Before she began her interview Lizzy jotted a quick note in the margin of her legal pad, "Pick up a book on criminal justice and give Bernice at the NYPD a call."

Emily's visit lasted just over three hours and ended with a quick bite to eat, but the information which she shared with Lizzy filled enough pages to appear to be notes from a full semester of studies. The name Tiffany Gould was the first and most valuable detail to come out of the interview. The other information hung on this young woman from Jackson Hole, and it spread out in strands leading in many directions. Tiffany was a young employee of the Brandywine Ranch who had caught the eye of Bill Pierce from the first moment of her employment interview with him. Despite having no education past a semester of college and no work experience whatsoever, she had been hired on the spot and was given a position of some responsibility. Her uncle, Harold Gould, had told Gerald Engleby that while he was delighted at his niece's good fortune, he was troubled by the fact that she had been hired so quickly and for a position which he felt was beyond her skills. Harold was very much a second father to Tiffany, and like any parental figure he questioned any situation regarding his niece which seemed too good to be true.

Harold was no saint, and he knew that his own hiring practices sometimes entailed ulterior motive when it came to pretty young girls. Over the years he himself had hired under-qualified young ladies for positions in his firm, and each of them had ended up on his office couch. The last of these new hires was now his third wife. So he wondered if the owner of the Brandywine Ranch was operating under the same modus operandi. In spite of his misgivings he realized that being half a continent away from Wyoming made his intervention nearly impossible, so he hoped for the best and offered Tiffany a long-distance shoulder to cry on should things work out badly. He had to admit that in the intervening months since her hire all her phone calls had been happy and positive. He began to think that he was being a foolish and doting old man over the whole matter, but when he learned of the murder his concerns were rekindled with a vengeance.

A quick flight to Jackson Hole and a long weekend with Tiffany confirmed his suspicions. There had been a romance, and his sweet little niece had just discovered that she was pregnant. Harold offered to bring Tiffany back to his home in Saddle River, New Jersey, but she would have no part of it. She had grown into her job, and that job was still secure. She had no reason to abandon her adopted home. An unwed mother certainly was no matter for scandal even in the conservative west which included among its residents the likes of Dick Cheney. She was happy with her life and was coming to deal with Bill's death slowly and gradually, so why should she throw it all away and run back home to New Jersey? Being the wife of the Brandywine owner was out of the picture now,

81

but to work her way up to being general manager was not out of the question with enough time and hard work. No. She would stay and make the best of it, so with a tear and a wave she saw her uncle off at the Jackson Hole Airport and returned to the task of keeping Bill's dream alive. The Brandywine was not Bill, but it was a part of his life which she could still hold on to.

Harold Gould reluctantly returned home, but he was not satisfied with what he had learned. Before he unpacked his bags he dialed the private investigator he had used for business reasons and set up an appointment to discuss this matter with him as soon as possible. He could feel in his bones that there was more to this tragedy than he had been told and probably more than Tiffany herself knew about. The Percy Manning Detective Agency would flesh out the story, especially since he intended to hire Percy Manning himself.

Within a month of their first meeting Manning presented Harold with a report on Bill Pierce, and what Harold read surprised and troubled him to no end. His departed and prospective nephew-in-law had been having a very open affair with a wealthy divorcee from nearby Greenwich, Connecticut, a woman who was also pregnant, presumably with Bill's child, and who had accepted a proposal of marriage from Bill. Their engagement was not a public affair, there was no notice in the society pages of any newspaper, nor had there been a party to celebrate the arrangement, but it was widely known in club society and among local people in the know. What Harold found most unsettling was the fact that the short engagement had been broken off because the Greenwich socialite had become aware of an affair which Bill was having with one of his young female employees, obviously Harold's niece, Tiffany. During a trip to Greenwich to try to repair the broken engagement Bill had been found dead. *What in the hell has Tiffany gotten herself into?* thought Harold as he closed the report and rubbed his eyes. Deciding that he knew as much as he cared to know he tossed the report into his paper shredder with a sigh of both disgust and, sadly, relief.

Gerald Engleby had related every minute detail to his wife after learning that the Greenwich socialite in question was Suzette Randolph, wife of the one man whom his wife hated with a passion. The information had lain dormant for some time before Emily discovered the GreenwichSecrets blog, and now it was in the hands of the blog's author. Hopefully, it would become one more nail in the coffin of J. Richard Randolph. Emily made no pretense to cover the fact that she firmly believed that Jack and probably even Suzette were tied to Bill Pierce's death. She hoped that Lizzy and her investigation would somehow prove it beyond a shadow of a doubt or, perhaps better said, beyond a reasonable doubt.

As Lizzy reviewed her notes late that afternoon, she felt that this was one of those times that she wished she had some formal investigative training. She now had three separate stacks of notes and files which badly needed to be integrated to delete redundancies and false avenues. That alone would be a gargantuan task, and it made her wonder how police detectives managed to keep all the facts clear and in order. Maybe that call to Bernice should be made sooner rather than later. A trained hand could be very useful to organize the Case and give her a focused direction to follow as she moved forward with her work. If she had made a final decision on anything at this point, it was her firm belief that Bill Pierce had, without question, been murdered, even if the police would not say so directly and the number one suspects in the Case were the Randolphs. Now all she had to do was fill in the blanks and prove it.

In the evening Lizzy and Joe had a quiet dinner alone, the kids were off on dates, and the house was totally still, so the two of them retired to the den and cuddled on the sofa in front of the lifeless television. Joe suggested that they leave the TV off and just have a pleasant conversation. He had no idea what he was in for by offering that innocent suggestion. In a calm and matter-of-fact tone Lizzy related all she had learned in torrents as Joe listened attentively, but felt somewhat stunned. The reality of how intensely Lizzy had gotten into this story hit home to Joe. He knew that she had devoted quite a bit of time to investigating the Pierce death, but he had not imagined how personally she was taking the whole matter. He hesitated to think of her actions as an obsession, but he feared that that was where she was headed. Unwittingly, he changed the subject to their upcoming vacation, not realizing that this whole trip was designed to dig deeper into the case. A light dawned, however, when Lizzy mentioned that Bill had been the owner of the Brandywine Ranch. In Joe's mind, the vacation lost some of its glamour.

Lizzy was gearing up for the trip and trying very hard to put the Case on the back burner. As is so often the case, she was the primary organizer and packer. Her perfectly able husband and two teenage boys seemed incapable of folding and packing a week's worth of clothes into luggage. Each of the household males was expert at packing the computers, video games, iPods, and Blackberries; socks, shirts, and underwear were the furthest things from their minds. In between packing for everyone in the house, Lizzy managed to make a few calls to Bernice as well as follow-up calls to detectives that Bernice had suggested might be of assistance to Lizzy. One in particular was especially helpful, Abel Ramirez, a retired sergeant from the Thirty-second Precinct up in Washington Heights, jumped at the chance to do a little police work again. Lizzy made a lunch date with Ramirez for a few days after her return from Wyoming. Although she would have preferred to get some pointers prior to the trip, she was satisfied that he was willing to remain in phone contact with her during the upcoming days and even during the trip.

The remaining days sped by; and before she knew it, she, Joe, and the boys were sitting at the airport waiting to board their WestAm flight to Jackson Hole. Lizzy did not look forward to the lengthy flight; with a two-hour layover in Chicago the entire flight time would be about seven hours, not counting any delays. The price had been right on the tickets, but after boarding the 737 she wished that she had spent the extra money for a first-class seat. Business class was all well and good; she did not need champagne, hors d'oeuvres, or a real blanket, but she dreaded the cramped seating with almost no room to maneuver her legs for comfort. She stowed her tote bag and computer travel bag under the seat and struggled to make herself comfortable. It was a losing effort, and she felt confined from the first moment. Joe and the boys seemed perfectly comfortable, but she could not find a position where she could feel at ease. *Seven hours of this is going to be hell,* thought Lizzy as the plane slowly taxied toward the runway. She decided that from this day forward she would splurge on better seats. In fact she would call and try to upgrade the return flight even if Priceline said no changes could be made on purchased tickets.

The flight was uneventful and smooth. After collecting all their bags Lizzy approached the Hertz counter hoping that things would continue to be trouble-free. To her surprise, things actually improved. The rent-a-car they had ordered was not in stock, so they were given a free upgrade to an SUV with all the bells and whistles that a person could ask for, and the price was definitely right. As they arrived in the lot to pick up their SUV they were greeted by a vehicle already running and with the air-conditioning on and functioning, a pleasant retreat from the dry heat of nearly one hundred degrees at the airport. All was going exceptionally well, but Lizzy felt achy and stiff after the long flight. She just wanted to stretch and jump into a warm bath, or maybe the Jacuzzi which was part of the Chief Seattle Suite. It had been a calm but physically trying journey. At long last, however, here she was pulling into the driveway of Bill Pierce's very own resort.

The resort was even more impressive than the photos on the Web site. It looked as if it had just been built while also reflecting the rustic western charm that was promised in its brochures. The boys were ecstatic at seeing the ranch with all its surrounding amenities. Stetsons were unpacked and donned before the bellman could even open the doors for the family. It was fairly obvious that Joe and the boys were going to make the most of this experience. Little known to them, so was Lizzy, but in a far different way than they had in mind. While Joe took the paperwork to the check-in desk Lizzy slipped away and followed signs to the resort's bar and luncheon area. When she pushed her way through the dark brown saloon doors she froze in shock and amazement. The bar was identical to the room in which she had spoken to Bill Pierce during her dream. With a trained interior designer's eye, she scanned the room and located every minute detail which she remembered from the dream; even the current bartender on duty was the same as in

86

her dream. Things were more interesting for her at the ranch than Lizzy had ever imagined.

The flight had left New York at 7:00 a.m., and for the Dawson family it was three in the afternoon, but in Wyoming it was just after one, and lunch was being served. After directing the bellman where to drop their luggage the four Dawsons were ready for a hearty meal as the meal on the airplane could hardly have been called a meal. Everyone was ready for a western-style meal of buffalo or some other Wyoming specialty. What they ended up with was New York strip steak sandwiches on hard rolls with some barbeque sauce. Anything tastes good after an airline meal, so they savored every bite and discussed plans for the rest of the day. Lizzy enjoyed her sandwich despite feeling under the weather. She still felt stiff from the flight and noticed a pain in her left leg. She thought hopefully that a nice dip in the Jacuzzi would fix that up in no time.

Lizzy fell asleep in the Jacuzzi and awoke at just before six, regretting having spent so much time relaxing. She had to admit to herself that she felt so much better, and the pain in her leg was gone, so it had been time well spent. Wondering how formally she needed to dress for dinner Lizzy dialed up the front desk and was shocked to hear a voice at the other end say, "This is Tiffany. How may I assist you?" The chances of there being more than one Tiffany were almost nil, so on her very first day at the Brandywine Lizzy was speaking to none other than Bill Pierce's young lover Tiffany Gould. It took Lizzy a moment to remember why she had placed the call, but after a few hesitant sounds she asked about the proper attire for dinner. Tiffany assured her that casual clothing was quite acceptable; after all this was technically a dude ranch. Lizzy thanked her and offhandedly added that she was so helpful that she would like to meet her at some point during their stay. Tiffany replied by saying, "Thank you, Mrs. Dawson. It would be my pleasure. I am the reservation manager, but I am filling in on the desk to give one of the staff a break. Just call back anytime and ask for Tiffany Gould, and we can set up a moment to meet. I would like very much to get your impression of our resort after you have had time to look around some."

Lizzy and the three cowboys that she barely recognized as her husband and sons had a delicious dinner at the outdoor barbeque café in the rear area of the resort's main building, where Joe and the boys had decided to eat. She had to chuckle at the sight of her three Greenwich city slickers all dressed up like Butch Cassidy and the Sundance Kid. She loved Joe and the boys so much and felt delight at the fun they were already having here at the Brandywine. She may have had ulterior motives for this vacation location, but it was obviously the right choice for her family to enjoy and in which to relax at. "Fun" was the ultimate word to describe how the male Dawsons were enjoying this vacation, and that made Lizzy very happy as a wife and mother. As a rookie detective Lizzy's choice of words for this trip had to be informative and productive, and she had not even begun to dig.

After a good meal and a scheduled square dance in the barn, Lizzy was ready for bed and headed off to the suite while Joe and the boys decided to stay out to see the nightly fireworks in the back forty of the ranch. Too tired to check her blog comments, Lizzy turned on the laptop and placed it next to her in the king-sized bed. She dozed off almost instantly but began to toss and turn within an hour of falling asleep. Around two in the morning Lizzy made a sharp roll and awoke to the sound of her laptop crashing to the floor beside her. The noise woke up Joe as well. He jumped up and retrieved the computer which had fallen partially under the bed. He sighed with relief that it had just been the computer and also at the fact that Lizzy had wisely brought her Panasonic Toughbook laptop on the trip. Lizzy was glad to see that the computer had not suffered even a minor scratch. Before she and Joe could settle back into bed she noticed a growing pain just under her left breast. Joe hopped out of bed once again and ran into the bathroom to return immediately with an ice-cold glass of water and Alka-Seltzer. Lizzy had occasionally suffered from indigestion, and he assumed that it had returned.

A grateful Lizzy swallowed the drink and after a quick burp decided that she felt a little better, so with some difficulty she tried once again to get to sleep. Joe nestled back into bed and feigned a quick return to sleep but remained awake for some time after watching Lizzy to make sure she was really all right. Joe sometimes gave the impression of being a gruff character, but he was still as much in love with Lizzy as the day they had married. Her well-being meant more to him than his own, and he knew that she sometimes downplayed her own distress, so as not to worry him. He worried nonetheless, and he wanted to be sure that her pain of the moment was only some indigestion from a heavy meal. When Lizzy finally was in a restful state of sleep, Joe closed his eyes and slipped away to a reassured slumber.

The alarm went off at 8:00 a.m. on the dot. Joe sprang up anxious to play cowboy again, but when he caught sight of Lizzy with a pained look on her face and a hand resting under her breast, he knew that something was not right. "Okay, baby, level with me. What's wrong?" he said as he lay back down next to his beloved wife. "Joe, the pain didn't go away, and it has gotten worse, but let's give it a little more time, okay?" was her reply. "Hell, no, we are not giving anything more time. I am calling for an ambulance right now. We aren't taking any chances. You are more important than any vacation." And with that said Joe called the desk and requested medical assistance. The resort nurse was at their door in less than five minutes, and before she knew it Lizzy was in a resort van speeding to the Jackson Hole hospital with Joe and the nurse beside her. Nurse Judy Regan was an experienced, well-trained medical professional. She did not like what she saw. It was definitely not a heart attack, but the pain was intense and close enough to the heart to warrant immediate emergency room attention. If it turned out to be a minor problem, so be it. Nurse Regan was not going to take any chances.

After several hours of tests the emergency room chief physician entered Lizzy's room and with a reassuring faint smile told Lizzy and Joe that her life was no longer in imminent danger. What they found, however, was a serious problem which would require treatment now and a regime of medication for the rest of her life. Lizzy had suffered a pulmonary embolism. A clot had formed, probably in her leg, broken loose, and traveled through her circulatory system before lodging in her lung very near her heart. The doctors had already given her a dose of Lovenox and a blood-thinning agent called Coumadin, which would relieve the pain and prevent the clot from being flushed into the heart where it would cause cardiac arrest. The condition was a serious one, but it had been caught in time, and treatment would dissolve the clot over time. The doctor told them that she could be released the next day. She could resume her vacation but should avoid strenuous activities for the next few weeks. He had already faxed details of her condition to her personal physician in Connecticut and spoken to Dr. Joyce Freiberg at her Greenwich office.

Feeling shaken at the news but noticing that the pain had dramatically improved, Lizzy insisted that Joe go back to the resort, reassure the boys, and return to the activities they had planned in order to put their minds at ease. Reluctantly Joe agreed but told her that they would all be back to see her within a few hours. Lizzy could tell that leaving her at that moment was one of the hardest things Joe had ever done, but she felt sure that she would be all right, and the boys needed to be comforted. Whatever was flowing from the IV bottle over her head was working, and right now she needed to rest and let it do its job. She closed her eyes and tried to get some badly needed restful sleep.

Lizzy's nap was restful and calm, but it did not last quite as long as she had hoped. The nurse informed her that a visitor wished to see her for a moment, a young woman from the Brandywine Ranch who wished to drop in and see how she was doing. "Would that be all right?" Lizzy agreed, and a woman with long dark hair and a bouquet of roses entered the room and introduced herself as Tiffany Gould. After arranging the roses in a nearby vase, she sat in the visitor chair alongside Lizzy's bed. "I heard about your emergency, and I had hoped to see you and find out how you are doing," said the smiling Tiffany. It was very nice that the resort showed such concern over a sick guest. The fact that the person now visiting her was Tiffany Gould delighted Lizzy. After the expected talk about Lizzy's condition and the pleasantries one expects from such a visit, Tiffany's smile faded as she asked, "I could not help but notice that you are visiting from Greenwich, Connecticut, and I was wondering if you have ever heard of a man named Bill Pierce who died near there

91

sometime ago?" That question led to a private chat which lasted well beyond the usual time allotted for a visit in the intensive care unit of any hospital. It was a chat which filled in many blank spaces for Lizzy and made the jigsaw puzzle she called the Case take a clearer form than Lizzy had ever hoped for from this little vacation.

Chapter Three

Two Families in Crisis

By the close of the last decade of the twenty-first century Americans had suffered through nearly thirty years of debate about family values and the definition of what actually comprised a "real" family. The divorced Ronald Reagan had introduced the subject to political debate and held himself and his second wife as paragons of familial virtue, despite estrangement from nearly all his children. Congressional leader Newt Gingrich spoke about the sanctity of marriage and family even as he sued his first wife for divorce while she lay dying of cancer in the hospital. On the other side of the political spectrum, we were told by First Lady Hillary Clinton that a child needed an entire village to be raised properly. So while the debate and redefinitions swirled around the heads of all Americans a few just dove in and started families. And some of those who started families did it right, and some did not.

Two cases in point would be the Dawson family and the Randolph family, both affluent and privileged clans in

Greenwich, Connecticut. One family are millionaires and the other are billionaires; both wanted for nothing and lived free of the specters of hunger, cold, and want. These families are studies in similarities and contrasts, each having areas in which they excelled and areas where they were found wanting. The children of both families were given the most nutritious foods, the best medical care, and the best education which money or circumstances could buy. One family opted for strictly private schools which boasted the highest of test scores but lacked in training its students to interact with the real world and the many characters which inhabit it. The other family opted for the Greenwich public school system whose test scores were slightly lower than private academies but excelled at socialization and teaching students to network and develop valuable talents in building useful relationships throughout life. Both sets of children were taught well and learned their lessons well.

The equality of education being a given, one could draw distinctions between the family atmosphere in which each set of children was raised. Neither had nannies or governesses, but they did have distinct levels of affection and interaction with their parents. Lizzy and Joe never hesitated to embrace their sons and tell them how much they were loved, while the Randolphs tended toward monetary rewards to express their approval of their children. While Lizzy kissed each child on the cheek as they departed for school every day, Suzette extended her cheek to each child to be kissed and added a warning for them to be careful of her hair and makeup. Suzy and JR eventually resorted to air kisses rather than risk disturbing their mother's polished look. Each set of children loved their parents deeply, but one set gave and received love, while the other offered love freely only to have it returned sparingly.

It is often said that money cannot buy happiness, but some might add that it certainly can make misery more enjoyable. In the case of the J. Richard Randolph family it also provided a buffer zone between family members and their severe patriarch. Internally the opinion was that the family was cripplingly dysfunctional because Jack teetered between tyranny and indifference, not a very comfortable situation for those who had to deal with him on a daily basis. The ability of a wife and children to spend a few thousand dollars on a getaway allowed the family to keep its sanity. But the same could be said for Jack who found little familial comfort in a wife he knew cheated on him; a lovely, athletic, and intelligent daughter who had not been a son; and a son who failed to live up to even Jack's most minor expectations. It could be fairly accurately said that none of the Randolphs were particularly close to each other, with the notable exception of Suzy and JR to each other.

The Randolphs were not poster children for the all-American family, but by all modern standards they could not be readily compared to the Manson family either. Dysfunction and estrangement are not all that uncommon among families of all economic and social levels. In fact the Randolphs might even be considered fairly "normal" by most psychologists, that is, "normal" notwithstanding their immense wealth and lavish lifestyle. The family often spent considerable amounts of time apart. Vacations were divided between husband and wife trips which often were business related or family vacations in which Suzette and the children went off together. Many times genuine family adventures were planned and even booked only to have Jack beg off at the last minute, placing the blame for his absence on some business problem. There were also the times when Jack would disappear for a week or more and leave word that he needed to attend a business conference only to return tan and looking very well-rested. Togetherness was not an overarching theme of the Randolphs, but close-knit family relationships are not all that common among the rich and powerful. In fact, some Greenwich couples maintain apartments in Manhattan as well as their mansions in town, but rarely are both marital partners in a single residence together at the same time. The Randolphs had never gone to those extremes.

Lizzy Dawson's family was quite an exception to the norm of wealthy Greenwich families. They were close, spent time together, and confided quite readily in each other and among the family as a whole. Troy and Scott often brought their problems to their parents, though they tended to seek out Lizzy's advice more often than not. Lizzy and Joe were both open to their sons' problems, but the boys more readily trusted their mother's advice, whereas they regarded their father's advice as both a bit gruff and not always showing a great degree of common sense. When Scott had been caught masturbating at age fourteen, Joe's way of dealing with it was to buy him several issues of *Playboy* and tell him to be more discreet when he needed to "relieve" himself. Lizzy confronted the situation from a different angle explaining to Scott that women were not simply objects designed to arouse and give pleasure to men. He should resort to self-simulation as an extreme measure and not as a recreation. Scott heard out his mom's advice, agreed to consider seriously what she had said, and turned over one copy of *Playboy* that his father had given him, hoping his mother did not know about the other half-dozen copies he kept. The small wink between father and son did not go unnoticed by Lizzy, but she decided to cut her husband and son some slack.

A similar situation in the Randolph household did not transpire in such a civilized and calm manner. Jack had quickly come in from the pool one evening and grabbing his copy of the day's *Wall Street Journal* headed for the nearest bathroom. Opening the closed but unlocked door he confronted JR furiously jerking at his penis with eyes closed and a pleasurable grimace on his face. Jack's roar could be heard across the estate as he threw a nearby bath towel across his son while shouting in disgust, "You vile little savage! How could you do such thing and not lock the fucking door? I would expect more from a tribesman in the jungle!" and then added in as stinging a voice as he could, "So who were you thinking about? What is his name?" JR's hot and bitter tears exploded across his face as Jack exited the room screaming at the top of his lungs, "Suzette my dear, come and see what your perverted little boy is up to. Come and see, goddamn it!" Although it was never mentioned again it left an emotional scar on JR which he would probably never forget, and it gave Jack just one more reason to despise the son that was such a bitter disappointment to him.

When Suzette addressed the matter her manner and concern seemed so superficial that JR wished she had not made the fledgling effort that she had. She came into JR's room several hours after the incident and patted him on the back as he lay facedown on the bed.

"Come on, JR, you know full well what kind of person your father can be, and yet you manage to run afoul of him at every turn. Had you simply locked the door none of this would have happened. Your father and I know that what you were doing is totally natural, but like all parents, we'd rather not have to face it. Let alone make an issue out of it. If this whole mess is really bothering you, why don't you discuss it with your coach or health education teacher at school on Monday?"

Instead of feeling comforted JR silently wondered how two perfectly asinine people had managed to find each other, marry, and produce him and his sister. Life was not just unfair, at times it was positively ridiculous, and this had been one of those times.

Suzy was privileged to be her daddy's little girl and escaped the wrath that Jack often reserved for JR; but she had a deep-seated resentment against her father because of his attitude toward her as a person on whom intelligence and agility had been wasted since she was simply a girl and was inevitably destined to marry a wealthy man who would protect her, provide for her, and make all decisions for her. Jack was, on several occasions, so tactless as to say aloud, "Why should a daughter have that going for her while her weak-kneed sibling withers in the sun like a sickly petunia?" As much as such words hurt JR they also sank like fangs into Suzy's soul and ate away at her self-confidence and self-esteem. By the time she was sixteen Suzy had learned to channel Jack's hurtful words into a challenge which fortified her determination to excel beyond what Jack himself had done in his life. He built upon a foundation given to him. She was bound and determined to build her own life and career from the ground up and without his help in any way.

By any measure the average person would have judged the Dawsons to be the more ideal of the two families. The nuclear family of two parents, both on their first spouse and happily married for about two decades, with two well-adjusted and sociable children, made a very nice picture postcard. There had been tensions now and again, but nothing earth shattering. There had been temptations over the years to cheat on each other, but neither partner had even fallen into the temptation. In the early years there had actually been some financial problems. Both Lizzy and Joe were from middle-class backgrounds, but in early life they had each done well, and together they were an almost unstoppable team in their professional and business ventures. Money had been earned and invested well. To the mix had been added a willingness, on the part of each of them, to roll up their sleeves and get their hands dirty in the interest of earning money.

Joe was the son of a neighborhood jeweler in the Greenpoint neighborhood on the border of Queens and Brooklyn. His mother was a second-tier opera singer who was never found wanting for a role in the Metropolitan Opera but who also never managed to land a starring role. They lived in a lovely one-family house in Bay Ridge which had a backyard garden and neatly manicured front lawn. The family lived within their means and provided four full years of tuition for Joe when he enrolled in Hofstra University on Long Island. Though Hofstra was a mere thirty minutes east of their home, Joe's parents decided that part of the college experience was to be away from home. They paid for room and board at the university in addition to his tuition, books, and miscellaneous fees. Joe held a part-time job in one of the dean's offices; but his salary was reserved for dates, beer, and the occasional ounce or two of marijuana. Having been able to go to a good school without the worry of paying tuition was a blessing that Joe always had appreciated as he watched his friends struggle with work-study programs, grant and loan applications, and multiple part-time jobs.

Joe's major was finance. He enjoyed helping his dad at the jewelry store, but he knew from an early age that retail was not the career he desired. The lure of corporate life with its high salaries and excellent perks stirred him to the business school, but being a bright and inquisitive young man in the midst of the computerization of the world he signed up for a minor in computer technology, a minor which consumed so many of his elective courses that he technically had a second major in it. Over the years this combination of expertise served him well as he moved from investment banking to being the chief financial officer for a small but prominent computer firm just across the Hudson in New Jersey. That position had eventually given Joe and Lizzy the capital to begin speculating on real estate in the Greenwich area. Their successes in this field permitted them to begin heavy investments in mutual funds and other areas of higher risk, gaining generous returns.

Lizzy, on the other hand, had come from what might have been considered an upper middle-class background. Her father having been a colonial governor in the Caribbean found the need for his kind of occupation waning severely with the fast-moving independence movement which spread across the old British Empire in the 1960s and 1970s. Having married an American wife, the former governor returned to diplomatic life at the United Nations in Manhattan and managed to purchase a respectable condominium on Fifth Avenue across from Central Park. Lizzy's education in America consisted of the United Nations International High School followed by a degree in design from the Fashion Institute of Technology down the street from Penn Station in Midtown. Lizzy had always been interested in art and design and very nearly entered studies to become an architect. But finding the tedious need for exact calculations boring and difficult, she decided to focus on the design of building interiors. Her interior design firm made quite a splash when it first opened; the British ambassador to the United Nations, a close friend of her father, asked her to decorate his country home in the north country of Greenwich. The results were featured in a two-page article of the *New York Times* arts section. From the publication date of that article the stream of business had always been good.

Like many young couples the Dawsons had occasionally overextended themselves and despite a steady flow of income managed to fall into pressing situations. Their strict allotment of earnings into investments sometimes limited their liquid assets, while at the same time their taste for expensive vacations and nearly weekly schedule of Broadway shows and post-show dinners dented their budget. The fights that erupted over finances were not terribly frequent, but when they did happen they tended to be loud and long. On one occasion there was a double surprise which led to a disaster. Joe had taken a very large amount of cash out of the family bank account and placed it an extremely high-yield investment recommended to him by the CEO of his company. The investment was short term, and the large return was going to be a surprise for Lizzy. Lizzy, however, had another quite different surprise in mind when she wrote a huge check on the same account to buy Joe a beautiful used Bentley for his upcoming birthday. When the check bounced the sparks flew at the Dawson house, and despite the good intentions on both parts, the sparks continued to fly for three days before calm had been restored.

That particular episode resulted in the ironclad agreement between them that no investment or major purchase could be made without the knowledge and agreement of each of them. They agreed with a wry smile that a breach of this agreement might result in a divorce at some future date. Once the boys had arrived Lizzy and Joe had managed to balance their spending and investments and learned to keep a respectable reserve of cash deposited in a mutual account in case of any emergencies. The appearances at Broadway theaters declined, dinners became more family style, and investments smaller and less risky as the years progressed. By the time the boys were in high school the family was in good financial health, and the future looked secure, as long as the rock-solid hedge funds kept performing as they had for some time. By the middle of the first decade of the twenty-first century the Dawsons had adopted a "What could go wrong?" and "What me worry?" attitude. The past few years had tested their mettle as a couple, but they had remained strong in the face of adversity.

In the Randolph household there was never any concern over money, except for the fact that Jack firmly believed that there was no limit to what he should possess. The family fortune had been huge when his father died and left the bulk to him, but he had worked magic with the funds and doubled the amount within ten years of his inheritance. The tensions within the Randolph family had more to do with Jack's ideas about how each member of his family should live, function, and contribute to the whole. He was an odd mixture of Puritan and libertine. He had very rigid ideas about the roles which a husband and wife should fulfill in marriage and an even stricter parental philosophy regarding the ways in which sons and daughters should act. And yet when the family did not live up to his standards he fumed like a mad man but did little in the way of punishing the offender. His reaction to most familial disappointment was to withdraw himself even further from the offending member of the clan. Now this was a double-edged sword since it was numbing him to any emotion toward his wife and children while they actually welcomed the distance.

Beyond each nuclear family the Dawsons and Randolphs had extended families which both seemed to contradict the circumstances of the nuclear households. That is to say, the Dawson extended family had some pretty serious problems, while the Randolph extended family seemed fairly sedate and stable. There were not many close relatives to the Randolphs, merely several grandaunts and uncles and a few cousins of differing degrees, but no one very close on either the paternal or maternal side. The relatives who did exist were rich and for the most part stable and contented. Jack was the only Randolph who felt an obsession with success and wealth accumulation. His cousin Bert who was roughly the same age as Jack and nearly as wealthy often chided Jack to stop making money until he learned to enjoy the money that he already had. Bert was retired by forty and simply counted the dividends and interest on his many well-placed investments. He owned a good number of businesses but had lost track of their exact number after he had hired a finance manager to oversee his wealth. On nearly every occasion when Bert ran into Jack he recited his financial philosophy mantra, "As long as there is enough for beluga caviar every evening, Monte Carlo every spring, and Tahiti every Christmas, everything else is gravy." The statement got deeper under Jack's skin every time he heard it and smarted all the more for knowing that Bert's untended billions were growing almost as much as his own well-tended assets.

Members of Suzette's family were rarely present at any Randolph events or holidays. One would have to say that somehow they and Suzette had simply drifted apart since there had never been a serious rift or outright argument between them. After Suzette's parents had passed away the funeral home had been sold and the money divided, and family members each went their own way. There were no hard feelings, just a general sense of apathy toward each other. Most of the family did envy Suzette's extreme success in landing a very wealthy husband, but the envy was neither so deep nor hateful as to prevent a friendly relationship. Family members just sensed that they were not important to Suzette and that they were part of a receding past which she did not wish to hold on to or cherish. Her family was comfortable and never found themselves in a position which would require them to ask for help from Suzette. That was the way they and she preferred to keep their relationships. Cards exchanged at the holidays were a sufficient link for all concerned parties.

Lizzy and Joe on the other hand kept close to their siblings and other relatives but found themselves more often than not lending assistance and sometimes financial help to their kin. Joe's family had been business owners. The ups and downs of business sometimes required that a relative might approach him for a loan to keep things afloat. Joe was always a ready ear to complain to, a shoulder to cry on, and sometimes a deep pocket to offer rescue money. Lizzy on the other hand had a family which was well-off, but also very self-sufficient, so much so that she often wondered if they would have reached out to her if they had been in need. Her family members were thrifty, wise in spending money, and very careful in their investments. For the most part they rarely found themselves needing her help, the one exception being Lizzy's sister Suzanne and her husband, Scott Delany.

Suzanne had married the handsome and promising young actor at age nineteen. Their marriage had been sudden and a surprise to most of the family. Scott had come to be well liked by the entire family, so much so that Lizzy and Joe had named their first son after him. During the initial rough times that most young married couples go through everyone in the family, especially Lizzy and Joe, helped them as much as humanly possible.

It was after Scott's career skyrocketed and the money flooded into the Delany household that things took a turn for the worse. Money had gone to Suzanne's and Scott's heads, as did the whirlwind lifestyle of a popular TV and movie star. None of the family begrudged the couple their success or their enjoyment of their wealth, but words were often whispered at family gatherings about their lack of gratitude to those who had been there for them in the hard times. It was sometimes noted that assistance which was supposed to be in the form of loans had never been repaid, even after the flow of money had become steady and massive. Some family members were hurt when the Delanys compared their Rolls-Royces to the BMWs and Cadillacs of other family members, but Lizzy would just shrug and calm feathers by reminding one and all that her baby sister was after all young and starstruck by her new lifestyle. What Lizzy and the family never fully suspected was the cocaine habit that Suzanne and Scott had acquired as part of their Hollywood lifestyle. They had always been free and easy with alcohol and marijuana, but that had never been very shocking since they were, after all, young and artistic types. The pressure to party as wildly as the Hollywood crowd had met with very little resistance from Scott, and Suzanne followed suit quite willingly as well. No one was going to out party the star of soaps and

105

cine and his lovely wife, not as long as there was enough money to keep the blow flowing.

Besides alcohol and drugs the third corner of the party triangle was never neglected, and that corner was sex. Neither Scott nor Suzanne could remember precisely when the whole thing started. It had been within a month of Scott landing a major role on the *Our Desperate Lives* soap opera, but which party or orgy it was when they took their first toots of cocaine was a blur to them now. In those first days of stardom the two of them were guests of other more established stars. Since the checks were only starting to roll in, much of their extracurricular activities were paid for by Scott's costars and their friends. People knew that Scott was going places, and they did not mind doing a bit of investment to get into his good graces. Were he to become a big star they could always rely on him to give their careers a boost or, at the very least, to be his guests when their stars were waning. Suzanne's beauty was always an attraction to men and women who enjoyed a libertine lifestyle, so the two came as a very attractive package.

Wherever the first sniff of cocaine had occurred and whoever the provider was at that moment did not really matter—it had been their first step on a thousand-mile journey, as the old Chinese proverb would say. From the first experience of cocaine the two were hooked, and while they managed to control it for quite some time, it ate away at their abilities to think straight and control their own lives. Despite the intense love which they felt for each other they began to allow their new friends and the aphrodisiac qualities of drugs to push them into a blur of sex parties and countless sexual encounters. Suzanne and Scott had many sex partners, some nameless, but they did not ever have an affair behind each other's back.

The sex was open and free when the cocktails and coke flowed, and the memories of exactly what they had done and with whom were a fuzzy recollection when morning would come. Their sexual promiscuity never bothered them morally and somehow, perhaps the quality of people they fucked, kept them pretty much disease free, despite the toll this wild lifestyle was taking on them in general. When the party had ended they inevitably went home together and woke up the next day in the same bed.

The toll that drugs were taking on their lives extended to the management of their money. Even when "sober" the two were easy marks for financial advisors with risky investments or "get-rich-quick" schemes. It was an advisor who straddled the fence between risky and outrageous who first suggested that they place their money in the Randolph Fund. The idea of a stable fund with high-yield returns struck a note with the young couple, and despite common sense suggesting a diversification of their investments they lumped a huge portion of their funds into Jack's hedge fund. Their investments did indeed remain stable, one might say static, since the large gains which they were seeing were quickly withdrawn and spent. Their funds were more than sufficient for a young couple to live and live well, but their habits were beginning to become costly, and their tastes became more expensive, if not more discerning as time passed. The one constant was their coke habit. They could get by with a lower-quality vintage champagne between dividend checks, but the quality and quantity of their drugs needed to be maintained at the highest levels. A wino may be satisfied by a cheap wine, but a coke addict needs quality to assure him of the right level of buzz. Nothing less than the highest quality could be tolerated by Scott and Suzanne as long as there was cash to buy it.

Lizzy had no idea of the downward spiral which Suzanne and Scott were traveling, but she did notice the distance which was growing between them and her own family. There had always been a close relationship between the Dawson sisters in spite of the few years that separated them. Lizzy had always been very protective of Suzanne, and in turn Suzanne had always been Lizzy's number one fan in everything that she did in life. When Lizzy tried out to be a high school cheerleader Suzanne had helped her practice and clapped heartily when she performed at the tryouts. No one was more disappointed when Lizzy was not selected than Suzanne. Lizzy had to take her sister out to a movie and ice cream to cheer her up that night. They were close and never kept secrets from each other. Suzanne knew about Lizzy's pregnancies before anyone else in the family, except for Joe. The fact that Suzanne was becoming more distant and silent disturbed Lizzy very much. She hoped that things were all going so well for her sister and brother-in-law that they simply did not have anything to complain about in life, but the nagging feeling that Lizzy had deep in her soul told her that there was something wrong. There were signs which bothered Lizzy, physical signs as well as changes in behavior, which seemed to point to something; but just what that something was, was beyond Lizzy to imagine. Respecting her sister's privacy, she did not pry into Suzanne's affairs, but she worried nonetheless.

Lizzy was unaware of how far her sister and brother-in-law had allowed their jet-set lifestyle to reshape their lives. The wild parties had led to more and more drugs and wilder sexual arrangements. The two were well aware of each other's activities and seemed to everyone concerned to have abandoned a normal life and marriage. While they did enjoy many lovers they also had a sense of marriage and loyalty which no longer included exclusiveness in the bedroom. While rumors swirled about the community and even ended up in the supermarket tabloids no one really knew what was going on in the lives of Suzanne and Scott Delany. At the height of the rumors Lizzy regretted that she and Joe had named their second son after his uncle Scott. As the distance grew between the two siblings and their families Lizzy wondered about the future of their larger family. Had her sister grown so different in such a short time? Being a very spiritual person Lizzy could not help but judge Scott's and Suzanne's increasingly libertine ways. Her concerns would have increased immeasurably had she been privy to the details of what was actually going on in the lives of the young Delanys.

While the young couple did in fact love each other, they also enjoyed the voluptuous and firm bodies of other sex partners. While Scott had a toned and lean body which was the envy of many of his fellow actors, it was not the kind of body which was favored by his lovely wife. Suzanne preferred firm pectoral muscles and six-pack abdominals. Oddly enough the physical build of the run-of-the-mill leading man was much like Scott's; but the aspiring actors tended to overdo the bodybuilding in a misguided attempt to gain the attention of directors, producers, and casting agents. It was from this vast pool of wannabes that Suzanne found the kind of man that she most desired in bed. The soap opera pickings were not only rife with handsome young bodybuilders, it was also close to home, being a Manhattan-based industry. And if the soap opera studs failed to please the aspiring actors, waiting tables throughout New York City served as a backup source of one-time lovers.

Suzanne never slept with the same man twice. It was her version of loyalty to Scott—no one would be a rival for her affections because she would never allow herself to know any one long enough to have feelings for him. Even the best lover would never be given a second night. It was a hard-and-fast rule. Suzanne fancied herself a connoisseur of the male form, and the lovers she chose were the best in form and beauty. A beautiful face was important, and a well-proportioned body came a very close second in her discernment process. Many times a young actor might approach her, and if he fit the criterion he would be given his chance at a visit to her bed. More often than not it was Suzanne who took the role of aggressor and propositioned the actor that most appealed to her at the moment. Scott did not mind the arrangement they had with each other since he too had a taste for other partners.

Scott's tastes ran to the long, lean, and leggy type, which was a slight contrast to Suzanne's voluptuous build. He preferred small breasts and an almost boyish figure. The love he felt for Suzanne was based on much more than physical attraction, and he actually considered making love to a woman who looked like Suzanne a matter of cheating, while having sex with someone totally different was permissible to his conscience. The Delanys had a very thought-out understanding about extramarital sex, and it served them well in satisfying their sexual appetites while not endangering their relationship. Such is the mind-set of such modern celebrities. When they shared a bed at home or on the road they were quite happy with each other, and their sex life was healthy by their own standards.

It had been Suzanne who first proposed this arrangement, and she was also the first to avail herself of its benefits. While visiting the set of Scott's daytime drama she noticed a young man playing the role of an orderly in a hospital scene. He was tall with a well-defined body, shaggy dark brown hair, and crystal blue eyes, the kind of beauty often described as being one of the "black Irish." His name was Sean, and he responded to her flirtations by slipping her his phone number between takes. She called him that evening and arranged for them to meet the next evening at the Kenyon Plaza Hotel. When he balked at the location she assured him that she would take care of the room and any other costs for their evening together. She quickly made a reservation for one of the hotels single rooms and charged it to her personal credit card.

The evening was well planned but did not go off as well as Suzanne had hoped. When Sean arrived Suzanne was already there with a room service meal awaiting them under domes of silver serving trays and a bottle of expensive champagne chilling on ice. When the covers were removed there sat two servings of filet mignon, done medium rare, and roasted vegetables. The horrified look on Sean's face tipped her off that he did not have the same epicurean tastes as her own. Sean explained that he was a strict vegan and could not possibly consume animal flesh. To make matters worse he also informed her that his health regime did not allow for alcoholic beverages either. With an exasperated sigh Suzanne poured herself a full glass of Moet and a glass of Pellegrino for Sean. The dinners were again covered and shoved off to the hallway to await their retrieval by the room service staff.

After downing half the bottle of bubbly, Suzanne decided that the time had come for more intimate activities. She took the glass of mineral water from Sean's hand, noticing a slight tremor in his grip. The water placed on the nightstand she proceeded to embrace Sean and nibble on his ear before placing her lips firmly on his. He responded halfheartedly, and again she felt a trembling of his entire body. Ignoring his shivers she kissed down his neck and began to unbutton his stylish sports shirt revealing a toned and hairless chest. Working her way down his firm torso she kissed his hard stomach as she began to undo his belt and the fly of his trousers. His shivering increased, and he began to fidget as she slowly lowered his zipper and spread his fly to reveal his black Calvin Kline boxer briefs. Looking up from her now-kneeling position she asked him, "Is there a problem here?" He sheepishly answered, "Well, this is kinda new to me, and I am a little nervous." With her mind racing with thoughts of Sean being a virgin she asked him if this was his first experience of sex. He answered that he had had sex before, but this time it was so different. She giggled at the thought that she was more than likely the first experienced woman he had ever had. He probably was accustomed to teenage girls who were as inexperienced as himself. Smiling she asked, "Am I the first mature woman you have had sex with?" Smiling back at her he answered in a squeaky boyish voice, "Yes, but actually you are the first woman," and trailed off to an unintelligible embarrassed murmur.

With another deep sigh she ignored his further comments and pulled down the front of his boxer briefs and engulfed his flaccid manhood. If he had never had sex with a woman before she was going to make her best effort to give him an experience which would encourage him to make women a regular part of his sex life from now on. She released his penis from her oral grip long enough to instruct him to lie back and close his eyes and then reengaged her mouth on his now-expanding organ. Before long a moaning Sean was encouraging her activities and thrusting his growing member into her welcoming mouth.

112

Before long his now nine-inch cock was actively seeking new depths, and his moans were increasing in volume.

The oral sex had been enjoyable for both of them, and Suzanne decided to skip any notion of reciprocal oral sex from him, instead suggesting they engage in regular sex. The moaning stopped, and the shivers returned as they removed their clothing, and Suzanne spread herself on the soft sheets of the bed. Sean, obviously nervous, but still fully erect, climbed up onto the bed placing himself between her outstretched legs. She began to giggle uncontrollably as he firmly grasped her legs and raised her feet, resting them on his shoulders. She continued to giggle as she informed him that he did not have to position her in such a way to enter her; she was, after all, a woman. The giggling became contagious as he realized what he was doing, and with that humorous exchange the ice had been broken, and his nervousness quickly passed away as he entered her to their mutual sighs and moans.

The floodgates had been broken as Sean began to get into the rhythm of the situation and found himself enjoying this new experience. As the night wore on they tried every position imaginable. They found that their favorite was Suzanne sitting astride the supine figure of Sean, supplying most of the motion as he fondled and kissed her gyrating breasts. She had met the challenge and guessed that she had won a convert to heterosexual sex. At the very least she had extended his horizons to include female lovers. When everything had been said and done the only thing that really mattered to Suzanne was that she had been brought to sexual nirvana by this handsome young man, and before the night had ended she found herself with no complaints. It could have been a more romantic evening, but the sex had turned out to be excellent, and what Sean had lacked in experience he more than made up for in his enthusiasm and eagerness to please. All in all Suzanne had been satisfied to the point that she promised herself that Sean would be the first of many such experiences.

It was nearly four in the morning when Suzanne decided that it was time to slip out of the Kenyon Plaza and drive home. The sex play had been wonderful, but also exhausting. She needed a little pick-me-up to make her way home, so she locked herself in the bathroom and opened the hidden compartment in her purse to pull out a tiny one-inch-by-one-inch plastic bag filled with first-class cocaine. Sean was peacefully asleep on the bed, his naked body partially wrapped by the white sheet. She might have woken him and offered him a sniff of her cocaine, but he looked so serene. She guessed that his health-conscious nature would have precluded his use of blow. She would never know that like so many of today's health-obsessed young people, Sean watched his carbs and forsook alcohol only to be a regular user of all manner of illicit drugs. So Suzanne decided to let him sleep and arranged for a wake-up call close to noon as she paid the bill at the reception desk on her way out. It had been time and money well spent for the experiences she had enjoyed with Sean. She would make an effort never to run into him again, but she would always remember being his first female lover and how quickly and well he learned to enjoy the opposite sex.

Scott had a somewhat different outlook on extramarital sex. He did not see a problem with seeing the same woman repeatedly over a period of time. It made for fewer lovers in the overall picture but created an atmosphere in which he could mold and shape the sexual relationship into experiences he craved. A regular lover could be coaxed into different activities such as scenario sex, one of his favorites being the role of doctor examining a lovely young schoolgirl patient. It was not beyond Scott to have two or even three ongoing relationships at the same time. Since none of them had any thoughts of any long-term or serious relationships, it did not matter how many lovers he had. Every prospective lover was informed of the game rules and went into the arrangement knowing what to expect.

Scott had been the strongest advocate of the use of drugs when he and Suzanne first encountered them in their party activities. It was Scott who tried the combinations of drugs and alcohol to enhance sexual prowess, and it was also Scott who was deepest into their use. While Suzanne was running up a sizable outflow of cash for drugs, her drug expenses were less than half of Scott's. As much as she enjoyed the endless stream of wild parties, she seemed like a piker compared to Scott's party animal persona. Suzanne almost always was back in their Greenwich mansion by the morning following any party, while Scott sometimes did not arrive home at all the following day. It was not very unusual for Scott to party all night, snort some cocaine in the morning, shower, and change in his dressing room at the studio, to be ready for another day of filming followed by a sleep in his dressing room, which led up to another party that night. His record for this kind of cycle was an entire week of filming and partying in Manhattan without being home a single night. He had a wardrobe of personal clothes in his dressing room which were cleaned and pressed, as needed, by his assistant.

Being a soap opera star proved to be a very handy way to meet women. There was never a party or bar scene in which at least one lovely woman did not corner him and

115

flirt with him using his character name rather than his own. In some ways Scott justified his sexual promiscuity by pretending that Dr. Richard Mayweather, his television alter ego, was having the sex instead of himself. It was a ridiculous mental ruse, but it made things more convenient in the early days when even the drugs could not completely quiet a guilty conscience. While Scott had jumped into the libertine life headfirst, he was also the one to feel qualms about what he was doing even as he enjoyed himself. At the beginning of their descent into the life of drugs and sex, Scott had been willing and anxious to take part in it, but somewhere in the deepest reaches of his heart he wondered if he was wasting all the good fortune he had found in marrying Suzanne and landing good roles in his acting career. The sheer pleasure of what was happening and the tired old excuse of joining in on "what everyone else is doing" overcame his moral reservations, and soon he was too numb with enjoyment to care anymore.

Scott had been asked by the producers of the *New York Morning Show* to judge a swimsuit competition which they were sponsoring at Jones Beach on Long Island early in one summer. Knowing that the gig would be fun and gain him some national television coverage he jumped at the chance. The day was hot and sunny as he sat in a wicker throne with two other judges and surveyed over fifty twenty-something young women clad in as little as possible. He even joked with one of the other judges that there was so little to the swimsuits that he wondered what they were actually judging. The other judge answered with a smirk, "Oh, I think we both know what we are looking at, my friend." And Scott was indeed looking for the smallest and most revealing bikini, so as to see more of the young flesh it revealed. The contestant

116

from SoHo quickly caught Scott's eye with her string top and thong. Not much was left to the imagination by this outfit of two shoestrings and three triangles no bigger than bar coasters.

She was a tall bronze goddess with no evidence of any tan lines and hair as bleached by the sun as her skin was tanned by it. Her breasts were small but shapely, and the thin fabric of her almost nonexistent top gave no place to hide her firm and extended nipples. Scott's mouth watered as he watched her promenade down the makeshift runway set up on the beach. As she spun around to give the judges a 360-degree view of her lanky and trim body, Scott felt his penis begin to lengthen and swell. He was grateful that he had chosen a baggy Hawaiian beach ensemble to wear to the event, knowing that anything tighter would have made his sizable erection noticeable to everyone present. She had not been the only contestant to impress him, but she certainly had been the one who affected him beyond all others. When the judging came he would, without question, vote for Ms. SoHo. It turned out that so did the other two judges. The newly crowned Miss Jones Beach wasted no time in asking Scott for his autograph, which he gave her as both Dr. Mayweather and Scott Delany.

As she bent over him watching him sign her program, she could not help but see the tent in the front of his baggy shorts and could not resist giving the little fella a covert squeeze. Her small peck on his cheek camouflaged her whisper in his ear telling him to meet her in changing cabana number 7 just down the beach from the grandstands. It took Scott only ten minutes to greet and quickly excuse himself from the producers and hosts of the event. He was quite sure the televised portions of this contest would be cropped and edited before Mr. and

117

Mrs. Average American would ever see them. Now he was anxious to see the X-rated sequel to today's activities. It did not take him long to find the right cabana and discreetly slip through the canvas entrance. There was Miss Jones Beach with her sash and tiara on the sandy floor, but her postage stamp bikini still firmly in place. She softly cooed that she thought he might like to be the one to untie its straps, much like opening a present.

Scott knew that it was very dangerous to engage in sex right there on the beach in a canvas tent, so he simply pushed the bra triangles off her nipples and quickly kissed each nipple and gave each a playful nibble while his right hand slipped into the third triangle covering her almost-hairless crotch. She moaned as he massaged her sensuously, eliciting her sexual response. He forced himself to pull away his lapping tongue from her now-stiff and tender nipples. She frowned at his withdrawing mouth and finger and wondered why he would stop so suddenly. His plan was to give her a taste of what he was capable of before he proposed that they leave the beach and rent a room at the nearest motel to finish this in a more comfortable setting. Her face showed disappointment, but also great interest in taking this action to the next level, even if it had to be somewhere else.

Scott left the cabana first after telling the girl where to meet him up the road from the cabana. He would drive up to her where she could hop in away from the possible prying eyes of the camera crew still prowling the beach for added footage for tomorrow's show. He was fully dressed in his beach outfit. Miss Jones Beach pulled a flowing beach robe out of her backpack, so both would be modestly dressed should anyone see them drive off together. Scott pulled up in his small Italian sports car, and in seconds she was seated beside him on the way to the nearest room where they could finish what they had started. The action could not wait for the room as Miss Jones Beach, now introduced simply as Rachel, began to massage Scott's penis through the soft cotton of his shorts. Before long her hand had snaked its way up his shorts and was stroking his erect manhood. A small spot of moisture now stained the flowered pattern of his pant leg as he began to physically respond to her caresses. If she did not stop soon it would be a huge stain as his pleasure slowly began to overtake him.

With one hand on the wheel Scott managed to slip his other hand into the top of Rachel's robe and with a quick tug pulled off the string bikini top which fell to her waist inside her robe. He began to squeeze each of her nipples while massaging the firm flesh of the rest of her breasts. He pulled her robe top open to see what his hand was doing, but to her surprise he stopped and pulled the robe shut. With a weak smile of frustration he explained that if he continued any further he would no longer present the appearance necessary to be seen in polite company, let alone at the registration desk of a decent motel. Rolling her eyes, Rachel withdrew her hand from his crotch and pleaded with him to find a motel already; she was ready for sex and knew that much more frustration and she would be past the "urge to merge," as she put it.

To their mutual delight a sign for a Holiday Inn could be seen above the treetops lining the highway. They registered as the Johnsons, but the desk clerk gave them the door pass card saying, "Thanks, Dr. Mayweather!" His cover was blown, but at this point he no longer cared, as he hoped that his cover would not be the only thing blown today. Before he could close the room door he was amazed to see Rachel on the bed in nothing but her bikini bottom. She had knelt on the bed and thrown herself backward onto the pillows, so she was arched with her shoulders and head on the pillows and her lower torso invitingly raised with legs spread as wide as possible. Scott did not need an engraved invitation to know where this was leading. He quickly shed his beach jacket and shorts, throwing them on a chair along with his sandals. He dove into position and with a single sweep ripped off the thong revealing the well-tailored and shaped pubic hair of this lovely creature. Without hesitation his tongue slipped effortlessly into her and hit home to her squeals of ecstasy.

As he pushed as deep into her as possible he ran his hands up to her breasts and down her long curving sides, bringing them to rest on her small hips. He imagined himself as a Greek or Roman god lifting a bowl of ambrosia to his lips and drinking deeply of that nectar so sweet that it was fit only for the gods. He noticed that she had stopped moaning and wondered if her awkward body position might be causing her to lose pleasure with the activities. He raised his head and peeked at her face from the side and was reassured to see her with dazed eyes and biting her bottom lip from the sheer enjoyment of his oral ministrations. He brought his hands away from her hips and once again found her stiff nipples, rubbing them with his fingertips and occasionally squeezing them as hard as he could without bruising her.

After nearly ten minutes of this combined oral stimulation and nipple play Rachel let out a scream of utter release as she was rocked by her first orgasm of the day. Scott promised himself that this would be just the first of many more before he was finished with her. Being a man of his word he gave his best efforts to bring her to the brink as many times as he could that day. She likewise brought him to climax again and again through the afternoon and evening. The two seemed to have been created for each other's pleasure. She knew what he liked and he knew what she enjoyed most and neither hesitated to provide their partner with their full attention and sexual devotion. Scott thanked his lucky stars that he had decided to accept the offer to judge the beauty contest. He liked the celebrity treatment and the national exposure, but he had never imagined that he would run into such a beautiful and sexually pleasing woman such as Rachel. This was the icing on his cake, and it was a cake he relished consuming, in more ways than one.

Scott was delighted when Rachel returned his oral loving and amazed him when she swallowed the entire length of his manhood. Scott had always enjoyed a deep penetration of a woman's throat, and Rachel seemed to enjoy giving as much as he enjoyed receiving. He felt that he could lie there forever, his head between her legs licking and kissing her vagina as she sucked his penis and licked his testicles. The joys of the 69 position had always delighted Scott, and now he had found a woman who enjoyed this form of sex as much as he did. This was Scott's first straying from his marital vows, but after this afternoon he knew that Rachel would be a long-term lover. It was that afternoon that Scott decided that he and Suzanne would need to sit down and hammer out some kind of understanding by which they could both enjoy other people and yet remain a loving and devoted couple. He wondered to himself if he could somehow include in the arrangement a place for Rachel, or some other partner, with him and Suzanne but quickly realized that this kind of deal would open the door to Suzanne asking for the same situation involving a second man in their bed. He wanted no part of that.

The Delanys were riding high for over a year, enjoying the success of Scott's career and the bounty of dividends deriving from their investments. It had been a simultaneous decision on their parts to sink a lion's share of their income into one of the many hedge funds centered in Greenwich. If these funds were good enough for Greenwich society, then they would be good enough for the Delanys. Scott knew that his career might stagnate into a decade's-long run on the soaps and that such an income would be limited. As long as his money was invested in a solid fund the movie roles could dry up without drastically diminishing their lifestyle. Both Scott and Suzanne were confident that the good times would roll on for the rest of their lives and that the alcohol, drugs, and sex would be unending.

The cracks in the dam began to show a while before the Madoff Fund collapsed. Despite warning from their financial advisors they kept their money evenly divided between the Madoff Fund and the Randolph Fund. Wasn't that what diversification was all about, putting your money in more than one place? Who could find two more solid and reliable funds than these two? If the returns on one fund were slowing down, then they had the other to fall back on until both funds were back up to snuff. The thought that both funds could falter was ridiculous and seemed as unlikely as a major downturn in the stock market! Old people liked to harp on the Great Depression, but people as young as the Delanys realized that such a catastrophe could never happen again. All the years passing since the Depression had cured the ills which allowed the 1929 collapse. As little as Scott and Suzanne knew about economics they knew at least that much.

When their bills started to rival their income the two of them assumed that the funds would correct their

122

mistakes and the returns would level off where they started, if not at a higher rate. The mansion, the cars, the trips, and the first-class meals might have to be slightly and temporarily trimmed back to accommodate the situation; but the drugs had so ingrained themselves into their lives that this would be an area sacrosanct to the trimmer shears. Fewer vacations in Cancun would allow for an undiminished flow of that delighted white powder they liked to refer to as "nose candy." It was not within the imagination to allow the benefits of cocaine to exit their lives. They had come to enjoy its benefits far too much to forsake them, never realizing that their "enjoyment" was lessening as they became immune to the drug's effect and only more of the stuff could satisfy their addictions. They were so hooked that they had to give up their family doctor and find a "user-friendly" physician who would turn a blind eye to the physical and mental effects the drug was having on each of them.

The first things to be sacrificed on the altar of drugs were the lavish vacations, then the extravagant meals at Connecticut's and Manhattan's finest restaurants. Soon all their cost cutting could not prevent them from facing the loss of their house and finally the habit which they had so deeply accepted into their lives. When the cars were sold for as much cash as possible they knew that they were looking over the edge of the abyss. The end of the Madoff Fund left them hanging on the precipice of that abyss by their fingernails. Something needed to be done and done as quickly as possible. The roles which were trickling in to Scott's agent's office dried up entirely. The soap opera producers were getting extremely tired of Scott's erratic behavior and flubbed lines. His costarring role on the soap was definitely in danger, so much so that the producers gave him a stern warning in the form of a future script which included the accidental death of Dr. Mayweather on the ski slopes of Aspen.

He was told that this alternate script would be shot in two months unless he pulled himself together and began to act like a professional again. If his role ended Scott knew that all would be lost. There was no other source of income which he and Suzanne could use to keep the house and whatever creature comforts they had managed to maintain since the bad times had begun. Suddenly out of nowhere money began to come slowly into the family coffers, and it was coming through Suzanne. Scott felt sure that Suzanne had tapped Lizzy and Joe for some financial help to get them over this fiscal bump in the road. Good old Lizzy would never turn down her little sister at a time like this. Scott would have been too proud to ask for help, and Suzanne knew that, so she must have taken it on herself to hit up the relatives for money. Scott already loved Suzanne, but at that juncture he loved her so much the more for her courage in seeking out help. Thank God her family had responded.

On the rare occasion that Scott saw Lizzy and Joe he could never bring himself to address the situation. It was best kept as a secret between the two sisters. Just once Scott found himself alone with Joe as they brought in packages from the car and told him how grateful he was to them for their help. He was somewhat surprised at Joe's puzzled look and comment, "You're welcome, for whatever it is we did for you." The moment passed and Joe never gave it another thought, but Scott wondered if this was a sign that Lizzy was lending them money without Joe's knowledge. He knew they were very open with each other about all their financial dealings, but he assumed that blood was thicker than water when it came to helping one's junior sibling. He could not have been more wrong

124

had he tried to be. Joe was puzzled because he and Lizzy had not done anything to help the Delanys, in large part because they had no idea what horrible financial shape they were actually in at the moment. They had their suspicions, especially when the Rolls-Royce disappeared, but they could only imagine what was going on.

Scott pulled himself together and tried hard to be prompt and cooperative at the studio. The alternate script including his character's death was tabled by the production staff, and his job once again seemed pretty safe. The house was brought back from the brink of foreclosure. The extravagant expenditures appeared to be gone for good, except, of course, for the double doses of cocaine picked up every week from the high-priced dealer headquartered in the village. The cars might be gone, but the lovers still were in good supply. Scott still managed to find ample interested partners at every party he attended. Suzanne was occupied and absent as often as she had been before the financial crisis, so Scott assumed that she was enjoying as rich an extramarital sex life as she had before. In fact, she seemed to be away more often than usual. Perhaps she was burying her disappointments and fears in the arms of handsome young men as an escape.

They say that while coke stimulates the sense during its use, its long-term effects are quite the opposite. The thinking process is dulled, and the regular user begins to skip details and lose their appreciation for all the most obvious events in their day-to-day lives. As their finances spiraled downward the quality of the Delanys' cocaine also declined. Since they need more powder to thrill and stimulate them, they needed to lower the quality to maintain the quantity of their addiction. Lower-grade cocaine seemed to dull Scott's thought process as to the point where he lived his life through a daze and missed so much of his surroundings that once again his job was placed in jeopardy. Flubbed lines might cause rolled eyes, but entire paragraphs of dialogue aroused much attention and comment on the set. Lines were not the only things being missed by Scott these days. When one of his costars pulled him aside to ask him a question Scott responded without grasping what the question had more than implied. Steve Roman, the star of a neighboring soap at the same studio, cornered Scott in the hallway and asked him, "Look, buddy, I am embarrassed to ask you this, but my sister wanted me to find out if you were on the market too and if you charge as much as Suzanne does?"

Scott responded innocently that he was always in the market for a role and he didn't even know that Suzanne was looking for acting work. Shaking his head Steve thanked him and told him, "Okay, friend, if you're gonna be like that fine. My sister is not going to beg for it." Never did it enter his mind that Suzanne had been selling herself to men in the very circles in which they had partied, before partying had become too expensive for them to engage in unless someone else was paying. Scott also could not fathom that Steve Roman knew how much Suzanne charged because he had become one of her regular clients. The money which had been flowing in was coming from Suzanne's life of prostitution and not from family loans.

Suzanne had come upon the idea when she was propositioned by a rather rotund and unattractive executive from Scott's network who had constantly flirted with her for months to no avail. Finally in desperation he had said to her, "Baby, I want you so bad I am willing to pay and make it worth your while." The price agreed upon was $2,000. Afterward Suzanne felt that she had earned every penny. The feeling of being penetrated by the short and semi-soft penis of a man old enough to be her father nauseated her, but she would never forget the difficulty which they had when his paunch prevented him from entering her easily, and they were forced into some awkward positions to satisfy his desires. When he asked her for oral sex she had gagged, and his offer to double or even triple her fee did not sway her from her refusal to place his penis in her mouth. They both left the situation with hard feelings. He had the memory and experience of having her beautiful body at his disposal even if it was only for an hour; she had the warm and fuzzy feeling of having twenty hundred-dollar bills tucked neatly in her handbag. There was a consolation prize for each of them.

The network executive had spread the word around that Suzanne Delany could be had for a price. Suddenly the offers began to roll in from all over the studio and the party set that knew the Delanys well from their past wild life. After being stiffed for her full price by a hot and beefy stagehand, Suzanne decided to go professional. She managed to find the name and phone number of the madam who had provided girls to the disgraced former governor of New York, who was forced to resign because of an ongoing relationship with one of the madam's ladies. Suzanne decided that this was the level at which she needed to be if she was going to engage in such a shameful career.

At the very least, she could pick and choose the men she would sleep with and not have to rely on the random propositions of men who "had always wanted to fuck Scott Delany's wife." Assuming an alias, she could even escape a connection with her husband's name and career. The men who would engage her services would do so because she was a beautiful, desirable woman, not because of whom she was married to. Although she did make quite a bit of extra money by selling herself to men who hated her husband and relished the idea of having his wife sexually. If Scott's enemies were attractive enough and offered enough payment why should she turn them down? It showed no disloyalty to Scott since she would be sleeping with men she felt were handsome and could offer the right price.

When the money was right but the man was not all that appealing Suzanne would take the advice she had given to Sean sometime ago. She would simply lie back and close her eyes, pretending the man making love to her was Scott or another past lover or, even sometimes, that he was Sean. Life had given Scott and Suzanne their share of the lifestyles of the rich and famous, and Suzanne had decided that she was not going to give up on that lifestyle without a fight. She had enjoyed her life too much to let it slip away. If the only means she had to continue it was by selling her body, then that is exactly what she would do. She had given herself to so many men for the sheer pleasure; now it was their turn to give her more than sexual gratification, it was time for them to pay.

Being in the employ of a Fifth Avenue madam gave Suzanne a sense of dignity and security, plus she had regular medical services to assure that she remained in good health and disease free. This might not be the best and most proper of occupations, but it paid the bills and kept the snow falling right up hers and Scott's noses. What the world thought of her was not any concern of hers. Everyone whored themselves in one way or another. No one got anything without paying a price of one kind or another. Who were they to judge?

Her only exception to that attitude was her family. She cringed at the very idea that her mother and father might find out. While she felt sure that Lizzy would understand and forgive her, she wondered if she could ever face the Dawsons if they knew what she was now doing. Oddly, Suzanne never had any problem facing Lizzy, Joe, or the boys when her name and affairs were splashed across the front pages of the tabloid newspapers or the trashy celebrity talk shows on television. The fact that she was taking money made her feel ashamed especially when she remembered a photograph on the wall of her father's den, a photo of a four-year-old Suzanne in a white lace dress shaking hands with Queen Elizabeth at the steps of the governor's palace in Saint Vincent. How could that little girl with her hand intertwined with that of the queen be the same woman that she saw in the mirror these days?

The times had changed, and they had changed her, but in a somewhat heroic way she was doing this to preserve herself and her husband. Ironically none of this would have been necessary if the lifestyle which she was preserving had been one without all that alcohol and all those drugs. She had fallen down a slippery slope and turned to prostitution to rescue herself, when all she had ever needed to do was turn to the very people she now felt too ashamed to face. Her family would have rallied around, helped her and Scott to get off drugs and turn their lives around, but Suzanne had chosen this path. Hopefully, in some way she would find her way out of this personal hell which she and Scott had created to find a good and decent life again.

Chapter Four

Trophy Wife

Suzette Benoit had been an ordinary girl growing up in small-town Ohio. In every town there is a wealthy area and a poor area. In Suzette's case she was from a family which occupied the middle ground between the two. Her parents, William and Frances Benoit, owned one of the town's two funeral homes, which made them comfortable, but by no means rich. The family house was next door to the business which was located at the east end of Main Street, the east side of town being the residence of the town's business owners and old money families. The Benoits were a family with deep roots in the community, being descendants of a group of French Canadian settlers who left Canada just after the American Revolution. In Lakewood, they were among the more prominent families who were members of the Catholic Church. Suzette was educated at the elementary and high schools of the Saint Francis Parish a few blocks from their home.

She had been a bright and promising student throughout her school years, and as one of the prettiest girls in town she was also one of the most popular. In her parish she had twice been selected to play the Virgin Mary during the ceremonies in May honoring Saint Mary. This honor was usually bestowed upon a pretty teen girl, but one who also had an impeccable reputation and a good school record. It seemed that everyone connected with her had a set of expectations for her. The pastor, Father Fitzsimmons, hoped that she would gain a sense of vocation and become a nun. Her parents hoped that she would one day take over the funeral home, while aunts and uncles varied from wanting her to become a lawyer to a nurse. One summer while assisting her father with arrangements for the burial of one of the town's wealthiest families, Suzette hit upon an ambition which would never be questioned as her goal in life. The arrangements were being made for the owner of the local power company subsidiary, Mr. Harold Pierce. With the family was their son, William. Being impressed by the ease at which the family agreed on every expense, Suzette decided that she would one day be the wife of a rich man, and at that moment seventeen-year-old William seemed like a good prospect for such a husband.

Suzette introduced herself to Bill, and a friendship began to take shape during the remainder of that summer. A whirlwind romance followed which went nearly unnoticed by the young people's families. It had all been innocent enough with dates at the fair, town dances, and the occasional movie. But by the weekend before Labor Day, Suzette found herself madly in love with Bill, so much so that she gave herself to Bill in the backseat of his father's car during a date to the local drive-in movie. Like so many young loves theirs was star-crossed. Bill left just three days later to go back to school at a private boarding school in Massachusetts. Despite scores of letters to him, she would receive only one response which told her that he would see her come the following summer, a promise he never kept.

The following summer, Bill spent in Europe. All that Suzette ever heard was that he had been admitted to a college somewhere on the East Coast. As her heart mended she turned her attention to other boys, who showed much more appreciation for her beauty and charms. She had never forgotten Bill, but life was too short to pine for a boy who obviously had not loved her as much as she thought he had. Boys and then men were plentiful for a lovely girl who had a calculating nature well beyond her age. Suzette knew what life could offer, and she had plans to take as much from life as she could. After high school, she had applied to several colleges and was accepted by all of them, but her first choice was Boston College. It was to Boston that she headed in the fall with two pieces of luggage and a year's tuition tucked in her bag. Higher education seemed like a silly pursuit to someone planning on finding a wealthy husband, so Suzette had no intention of using her money for the expenses of her first year at college.

Arriving in Boston she immediately took a room at one of the city's nicer hotels and set out to find an apartment central to the cluster of universities nearby. On her second day she had found a cheerful one-bedroom flat with a terrace and a view of a park across the street. The next three days she visited the employment offices of Harvard University, Boston College, and MIT, filling out applications for secretarial jobs and even being granted two interviews. The good economic times made jobs plentiful, and within a week she had been offered two jobs, one at MIT and the other at Harvard. When the employment office at Harvard mentioned that the job which they were offering was in the dean's office at the school of business, her mind was made up. She spent the weekend at the local shops buying several business suits and matching shoes so that she could make a good impression at her new office. Harvard was the place to find a solid and promising husband, and she was going to begin her pursuit from the very first day.

It had occurred to Suzette that a likely school for an up-and-coming young businessman would be Harvard, so it was with great expectations that she scanned the list of students on her first day on the job, hoping to find the name of Bill Pierce. To her disappointment, it was nowhere to be found. The ulterior motive of finding Bill was not to be accomplished. Life would have been ideal with Bill as a husband, but it also would have had its limitations. She assumed that after his schooling Bill would have headed back to Lakewood and picked up where his father had left off. While being the royal family of a small town had its appeal, so did the more exciting life in the big wide world outside Ohio. Finding a business student with potential would not be very difficult, not at Harvard, anyway, and the added attraction for this esteemed establishment was the fact that most of the students there were already the sons of privileged and extreme wealth. She might even be able to land one of the younger Kennedys.

A young woman as beautiful as Suzette gained attention from her first day on the job. The deans as well as most of the professors did not mind her presence whatsoever, and the fact that she was a bright and competent worker made her very popular with the entire staff. The older assistants and secretaries took a liking to her, adding some maternal care and concern for her into the mix. Before long her apartment was replete with every comfort imaginable and a good bit of homey charm as well. To launch her entry to the office community Suzette had hosted an open-house dinner party at her new digs and made sure that every possible office member was given an invitation. She asked the dean for a list of employees and hand-addressed invitations to each person, even those with whom she did not have direct contact in the course of her duties. Even the maintenance staff made the list for the party, and just about everyone showed up. Suzette was already a consummate hostess from years of helping her mother and father deal with grieving families at the family funeral home.

Her popularity at the office skyrocketed in the days that followed her soiree. People talked about how lovely she was and what a beautiful personality she possessed. Some of the older ladies began to try to introduce her to their sons and nephews, but what they did not realize was that their sons and nephews were unsuitable for the intent which Suzette had in mind. She was polite and loving in her refusals to be set up with various relatives of officemates, but she was steadfast in turning down every offer. She sometimes rued her game plan when an office friend would have her gorgeous son drop by the office, conveniently to bump into Suzette. Gorgeous or not, these boys did not have the sort of wealth that was a key requirement for attention from Suzette.

Only once did Suzette deviate from her long-term plans when Helen McMahon brought her twenty-three-year-old son for a visit to the office. Jimmy McMahon had graduated from Boston College the year before and was now in his first year of studies at the Massachusetts Institute of Technology working on a PhD in electrical engineering. He was a strapping young man and had the physique of the quarterback position he had held in the last two years of his tenure at Boston College. He was a strawberry blond with piercing green eyes, almost stereotypical of what most people think of when they envision a young Irishman. He was tall and broad with an almost-feminine face, full pink lips, and freckles on the rosy tops of his cheekbones. Suzette felt lust at first sight when Helen introduced her to Jimmy. She sized him up as they spoke and noted the smooth round curves of his butt cheeks and the robust bulge in his crotch through his tight Levi's jeans. Up to that moment Suzette had only had sex with one man, and that was William Pierce. Although her heart still belonged to Bill, she could easily imagine her body belonging to Jimmy McMahon, at least for a wild fling or two.

It took only two dates for Suzette to unwrap the package neatly concealed by the button fly of those Levi's. Jimmy had taken her to a school gather at MIT, which she had found rather dull and boring. Scientific types were intelligent, there was no denying that, but they also tended toward two distinct types. The first group were social misfits who could relate better to quantum physics than young women. The second group might have been able to make great progress with the opposite sex if not for their fanatical devotion to their work. Luckily for Suzette, Jimmy was quite different from either extreme he could talk about academics as easily as make sweet small talk with his date. Suzette decided that a drive to the shoreline might be more conducive to her interests than remaining at the gathering. It did not take much effort to talk Jimmy into a drive by the shoreline, so off they went in his restored 1957 Chevy convertible. It was a cool night. The seaside breezes made it feel colder than the actual temperature, so the top was up and the heater set on medium as Jimmy's hands made their first contact with Suzette's rigid nipples. He had made first base without any real effort and was now nearly at second. He wondered if he would drive in a home run before this first date came to an end.

As luck would have it, Jimmy steadily made his way into and down Suzette's outfit. He managed to slip a wiggling index finger into her before fatigue and a chilly shiver caused Suzette to murmur, "Not tonight. I am just not ready for it yet." She was not playing the tease at the moment; she actually did feel cold, and the long day was closing in on her. She felt disappointment with herself that she was pulling away from a situation which she really wanted badly. She also knew that it was better to hold off for a far better future experience than push ahead halfheartedly and risk a sexual disappointment for herself and Jimmy. Her partner, on the other hand, being a horny young man, was ready to rumble with little or no concern for the consequences. having bad sex with a beautiful girl was far superior to not having sex at all. Suzette could see the disappointment in his eyes, and she could also see the strain of his manhood against the denim material of his jeans. The swelling was impressive. She mentally ached to get acquainted with the frisky little fellow, but what her mind craved just did not sit well with her tired and chilly body. As Jimmy drove her home she hoped that this would not be the end of their growing relationship. She was relieved as Jimmy kissed her at her door and said, "I've got a study session tomorrow night, but can I pick you up on Friday for dinner, a movie, and maybe a continuation of tonight's session?" Her return kiss gave him just the answer he was hoping for.

Life at the dean's office was not particularly exciting, and Suzette found herself daydreaming about Jimmy McMahon for the next two days. He was beginning to take on the characteristics of a Prince Charming ideal in her mind as she counted the minutes until they would be resuming their physical exercises. Suzette had always enjoyed fairy stories about fair damsels and handsome princes, but after about age thirteen she began to fantasize about what living "happily ever after" actually meant. She had envisioned the usual scenes of domestic bliss with the happy couple sharing every aspect of their lives with great relish and affection; but it had occurred to her that bliss between a boy and a girl had to entail more than eating dinner, walking hand in hand, and kissing. Having learned the rudiments of sex education from older girls and the occasional adventurous boy, Suzette determined that fair maidens and handsome princes were having some excellent sex in addition to all the romantic touches implied by adept storytellers of old.

By 3:00 p.m. on Friday afternoon Suzette's imagination had gone into overdrive as she stared out her office window over the silent typewriter at which she was seated. In her mind she was millions of miles away in some mystical kingdom in which she was a noble and beautiful lady waiting for her knight in shining armor to charge over the horizon and sweep her onto the back of his horse. By three thirty, the fantasy had progressed to the bedroom of some ivory palace whose occupants had already shed their uniform and flowing dress. She saw Jimmy discard a royal blue jacket smothered in ribbons and sashes and quickly unbutton the fly of white military trousers with golden stripes down the sides, revealing a sharply curved member glistening with tiny bead of sweat. His chest was defined and firm with wispy traces of reddish blond hair at the nipples and around his navel. A small patch of equally wispy hair crowned the top of his majestic shaft and appeared to be a small flame from which his penis grow, like a phoenix towering above the flames from which it arose. She might have daydreamed well beyond her four o'clock quitting time except for the entry of Dean Wentworth into the room. The dean rolled his eyes at the idle fingers of his secretary resting on the typewriter keyboard; but this was, after all, Friday afternoon. With a sigh he bade Suzette goodbye with a wish for an enjoyable weekend. She returned the salutation and reached for her jacket and handbag as the dean stepped out of the room. *I hope the poor girl isn't coming down with something,* thought the dean, having noticed her blushing complexion, mistaking sexual arousal for a fever.

As she covered her typewriter and arranged her desk, Suzette glanced out the window to the street outside. There was her handsome prince astride his candy apple red '57 Chevy steed. She felt sure that inside his pants was another steed—equally shiny red and ready to be revved up and manually shifted into overdrive. Suzette was by no means a shrinking violet, some might have termed her brazen, but above any labels or categories she was a young woman who knew what she wanted from life and had a good idea of how she would acquire every last bit of it. Wealth and a comfortable life were her ultimate goals, but at the moment she was hungry for satisfying sex with a man that she was beginning to think could become both a means of sexual relief and a solid provider for her more material hungers. Tonight she planned to test out his abilities to satisfy her physical needs. That would be a good start, and the harder, faster nitty-gritty details could be explored in the morning.

The movie was called *Love Story* and starred Ali McGraw and Ryan O'Neal. It was romantic and a considerable tearjerker. Suzette loved it and Jimmy tolerated it. Their dinner consisted of a pizza at Giovanni's Pizzeria off the Harvard Yard and was followed by a bottle of wine on Suzette's couch. After the requisite time of kissing, fondling, and petting they were both ready for the main event. Jimmy fumbled with the buttons on her blouse until he accidentally tore one from its place. He laughed nervously as he apologized for the mishap, explaining that it was his fierce anticipation which was playing havoc with his normal coordination. Suzette joined his laughter and told him to do whatever he felt like doing with her blouse and with her. Needing no more prompting Jimmy grasped the blouse at each side of its collar and tore it in two with one swift and violent jerk. Buttons flew in all directions, and two perfectly shaped breasts nestled in a low-cut bra came clearly into view. Not bothering to fumble with the clasp of her bra Jimmy wrenched down the cup of each side of the bra and exposed her two succulent brown nipples. Before they were fully exposed to the light of day one was covered by a masculine hand with a tight and strong grip, and the other was pressed between two eager young lips.

Her head flung back from sheer sexual excitement and pleasure. Suzette moaned as she greedily pulled Jimmy's head more deeply into her bosom. "Don't be afraid to nibble on them, Jimmy," she instructed as she mashed his face into herself. Her hands ran through his thick strawberry-colored hair again and again as she massaged his head and kept it locked into its position on her breasts. It seemed as if Jimmy had ceased to require oxygen as his face rolled from nipple to nipple while coating her chest with warm saliva. When he finally came up for air Suzette immediately turned the tables as she ripped open his shirt and clawed at his chest which was coated more heavily with hair that she had imagined in her fantasy earlier that day. His nipples were large and hard with excitement as she too began to suck and bite at them. To his surprise Jimmy was enjoying the sensation and repeated her actions on him during his nipple play with her. His hands now massaged her head and held it firmly locked to his chest. He suddenly understood the old adage which said that "turnabout was fair play." He was receiving what he had given and was enjoying every tingling moment of it.

The sexual play was progressing to the point where skirt and pants were now to be found across the room and behind the couch. Panties and briefs lay in shreds on the floor below them as the young couple assumed the 69 position and began to orally simulate each other's sexual organs. Suzette could not believe that she was able to feel Jimmy's organ head at the very back of her throat, but the coarse brown pubic hairs tickling her nostrils were ample proof that she was indeed deep throating a large penis. Likewise she marveled at the depth to which she could feel Jimmy's tongue ministering to that delightfully sensitive spot within her, called her clitoris. Before long each of the young lovers was gasping from their own orgasms and lapping up the results of their lover's equally powerful reactions.

Jimmy was covered in nothing but sweat as he sat up on the armrest of the couch, his face was ablaze with a toothy smile as he gazed down on the sprawled body of Suzette, her legs spread open as far as the couch would allow. She gazed back at him, and her smile broadened as she noticed that his beautiful penis had not softened in the least nor had it lost even a fragment of its length, despite his ejaculation just moment before. "Looks like Junior is up for another round," she whispered to him as she reached out and grasped his penis, pulling him on top of her for further lovemaking. With amazing ease he covered her body with his own and slid his member smoothly and completely into her. Despite his copious

140

ejaculation, he remained perfectly hard and began a long, slow, and romantic rhythm of penetration that would last for over twenty-five minutes before a second and more violent orgasm. This time his orgasm would be within her, and the thought suddenly occurred to him that it might not have been a wise move since it had been without the benefit of a condom! As if reading his mind she spoke calmly to him, "Don't worry, lover. Suzy is on the pill." He breathed a sigh of relief, and Suzette remembered with gratitude how her mom had talked her into taking birth control pills just before her move to Boston. *Thanks, Mom,* she thought as she pulled Jimmy in position for what she hoped would be round 3.

Jimmy and Suzette remained a couple for nearly two months. The sex was outstanding, and the company being kept was mutually satisfying. Suzette began to talk with him about what plans each had for their lives. Jimmy had high hopes for a career as an electrical engineer with a specialty in research and development of new technology in the growing field of computers. When she asked what his ambitions were in the area of future financial gain, she was disappointed to hear that money ranked as less important in his mind than the thrill of creating new technology. She recoiled just a bit when he said, "How can money compare to the thrill of knowing that I might someday be the man who creates a computer small enough to fit on the top of a person's desk?" The very thought of deriving satisfaction from such an achievement without concern for financial gain seemed absurd to Suzette. Her mind was reluctantly made up, and Jimmy had become expendable. She saw no future in a computer technician and began to concoct ways slowly and gently to distance herself from Jimmy. Luckily for Jimmy his attachment to Suzette was more sexual than romantic, and he took the breakup better than his mother did. Suzette had come to a junction in her life and decided that money without question was much more important than love. It would also be the point at which she would make her first major mistake in life. She would never find out that within ten years Jimmy would be a close business associate of one of the foremost computer pioneers in history. She might have had both money and love.

This was to be Suzette's first mistake, but not her last. Nor would it be her greatest error. She had passed up the opportunity for love and did so in a frantic attempt to land a husband as rich as possible, as fast as possible. Somewhere along the line she had decided that an instant jackpot was more desirable than hooking up with someone and mining his potential. Despite all the assets which she possessed, Suzette seemed in capable of realistically evaluating her own potential. Were she ambitious enough she could easily have launched herself on a pathway to fame and fortune in any number of possible fields. Even in her chosen career path of marrying money she seemed destined to become the power behind someone else's throne. Her ability to win over people and befriend them was uncanny; people took to her and felt genuine affection for her. It said something about her personality that Helen McMahon was more deeply traumatized by the breakup of Suzette and Jimmy than either of them.

The dean and his staff were well aware of the abilities and potential which Ms. Beniot showed in her job, but many were also becoming aware of her abilities in bed as well. Rumors were rife as professors, teaching assistants, and students were added to her list of conquests. Finally, the dean himself called Suzette into his office to bring up delicately the matter. Being quite a bit older than Suzette he felt a fatherly interest in her as well as an interest in her ability to remain in his employ.

"Suzette, my dear, I am loath to bring up this subject with you, but I feel that while it is personal this matter also is having its effect on your performance here in my office," began the dean quietly.

Suzette was dumbfounded and could not imagine what this "matter" could possibly be. The last thing that ever crossed her mind was her personal life, let alone her sex life. She sat stunned as the dean revealed his concerns and made no comment until the dean added a heartfelt, but misguided, personal note.

"Suzette, as your reputation spreads, you will acquire what might be called a 'used merchandise' label; and no young woman wants that."

Suzette abruptly interrupted him saying, "I am touched by your concern, but I resent this conversation in so many ways. Not the least of which is that you would not be having it with me were I a male member of your staff."

The dean fidgeted and cleared his throat before answering, "Suzette, as your friend I must apologize, but as your employer I simply have to ask you to be more discreet in your actions and hopefully more discerning in your choice of acquaintances."

Suzette felt the sting of his pulling rank on her and merely nodded her assent to his request. They stood, shook hands, and parted company, having a much different relationship between them than they had had before Suzette entered the room that day. Suzette was hurt and angry, but much angrier than anything else. When a woman sought and found sex, she was a tramp at the worst and "used merchandise" at best. The same situation with a man brought him epithets such as "experienced" and "man of the world." It just was not fair. Despite the progress that women had made in the last ten or fifteen years there was still a double standard which painted women as wanton and brazen when they were seeking the same pleasures as their male counterparts. The time of such sexist nonsense was beginning to end, but despite the cigarette slogan "You've come a long way, baby," there was still a lot of ground to cover before Suzette would be satisfied with the situation.

All that was about to dramatically change in Suzette's life. A sweeping sea change was on its way, and within just days of the unpleasant conversation with Dean Witherspoon she found herself in a position above reproach, or at least a position which no one had the ill manners to question. It was a Tuesday morning with several students lined up in her office to request special permission to drop classes after the deadline which had ended the day before. The procedure was routine; each student filled out a short form and was then told that their request was denied. Students of Harvard were expected to have the wherewithal to deal with deadlines. One student refused to accept the required form and sternly asked to speak directly to the dean. Suzette knew that Witherspoon rarely spoke to students about such trivial matters, but at the student's insistence, she dialed the dean's extension. As she explained the request to the dean, she asked the student for his name, almost as an afterthought. The student's reply was strong and firm, "Inform the dean that Jonathan Randolph requests to see him, immediately."

Expecting the dean to explode with indignation, Suzette was caught by surprise as Witherspoon instructed her to usher the young man into his office at once. Upon closing the office door behind the student, she sat at her desk and glanced down at the stationery in its tidy little stack to the right of her typewriter. For the first time she noticed that the street address of this office contained a line reading Randolph Hall. If her guess was correct she now understood why this single student warranted such personalized attention from the dean. She slipped out from behind her desk and pulled open the "R" drawer of a rather large file cabinet and within seconds was perusing the J. R. Randolph file. It confirmed her "best" suspicions. This handsome young man was the scion of an extremely wealthy Connecticut family with deep roots in American history and even deeper roots in America's finances. He had struck her as a handsome man from their first encounter, but she now felt an overpowering attraction to him. She counted the seconds until he reemerged from the dean's office and considered just how she should approach this slightly older and much richer prospective future husband.

By the time the door finally opened Suzette's hair had been freshly brushed and her blouse unbuttoned one additional button. She even pinched her cheeks mildly to give herself just a tad more color and smiled her sweetest and more alluring smile as the door began to slowly edge open. Randolph was exiting with warm words and a bit of laughter for Dean Witherspoon. It seemed that the conversation had been genial and that Randolph was leaving a happy man. "Be well, my boy, and never hesitate to see me should you run into even the slightest of problems," shouted the dean as Randolph stepped into the outer office. It was apparent that even by Harvard standards this was a rich and powerful young man—just the kind of man that interested Suzette the most. The fact that he was easy on Suzette's eye did not hurt the matter. While she felt physically attracted to him Suzette did not rate him as the best-looking man she had ever seen. He was as handsome as Jimmy but did not quite measure up to Bill Pierce. But then again why should she make that comparison since Bill had removed himself from the equation? That removal appeared to be a permanent one.

Going to the extreme of batting her eyelashes Suzette endeavored to catch Young Randolph's attention, and she did. Jack formally introduced himself to the young secretary by his full name but quickly added, "Just call me Jack." She nearly swooned as she made the comparison between Randolph and a Harvard alumnus named Jack Kennedy. With her French heritage in mind Suzette found herself imagining herself as the new Jackie Kennedy. This entire scene was developing into a fairy-tale dream, and she knew that she must act and do so quickly if there were any chance of this dream becoming a reality. She decided that a straightforward approach might be the best, so she looked into Jack's eyes and said, "I have never seen you around campus before, but I am certainly enjoying the view now." Jack burst out in laughter and complimented her on what he assumed was a Mae West imitation adding, "That calls for my treating you to lunch at the University Club. Let's go." Suzette explained that she could not leave for lunch for another hour and one half. Jack ignored her totally. Striding over to the door of the dean's private office, he threw it open and shouted in, "Your secretary will be joining me for lunch just now. Don't expect her back this afternoon," and, turning to Suzette, continued, "Now that that is taken care of let's get going."

Suzette was swept to the University Club in downtown Boston in a shiny new black Aston Martin sports car. The attendant at the club entrance greeted Jack formally but cordially as he took the keys to the car. It was obvious from his reaction and that of the maitre d' that Jack was a respected regular within these hallowed halls. When the waiter arrived at the table, Jack ordered for both of them, a habit he would exercise their entire married life. "Roast duckling for the lady, and I'll have my usual filet done rare, very rare," he instructed the waiter, adding an order for a bottle of their most expensive French red wine. Luckily, Suzette quickly acquired a taste for duckling, which she had never had before, and decided that she could become accustomed to this sort of treatment with very little effort. If her tastes actually leaned more toward a filet of her own done well, she could indulge herself while dining out alone as Mrs. Randolph one day soon. By dessert, she knew that she had charmed Jack, and all that was left was the act of reeling him in. She decided that she would step up her plan of action by charming the pants off him, quite literally, by the end of the afternoon.

She made her move in the car on the way back to Cambridge—a slip of her petite hand onto the center of his crotch. This plan had worked exceedingly well with Jimmy McMahon, but Jack was a horse of a different color. Suzette was surprised to have her hand silently lifted off Jack's trousers and returned to her own leg. Nothing was ever said, but she began to get the message that when the time was right for a move toward sex, it would be Jack who made that move. Suzette gave a deep mental sigh realizing that this man was at least twenty years behind the times, and for him the sexual revolution had not yet heard its first shots. If the dean had seemed archaic in his attitudes, on sex, then Jack was a throwback to the Tudor understanding of the role of the man as superior in sexual situations. *Oh well,* she thought, *a step back from the edge of sexual liberation was a small price to pay for a*

*place among the elite families of Greenwich, Connecticut,
and Harvard alumni.* To get anywhere one had to pay the
fare, and she was ready to pay whatever price she needed
to in order to get where she was hoping to go.

The rest of the afternoon was spent walking along the
Charles River and watching the crew boats glide silently
along. They walked hand in hand along the pathway. At
one point they stopped to look at the selection of flowers
being offered by a woman with a floral pushcart. Jack
whispered a few words to the woman, and she handed
Suzette six bouquets of flowers, one for each variety
of flower which she sold that day. Suzette smiled and
considered that even if Jack were some modern-day
Puritan he was a sweet and thoughtful one. She leaned
into him to deliver a small kiss to his cheek and was
delighted when he took her into his arms, flowers falling
to ground all around them, and gave her a passionate
kiss. She had somehow managed truly to break the ice
but decided to leave him in the driver's seat rather than
risk making a wrong move and setting back her progress.
This time she definitely made the right decision.

Their romance could hardly be called a whirlwind. Jack
made it clear that he was interested in Suzette, but such
things took time, as did the move to committing premarital
sex. Jack was not really a prude, but he also felt that
taking the step of having sex with someone was one which
should be thought out and not be the result of raging
hormones or drunken empty passion. It was during the
few months of this chaste courtship that Suzette entered
into a pattern of serial cheating which would become her
trademark as a girlfriend, fiancée, and wife. Young Mr.
McMahon stopped by the office one afternoon to pick up
his mother, only to find that a friend had already given
her a lift home. While leaving the building, he bumped

into Suzette standing on the portico waiting for the heavy downpour to ease up. Being a gentleman, he offered her a lift home which she accepted. In the car she glanced over at his lap and remembered the magnificent sexual organ lying asleep under the cloth of his jeans. It had been so long since she had had sex that Suzette felt as if she would become wizened and die if she did not have sex soon. There she was alone in a car with a handsome ex-lover, and there in plain sight was that delicious bulge beckoning to her. The course of the next few hours were the result of an obvious choice and one which took her less than sixty seconds to make as she gingerly slid her hand up the thigh of Jimmy's leg to let it come to rest on what felt like a lead pipe in his lap.

The late afternoon flowed into the evening and then into the night with Jimmy buttoning his fly and slipping out her front door just as the first few rays of the rising sun breached the eastern horizon. She rolled over to watch him patter down the path to his Chevy and wondered why she felt no guilt at what had just taken place. She didn't think about it for very long. She simply rolled back over, hugged her pillow, and basked in the afterglow of a night of wild, passionate, and satisfying sex. She knew then that one man could never be enough. There would always have to be lovers hidden in the landscape ready at her beck and call to satisfy her. She would not love any of them as much as her husband, she promised herself, but they would share in her physical love. They would be amply rewarded for their sexual duties as well as their utter discretion.

Suzette never intended to cheat on anyone, mostly because she never took sex very seriously. To her it was a sport to be engaged in and to enjoy. Much like a high school, college, or professional jock, she relished any opportunity to jump onto the playing field and compete with a partner to see who could win the game by exacting the most pleasure from their opponent. When thoughts of marriage occurred to her, she thought more along the lines of a business relationship or partnership. To have a husband meant that she had a means of sufficient support and, by pure chance, also a bedroom companion. When the thrill of that companion grew thin, it seemed quite natural that he and she would seek the sexual company of someone else. The couple would stay married and share a bed, but their sex life would simply be a bond between them which cemented their arrangement. She had often read about loveless and sexless marriages which endured the test of time and, even at times, bore the fruits of accomplishment. As a child she had been fascinated by all types of European royalty and recalled the rampant stories in the 1960s and 1970s of the supposedly loveless marriage of England's Queen Elizabeth and her husband, Prince Phillip. There were rumors of separate bedrooms and Phillip's affairs, and yet the royal couple remained firmly together through thick and thin.

Such was the future she anticipated with Jack. Jack had been a sportsman in his undergraduate days and had the physique and bearing of a man with a well-proportioned body and one in good physical condition which impressed Suzette, but which she recognized that as an asset which, even if well maintained over the years, would become too familiar and would bore her, given enough passage of time. She looked upon her own attitude as being much like a coin collector; the thrill of finding and purchasing a rare old coin quickly gave way to the complacency of ownership. The future thrill was the pursuit of the next coin to be had. Somewhere between Bill Pierce in the backseat of his father's car and now, Suzette had grown

150

cold, not in the sense of sexual desire but in the sense of romance and love. She could envision a lifetime of weekly sex with a husband to do her wifely duty, but she knew that it would never be enough. She grew perfectly satisfied with the prospect of a husband at home and countless one-night stands and occasional lovers all over the landscape.

She could tell that Jack was no genuine romantic; even his purchase of multiple bouquets was not so much a gesture of abiding affection as it was a show of net worth designed to impress Suzette. He had the moves of a lover down pat, but he somehow lacked the emotional follow-through to make his actions really count. Suzette was happy to receive the expensive gestures and lavish dates without any deep affection behind them. Her expectations were to live well, get along with a husband, and do whatever it took to keep the home front calm and cooperative. Even when her mother told her endless Camelot stories of the Kennedy family, she always found herself admiring how well Jack and Jackie looked and acted together whether or not there was any real love between them. She did not have any reason to think that the Kennedys were not in love, but to her that was a point which really did not matter, as long as they worked together for common goals. She hoped that he and her Jack would develop such a relationship and work toward the goals of more wealth and more power.

Almost from their first day together Jack allowed his chauvinism to blind him to the fact that Suzette was much more than a pretty face. He assumed that she, like all women and his mother, would be vapid creatures to be regarded as an ornament hanging from the arm of their man. Jack's father had underestimated his wife during their entire marriage, so Jack assumed that this was a natural pattern for a husband and wife, never stopping to think how masterfully and powerfully his own mother had dealt with family and business matters during his father's several bouts with ill health. Jack's failing to appreciate all facets of his wife's personality would cost him his domestic tranquility on many occasions, and eventually, it would be his downfall, but he persisted in writing off any show of independence and insight on his wife's part as a fluke. After all just how much ingenuity could one expect from the fairer sex? His naiveté would be Suzette's greatest weapon in her arsenal of marital combat, and it could eventually carry the day for her.

Dean Witherspoon gave Suzette great latitude in her position in his office knowing that she was steadily becoming a prospect for the title of Mrs. Jack Randolph. He also shook his head in silence at all the sexual indiscretions he was aware of on her part. The single exception he made in meddling in her affairs was when he put his foot down and ended a tryst which had developed between Suzette and his nineteen-year-old son. There had to be limits to what he would tolerate, even while he recognized that there were no limits to what Suzette was capable of in her sexual prowling. Despite all the rumors and gossip Suzette remained ever popular with the other staff members in the dean's office. She held the occasional dinner party for her coworkers. Although they might gossip about her behind her back, no comments were vicious, and a few were made with the admission of a good dose of envy on the speaker's part.

Finally, after a semester and a half of dating Jack made a decision. First, he asked Suzette to come to Greenwich during the Easter holiday to join his family in their spring gathering at which time he would seek their approval of her. To Suzette's disbelief he also decided to make love to her for the first time on his family estate and, naughtily, on his parents' bed during their absence one afternoon. Suzette was thrilled finally to couple with the man that she was beginning to assume would be her husband in the near future. Her delight was tempered by the way in which the first sex was to be made. Jack sat at the edge of the bed slowly removing each article of his clothing, with his back to Suzette. When he finally looked over at her and realized that she was still clad in her summer dress, he grunted and said, "Well, those clothes are not going to remove themselves, and I don't plan to screw you like that." Suzette explained that she anticipated that he might enjoy erotically removing her clothing, but his response was to tell her gently that she should get on with it, because they would not have all day to do this.

By the end of their time in bed Suzette was ready for a nap, not out of physical exhaustion but out of boredom. Jack had rebuffed attempts at oral sex of any kind saying it seemed so unsanitary. His single sexual position was to enter her in the missionary position and pump away. She would not say that the sex was bad, but it definitely was not an exciting experience to be cherished for the rest of her life. As he finished his push-ups inside her she thought to herself that she could put up with a lifetime of this for the sake of comfort and financial freedom. So she simply grinned and bore it through the entire forty-five minutes it took. She hoped that as time passed she could introduce him to different and more exciting sexual conduct, but she knew that it would be a very long time before she could expect him to even read the Kama Sutras. After they finished their activities Suzette fully expected Jack to ring the maid and have the linens on his parents' bed stripped and replaced. Instead he cracked a mischievous grin as he straightened and refolded the bed linens and tucked bed coverings under the edge of the pillows. Maybe there was a glimmer of hope after all.

The Easter break went very well. The senior Randolphs took a liking to Suzette and invited her to come and visit with Jack on some weekend before the end of the school year. Jack would be graduating with his MBA in June, and Suzette wondered if their invitation might be a hint that they planned to see her again before too long. As they prepared to pile into Jack's car for the return ride to Cambridge she noticed that Jack's mother took him aside for a moment and whispered in his ear. Both shared great smiles as she did so, and Suzette noticed that she also slipped a small box into Jack's hand which he quickly shoved into his jacket pocket. It appeared to be a small velvet box of the type that one uses to store rings, perhaps old family engagement rings. The entire ride back to Harvard was a wonderful few hours of laughter and enjoyment. She only wished that their inaugural sexual encounter might have been as carefree and affectionate. It was obvious that Jack had a strange attitude regarding love and romance, but like so many women, Suzette promised herself that she would work on loosening him up and expanding his attitudes somewhere down the road of life.

The weekend following their return to school Jack took Suzette out to the University Club, ordered identical meals to their first date, and sat back with a glass of wine to talk about his plans for life after his upcoming graduation. He spoke of his return to Greenwich and the plan for him to enter his father's banking firm on a very high level. Suzette began to become alarmed that, as yet, there was no mention of her in any of these grand plans for the future. The concern began to show on her face. Jack seemed to be ignoring her growing gloom until he reached in his pocket and placed a small velvet box on the table without a word. He then seemed to ignore the box entirely as he said, "And I plan to purchase a house in Greenwich near my parents but far enough away to afford some privacy. I have nothing picked out as yet. After all I think it only fair that Mrs. Suzette Randolph should have some say in the matter." At those words he opened the velvet box, producing an antique Victorian engagement ring, and reached for Suzette's hand. "So, my dear Suzette, what do you have to say?" he asked. The answer he received was a muffled, "Yes!" as she pressed her face against his in a long and passionate kiss. Perhaps there was some hope for romance between them after all.

Within a few short months Harvard was a memory, as was the wedding of the year at Saint Saviour Church, Greenwich. Suzette remained Catholic, and much of the ceremony at the huge Episcopal Church was tailored to her tastes. Episcopalians, even ones at the upper stratosphere of society, remain slavishly adoring of Catholicism. The clergy of Saint Saviour Church quickly agreed to allow a Catholic priest to participate in the elaborate ceremony so that Suzette and her family could feel duly comfortable with the sacred union. The church in spite of its size was filled to the rafters with everyone of any note who lived in the tri-state area. Several retired governors, captains of industry, and the crème de la crème of the Social Register attended the rite, joining the happy couple at the Bentley Cove Club for a sumptuous reception which rivaled that of any sitting monarch of Europe. Suzette knew beyond any doubt that she had made the right decision, and her life was going nowhere but up from now on.

Their first house was a French chateau in the northernmost reaches of Greenwich proper. It was roughly

155

fifteen minutes from the elder Randolph's estate and, while grand in and of itself, paled a bit when compared with the paternal estate. That seemed appropriate since one day it would be replaced as their residence by that very same paternal manor. Suzette proved herself a capable and expert hostess from early on in their marriage by throwing grand parties as well as intimate gatherings where she endlessly networked on her husband's behalf as well as her own. The tragedy of the matter was the fact that such grand affairs brought her into steady contact with attractive young chefs, caterers, and waiters. The endless stream of toned young bodies and Adonis-like faces inevitably led to a stream of quickies and blow jobs in pantries and even kitchens under the very noses of other staff and visitors. Jack went about his merry way never suspecting what was going on. At least unaware of the extent to which it was going on. It was not until a young tutor was hired to bring Suzette into the business world that Jack would comprehend what his wife's needs and appetites encompassed. By that time he decided that the best course of action was inaction; a blind eye was preferable to accusations and constant bickering, and so the pattern was set.

It was just a few months into their first year together that Suzette began to feel under the weather and stopped in to see her doctor at Greenwich Hospital. After spending the afternoon undergoing several tests, she was told that in all likelihood the test results would confirm that she was pregnant. That evening Suzette decided to break the news to Jack in a dramatic and romantic way. She asked the chef to prepare a meal of duckling and filet. She rummaged through the wine cellar and found Jack's favorite wine. As evening approached, she sent the servants off to enjoy a night at the cinema on her. She then set an intimate table replete with candles in one of the parlors and waited for Jack's arrival from Manhattan. When he arrived he was bursting with happiness and greeted her with a warm embrace. Before she could react, he announced that he had made reservations at his favorite restaurant to celebrate the delightful news that he was soon going to have a son or daughter! Suzette recoiled in horror as she fumbled with her words to ask him how he had known. In his usual paternal way, he tut-tutted her and explained to her, as if she were a child, that their doctors were all instructed to telephone him immediately at any sign of good or bad health news.

He wondered to himself how this silly girl could have ever assumed that such news would be kept from him. Suzette, crestfallen and disappointed, slipped from the room to blow out the candles on the impromptu dining table in the parlor. Returning to him, she told Jack that while she adored him for making reservations at "their" favorite restaurant she could not possibly go out that evening. She was after all still feeling badly from the effects of her condition. She insisted that he call some friend and go off to dinner to celebrate this auspicious occasion. After a moment of hesitation he agreed with her suggestion and called a local business associate to join him for dinner. After he left Suzette went to the kitchen, poured the duckling and its sauce into the kitchen sink, and crammed it down into the garbage disposal. She then took the filet out of the warmer and tossed it into the broiler. As soon as it was sufficiently charred, she piled it in a heap alongside double helpings of side dishes and smothered the meat with A1 Sauce. She would eat what she wanted and how she wanted this evening. This would not be the last time she struck a blow for her own independence.

After her satisfying meal Suzette dialed several 800 numbers to twenty-four-hour medical referral services and, before retiring for the night, had chosen several names of potential physicians to contact in the morning. From tomorrow on, she would have her own personal doctors, and their names would not be shared with Jack. While she could heartily enjoy the good life of being a rich man's wife, she had no intention of assuming the role of the proverbial "bird in a gilded cage." Jack had gone too far, and this entire situation unnervingly reminded her of a scene from the film *Rosemary's Baby*. She was not about to stand for that creepy kind of invasion of her privacy. Within days Jack would rave and rant demanding the names and numbers of her new doctors to refrain from trying to strong-arm every doctor in Greenwich to find out who was treating his wife, after his lawyer told him that the invasion of medical confidentiality was not only illegal but would boost any other related grounds for divorce.

With the medical privacy issue behind them Jack and Suzette settled into a future of marital peace and cooperation. She gave him a son to be his namesake and a daughter to be hers. Before even being asked, Suzette provided DNA samples of each child to be tested for paternity. Jack protested that he did not even want such a thing done but studied the results of each testing to determine the exact DNA match percentiles to assure himself that each child was the genuine product of his loins. He might love a child who proved not to be his own, but he'd be damned before he would share the Randolph heritage and wealth with such a bastard child. Suzette was very careful to keep any children strictly in the family. She allowed the tests with every confidence that the results would satisfy all concerned parties. Grandpa and Grand Mamma Randolph were mystified by the need

158

for such testing; but they, much like their son, preferred to turn a blind eye to questionable situations in order to avoid any possible embarrassment.

Almost from the hour of their births, Jack began to decide the futures of his two children. His son would go to Harvard to earn a degree either as a master of business administration or as a doctor of jurisprudence. His daughter would earn an undergraduate degree in some ladylike subject and eventually be married off to a rich young Connecticut businessman to serve much as her mother did as a trophy wife to be paraded about and flaunted to friends and, more importantly, to business associates. To Jack that was the natural and God-ordained order of things: each sex had its proper roles and duties. No amount of social upheaval or liberation movements could change the bedrock of society. Minorities and their taste for equality might live in whatever manner they saw fit, but the blue bloods of American society would hold fast to tradition and proprieties. No one ever asked JR and Suzy what they felt about these "ideals," and Suzette set about from their earliest childhood to thwart their father's influence upon them.

Putting aside the major and minor tensions at play in the Randolph marriage there was actually a general everyday calm to the household. Each family member went about their life pretty much doing as they pleased. One of the amazing social glues which tend to keep wealthy families together is the ease with which each family member can buy themselves a niche and stay out of the others' hair. A family of four in a four-bedroom Cape Cod would find themselves vying for a quiet nook to relax in, a place at the table to do homework, and, of course, a reservation for time in the communal bathroom. A rich family had dozens of rooms to retreat to and do their own thing, so to speak. There are no knock-down, drag-out fights over what program to watch on television when there are half a dozen televisions scattered about the house. The same can be said about arguments over who gets to use the family car when a family has a family fleet and not one, but two, full-time drivers at their command.

As life settled down to a tranquil pace Suzette came up with an idea that Jack was slow to warm to, but which he eventually embraced. Always fancying herself and Jack as a potentially new Kennedy couple, Suzette set out to encourage Jack to enter local politics in the hopes that they would move up the ladder of political offices and, someday, be the founders of a new Camelot on Long Island Sound. The thought never really occurred to Suzette that there were striking differences between them and the Kennedys. For one thing, Jack Randolph had almost none of the charm and wit of Jack Kennedy and Jackie Kennedy had none of the nymphomaniacal reputation of Suzette. Their major similarity with the Kennedys was their seemingly unlimited bankroll with which to buy elections. Jack often quipped about Joe Kennedy's comment to John during the 1960 presidential election, "John, spend whatever it takes to win this thing, but be reasonable. I'll be damned before I pay for a landslide." It had never been beneath the Kennedys or the Randolphs to pay for enough votes to get them elected.

When the Greenwich municipal elections rolled around one year Suzette pushed Jack hard to throw his hand in the ring for the office of first selectman. It never occurred to Suzette or Jack that most local politicos ran for and held the office of selectman for a number of years before running for first selectman. Such details did not really matter. There were enough Republican voters in

Greenwich to elect a conservative to the post, and Jack had more than enough money to buy enough of those votes in the party primary. He won the primary by a landslide. Most observers credited his lovely and driven wife with garnering more votes than had his liberal application of over $1,000,000 to an election involving less than thirty thousand voters. The *Greenwich Time* gushed over Suzette. To her chagrin none of the comparisons were between her and Jackie Kennedy, but rather they compared her to Evita Peron!

It really didn't matter whether she was regarded as the new Jackie or the new Evita because she had no intention of filling either woman's shoes. Suzette had visions of having her name ranked equally with those two powerful ladies. Had Suzette's grandiose dreams been realized, she might have been the first female candidate to win her party's nomination, unlike Hillary Clinton who was an "also ran." Her only major stumbling block to fame and political power was the rather stiff, staid, and elitist husband who led her about on his tuxedoed arm. They were a royal pair considered symbols of the kind of life Greenwich offered to those who could afford it. They also displayed a strong distaste for the common people and, more especially, the everyday problems of people who worked for a living. Well into his term as first selectman, Jack was asked about a growing financial crisis brewing in the town's working-class borough of Cos Cob. Jack was asked what he thought about the increasing complaint that local property taxes were forcing some Cos Cob residents to sell their homes and move out of Greenwich. His response spoke volumes about his class-conscious values when he said, "As I see it, if they can't afford to live in Greenwich, they should just get out and sell their homes to people who can afford them."

No amount of charm on Suzette's part managed to smooth the ruffled feathers of the Cos Cob population. It was evident that the next election would have to be won without the staunchly conservative votes of Cos Cob's workers. But despite his alienation of so many of the town's average citizens, Jack remained steady in the polls and was expected to win reelection by a respectable, if not landslide, margin. Jack, however, grew visibly weary of his constant debates with the board of selectmen and with the working-class residents. When two scandals hit, one following the other, things became too much for him to bear. First, a group of female African-American millionaires had organized a weekly exercise group at Todd's Point, Greenwich's exclusive beach and wildlife preserve. At the second gathering of the group Jack instructed the park police to remove the group from the beach under the pretense that they did not have the required permits for such a regular gathering. The courts were to decide that situation clearly in favor of the ladies' exercise group. Shortly thereafter, a Caribbean-American police officer on the town's police force produced evidence that while he held the highest scores on the civil service sergeant's test, he had been passed over for promotion not once but three times in the course of three years. Memos were produced showing that Jack was the power behind the decision to pass over the officer each year.

Even though polls continued to forecast Jack's reelection the following year Jack announced that he would not seek a second term as first selectman. Suzette's dreams of the governor's mansion and then the White House were over in one terse announcement. She would be forced to be content with being the first lady of the Randolph financial empire. A consolation prize was the fact that her private life would no longer be in the

162

public eye, and she could once again prowl for exciting young sex partners with no concern for her public image. In every dark cloud there was, indeed, a silver lining. Suzette was the kind of survivor who sought and found those silver linings. Jack had tried his hand at politics, and while he had not by any means failed miserably, he did prove that he had neither the temperament nor the finesse to keep even a majority of the people happy at any given time. He might have been a Republican, but he was most decidedly not cast from the same mold as Abraham Lincoln. Considering Jack's thought on racial equality, he was probably quite satisfied with his distinction from old Honest Abe.

When the day came for Jack to turn over the office of first selectman to his successor he made a speech filled with his usual hyperbole calling his departure "the end of an era." Suzette picked up on the theme and hosted an "end of an era" party at the huge atrium of the Greenwich Biltmore. The atrium is similar to one of those old Zeppelin hangars from the 1930s and can easily hold a thousand partiers with masses of room to spare. The night of the Randolph party it was overflowing. Suzette had reserved every room in the hotel so that guests could drink themselves senseless and not have to be concerned about transportation home. She had thought of everything. The alcohol which flowed into every glass was the top-of-the-top-shelf brands. The food was limited to four choices—all gourmet selections, there would be no second-rate entrée to spoil the delightful smell of opulence hanging over the guests. The venue was so large that two grand pianos played simultaneously, one at each end of the atrium, but synchronized to play identical pieces in perfect time with each other. It was a grand fete even by Greenwich's standards.

If ever Suzette proved her worth as a grand dame it was that night. One would have thought that a king had abdicated in favor of his crown prince; such was the grandeur of the affair. Suzette shared in the glow as she took her place like a consort next the man of the hour. They had not celebrated like this when Jack had won election. For him this was a greater day for he was finally free of the vile common people who dared to call him their civil servant. The festivities lasted all night. Around midnight—with the salmon, Delmonico steaks, and caviar past—it was time to divide up, gentlemen with cigars and brandy on one side of the hall and ladies with after-dinner wines and cheeses on the other side. Each side had a piano which continued to match its twin's every note, but at much lower tones than it had earlier. Some of the guests were a bit taken aback by this Victorian arrangement. Since most guests knew Jack, they understood why it was taking place. After all, this was his night.

Jack himself had not been the architect of this gender division. It had been the suggestion of Suzette and recommended as a way for Jack to display his sensibilities in a grand show of statecraft at the end of his "reign." Such talk always appealed to Jack, and he was easily recruited as it biggest advocate. He eventually came to believe that he had originated the idea. The whole idea had actually been a very cunning way for Suzette to be out of Jack's sight in order to slip away to one of the rented rooms with any gentlemen interested in clandestine sex with the former first lady of Greenwich. She congratulated herself on her own ingenuity as she took an absolutely delightful young busman by the hand and led him off to a convenient guest room on the other side of the hotel. She wished that they had been able to have a swim in the nude at the hotel's indoor pool, but she knew that such a daring act would be far too risky with friends and associates prowling all over the hotel in various states of intoxication.

The busman could have been no older than twenty, but he was stunning and appeared eager to shake off his job-related boredom with a sexual romp with an older but ravishingly beautiful woman. A former first lady no less! His name was Manuel, and he was a second-generation Mexican American with piercing dark eyes of a shade of brown which neared blackness. These onyx jewels were set in a long lean face with very decided angles to it which seemed more Welsh than Hispanic, but with his pale ivory skin it was a good bet that his heritage included Basque blood from the north of Spain. No matter what the combination of heritage, it added up to a magnificent example of the male human form. Suzette decided that such a man must be had and not just for some one-night stand of sexual release but kept in reserve for times when urges needed to be met. He would be an investment in pleasure. She expected that with the right level of investment, he would pay excellent dividends for years to come.

His body was long, firm, and lean, a kind of cross between a college athlete and a lovely young schoolboy. When she cornered him for a moment she was delighted to hear his words come out in a valley-boy accent of sing-songy tempo and intonation, the kind of speech pattern which was both charming and invoked images of surfer boys on some California beach. Suzette had reserved a room in the hotel for just such an opportunity, and she was not about to pass this one up. Manuel's body made his black polyester slacks and vest look as good as any tailored tuxedo. She decided that she needed to see more of it. A conveniently dropped napkin gave cause to ask him to bend over and retrieve it. When he did so she scanned every inch of his firm and roundly smoothed buttocks. His ass cheeks were small, compact, and looked as if they had been poured into the perfect mold of his slacks. Suzette took it as a very promising sign that he lingered in that position far longer than required to fetch the errant napkin. He was responding to her interest, giving her ample time to peruse his assets.

Suzette had all the confirmation that she needed to put a plan together and into action. She pulled Manuel aside and instructed him to return to the area in twenty minutes. She then put herself to the task of mingling with friends and associates making sure to give each important friend at least a moment of face time with her. It seemed very impolite to rush out of the festivities without giving everyone a bit of attention. About two minutes before Manuel was scheduled to appear, Suzette announced loudly, "Good heavens! Now where did my diamond earring go off to? These were a gift from Jack on our first anniversary, and I would hate to lose one." When several of the gathered ladies offered to assist in a search for the missing earring, Suzette politely brushed off their offers stating, "Oh my no! Isn't this the very sort of thing we pay the help to do for us?" And with that, she turned to Manuel who had just arrived and told him that he must assist her in locating the earring, which was actually safely tucked in her handbag. "I believe that I may have lost it over one of the serving tables, so we had best go off to the kitchens and check the serving trays before my little bauble is tossed into the trash."

Having given her excuse for an abrupt exit she led Manuel off toward the serving entrance of the hall. Once the door closed behind them she took his hand and quickly moved into the corridor which connected to the accommodations area of the hotel. As they silently trotted to the reserved room across the building Suzette looked longingly at the indoor pool as they strode past it. She imagined their nude bodies entwined poolside or even in the cool waters of the shallow end of the pool. The very idea that they might well be caught in the act of copulation aroused her. Danger was a powerful aphrodisiac, and even the hint of it made Suzette moist in a most personal place of her body. This man/boy beside her looked more and more appealing as they drew near to what would be their love nest for the evening. His presence made her feel nearly as giddy and excited as she had in the car so long ago in Lakewood when Bill Pierce had claimed her virginity.

Once inside the room Suzette slowed things down as she insisted that Manuel lie on the bed and watch her perform a slow and sensuous striptease for him. As each piece of her clothing fell to the floor Manuel groaned and showed his pleasure. When the last article left her body, that being her panties, and she stood before him totally bare he gave out a long whistle and in his giddy valley-boy dialect exclaimed, "Like, totally radical!" Suzette felt like a schoolgirl again, a faint blush coming over her body, as she was ready to move this situation to the next level. Climbing on the bed next to Manuel she pushed him back onto the pillows, when he tried to rise. This was going to be her show, and she made that clear. He gave no resistance and made no argument to the contrary. She began to kiss his mouth and face passionately as she removed his tie and vest. She slowly undid each button on his shirt kissing the flesh exposed by the undoing. She was amazed and delighted to find his chest hairless even around his tiny rose pink nipples. Her kisses aroused him, and his hands began to explore her body as she worked her way down his torso.

Before very long his shirt and slacks were crumpled on the floor next to the bed, and Suzette was facing a ten-inch smooth and erect penis. She ran her fingers up and down the magnificent shaft enjoying the fact that his member was devoid of the veiny bumps so many men possessed on their penises. Some women craved the extra sensual simulations that such veins gave when coming in contact with her flesh. Suzette preferred the smooth and shiny surface of a penis to slide effortlessly and quickly in and out of her. In every way Manuel seemed perfect, and she would enjoy every inch of his body and relish it as long as she could. They joined their bodies with Suzette astride Manuel's trim middle section enjoying the gliding of his member with so little friction. She would provide the necessary friction by tightening herself around him, and his increasing gasps proved that her method was resonating with him. The night's lovemaking was long and intense, resulting in multiple orgasms for each of them.

Had this been a different world with a totally different set of circumstances she would have agreed to stay there with him forever, but they were in the real world, and the circumstance in which they both lived made their revelry limited. Yet there must be some way to make this joyous situation last beyond this single episode. A thought came to Suzette just as they fell into each other's arms and into an exhausted sleep. That thought made Suzette smile contentedly as she rested her head on Manuel's chest, taking in his aroma much as one would sip exquisite wine. His scent was a combination of perspiration born of lovemaking lightly mingled with what she felt sure was Cool Water cologne. It proved intoxicating, lulling her into a deep and restful slumber.

In the morning it was Suzette who rested on the bed as Manuel performed a little erotic show for her. He stood dressing with his shirt, tie, and vest on his upper body, but totally nude from the waist down and his ten-inch uncircumcised erection waving slightly in her direction. When the show had concluded and both were completely dressed she reached into her handbag, retrieving both her earring and a small social calling card. As she nuzzled her face into his neck, she whispered in his ear, "Come to the address on this card around nine on Monday morning. You will be starting a new job at the Randolph estate at that time, at double your current salary." Manuel took the card and after reading the address asked, "And what am I am expected to do for that kind of salary?" Suzette smiled as she said, "Oh, I can think of duties that you won't mind so much. Just be there." As she slipped past him and out the door, she was ready to head home to start planning the many and delightful ways in which Manuel would become an integral part of her household.

Chapter Five

A Cowboy's Girls

William Pierce had been a beautiful baby from the day he was born, even the delivery room nurses joked that this one would leave a trail of broken hearts by the time he reached the age of twenty-one. They were not too far off on this one. Born into a wealthy and prestigious Ohio family, he had quite a bit going for him from his first day on this earth. He was handsome, he was intelligent, and to complete the trifecta he developed a charming and extremely likable personality. While he was not an only child, having an older sister and a younger brother, he was the gem in the Pierce crown. Mother and Father Pierce treated him like royalty, even nicknaming him their "Golden Boy." During childhood and adolescence Bill was totally unfamiliar with the word "no" in regard to any of his wants or needs. Fate treated him as well as his parents did; every effort he made was rewarded with success. It was not all magical, however. One could not fault him for failing to put his best effort and intelligence into every project he undertook, despite knowing that his parents would make it succeed.

The very first tragedy in his life came when he was eleven. Michelle, his sister, had been killed in a school bus accident during her first year of high school; and the loss would stay with Bill and his brother, Timmy, for the rest of their lives. Shelly had been a protective and doting sibling to the boys, and her death shook their idyllic lives to their cores. Neither boy ever rode a school bus after the tragedy, as their mother would not allow it. They were driven to school by their father on his way to the office and picked up by their mother each afternoon. This routine was carried on throughout their grade school days until each went off to boarding school for high school. It took some time, but each boy eventually recovered from the loss of their sister, and yet a certain seriousness had been infused in their young lives by her death.

Bill, who had always been a good student, continued his academic excellence through high school and on to college. Timmy eventually lost interest in school when he took up the study of the guitar in his junior year and formed a grunge band which became fairly successful and provided him with a decent living after graduation and his relocation to Philadelphia. This career choice did not sit well with Mother Pierce resulting in an amicable estrangement which continued to the present. Bill, on the other hand, chose a career path which delighted his parents. By the time his father died in Bill's junior year he had already been granted early admittance to Princeton University and a spot in the business program. Before his death Father Pierce had bragged to his business associates that Bill was well on his way to becoming his well-qualified heir to take over the power company. At his funeral many comments had been made that Harold Pierce had died a happy man, and the lion's share of that happiness was his pride in his son Bill.

After the death of Harold Pierce, his wife felt no interest in assuming the presidency of the power company and sold off the controlling interest in the utility subsidiary to its vice chairman, so Bill would have to find other business interests to pursue. It did not take long for Mrs. Pierce to decide upon investing her liquid cash in another field which she found more genteel and appealing, and one which as a gracious hostess she had some experience doing. She purchased a small chain of hotels. There were three hotels, one in Lakewood and two in other nearby towns in Ohio. The three establishments were grand and elegant places with a Victorian charm, not found in more modern hotels, and they were all showing profits despite America's growing love affair with low-cost chain motels. Part of her motivation was to preserve a traditional elegance in their field and to make a good living at the same time. She also hoped to create a family business which Bill could one day inherit and apply his increasing talents to.

The hotel and hospitality industry proved to be the perfect career situation for both mother and son. Lillian Pierce blossomed in her role as grand dame and gracious hostess in what she regarded as her hotel empire, such as it may have been. One man's pittance is another's treasure trove, as they say. For Bill this was an escape from the captivity of the corporate boardroom, a welcome change of plans. Business was in his blood, but the thought of spending inordinate amounts of time dealing with staid old codgers did not appeal to the young and exuberant Mr. Pierce. Bill preferred the company of females. It didn't much matter their age or degree of beauty. Just the fact that they were women gave Bill an energy which charged his personality and brought out his natural charisma, although he had no problem fitting in when it came to dealing with other men. But his talents were at their best among the ladies. If one might use a rather passé expression, Bill was by all measures an old-fashioned ladies' man, par excellence.

In the hotel business, charm is an incredibly valuable asset, and it was one both the Pierces had in abundance. Following his graduation from Princeton Bill returned to Lakewood and the new family business. It was a natural for the gregarious young man with his newly learned business acumen. It helped the hotel business prosper far beyond the expectations held even by his mother. The trio of hotels began to prosper, not as direct competition to the large motel chains but as a niche service. They became places that one came to visit as a unique experience. They took on the air of semirural resorts which offered weekend getaways from the urban areas of Ohio and surrounding states.

The Pierce family was made up of people who had no problem with risking their capital and did not hesitate to back up their investments with the hard work it took to make them a success. Harold Pierce's father, Stuart, had invested in the power company at a point in time when many rural areas surrounding Lakewood had not yet electrified their homes. It was Stuart Pierce who had traveled the back roads of the nearby counties to urge people to buy into the convenience of electric lighting. That had not been part of his job description. But he realized that the more people he got to electrify, the greater his client base and the larger his profits. Such was the stuff which Pierces were made of, and Bill was no different from the Pierces who had gone before him. He threw himself into the hotel business with his usual ardent fervor, and equally as usual he made a success of his efforts.

Though his mother was the actual owner of the hotel enterprise, Bill was given almost total control of the two hotels outside Lakewood. Mrs. Pierce preferred playing the grand dame at the flagship hotel in Lakewood. It was there that she ruled the roost while the two other inns were left to Bill's tastes, ideas, and management skills. All things considered, the Lakewood Hotel was the grandest of the three, but it was also the least profitable as well. For Lillian Pierce style meant much more than profit. She had her son to provide the profits to keep the business solvent. Her mission was to keep a tradition of excellence alive, and to her excellence meant luxury and some degree of glamour as well. Her idea of success involved a visit from a Hollywood star more than a large profit margin. She was old school when it came to style and elegance. The china and crystal had to be genuine, no stainless flatware, but sterling silver sat beside her Noritake China.

Her guest list always included recognized movie and television stars. Even the stately Mrs. Pierce knew how to have fun. No one in Lakewood would ever forget the gala she hosted for one of her favorite TV stars. The television comic Paul Lynde was a native of central Ohio and had friends in Lakewood, so he was familiar with the Lakewood Hotel. Every summer Lynde returned to Ohio for summer stock productions, and during those tours he would stay at the Lakewood, commuting to dinner theaters around the state. During one season he and the troupe put on an unscheduled performance of their revue in the ballroom of the Lakewood. The show was a raging success. People came from all over the tri-county region to see it. Despite his ribald sense of humor, he and Lillian had hit it off

174

from their first meeting. Paul often toured the Ohio area with Broadway show summer stock troupes and made the Lakewood Hotel a regular stop on his tours.

Mother Pierce instilled in Bill a love for the finer things in life as well as a lifestyle of elegance in which to appreciate those finer things beyond their expense. Such a taste for the pleasures of life extended to all facets of Bill's life, even down to his taste in women. The most beautiful women come to be nothing more than sex partners unless they possessed a refined style and worldliness which appreciated the beauty in life. He was a renaissance man and intended to have a renaissance wife, but one of his faults was a decided shallowness when it came to female beauty. Few cultured women were possessed of the type of beauty Bill craved and lusted for so badly. Even from his earlier years he found himself fascinated by women of élan and elegance. But more times than not, he also found himself bedding down their maids. It seemed to him that the beauty he wanted sexually was vastly different than the cultural beauty he admired.

Having always been a handsome and well-built man, Bill was never short of female admirers and sexual partners. The hotel employees were a handy harem of pretty young girls ready and willing to provide all the sex that he could handle. And handle it he did, with almost every maid, waitress, and secretary in the business. Every one of the young ones dreamed of being the wife of the Pierce heir, but as the years passed none of them made it past his bed. After the death of Mother Pierce, the bulk of the hotel business was left to Bill. His decision to sell the hotels to the Four Seasons Inn Corporation raised many eyebrows, but his personal decision to relocate to the west left many of the local women teary-eyed and seriously disappointed. Such was the sex appeal of the Pierce scion whose charm was matched only by his virile good looks. Ohio's loss would be some Wild West state's gain. On the day he left Lakewood, after completing the sale of the family's assets, Bill was seen driving a brand-new Bronco down Main Street and out of town with a white cowboy hat perched on his head. The small-town rich boy was about to become a dashing cowboy in the rather luxurious and tony resort town of Jackson Hole, Wyoming—a town better known for more celebrity stars than cattle rustlers these days. The acorn had not fallen too far from the tree. The glamour loving Mrs. Pierce would have been very proud.

Upon his arrival in Jackson Hole, Bill adopted a new persona, one of a confident but struggling newcomer. No one ever understood the motivation behind this role-playing, but it certainly led to the establishment of many solid new friendships as locals befriended and rallied behind this charming newcomer. Several of the friendships did not survive the eventual revelation of Bill's true monetary status, but for the most part his friends accepted him equally warmly as a rich man as they had when they thought he had nothing. One exception was the manager of the Brandywine when he realized that the man he had hoped to groom for better things was now going to be his boss. He eventually got over it, but their relationship was never quite the same. It might have also had something to do with Bill's interest in a young female employee whom the manager saw as a prospective plaything, a girl named Tiffany Gould.

From the first moment that Bill saw Tiffany he felt a strong physical reaction to her. His chino trousers were tented from his erect penis, and he was large enough to attract the immediate attention of Tiffany Gould. Tiffany was no choir girl, and she was fond of men in general, but most especially of men with large endowments. From the swelling in the front of Bill's pants, she knew he was the kind of man she would enjoy having. It was not that she was a shallow person attracted simply by physical attributes, but she also did not ignore her own sexual likes and dislikes. Loving a man was serious business, but fucking a man was a whole different matter, one that had much more to do with pleasure than thoughts of compatibility or personality.

It would be a safe judgment to make that in its initial stages their relationship was purely a sexual one. To assure herself that Bill and she were on the same page Tiffany excused herself from Bill's office and headed off to the ladies' room. She hiked up her already-short skirt before returning to the office. Before very long she found an excuse to pick up something from the floor, making sure to aim her backside toward Bill as she bent especially deeply. Bill noticed, and the tent arose even more pronouncedly than before. They were most definitely on the same page. Their discussion of seating arrangements for that evening's party soon gave way to a quick lunch in Bill's private suite. The luncheon gave way equally quickly to enjoying each other's body. She was the kind of girl he had always enjoyed making love to and yet the kind he never seemed to become serious with. Tiffany enjoyed the look of Bill's square jaw, firm toned torso, and lightly furry chest. His nine inches of firm manhood closed the deal for her. Initially it hurt her considerably to have Bill enter her. She never could handle all of his nine inches; nonetheless she found herself experiencing multiple orgasms every time the two of them had sex.

As time went on their sexual escapades became more random and adventurous. Afternoon trysts became a daily standard, but peppered between those scheduled sessions were an increasing number of impromptu encounters.

Probably the most outrageous of their episodes was a Saturday afternoon encounter in the ranch's outdoor Jacuzzi. The Jacuzzi being located between the swimming pool and the kiddies' wading pool just behind the main building in a very dangerous spot, one could easily be seen by guests on either side. It had started as a simple soak. Being alone in the hot water, one hot and sunny afternoon, a game of footsy developed into lowered trunks and alternating exercises in oral sex. No one seemed to notice as each of them took turns diving beneath the swirling water emerging with guilty smiles.

Another equally daring sexcapade took place in the lobby of the resort just after the closing of the dining room. The staff was heading home except for the night bartenders, so the lobby was deserted by one o'clock in the morning. Both Bill and Tiffany had had several drinks. Caution was easily tossed to the wind as their passions became enflamed. The thought had crossed both their minds to make love on the check-in desk, and this seemed like the perfect opportunity to do so! Placing Tiffany on the counter Bill ran his hands up her elegant black evening gown, sliding his hands along her cool and smooth flesh until he came to the waistband of her flimsy panties. He gently tugged the silk garment down her legs until it fell to the ground from her now-bare feet. Retracing his way up her legs, Bill smoothly hiked the dress up to her waist as he buried his face into her. She moaned so loudly that both of them caught their breath sure they would be discovered.

With great effort Tiffany muffled her moans as Bill's tongue found her most sensitive spot. He mercilessly fondled her clitoris with the tip of his invasive tongue as she squirmed in ecstasy on the counter. When he thought she was ready for the main event he gallantly lifted her by the shoulders and waist, keeping her dress around her midsection and keeping her totally exposed from her navel to her toes. He brought her to one of the divans in the center of the lobby, placing her shoulders on the seat and her buttocks on the armrest, preparing for one final oral assault before entering her. She again stifled her moans as he finally replaced his tongue with his swollen manhood. They enjoyed each other's bodies for over an hour, knowing that at any moment a late arrival, a wandering bar patron, or an employee might happen upon them. But that was the whole point, now, wasn't it?

Having the sort of relationship which is based purely on sex, neither Bill nor Tiffany felt any compunction about carrying on affairs with others, be they fellow employees or guests. Bill often found single guests looking for more than companionship after the nightly barbeque and square dance. In some ways he thought of his sexual ministrations as just another of the many services provided by the resort. On occasion he substituted for the resort's masseur and found that many an innocent massage could easily be turned into an afternoon of sex, given the right approach. It was during one of these seductive massages that Bill found himself in bed with an old friend from Ohio. Suzette had realized immediately upon her arrival at the Brandywine that its owner was none other than her old flame William Pierce, but Bill did not recognize Suzette or her new last name.

Jack, Suzette, and the children had come out to the Brandywine Ranch for the first time while Jack was the Greenwich first selectman. The trip had been a getaway following his first year in office and was the suggestion of one of the other selectmen who often headed out west for a little roughhousing away from the rarified atmosphere of Greenwich society. Jack found the whole place grandly amusing—people as urban as himself dressed up as cowboys and doing the sorts of things one sees in movies, but at a much slower and safer pace. Despite himself, he loved the place and was glad to find at least one activity which the entire Randolph clan seemed to enjoy, not initially realizing that Suzette was relishing their trips for her own ulterior reasons.

Bill had long ago forgotten about Suzette, but she had never forgotten him. Part of her motivation in moving to the East Coast had been an attempt to find him, but it had been in vain. Now all these years later, there he was, older, more mature, but just as handsome as ever. The very first time they made love while he pretended to be a masseur she had felt as if the intervening years had never happened at all. She did not care in the least if her beloved Bill was simply a resort masseur. In fact, she rather liked the idea of having the financial upper hand. There was a hint of bitterness in Suzette from years of waiting and hoping for a reunion with Bill. After all, she had waited right there in Lakewood where he knew she would be, but he had disappeared. She never realized that he had come back to town just months after her relocation to Boston.

Bill had gone off to college directly from boarding school. His visits home were short and infrequent, so there had been little chance of running into Suzette. Even if he had seen her again, the passion which they had shared was a passing infatuation, at least for him. Suzette, on the other hand, had fallen in love deeply and hard with a man who so neatly fit into her profile of a future husband. She had never abandoned her hopes to land a promising and wealthy man, preferably one who was also handsome. Bill had fit that bill from the moment she had laid eyes on him at her family's funeral parlor.

Time, marriage, and children had not dulled her desire for him. Years had passed, but each of them remained as attractive as they had been in their youth. Bill was more ruggedly handsome and more muscular. Suzette had filled out her figure from a girlish pixie to a curvaceous woman. They were well-matched as young adults and were now equally well-matched as middle-aged adults. Time had been kind to both of them, as if saving them for each other.

There had been many women in his life since his teen years. Some had been contenders for marriage, but none had managed to fulfill all the criteria so very important to Bill. Beauty and sex were important parts of his ideals for a wife, but there were social and cultural aspects he regarded as even more vital. To become Mrs. William Pierce was an honor for any woman in Bill's mind. There was no shortage of ego in the Pierce line. Like his father and mother before him the family name and history are held in very high regard, if only by the Pierces themselves.

Although Bill would hardly have considered Suzette his lifelong love it was a strange fact that he never had engaged in any truly serious relationship with any woman. There had been scores of flings and too many one-night stands to keep track of. No one ever lasted more than a few months. Women came and women went in his life to the extent that one might have referred to Bill's love life as a revolving door. There was always a sense of loneliness in Bill, and he knew it. It was the one area of his charmed life which refused improvement. It was not as if he didn't try to find someone. Yet the right woman never appeared. His handsome face was a regular sight in all the "right" nightspots in whatever locale he happened to be living at the moment. For a man who appeared to have everything there was one glaring absence in his life—someone to share it with and grow old together.

For a man in his fourth decade on earth things were still very good, but Bill's thoughts were beginning to turn to the future. Having Suzette suddenly reappear in his life seemed providential. It was true that she had a husband and kids in tow, but that kind of situation had never posed a problem of much substance before. So why should it now? Bill was accustomed to having things his own way all of his life. If charm could not acquire what he wanted, then money usually did the trick. In the case of women he never failed to "plant his flag" in whatever "territory" he decided to claim. Sex was never a problem, nor was finding someone to love him. The problem was finding someone whom he could love with the kind of love which would last a lifetime. Maybe, just maybe Suzette could be such a love. And to think she had come from his own backyard!

The matter of breaking up a marriage was something Bill had done several times before, and it seemed to get easier with repetition. It was not as if Bill were an amoral person; in so many ways he was a kind, caring, and just person, but his entire demeanor and attitude transformed when a beautiful woman was involved. At those times his mind shut down and his penis took command. There is a sexist adage which states that "all men are dogs," inferring that a man will do anything for sex and will have sex with almost anyone. In Bill's case that was nearly true. Bill was a man of reason and liked to look for guidance from reason. For example, he reasoned that a man had a penis for sexual activity, be it for procreation or not. Therefore if a man such as himself was endowed with a large penis, he had every right in the world to use it as much as humanly possible. It would be a waste not to do so. With logic like that, there was little doubt that Bill would always be a "swordsman" and a totally uninhibited one at that.

From his early teens, Bill had used his looks, charm, and social standing to bed down almost anyone he chose. One of his favorite activities was to screw the sisters of each of his best friends from school, and when he became bored with that, he managed to bed down a few of their mothers as well. He was the perfect gentleman which sat well with the ladies. It impressed adult ladies even more than those in his age group. There was the case of poor Ms. Phillpotts, Bill's junior year chemistry instructor. She was thirty-five years old and had never been married, despite being a rather pleasant-looking woman. In the spring semester of that year, Bill took a liking to her and began a process of seduction far more advanced than one might have expected from a teenage boy.

For several weeks Bill observed where Ms. Phillpotts parked her car and when she left for the day. Luckily for him Phillpotts was as regular in her routines as a train schedule in Mussolini's Italy. Each day at exactly 3:20 p.m. she would lock her desk drawers, leave her office, and head for the parking lot. Her little Honda Civic was always parked in parking spot 9 in the corner of the lot near the wall of Burke Hall, a somewhat secluded spot away from the main doors of the building: the perfect spot for Bill to put on a little show for his teacher and object of desire. At three twenty-two on a warm and sunny afternoon Ms. Phillpotts arrived at her car only to find Bill urinating on the school wall near her car and with his back toward her. Indignantly she called out to him, "Just what do you think you are doing, you young savage? There are restrooms inside for that." To her shock Bill turned around, his erect penis in hand, smiling at her with a broad grin that was as inviting as he could muster.

"Sorry, Ms. Phillpotts, but I just could not hold it any longer, and as you can see I really needed some release." He said this to her maintaining his coy smile as he spoke. Clearing her throat nervously she had to agree that it was pretty obvious that there was an urgent need for release for Bill, although she doubted that it was urine that he had in mind. No words were spoken as the teacher and the teen entered her car to drive away from the school and off to Phillpotts's apartment about a mile from the school. There was silence as they rode the distance, but Bill had not returned his erect penis to his trousers. Phillpotts's free hand was caressing and stroking Bill's manhood, seeking to encourage even further growth. She might have been unmarried, but it became quickly apparent to Bill that Ms. Phillpotts was not without her share of sexual experience as she quickly bent over at one stoplight to enwrap his erection with her lips. *This is going to be one wild afternoon!* thought Bill as the car pulled into the underground garage of a well-groomed apartment complex.

Before the apartment door had fully swung shut Phillpotts had Bill's trousers and boxers down around his ankles and had slipped her hands beneath his shirt and blazer, massaging his chest and stomach as she swallowed his swollen member. Bill thought he was in nirvana at that moment. This older woman was providing him with the best sex he had ever had in his young life. Between groans he considered that perhaps he was falling in love. Bill had already had a good deal of sexual experience, even some with older women who enjoyed his massive endowment and his endless sexual energy. Ms. Phillpotts was different. She was ensuring that the pleasure she was enjoying would be shared between them. The other ladies had made use of his sexual ministrations and cared precious little how much he had enjoyed the experience. This woman was different. She matched his pleasure-giving prowess point by point and left him panting for more. For years to come Bill would brag that Ms. Phillpotts had led him to no less than six orgasms in their three-hour love session, somewhat of a record for a teenage boy.

After a thorough exercise in fellatio which accounted for the first two of Bill's six orgasms, Phillpotts led Bill from the living room couch to the bedroom. Although Bill stood nearly four inches taller than Ms. Phillpotts, she threw him unto the bed with one heave and had removed all of her own clothes before he could recover from her seeming judo move. There he lay stripped down except for his shirt, tie, and blue school blazer. It seemed that Phillpotts enjoyed what she considered the "deflowering" of one of her students while he remained in at least part of the school uniform. Unbeknownst to her this teenager was a long way away from any deflowering. Bill had a track record stretching back to the tender age of thirteen when he had lost his virginity to a high school girl three years his senior. She, like Ms. Phillpotts, had succumbed to the "charms" of his sizable and thick penis, which he was never hesitant to display to a prospective lover.

Bill was flat on his back, half dressed and nine inches of erection pointed directly at the ceiling. Phillpotts wasted no time in climbing unto him and mounting herself on all nine inches of penis in one motion. Simultaneously each of them let out an erotic groan of sheer pleasure. Bill had never experienced such an active and aggressive lover. She smiled broadly as she realized that Bill had no intention of letting her do all the work As she drove her body down on his erection he rose to the occasion and met her every stroke with an upward thrust. The

185

combination of the two motions gave each of them extreme pleasure leading to competing cries of sexual ecstasy and intense releases for each of them which left them nearly incoherent with pleasure. During the entire three-hour session no words were exchanged between them. When the roller coaster ride of sex was over, Phillpotts simply rose, grabbed a towel from her linen stand, and headed off to the shower, much like a jubilant pitcher after his first no-hitter game.

Bill, the experienced and yet still-young lover, felt disappointed by his successful seduction of his teacher. Perhaps he sensed that while he had made the first move, the rest of the game had been utterly in her control. Now in the aftermath, he had expected fondling, kissing, and snuggling; but he had not even gotten a comment, let alone anything romantic. As he stumbled up from the bed he used the bed sheet to wipe himself off as he looked for his pants and shorts. Above the hiss of the shower he heard Phillpotts shout, "I'll be done in a minute. Then you can take a quick one and I'll drive you home, honey." Bill's mood totally reversed itself. The simple word "honey" was an affirmation of what he was looking for, a small indication that this woman was pleased with his sexual performance. Suddenly he felt a bit guilty for wiping his sweat and semen on her bed sheets even though it was clearly obvious that the entire bed ensemble was in need of a wash after their strenuous physical activities that afternoon.

Over the course of that semester and the summer session these long and steamy sexual encounters were a regular event of the week. The sex was always excellent, and as time passed a romantic bond began to develop between the two mismatched lovers. Near the end of the summer they began to expand their experiences, even including other partners in the encounters. It was that experimentation which eventually led to the abrupt and tragic end of their affair. In a small orgy arranged by Ms. Phillpotts two other teachers had joined them. Mr. and Mrs. Ghent were the school's French and literature instructors. The Ghents were in their late twenties and rather attractive, as well as considering themselves sexual libertines, so they had no qualms about joining Ms. Phillpotts's little "arrangement." During one afternoon's lovemaking the two female teachers engaged in a bit of lesbian activity to the delight of the males, but in the tumble of bodies Mr. Ghent saw the opportunity to try something quite new. He entered Bill as he entangled himself between the women. Bill let out a scream mingled with profanity that ended the session and the "arrangement."

The following day Ms. Phillpotts was summoned to the headmaster's office and accused of sexual misconduct with a student. She was informed that the Ghents had become aware of her misbehavior and had reported it immediately. When she protested that they themselves had participated in the sexual misconduct the headmaster would hear none of it. Years later the headmaster and the Ghents would be exposed as serial sexual predators and be arrested as well as being dismissed, but at the moment that did not help Ms. Phillpotts. She was given the choice of a quiet and immediate resignation or a scandal which would ruin her career forever. Her office was cleared and her name struck from the faculty registry in the main hall that day. When Bill dared to sneak over to her apartment several weeks later, there was no answer at the door. When he returned well into the fall semester the apartment was vacant.

Bill never forgot Ms. Phillpotts and for years to come would use her as the template for his idea of the perfect

187

prospective wife. She had been beautiful, although her beauty seemed to increase with more distant memories. She was as well highly intelligent, cultured, dignified, and an absolute fantasy in bed. No woman could reach those standards for years to come, and when one did, she happened to be a married rich woman from Greenwich, Connecticut: a woman that he could have married right after secondary school, if he had only recognized her for what she could have been to him. As a successful hotelier and social magnate in his own bailiwick of Jackson Hole he had come a very long and circuitous route to find that Suzette Benoit was the right woman for him after all. She could have told him that back in Lakewood, but she knew that back then he would have never listened or understood. For Suzette the old adage "Better late than never" had a very rich and full meaning.

At the ranch, Bill had always been quite popular with the women. He was an incurable flirt and had a knack for making every woman feel very special to him. Even the young daughters of employees had secret crushes on him as did many of the church youth group he led after church on Sunday mornings. The guests at the Brandywine were off limits when he was simply an employee, during the time that he was studying the operation, determining how profitable the ranch was currently, and could become under his ownership. In that year or so, one could have classified Bill as the ideal employee—never late, nearly never absent, and always on top of his game. He anticipated problems and often took preventative measures to head them off, saving the ranch time and money. That is why he was being considered for grooming as a future general manager at the time that he decided to purchase the Brandywine chain of resorts. His master plan would have been to expand the number of resorts to ten, spread across the fashionable areas of the western states and into the southwest.

Once he had become the owner and general manager of the Brandywine resorts he decided to keep the Jackson Hole resort as his headquarters and send his friend, the former general manager, to the Nevada resort. Bill liked Jackson Hole, and the clientele which it had built up was the kind of people he enjoyed rubbing elbows with on a regular basis. They were mostly easterners looking for a western adventure, but not so authentic an adventure as to strain them physically or mentally. These were the sort of people who had visited the Lakewood Hotel back in Ohio. They were moneyed and refined, but not as arrogant or stuffy as the Boston Brahmin types. While Bill was an athletic and strapping kind of man he did not appreciate the rough edges of many of the working-class citizens of Wyoming. Although he detested his politics, Bill would rather have entertained Jackson Hole resident Dick Cheney than the Harley-Davidson-riding modern cowboys of the rural areas surrounding Jackson Hole. He was no snob, but Bill identified with the upper classes for no other reason than the civility he found in them.

By the time the Randolphs had found Brandywine Suzette had a long history of cheating on Jack. By this point in their marriage he was never surprised when he found the telltale signs of her cheating. At the Brandywine the first thing he noted was her absence at almost all their family events. Every event which they had planned to attend together and with the children was always brushed off with the most flippant of excuses. That had always been her pattern, and she was true to form even during their first visit to Brandywine. Jack had no idea who the secret lover was, but he had several candidates in mind. One of them was the handsome general manager who seemed to double as the resident masseur. Jack was no fool, but he had ceased to care about Suzette's cheating after the first few years of marriage. Yet another lover would make no difference to him. He actually appreciated the opportunities this arrangement gave him to enjoy the ranch and its rustic amenities.

Bill seemed to have very little trouble with mingling among the husbands and families of women he was "servicing" sexually. He and Jack had spent some time together playing golf and poker and doing a bit of hunting on the resort's properties. It would have been a stretch to say that the two had become friends, but they certainly had no problem enjoying each other's company. If Bill did find any situation uncomfortable it was when he attended events with both a lover and her husband. There was an evident awkwardness to the situation and to the conversation between them. In the case of Suzette and Jack, there were only rare occasions when the two were together with Bill, except for the times when Jack would invite Bill over for a drink after dinner. Suzette had the good grace to excuse herself from the room on those occasions. It seemed that they all had a good thing working for them, and each maintained enough of a distance from each other to keep it going sans complications. They were a civilized lot, and oddly enough, none of them found anything strange about this "convenient" arrangement.

There were times when Jack and Bill went off into the wilderness to do some fishing and, at times, hunting. There were more than a few occasions when Jack crouched in a bush a few yards from Bill holding a high-powered rifle, a perfect situation for a jealous husband to dispatch his wife's lover and chalk it all up to an unfortunate hunting accident. No such action was ever taken. Jack had his suspicions, but he was not 100 percent sure if Bill was fucking his wife; then again, as long as the arrangement did not become embarrassing, he was not all that concerned. A happy Suzette was a quiet one. For domestic tranquility, he had no problem putting up with her infidelity. Although Suzette was a born cheater she might have made some effort to be a loyal wife had Jack shown some form of jealousy or anger over her affairs. He never did, and she felt that he actually gave her license to carry on as she pleased.

Just a year before the Randolphs had decided to take a late autumn trip to the ranch which included Halloween. The Randolph children had purchased costumes before leaving Greenwich. JR dressed as the 1950s children's show puppet Howdy Doody and Suzy as a vampire from the Twilight books and movie. Jack's halfhearted effort was to wear jeans, flannel shirt, bandanna, and cowboy hat. None of them would be noticed at the Halloween festivities, however, when Suzette stepped out of her robe as they entered the ballroom. She wore a blonde wig much longer and fuller than her own hair and a one-piece swimsuit from the television series *Baywatch*. Her likeness to Pamela Anderson was quite striking. While her breasts were not quite as ample as the TV star's they were impressive enough to stun the assembled crowd into momentary silence. They immediately caught Bill's undivided attention. Her costume had crossed the line with Jack. After two drinks he excused himself and returned to the family suite where he had several more drinks and watched Fox News until he fell asleep alone at well after three in the morning.

The interior of the Brandywine was quite modern and well heated, but the October weather could be felt in draughts and cooler corners of the ballroom. Suzette's bathing suit provided little warmth, and her nipples were extended beyond what one would think was humanly possible. Bill, being the gallant gentleman that he always was, had dressed as a musketeer and offered his cape to Suzette for a bit of covering, using the flourish of the cape to camouflage a discreet pinch of Suzette's distended nipples. She knew without a doubt that the two would be making love before the night was ended. She smiled at how well her blatant costume had worked in both getting rid of Jack and attracting Bill away from his duties as host of the evening's events. She had honed her seductive skills over the years using them on as diverse a crowd of lovers as teenaged delivery boys to Jack's business associates, but Bill was different. He was her ultimate goal, a prize that had slipped out of her grasp some twenty years ago. She meant to have him permanently this time, even if it took months or years to do it. There was more than sex at stake this time, and she meant to have it all.

During the same trip a small incident made Suzette stop and ponder what she was doing and where she planned to end up regarding Bill, Jack, and her future. Being a quite self-centered creature of luxury it had never occurred to her that while she might indeed have Bill, he might not be the obedient or loyal husband that Jack had been all these years. As she left the gym, heading for her suite, she passed the indoor pool and noticed that despite the early hour of 6:00 a.m. there was a sole occupant in the pool resting her head against the pool's edge apparently enjoying a rather satisfying soak. The girl was young with long dark hair. As she rested her head on the ledge of the pool she rocked it back and forth as if moaning. It was impossible to be sure through the glass walls enclosing the pool. For a moment Suzette considered going into the enclosure to see if the young woman was in some form of distress, but thought better of it and turned away. As she reached the door at the end of the hall she glanced back and was startled to see Bill popping up out of the water directly in front of the girl. She realized with a jolt that Bill would be quite a different kind of man and future mate than Jack.

Bill and Tiffany were becoming quite an item among the Brandywine staff and the surrounding community, so much so that a good number of folks were patiently waiting for wedding bells to be heard at the resort. Tiffany certainly had long-term ideas for the two of them, although marriage was not necessarily the ideal conclusion to her plans. She was a very mature and practical young woman. She believed much more in a professional relationship with sexual benefits than true love. She knew that legal arrangements, such as marriage, hung on two things: first, an infatuation with each other that would eventually fade, and second, a legal contract which bound individuals together with messy financial entanglements that had nothing to do with love. She had seen her parents live out a loveless marriage at the same time as interacting in a flourishing and positive business partnership. For Tiffany the loving side of any arrangement suited her just fine, but with the understanding that when the romance was gone the financial agreements stood firm. She would like quite well to be Mrs. William Pierce, but it would be a side benefit of being a partner in the Brandywine resort's operation.

Bill, on the other hand, saw Tiffany as a beautiful young playmate who had an amazing ability to satisfy his sexual needs and be pleasant company to boot. He saw no great plan for sharing his assets or any type of partnership growing out of this relationship. At the very most Bill had given passing thought to the idea of marrying Tiffany with the expectation that she would leave his employ and be a stay-at-home wife. Neither of the two of them had any idea of how their attitudes toward each other were at such cross purposes. The single item which bound them together was their amazing sexual compatibility. They each enjoyed the sex that the other provided and earnestly enjoyed each other's conversation, personality, and presence. Each, however, was an ambitious creature who held his or her own success over all other concerns, including each other.

For Bill a wife would be a domestic partner, not a co-owner of the Brandywine. It was just one way he compartmentalized his life into very neat and distinct areas. There was always the possibility that one day he might encourage someone to invest in the resorts and buy their way into a partnership. That partner could just as easily be a woman as a man, but they would need to buy that partnership with cold hard investments. With regard to a wife, she would be his lover and household partner quite distinct from his business life. Some might have regarded Bill's attitudes as a bit archaic and possibly even sexist, but such an attitude would miss the whole point. Bill did not hope for a barefoot and pregnant slave for a wife, but he also did not plan to marry someone expecting to sleep their way into his business accomplishments. Any woman he might consider marrying would have to be an intelligent and independent individual, as well as being socially and culturally sophisticated.

As Suzette began to enter the picture, Bill was in a full-bore relationship with Tiffany, but without any plans of commitment or in any way formalizing the relationship. Bill had a boyish ability to regard things as if they would go on unchanged forever. As suave and worldly as he was, there was also a good dose of the Peter Pan syndrome in his personality. When a situation pleased him, Bill would allow it to continue without preventative or calculated measures to preserve or modify it. Like a schoolboy expecting every day to be much the same as the day before it, Bill acted as if Tiffany would always be there beside him in his bed or on the check-in counter, no matter how life changed for each of them. Such an attitude can work for a surprisingly long period of time. Couples have been known to be engaged for nearly twenty years before marrying or breaking up. When, however, relationships are as complex as the one Bill and Tiffany enjoyed there was always the threat of something throwing it all off balance. The arrival of Suzette did just that.

If Suzette's discovery of Bill performing underwater oral sex on a young woman in the pool got her thinking about the situation, then Tiffany had far more things to set the gears of her mind in motion during Suzette's visits. How often did she see Bill dressed in the white jeans and tight-fitting white tee shirt of the resort masseur heading for Suite 609, the large suite which the Randolphs reserved for each of their visits. Equally disturbing to Tiffany was the attention which Bill had shown Suzette and her *Baywatch* swimsuit during the Halloween party. She had cursed herself that evening for wearing a Cinderella costume with tons of frilly lace, but no cleavage or revealing bodice. While she was a hit among the many attractive male guests that evening, she noticed that Bill's attention had been devoted entirely to the ersatz Pamela Anderson, so much so that by midnight they had disappeared, and Cinderella found herself alone at the ball.

Tiffany was not the kind of woman who could get accustomed not to being the center of attention. She had always been a lovely girl with a charming personality. Added to her looks, she often found herself admired and

195

liked by males and females alike. She had been popular throughout her school years often finding herself elected to some office or station which other girls only hoped to achieve. From a very early age she had become a goal-oriented personality. Rarely was she content except when she was pursuing some distant and challenging goal. In her schooling she had been an above-average student, but overly fond of fun and games, often sacrificing her study time for a date which always lasted well past her curfew. By her senior year of high school she had managed to maintain a B+ average, with the exception of failing her physical education classes, not once but two years in a row. When her school counselor broke the bad news to her that she could not make up two physical education classes in the summer session of her senior year, she did not quite understand all the fuss over such trivial classes. She did come to understand that she would be required to attend an additional year of high school in order to take and pass two such classes.

Being the goal-oriented person that she had developed into, the thought of her entire education being thrown off for a full year for such a trivial reason was intolerable. New Jersey educational laws be damned, she would quit school and take a high school equivalency test and achieve her diploma right on schedule. After acing the test and getting her GED certificate she had not counted on the effect it would have on her college applications. She had been turned down by every major university to which she had applied. She devised a plan B and entered Thomas Edison Community College, a small junior college in suburban Newark. Completing her two-year degree in a single year, she applied to Rutgers University and gained entry to complete her bachelor's degree as if she had never had any problem at all. Her determination and effort paid off when she learned that she had been admitted to a master of fine arts program at Columbia for the following fall. By that point Tiffany decided that life was more than degrees and declined the offer in order to set out for Wyoming where she hoped she would find a life more exciting and personally rewarding than what she saw as her prospects in northern New Jersey.

One of the things which Bill noticed about Tiffany, besides her beauty, was her serious attitude about being a success in life. They had met while Bill was still working for the Brandywine. He had been one of her interviewers and had been impressed by her presentation more than by her resume. The manager took Bill's recommendations seriously but also considered in the back of his mind that Bill's judgment might have been clouded a bit by this flirtatious young woman. Tiffany explained that she had relocated to the Jackson Hole area after doing her homework on several municipalities in the general area. She had researched per capita earnings and average incomes when considering her new location, hoping to enter the hospitality industry among people of means, so as to earn the highest salary possible. After considering the financial aspects of her prospective homes, she then weighed in with the amenities which each offered. After some visits to each location she decided upon Jackson Hole. Such a thorough plan of action sat very well with Bill. For once his recommendation had very little to do with sexual attraction.

There had been other female employees at the Brandywine who had caught the attention of the assistant manager and then owner. It was said that at one time or another Bill had romanced every woman on his payroll under the age of thirty-five. Most of the ladies at the ranch were modest and discreet, but one could not help noticing the dreamy look in their eyes when they spoke about Bill, some from experience and some from unfulfilled fantasies. No one would deny that Bill was a good catch. What most people comprehended, especially his many lovers, is the fact that he had no intention of being caught, at least not by anyone except his ideal woman. That person seemed to be just a phantom, until Suzette stepped back into his life. All the others would be fondly remembered and some even kept on his active "waiting" list, but none of them would ever fill the niche in his life the way he hoped Suzette would. She was a beautiful woman who had matured into an intelligent and cultured princess in his mind. The cold and calculating side of her personality had not yet made itself evident to him. No woman was perfect, nor any man, so one must settle for a rose with its thorns. Bill was satisfied to have both in Suzette.

After their reunion Bill often questioned why he had ignored her so long ago in Lakewood. He had enjoyed being her first lover and taking away her virginity, but the lure of so many bodies back at school and so many potential romances at Princeton had dulled him to the great compatibility which they had shared for a few short weeks in their high school years. He often compared himself to Dorothy from the *Wizard of Oz* who ran off searching for an ideal life, only to discover after so much wandering that what was desired and needed most was right there at home—in Lakewood. During their first encounter when he posed as the resort masseur there had been a great physical attraction. As they began to spend time together, both sexually and simply in friendship, he fell in love with Suzette all over again for all the qualities he never saw in her during their youthful romance. Bill was a very complex personality, but so was Suzette; somehow against all odd their peculiarities fit together like a finely

198

cut jigsaw puzzle. If there were two people "made" for each other, it seemed that these were the two.

After finding Bill again Suzette wondered if the saying was true, that all things happen in their own good time. She had been without Bill for so many years, but she had married well and had two children whom she loved very deeply. Jack had been a lackluster husband, but he had always been kind and generous to her. She had been from a respectable family back in Ohio, but Jack had honeymooned her in Paris, and in their years of marriage she had seen the major sights of the entire world, eaten at the finest restaurants on five continents, and lived in the lap of luxury as a backcountry matron of Greenwich. She had done well for herself; and she had been a good, if not loyal, wife to Jack. She had always been an asset in his political and business affairs, greeting his associates, even bedding a few of them down for her pleasure and his advancement. Had he not been so disdainful of the common people they might have ended up in the governor's mansion in Hartford, or even a Georgetown town house, residence of the state's junior senator. So many things could have been achieved by Jack with Suzette's support and drive. In the end, it all would still have been loveless and somehow even beyond all the success in the world, Suzette still longed for love.

It could truthfully be said of Bill that he had the sexual appetite of a hungry alley cat, but the taste of a consummate connoisseur. He fucked a wide variety of women of every race, creed, color, and economic status; but the women he actually loved were class acts. Each one had a charm and intelligence which gave them the air of another Princess Grace, warm and yet aloof, beautiful and yet down to earth. Such were the many loves of William Pierce. Many years before his death his concerned father had told him, "William, women are a wonderful part of a man's life, but mark my words when I tell you that when a man becomes obsessed with them, or even just one of them, it will be his downfall. And you, my dear boy, are becoming obsessed with all of them." Had his father lived to see the multiple affairs Bill had going on at the Brandywine he would most likely have shaken his head and sighed at the fulfillment of his prophecy.

Women had always been a major part of Bill's life. Oftentimes when he found himself in some predicament or another it was the result of some misstep regarding a woman or a woman's husband. During more than one of his massages a client's husband would arrive unexpectedly to find the couple in a compromising situation. Each time the husband was contented to speak to the resort's owner by telephone and be assured that the philandering masseur would be fired immediately, never realizing that the owner was in fact the same philanderer as the offending masseur. Bill recalled fondly the time that a husband had walked into the room just as Bill had inserted himself into the man's wife. Expecting violence, he quickly withdrew and began to apologize only to have the husband plop into a chair and cheerfully instruct them to "Carry on! Do carry on!" and watch with apparent glee as his wife enjoyed the inflamed organ of an overheated Bill. Such was the life of a resort owner among the rich and famous clientele of a tony retreat getaway.

Life was very good to Bill, and the Brandywine Ranch had turned out to be a gold mine financially and socially. One would have thought a fairly rustic and rural setting in Wyoming would be a social graveyard; but one of the amazing things about the rich is their willingness to travel to trendy meccas to rub elbows with the very same people they usually socialized with in Hollywood, South Beach, and the Hamptons. The rich are an odd lot, and Bill knew he could count on that fact. The other fact about the rich which he counted on was their insatiable appetite for sex. A fact he used for his own amusement rather than for the good of the business. For most "red-blooded" men sex is a commodity often sought after and desired, even obsessed about. For Bill it was more of a gentleman's hobby, something like collecting rare stamps or coins. There was no trove of pornographic magazines in his apartment or gigabytes of lewd, distasteful material on his computer. Those were the trademarks of amateurs, not the refined collector.

That was the distinction about Suzette. She was not just another piece in a collection. Rather, she was the replacement for the entire collection. Once they were together in a permanent situation the collecting would come to an end, or least that was the romantic notion which filled Bill's mind when he considered his future with her. The problem which proved to be a thorn in his side was Tiffany. He did care about Tiffany and might actually have admitted to being in love with her except for the fact that he now saw a definite future with Suzette. Her return to his life had caused him to reconsider and redefine large portions of his life. With the bluster of a man in love he made vows to himself to reform his life and center it around his beloved Suzette. The problem was the fact that a man of over forty years of age with a habitually promiscuous lifestyle can rarely change his appetites so quickly and so thoroughly even for the woman he truly loves. Suzette had taken center stage in his life, but Tiffany was not going away, and a very large part of him did not want her to exit from his life. He was quickly becoming a torn man, led in two different directions by two very appealing women.

Somewhere along the line of building a life and career Bill had allowed an idealistic notion of settling down to harbor itself in his mind and heart. The ultimate playboy had all along nurtured a dream of finding the perfect wife and finding bliss in her arms, rather than in the beds of dozens of different women. All in all that was by no means a bad thing for a man to aspire to, but in this particular case there were complications. First, there was the woman with whom he had enjoyed a regular and heated romance over the past several months. Second, there was the woman of his dreams who fell back into his life after years of absence but who was married to a very rich and very powerful man. Lastly, there was a complication which Bill did not even consider. Suzette was not the naïve young Lakewood, Ohio, girl anymore. She was a complex and strong-willed woman whom he really did not know as well as he told himself he did.

Much water had flowed under each of their bridges in the years between Lakewood and now. His life had undergone many changes, and he certainly could not have predicted back in Lakewood where he would find himself today. He was supposed to have been the CEO of a power company in central Ohio, married to one of the daughters of his father's business associates, living with his wife and children in the big house on the hill in Lakewood. If his life had taken so many and varied twists and turns how much more had Suzette's? He did not stop to consider how she had grown and developed before and during her marriage to Jack Randolph. She had tasted not only wealth, but to a certain degree she had also tasted power, and at least the power would be something she would have to give up to "run off" with Bill. Being the mistress of a resort for the rich had its appeal, but it was not quite the same as being the first lady of

202

one of America's wealthiest hamlets, hobnobbing with the likes of the Bushes and Kennedys.

All the intense love in the world cannot erase more than twenty years of personal history, but Bill was in the process of selling himself on an idealized picture of life with Suzette. One could not fault him for his blind optimism, but they might also pity him when it became so painfully obvious that all his rakish legend was a façade behind which hid a man in need of the simplest of life's necessities, someone to love. The countless sexual escapades had all been great fun, but they had never fulfilled him. Deep down Bill was an old-fashioned gentleman, someone who needed family and the sense of a home as his retreat and source of strength. That is not to say that he had any archaic notions of being the "king" of his castle, but he did feel a deep-seated need to belong to someone. Such feelings conflicted with his devil-may-care outward attitude, but it resonated to the sensitive and caring side of his personality. He wanted to belong to someone and likewise feel that they belonged to him, not in a master-and-slave relationship but rather in the sense that two parts could constitute one whole.

In her own way, Tiffany fulfilled his desires beyond sexual gratification, because she had a sense of belonging which in many ways agreed with his desires. She, however, took that possessiveness a step further, moving from the emotional to the mercenary. She definitely loved Bill, but she also had very definite desires toward Bill's successful business ventures. Although Tiffany had not singled out Bill because of his money, she did find the prospect of marrying a wealthy man a very attractive option. In some ways Tiffany did not fit the idealized image of the cultured and sophisticated "lady of the house" which played such a major role in Bill's search for a wife. The choice between Tiffany and Suzette would be a difficult one. While Tiffany had youth, beauty, and charm in her favor, she also betrayed enough of her ambition to temper the physical attraction Bill felt for her. Suzette appeared more and more as a soul mate to Bill, even if he never acknowledged even to himself that he was idealizing her from past memories and his own subconscious desires.

It would be anyone's guess how Bill would reconcile his emotional struggle. Had he sought advice and counsel someone might have led him to a more realistic and balanced set of values by which to weigh his decision. For an intelligent and composed man in his forties, Bill was approaching this situation with the emotional maturity of a starry-eyed teenager. Even worse, like a child given the choice of two candy jars to select from, he wanted both for diverse reasons, but could only have one. As many men do, when faced with a difficult decision, Bill considered all options by which he could have his cake and eat it too. Wild schemes ran through his head about marrying Suzette and living in the east while keeping Tiffany and the Brandywine Ranch as a separate western side of his life. He knew that such a scheme would never work and yet found himself daydreaming about such an arrangement more and more as the two relationships developed.

Strangely enough, while Bill obsessed over his choice of future wives, he spent no time at all considering another major player in what he regarded as his love triangle. Jack Randolph was another human factor which also needed to be dealt with before Bill could settle down with Suzette. He had put Jack out of his mind and the equation, a very silly and dangerous thing to do. As a dedicated "ladies' man" the consideration of the other men in situations rarely occurred to him. If it did, he usually could not be in the least bit concerned about that man's feelings or actions.

In the past, situations just seemed to work themselves out, much like the husband who played voyeur after catching Bill servicing his wife at the ranch. Bill foolishly underestimated the reaction of Jack Randolph. Jack might be a man who tolerated a cheating wife, but only if that cheating wife was discreet and gave the appearance of loyalty. The idea of Suzette leaving him as the result of an ongoing affair would be a whole different matter. Such a development would mean that Jack's blind-eye attitude would be exposed and made public in a divorce trial. It never occurred to Bill that such exposure would matter to another man; romance was not the hard and solid matters of business. Why would a man be bothered with such trivial things as affairs and personal relationships? In that way he had underestimated the pride of a man like Jack. For Jack, Suzette was a property or a valuable commodity which he had partially bought and partially earned. Taking her away would be theft in his mind. Bill and Jack were very different men when it came to their attitude toward women, relationships, and marriage; and Bill made no effort to understand the other man's position, probably because he could never fathom it. It may well have been this fundamental disconnect in their worldviews that would lead to a confrontation of classic proportions and a tragic end.

Chapter Six

Even a Monster Needs Love

Almost every person in Greenwich knew the name of Jack Randolph. Few actually knew him personally; but everyone who knew him through business, social engagements, or simply by reputation would never go so far as to say they liked him. Lizzy knew Jack as a client and beyond that had met the man many times at country clubs, social affairs, and even charity benefits. While she could not point out any obvious characteristic which annoyed her, she had to admit that the sum total of his characteristics made for a very unappealing personality. He was a genuine New England snob who would use any excuse to mention his descent from one of the early governors of the New Haven Colony. Even in appearance he just did not impress, despite a trim and athletic build which was holding up very well as he headed toward fifty years of age, he was simply not a striking person. No one could honestly say he was unattractive of face, and yet again nothing made him stand out. He was never the subject of conversation among even the most lustful ladies of town society, and none of them sighed in desire on the occasions when he swam at the club pool.

Lizzy had a profound dislike for the man ever since their exchanges during her interior design contract over a year ago. He had never been overtly rude, but he had managed to give the impression that home decoration was purely a female matter. He became involved in the project only in so far as he was assured that his personal space in the house was kept precisely to his liking. During her measurements of Jack's den and office she remembered how austere and impersonal each room was before she redesigned it. The rooms could have been generic to any wealthy man. The furnishings were traditional and had all been very expensive in their day. Jack had said that he was perfectly happy with things remaining exactly the same but allowed the redecoration to proceed to mollify his wife. Looking back on the comment, Lizzy wondered if this was an attempt to appease his wife and save their marriage.

With some research at the public library and old online yearbooks from Jack's primary and secondary schools and college years, Lizzy had produced a profile which any private detective would have been proud to present to a client. Jack had been an athlete throughout his school years and appeared to have been a fairly popular person among his peers. In the pages of his secondary school yearbook, during his senior year, he had been voted numerous accolades, including Most Likely to Succeed, Student Body Vice President, Best Lacrosse Player, and even Most-Sought-After Prom Escort. Lizzy wondered how such a "big man on campus" could have morphed into the rather dull and plain character who now bore the name J. Richard Randolph. Even his college years at Yale's Ezra Stiles College seemed to be a time of popularity and success. Like his hero, George W. Bush, Jack had been a major force on the Yale baseball team. As best as she could gather from old resumes and records open to the public Jack had also been a solid student with better-than-average grades, although never making any of the honor rolls.

The change in Jack seemed to be rooted in his graduate work at Harvard Business School. Like many Greenwich businesspeople Jack had taken his undergraduate degree at Yale and his business degree at Harvard. It was considered a plum to have a degree from each of the top Ivy League school, and the resulting set of double business connections was invaluable on Wall Street as well as in Greenwich. Such a standing also made the embarrassment of a loss at the annual Yale-Harvard game a total impossibility; either school's victory could be claimed as one's own. Jack was not a football fan, but certain games were a social must among the financial magnates. Though not a football fan, Jack was known in his student days to participate in an old Harvard and Yale football tradition. When one of the Ivy League schools lost to a lesser school the losing team's fans would pull out their handkerchiefs and wave them at the victors with the cry, "That's all right. That's okay! You will work for us one day." Now that sounded very much like the Jack Randolph that Lizzy knew today.

It was just after earning his MBA that Jack had married Suzette. There seemed to be no record of her in Greenwich society prior to their marriage. Lizzy wondered about that and decided a check with the registrar of marriages in town hall was in order. After a quick search on an antiquated microfiche machine at the back of the registrar's office she found the license and jotted down the details. At the time of the marriage, performed at Saviour

Episcopal Church in Greenwich, Suzette Benoit was a resident of Cambridge, Massachusetts, home of Harvard University. Her place of birth was listed as Lakewood, Ohio, so Lizzy assumed that she may well have been a freshman at Harvard while Jack was a senior graduate student. A little online research in the Harvard yearbooks would reveal the answer in no time, or so she thought as she typed away on her laptop while still parked in the town hall parking lot. After scouring all four relevant years, she came up with nothing.

Back at home and at her desk, Lizzy decided that for now Jack was the person to investigate, so she returned to the Harvard Business School yearbook site. While scrolling through the opening pages a name caught her eye as it rolled up the screen. Going back slowly she could not seem to find the name Suzette, which she was sure that she had seen. As she reexamined the page on the dean's office she told herself that she must have been mistaken. Then she noticed the name of the dean's secretary, Suzette Benoit! Suzette had not been a Harvard undergraduate student but had actually been a school employee in the administration. Wheels began to turn in her head as Lizzy realized what this all meant. Suzette was not a wealthy schoolgirl who had turned the head of Jack Randolph at all. She had simply been an employee whose beauty had won her an up-and-coming MBA with a bright future on Wall Street. It was the familiar old Cinderella story of the middle-class secretary who marries the handsome prince, although that revelation came as quite a surprise since Lizzy had never pegged Jack as any kind of romantic who could marry for love over class and money.

There was a somewhat romantic side to Jack that Lizzy would not discover just yet despite her growingly intense research. There had been the gossip some weeks ago from Lucy Provence about a sudden change of heart in the mood of the Randolph divorce. The rather pitted initial dustup between the couple had suddenly and inexplicably become a very quiet and amicable settlement in which Suzette had gained greatly. That was a thorn in Lizzy's side for some time now. Knowing Jack Randolph, there must have been a very large and serious reason for him to lay down arms and declare a truce with Suzette. It would seem that if even half the stories Lizzy had heard about Mrs. Randolph were true then Suzette was what an unkind person might term a sexual alley cat. Were Jack an equal wanderer from the matrimonial bed, he had been so discreet that there was not a trace of evidence or even rumor to disclose such conduct. What could she have held over his head? Perhaps there was some business deal which she knew of that he feared more than a generous divorce settlement. *Of course,* thought Lizzy, *the pending Securities and Exchange Commission's investigation of the Randolph Fund. That must be the answer.* In fact, that was only part of the answer.

Lizzy now knew a great deal about Jack Randolph, but what she knew was about the public figure and ever so little about the private man. Later she would learn about his private life, but at the moment she could only make guesses. Her guesses were educated ones, and she was hitting near the target, but not making any bull's-eyes as yet. The staid and ultra-prudish man she knew and disliked displayed those qualities at home as well as in public which made for a rather uncomfortable home life not only for his wife but also for his son and daughter. The brunt of his overbearing parental style fell primarily on his son; his sexist attitudes made his concern over his daughter much far less important to him than the need to tailor every aspects of the son he called JR for

210

junior. For all his concern over JR he never seemed even to like the boy when they appeared together in public. Father-and-son golf tournaments at the club were neglected while father-and-daughter events were a must for the Randolphs.

JR was a handsome boy of seventeen. His dark brown hair and piercing blue eyes were a hereditary trait from his father, but his slight and smooth build were the contribution of his mother's gene pool. Perhaps Jack was disappointed in JR's expertise in swimming rather than in a more manly sport like lacrosse or baseball to begin with, but a certain incident over a year ago had turned Jack's disappointment into bitter scorn. JR having just turned sixteen at the time was a star member of an independent swim team which represented the junior members of several Greenwich country clubs. Their team was a good one which dominated regional play against neighboring teams. After an impressive victory over the Westchester, New York, team JR and his team were treated to an evening of swimming and partying at the Kitcahawk Club in Rye, New York. A bet had been made by which the losing team's club was compelled to host such a party for the victors. JR proved to be the star of the party and returned home just after 2:00 a.m. JR worried that the late hour would trouble Jack, but his father had had no concern whatsoever; the boy was a healthy sixteen-year-old, and he had many wild oats to sow.

Several days after the party Jack was approached by one of the maids, named Ernesta. She and her common-law husband lived on the estate in a servant's cottage among the trees of the back grounds. Ernesta's Jose worked for Randolph as needed in the gardens and with general maintenance. His primary job, however, was that of night shift cleaning man at the Kitcahawk Club. In her faltering

English, Ernesta addressed Jack, "Senor Jack, I have a question to ask of you from my Jose." Randolph quickly corrected her with "I am Mr. Jack. We are in America and English is spoken here." She hesitatingly began again, resenting Jack's comment, "Meester Jack, Jose has a question that I can no answer. Will you explain to us, please?" Jack may have been somewhat of a tyrant to his servants, but he was paternal enough to help them with problems as needed. He nodded to the maid and gritted his teeth for what he knew would be a question expressed in Spanglish, broken English he so vehemently detested. Were it not for his impatience he might have lectured Ernesta on the injustice of American immigration laws which had allowed her and Jose to come to Greenwich.

The question was in reference to the swim team party held at the Kitcahawk Club and a mystery which Jose could not solve. It seems that Jose was working near the private party room as the team and their coach, Joe Moffet, entered the club. He watched with amusement as the boys and their coach frolicked in the water. He also saw them dry off about two hours later and change into dry clothing out in the open air of the pool area before entering the wing of the club which contained a sauna, locker rooms, and the wood-paneled "private" party room, a room from which other members could be excluded. At this point in the story Jack stifled a yawn and wished Ernesta would just go away, but he thought, *Why waste even more of my time without even answering her damned query?*

Ernesta droned on telling him that Jose had puttered around near the party room all night, knowing that he would have to clean up the mess left by the boys before leaving at four the next morning. Becoming totally bored by this point Jack interrupted, "Oh, for Christ's sake! Cut to the chase, woman!" But seeing the look of puzzlement on her face over the use of a purely English expression, he simply sighed and instructed her to "Just go on, already!" In her next sentence she explained that at no time did Jose see any girls enter the club or the party room. That caused Jack to raise an eyebrow as he now said, "Do go on, dear Ernesta," in a feigned show of friendly concern. When Ernesta added that during his cleanup Jose had found some rather unusual objects, Jack immediately thought to himself, *If that boy is doing drugs, I will throw him and his entire team into rehab before they can do another line.*

But Ernesta made no mention of any type of drug paraphernalia; instead she struggled with a word which finally came out as "drubbers" and added that the "drubbers" had been used. In a sputtering voice which Jack always fell into when angry he shouted, "Do you mean used rubbers, as in condoms, madam?" When Ernesta nodded her head yes, Jack fled the room as if it was on fire. As he locked the door of his den, Jack punched the door hard enough to crack its panel and draw blood from his knuckles. His son and the swim team, twenty nine year old coach included, had partied in a private room and emerged only to leave behind what Jose had described as some two dozen soiled condoms. Jack suddenly wished to himself that JR and the team had instead engaged in some form of drug use, something mild like marijuana. That would have been more acceptable than this.

Later in the day when JR and little Suzy arrived home they were met in the foyer by their father. After a greeting from Suzy, Jack gently kissed her on the cheek with his usual salutation of "Hello, little girl." As JR approached his father and said, "Hi, Dad!" he never expected the powerful slap across the left side of his face which he received. A slap so hard that JR toppled over onto the floor, knocking over a large brass umbrella stand in the process. Jack turned to Suzy and said calmly, "This has nothing to do with you, sweetheart, so just go to your room like a dear." Turning his attention back to JR he spat, "Get up, stop your tearful babbling, and get into my office right now, you little bastard." JR may have been terrified, but he knew disobedience at this moment would only make matters worse, not that things could get much worse. That slap had been the first blow he had ever gotten in his life from his father or any other family member. Trembling and holding back further tears he wondered what he had done as he scurried like a wounded dog into his father's den. The door closed, and the screaming began as he took a seat on one of the office's guest chairs.

After the screaming ended and the door reopened, Jack and JR never once explained any part of the situation to Suzette or Suzy. But they both imagined that Jack had finally realized something which they had suspected about JR for some time now. While nothing was said on the subject by father or son, some major changes soon followed. JR's canvas-topped Jeep was put up for sale. He quit the swim team and, when his Internet privileges were restored several days later, read on the team Web site that Coach Moffet had been replaced by the trustees of the swim team and reportedly had moved to an undisclosed location somewhere out west. San Francisco was one suggestion made on another chat forum, by an anonymous team member who seemed to be in the know. Jack brooded for almost a week before he returned to his usual beneficent tyranny over the Randolph clan. After that week from hell the entire family welcomed Jack's return to "normal" as if he had been Scrooge on Christmas morning.

While subtle hints of this episode would emerge much later in rumors and unsubstantiated gossip, it would be never be found in any confirmed reports. Lizzy had no idea of what had occurred between Jack and his son, but she did sense a new coolness between them. She had heard the rumors about JR's sexuality from her boys and knew that that could not have sat well with Jack. She also smelled sexual scandal in the air, but it did not come only from Suzette. Had she known of it this incident would have made Jack's personal life seem even more hypocritical and dishonest than even she might expect of him, and exposed a greater degree of cruelty than anyone would expect from one's father. When Lizzy would piece this story together in the not-too-distant future, her dislike for Jack Randolph could turn to abhorrence and disgust. For all the fleeting clues which lay barefaced on her laptop and in her notes she would have never dared guessed what was eating at Jack. Something beyond JR, something beyond Suzette's cheating, something which ate at his insides and which may have been a prime motive for his participation in the death of Bill Pierce. There was something that Jack had to hide, and judging by his reaction to JR's homosexuality, things seemed to point toward a sexual matter.

If Jack did have something to hide, did Bill suspect that Jack had been engaged in a sexual dalliance of his own? Had Suzette shared some indiscretion of Jack's with Bill unwittingly made him a target by making him a man who knew too much? These possibilities would be on the mind of Lizzy Dawson shortly, but at the moment she was following a trail which reasoned that perhaps Suzette had shared information with Bill about the Randolph Fund. After all, Bill had invested in the fund. Whatever she may have told him he might never disclose, but could

Suzette or Jack ever be sure? Whatever the information was it would surely spell ruin for the great financer Jack Randolph. Lizzy smelled sex on the trail, but financial intrigue seemed much more promising. She had not yet realized that there might be two parallel trails both leading directly to the possibility of cold-blooded murder.

Lizzy was aware that the Randolph estate housed a veritable menagerie of people who were all possible contributors to the situation which she referred to as the Case. There were live-in maids, a live-in butler, and an assortment of other household help who counted among their compensation packages residency somewhere on the estate. One of them was a pretty maid named Jackie Lewis and her son Evan. Lizzy knew Evan as the Randolphs' pool boy and all-around handyman. Evan Lewis was a handsome young man of twenty-four with a pair of stunning blue eyes set in a gentle face with a stunning light mocha complexion, a mixed inheritance from his Caribbean-American mother and Caucasian father. Twenty-five years ago Jackie had been a lovely young woman of sixteen. She had lost an ounce of beauty as she aged. As a girl, she was a devout Episcopalian and had attended Saint Alban's Church in Port Chester, New York, when her rector had become ill and the parish had hired a past middle-aged and semiretired priest from Boston to serve as interim rector. His name was Jeffrey Lewis, and he was a silver-tongued New England gentleman with an eye that favored beautiful young women.

During his seven-month stay in Port Chester it was rumored that this white-haired and huskily built cleric had managed to deflower several of Saint Alban's prettiest maidens. Lewis was an open-minded rogue, and the objects of his lusty desire crossed racial and ethnic lines quite freely. Jackie had been one of the confirmed cases

216

of his activities and the only flower to have conceived with the randy priest. A gentleman to the end, he paid for the birth and had sent support funds for Jackie and Evan right up until his death several years ago. He had showed no shame for his actions and actually legally married Jackie while telling her honestly that he had no intention of ever living with her. His parting gift was to bestow upon his legitimate offspring the name of his own father, Evan William Lewis, a Welsh moniker to carry on the family name and line.

Evan had been an active part of the Randolph household since his childhood, helping Jose and the other outdoor workers in keeping the estate well trimmed and beautiful. Jack insisted that the boy be paid a regular wage out of the household budget even before Evan was of legal age to work. As the years passed Jack had been kind to Evan but showed no favoritism to him or his mother. They were workers, and one must be pleasant and fair to those in one's employ. That was ever Jack's motto. While his treatment of subordinates on Wall Street could be compared unfavorably even to those of Donald Trump on his show *The Apprentice*, no one would question the way he treated his workers on what Lizzy now thought of as the Randolph plantation.

The huge house had two swimming pools, and Evan maintained both of them. As part of his duties, he would change into swimming attire to skim debris off the surface of the water and dive in to remove objects which had sunk to the bottom of the tile-lined pools. On a particularly hot Saturday last summer Evan had finished his cleaning routine and lingered in the outdoor pool enjoying the sun and cool water when he realized that the Randolphs might soon be arriving for an after-lunch swim. Storing his tools in a nearby shed, Evan strode into the cabana feeling rather dry from his chores in the hot sun, but he noticed that his baggy trunks were still quite moist and needed to be removed before he put on his khaki uniform again. He had just removed his trunks when he heard the cabana door open letting in the bright sunlight fully exposing his nakedness.

It was Jack Randolph entering the small room, swim trunks in hand. With a somewhat surprised look he closed the door behind him and sat on the small stool across from Evan. The thought of Mr. Randolph casually taking a seat while he stood totally nude before him made Evan uncomfortable. Turning his back to Jack, Evan assured him that he would be dressed and gone in just a moment. Jack laughed and said, "Come on, Evan. We are both men, and there is no reason to be shy. It is nothing I have not seen in locker rooms all across town." As Evan turned around he was relieved to see that Jack had evened the playing field and had removed his own white tennis shorts and polo shirt. What Evan saw impressed him to a surprising degree. Jack Randolph was in excellent physical shape and showed very little signs of being so near to fifty. What drew Evan to look at Jack's penis he could not say. Perhaps every man wonders about every other man's size, but for whatever reason, Evan was now looking directly at Jack's manhood, and he could tell that Jack had noticed.

Jack reassured the young man with the very logic that had crossed Evan's mind, "Every man wants to check out the size of the competition, you know. So how do I rate, my boy?" Evan who had never seen a naked man before in his life smiled and feigning experience said confidently, "Not too shabby, Mr. Jack. Not too shabby at all." Suddenly Evan felt his penis becoming rigid and growing in size, and he knew that at this juncture there was no way to hide the seven slender inches which were inflating below his navel. He hoped that Jack would play the gentleman and excuse either Evan or himself from the cramped cabana. Jack did no such thing, but suddenly he fell quite silent. Evan noticed that Jack's penis was now erect. Jack's silence was due to a mental and emotional short circuit which had stunned him speechless. Never in his life had any man's body been the least bit attractive to him. While being casual in locker rooms and gymnasiums he had actually felt a tinge of revulsion at the sight of the male reproductive organs, so why was he aroused and beginning to sweat right now?

Without a word and in a dreamlike state Jack reached for a bottle of suntan lotion and squeezed a generous dollop on his erection. Evan knew that if he was going to leave, he should do it now. Yet he stood utterly still as if he had suddenly been turned to stone. Jack took the two steps between them and reached out for Evan. Before he knew it Evan had been gently turned around and bent over the stool on his side of the room. Hands were now caressing his back, sides, and chest; and he let out a low sigh. As if the sigh had been a signal or an indication of consent, Jack moved his hands to the young man's firm and hairless buttocks. Working a bit of lotion into the space between his cheeks, Jack too let out a cross between a sigh and a moan. Within moments Jack had penetrated Evan and begun a slow and gentle motion. It struck Jack that he had never been as reverent as this in his approach to sex with Suzette, or any woman for that matter.

His mind was numb, and the movements he was making inside Evan brought a sexual rush to him that he had rarely felt in his life. As he climaxed a screaming thought raced into his head, *What the fuck am I doing!*

Have I totally lost my mind? The thought was interrupted by grunts and moans of ecstasy from both participants in this forbidden sexual encounter. What had just happened had been insane, but at the same time Jack knew that it was something wonderful and fulfilling for him. Still wordless the two parted, Evan hurriedly putting on his khaki shorts and bush jacket uniform before heading off to the house and Jack slipping on his trunks for his now-overdue swim. Jack broke the silence as he shouted after Evan, "Not a word! Not a goddamned word, I tell you!" Evan understood and nodded subserviently while asking himself, *Why in the hell would I ever mention this to anyone anyway?*

As Jack dove under the sparkling water of the deep end of the pool his mind raced, and the episode with JR flooded his mind. He pushed JR out of his mind, reciting a litany of denial to himself to justify his treatment of JR and the incident which he had just participated in.

"JR is a weak and feminine milksop. He needs to learn to be a man. I cannot tolerate a faggot in my family, and I am goddamned well not a faggot! I simply tried something new and different. Most men try it at least once in their lives. Why should I be any different?"

His denials sounded hollow even to his own conscious mind; he knew he had enjoyed the encounter, and were he honest with himself, he would admit that Evan was a far better sex partner than Suzette. He was someone who actually seemed to enjoy the sex, unlike Suzette for the past decade.

The sexual incident in the cabana was not the last such encounter between Jack and Evan. In fact, it had become almost a routine in the weeks following their first episode. Each time they met the lovemaking followed a set pattern. It was in total silence, Jack was the active partner, and though he made no effort to kiss Evan, Jack did fondle him with a tenderness that surprised even him. Oral sex had been included in their repertoire, but once again Jack assumed the masculine role. The domestic situation was never discussed, and nonverbal nods were used to communicate a desire by either partner to initiate an encounter. Only on one occasion did Jack utter words to Evan as they prepared to make love. Jack had had a bit too much to drink and turned to Evan and kissed him saying, "Your skin is as soft as velvet, the color of rich milk chocolate, and your lips are as sweet as Godiva's finest." Evan's only response had been "You're drunk and you certainly are no poet, Mr. Jack, so let's just do our thing." With a shrug Jack complied with no further conversation being necessary.

The affair was in full swing as the Randolphs' marriage began to totally unravel. It was by no means a cause of the tension, and Jack was confident no one had even the slightest idea of what was going on. He felt secure in his position on the divorce. Suzette had contributed nothing. She had played the tramp for most of the marriage. She would leave with an extremely modest settlement whether she liked it or not. She may have hired Abernathy as her attorney, but there were bigger and meaner sharks than her in the legal oceans, and he could afford the biggest and the meanest of them. When a man holds four kings and a deuce in poker, he might just forget that there are four aces floating around in the rest of the deck, and as unlikely as it might be, his opponent might be holding them. Jack Randolph made that very mistake when he decided to play hardball with Suzette. He knew he had photos of his dear wife entering motels in far-flung towns over in Massachusetts and upstate New York. He even had some shots of her engaged in sex in cars and outdoor locations. "What judge would have mercy on such a harlot?" He chuckled to himself in self-satisfaction as he entered his den with Suzette.

Jack fully expected a concession and a plea for mercy from Suzette that afternoon. What bothered him at that moment was the fact that she did not carry herself as one who had been defeated. Jack's overconfidence carried him so far as to have a chilled bottle of champagne ready to toast their agreement at the end of this meeting. He popped the cork quite prematurely, poured out two portions in the most delicate glasses at the bar, a choice he would come to regret, and offered Suzette a glass. She accepted the offer with a smile and after a quick sip commented, "Not the best of vintages is it, dear?" Jack did not show his annoyance at her criticism but simply smirked as he retorted, "Good enough for the likes of you, my dear. Enjoy it while you can still afford to." The sparring had begun, and Suzette generously offered to let him begin the discussion of an out-of-court settlement.

A tirade of resentment flowed from Jack's mouth for well over ten minutes, never once interrupted by the still-smiling Suzette. His final line included his contention that what little he was offering in the way of a settlement would be lost entirely were she so foolish as to drag this matter any further in the courts. Suzette seemed to beam as she asked, "Are you completely finished, darling?" A nod from Jack was accompanied by a lifting of his glass in mock salute to his soon-to-be ex-wife. At that signal Suzette took aim and launched her verbal salvo. It was a calm and quiet salvo, but she knew it was a deadly one. She began, "Tell me, dear, what is your desire as far as custody?" His response seemed utterly generous to him. "We will share custody. I am not a monster, you know." She smiled again, which was beginning to get deeply under his skin. "Oh, I am quite aware from the paperwork that you are willing to share JR and Suzy, but I am afraid I was not being clear enough. Who will have custody of Evan?" She nearly hissed at him. "What in the hell are you talking about, you lunatic? What has the house boy have to do with matters of family custody?" Jack shouted at her.

Her response would change Jack's life forever. In a low, calm, and steady voice Suzette said, "Allow me to give you just a small bit of advice for future reference, darling. Never fuck a man who is also fucking your wife." Jack's grip on the fragile glass became so intense that it shattered in his hand; champagne and blood splattered across the blotter pad on his desk and ran in tiny bubbly pink streams unto the hardwood floor beneath. "Have you lost your fucking mind, you bitch?" he raged at her. His expletives betrayed the panic he was feeling, as he fought with a superhuman effort to regain his composure, only to find that it was decidedly gone. With a bloodied and champagne-drenched hand he wiped his brow and shook his head as he quietly uttered those unthinkable words, "All right, you bitch. You win." The game had ended before it had begun, he had mated, and she had checkmated. All was lost. Well, in all honesty, roughly half was lost—half of his fortune and properties.

Half of his wealth meant less to him than allowing the world to find out that he had willingly and repeatedly engaged in homosexual sex. He still could not acknowledge it as romance or even an affair. It had been and still was simply sex in his mind. Suzette had delivered a death blow. He knew that nothing would be more humiliating for Jack than having to face JR were he ever to find out. With this concession at least he reasoned, he could be spared that. Surely Suzette had enough common decency to not

223

tell JR. Suzette straightened her outfit and prepared to leave the room as she told Jack, "I am taking Suzy and JR to Martha's Vineyard for a long weekend. The least you can do is come out and say goodbye to them." As Jack stumbled out the front door into the driveway he was surprised to see Suzette enter the passenger seat of a brightly colored Jeep much like JR's old one, except that this one was a better model. JR sat at the wheel, and Suzy sat in the rear with several pieces of luggage. The canvas roof had been removed, so everyone was quite visible. Suzette directed her words across JR to Jack, "This is JR's new Jeep. He would like to thank you for paying for it." With a grimace Jack wished them a safe trip. As the Jeep began to move slowly forward JR leaned toward his father and said softly, "Don't worry, your secret is safe with me, faggot." The laughter of all three occupants as they drove away would surely haunt Jack right up to his grave.

Jack had been defeated, and he knew it as he limped back to his office. One of the maids had already wiped up the blood and champagne from his desk and the floor. He noticed that the ruined blotter had been completely removed from the room. As he threw himself into the desk chair his eyes ran across the flat screen of his desktop computer. How could that be on? Only he and Suzette knew the password. Oh, why the hell had he not changed the fucking password? If he was recovering in the least bit from the trials of Suzette's assault, that recovery was about to turn into a major relapse. The screen contained a page of extremely sensitive information from the Randolph Fund dossier, and in the center of this information there stood a small bright box which read, "Download Completed." Jack eyed the middle side drawer of his desk; that was the drawer where he kept his revolver. Should he take it out, turn off the safety, and take it to the shower stall in the adjacent hall bathroom? If he was going to kill himself he would do so in an enclosed shower stall, assuring that the gore would be contained and not damage the resale value of the house. If anything, he was still a businessman, and a businessman he would remain to the bitter end.

It was because he was a businessman that Jack decided against killing himself. By a businessman's logic, he calculated in his mind how much he was worth, the chances of his fund collapsing and the profits which could be earned annually both as interest on his current fortune and as return from continued investment. Thoughts of his wife, children, and other family never entered into the equation. Giving a slow and low-keyed whistle, he decided that life was still worth living, even if moments ago half his worth rode off in a brightly colored Jeep headed for Cape Cod. He even silently hoped that by pure chance the Jeep might be involved in an accident and his losses would be recouped in an instant. He felt sure Suzette had not as yet changed their joint will. The fact that his two children might also be killed in an accident perturbed him for an instant. But he reasoned Suzette was sitting in the front passenger seat, and they did call that the death seat, didn't they?

Jack walked over to the bar and rummaged through the many bottles until he found what he needed, a bottle of fifty-year-old Scotch, and poured himself a good long drink. The first glass burned like hell as he consumed it in one gulp, but the next few were sipped and savored. One had been enough to restore his courage, and now he would not waste the rest by drinking in undue haste. He reckoned that he had avoided jail for over ten years now, and even though the heat was on, he was still the same clever and resourceful man that he had always been.

Before he took any financial steps he wanted to solve one personal problem. Reaching for the house phone he dialed Jackie Lewis's extension, and when she picked up the phone he greeted her casually and asked to speak to Evan. "Evan, I need your assistance with a little matter. I am in the office. Be here in five minutes," he instructed the young man whom he had made his aide and who was his secret lover.

Evan arrived promptly five minutes later dressed in chinos and an opened collared dress shirt, a considerable step-up from the uniform he always compared to a safari suit. "You need me, Mr. Jack?" he said even before he had fully crossed the threshold. "Please close the door and have a seat, dear Evan," instructed Jack in a warm and friendly tone. "My boy, in my own way I have loved you. I am not a sentimental man, and you might say I have also never been a warm man. Still, I have cared for you, and I still have a fondness for you at this moment, although I know that you have betrayed me. Mrs. Randolph and I are finished, and so are we. I never cared if you slept with women while being with me, but my wife is quite another story." Showing not the slightest bit of emotion Jack dropped a bomb on Evan. "I want you out of this house before midnight. I don't care where you go and how you get there, you just need to be gone." Evan interrupted to ask how he could move himself and his mother in such a short time, but Jack had already taken care of that. "Your mother is one of the best employees I have, and I do not want to lose her. I only want to lose you."

Before Evan could say another word, Jack walked over to a small Monet which hung on a side wall. He removed the painting to reveal a wall safe, and in a few turns it was open. He pulled out several bundles of bills which appeared to be hundreds and tossed a stack to

Evan. "That is a bundle of one-hundred-dollar bills. There are a hundred of them for a total of $10,000. That is your relocation money. Allow me to write you a check. I'd better make it several, for an amount of money which I believe will assure me that the story of our friendship will die right here and right now." Scribbling on a number of checks he handed them to Evan. There were eight checks, seven for $100,000 and one for $50,000. The size of the payment stunned Evan, but he still needed to know what would become of his mother. "What about my mother, will I be permitted to leave her part of this money?"

Jack's response was kind. "You mother will remain here as long as she chooses. As long as she does, she will want for nothing. I will provide for her, and I will see to it that she lives well and is sent home to Trinidad for a month every year at my expense. I will tell her nothing beyond my opinion that you had hooked up with a young woman and told me that you were eloping. One way or another I will find a way to convince her that you are safe. And now, my beautiful friend, I must say goodbye and ask you to leave." With that he crossed the room, approached Evan, and for only the second time kissed him deeply on the lips. His only parting words to this tender part of his life were "Now, go!" Evan did not respond but simply walked out of the office and out of the life of J. Richard Randolph and the life of his mother as well. He would miss his mother and was surprised to realize he would also in some small way miss Jack as well.

With Evan gone Jack flopped heavily into an overstuffed leather chair and quite unemotionally sighed. "What's done is done." He would miss the young man and he would miss the sex, but when a problem arises it needs to be disposed of, and he trusted that the money he had just spent for silence would dispose of this problem for good. *Now, to see exactly what that bitch has downloaded and how much work it will take to remedy that situation,* thought Jack. He knew that he was in trouble with the government, but he also knew that he had been wise enough not to engage in a full-blown Ponzi scheme as his friend Bernie had. His fund was dirty, but not Madoff dirty. With some well-thought-out scheming and financial maneuvers he could salvage most of the money and, hopefully, avoid any jail time. He knew he would lose his trading license, but there were always brokers to make his investments in the future. Life was beginning to look brighter than it had an hour ago. Although he had lost quite a bit of money and Evan, he had also lost Suzette and that he would never consider a bad thing.

Evan had been gone and the divorce agreement settled some eight months ago. Things had not turned out exactly as Jack had hoped. Suzette and the children continued to occupy half the estate. Jackie continued to be worried sick over Evan. Just a few weeks ago he had received official notice that the SEC was looking into his investment fund; just looking for now. If no audit was deemed necessary he might still survive the process unharmed financially. Jack was glad that he had begun to divest himself of a good number of investments over the past few years and was even happier that much of his liquid funds had been deposited in accounts in the Cayman Islands and Switzerland. There was no way that he would go down like Bernie Madoff had—the disgrace, the public humiliation, and the new experience of poverty would not be their shared fate. There were out-and-out scams, and then there were more subtle ways to bilk people out their money without leaving a clear trail back to you. Bernie was richer; but Jack was content knowing that he, J. Richard Randolph, was smarter. In the end, that would carry the day for him.

Whatever Suzette had copied from his files would be damaging, but it would not be deadly. From the beginning of their marriage Jack had allowed Suzette free access to his computer files. He had even tried to explain some of the basics of his investments to her but found that he did not have the patience to teach her basic business skills. In the beginning he had deeply loved her and had hoped that they would work together to amass a fortune greater than he had ever cared to work for alone. She seemed earnest in her desire to participate in their financial dealings, so Jack made an enormous blunder and had hired a tutor to teach her the ins and outs of investing. That had been after just two months of wedded bliss and would mark the beginning of Suzette's affairs. The tutor had been a graduate student in an MBA program at a school in New York. He was about twenty-three years old, with black hair and dark brown eyes, probably Hispanic in spite of the last name of Martin. From all outward signs Mr. Martin was a serious student and an equally serious tutor with no signs of being interested in any type of sexual activities with his students. Jack was, in fact, rather impressed by his professionalism and rather muted mode of dress. Upon hiring him, Jack noted his information for future reference. This young man struck as a potential employee after earning his MBA.

The affair going on right under his nose might never have been discovered by Jack were it not for the noticeable lack of improvement in Suzette's business acumen. A full six months into the tutelage she seemed as unable to grasp investments as she had when Jack first began to include her in his financial decisions. She seemed quite happy to be included in investment considerations but tended to select potential investments in the same manner as she chose horses to bet on during vacations at Sarasota, simply because she liked their names. Something was going on with her classes, of that Jack was sure, but the very last thing he ever expected was a romantic arrangement. Mr. Martin, probably Martinez, thought Jack, was a perfect gentleman and so intense in his financial discussions with Jack that it seemed unlikely that such a man would jeopardize his well-paid tutor's position, or his good name, just as he was about to enter the financial community.

Jack thought he had sized up Mr. Martin pretty well. The truth be told, he had, except he mentally refused to add his beautiful and seductive wife into the equation. Suzette had been known at Harvard Business as a woman who liked men and liked them a lot, but Jack assumed every lovely woman who doesn't put out is given a reputation by the suitors who left her presence with disappointment. The reality of the situation was that Mr. Martin was a serious businessman, but he was equally serious in his desire to satisfy his perpetual horniness. A man on the make and a woman hunting for her next sexual conquest are a volatile combination, one which Jack had never become accustomed to in his rather reserved and yet active sex life. The thought of a woman being aggressive and forward in sexual matters still seemed to stun the old prude right up to the present day.

The reality of the situation came home to Jack on a gloomy afternoon when a sudden and unexpected rain had cancelled his weekly golf outing with friends from Wall Street. In those days Jack had a silver Rolls-Royce Corniche convertible. It was elegant. It was fast. And it also ran quieter than even the average Rolls. Jack cared most about the comfort and elegance of his ride, but on that day its quietly humming motor would serve the unexpected purpose of covering his arrival at the estate. There in a corner of the driveway was Mr. Martin's already well-used Ford Mustang, telling Jack that a lesson was well in progress somewhere in the house. With a multiplicity of rooms to choose from he decided not to play hide-and-seek with the scholar and her mentor but rather let them be and head up to the bedroom to make a quick change out of his golfing attire. As he made his way along the hall he heard a sound, a muffled moan to be exact, coming out of the guest room which they called the French Room because of its white French provincial furnishings and baby blue walls. He approached the door, opened it, and entered the antechamber, a small sitting room which guests could use to entertain friends out of sight of the sleeping chamber.

The moan was now more pronounced and was clearly made by two voices, one male and the other female. The bedchamber door was open, and with a slight crane of the neck Jack could look in and see a large mirror on the left wall. In the mirror was the image of Suzette and Mr. Martin engaging in what appeared to be extremely intense sex. Neither figure had on a stitch of clothing; the bed sheets were under them falling in drapes from the bed onto the surrounding floor. Mr. Martin was on top of Suzette with her legs around his waist, tightly locked behind his back. Martin was pumping his entire torso onto Suzette, withdrawing his manhood slowly and deliberately from her and then crashing down and back into her with brute force. Each withdrawal was accompanied by echoed moans of man and woman, but

231

each penetration elicited a sharp and urgent cry from Suzette alone.

Jack's reaction to all this was a stunned state of disbelief. He thought to himself, *I should rush in, slap her face, and strangle this impertinent little schoolboy.* But something was stopping Jack from acting on his thoughts, something very staid and proper instilled in him by private school and something he might have called breeding. His only physical reaction was a stifled gag at the sight of Martin extracting himself from Suzette, only to ejaculate on her lovely bosoms. Never had he ever considered doing such a thing to Suzette, nor could he accept the fact that she was now smiling and appeared to be utterly enraptured in sophomoric delight. Feeling no rage, but only an empty deadness in his chest, Jack quietly stepped away from the door and crept quickly and stealthily to the antechamber door, closing it without making a sound.

Walking back to the driveway Jack strode back into the house, making as much racket as he could, but upon finding no reaction he placed a record of classical music on the stereo turntable and played it at a higher-than-usual volume. Assuming that the lovers would not want to come down the grand staircase together he withdrew into his office and waited to hear their footsteps. Suzette entered the office with a flourish and greeted her husband with feigned delight at his early return home. Jack greeted her with equally feigned enthusiasm but asked if she was feeling all right, asking, "Are you feeling under the weather, darling? You look so flushed. Do you have a fever of some sort?" Her assurances of her good health sounded hollow to Jack as he considered that the thrusts of another man were the cause for her rosy complexion at the moment. Jack expressed his relief at knowing she was feeling well and asked that she send in Mr. Martin, as he had a check for him.

Martin, being less shameless than Suzette, came into the office in a nervous and embarrassed state. Jack imagined that the redness in his cheeks might have been shame more so than the aftermath of lust. Jack sat the young man down and got to the point. "Mr. Martin, after months of your instruction I must rate your performance as piss poor. Suzette is as ignorant as ever of finances, and I have been, evidently, wasting my money on you." Walking over to the wall safe, as he would years later with Evan, he withdrew ten $100 bills and tossed them into the young man's lap, a lap he noted appeared to be still slightly swollen from the day's screwing. "There is $1,000, your weekly rate plus severance pay, as your services will no longer be required." Martin appeared stunned by the news and began to defend his tutoring skills when Jack spoke without looking up from the papers he was now examining, "Perhaps part of your problem was the venue you chose as a classroom. The French Guest Suite is not a place that I would think was conducive to business lessons. Good day, Mr. Martin."

The Martin episode was never discussed with Suzette, and she never inquired why Mr. Martin ceased to be her tutor. Some things were better left unsaid. The only allusion made to the matter was during a session of lovemaking several days later when Jack withdrew from her before his orgasm and knelt over her while tugging on his penis to produce a stream of semen across Suzette's face, delivered with the comment, "I know how much you seem to enjoy that, my love." Mr. Martin was only the first of what would be a long list of known and unknown lovers which Jack would endure over the coming years. One of whom would be a businessman, named William

Pierce, who owned a resort which the family had visited a number of times prior to the Randolphs' divorce and Pierce's tragic death in Port Chester.

Over the years Jack and Suzette would produce two children, JR and Suzy. Their sex life was more than adequate in Jack's mind. Suzette was quite a different story. Jack's count of his bride's affairs stood at fifteen long-term lovers and scores of one-night stands over the years, and he shuddered to think of how many others there might have been that he did not know of as fact. He had always suspected that even the seventeen-year-old delivery boy from the nearby gourmet market on North Street had shared in his wife's sexual favors, but he could never quite prove that one. After so many others what did it really matter? Knowing his wife's proclivities Jack reexamined the DNA tests which Suzette had done after each child was born to assure himself that they were indeed his children. Jack had decided, long ago, that if either of the children had not been his, he would raise them and care for them nonetheless, but the offending child would receive simply a servant's share of his fortune from his will upon his death.

There were two things which Jack Randolph could never be accused of: being a fool and being a romantic. Jack loved Suzette, but not so blindly as to accept her cheating ways for the sake of love. Suzette was beautiful and would likely remain so in old age which was a pleasant fact to consider; but her greatest asset was the fact that she managed his house well, she raised his children well, and outside her sexual wanderings, she always seemed to be the perfect complement to his stature and image. For all her lack of financial prowess she possessed a manner and charm which served him well and an intelligence which impressed his business associates and bowled over the voters during his forays into the political arena. The businessman in Jack kept a mental ledger of pluses and minuses on Suzette. The pluses had always outweighed the minuses, and as long as the ledger stayed that way he would endure the cheating.

Jack had known about Bill Pierce being Suzette's lover for some time now. The Randolphs had made yearly vacations to the Brandywine Ranch as a getaway where they could relax without the usual concerns of running into business associates or friends from Greenwich. It was a quiet little retreat, and they regarded it as their little secret. During trips to the Caribbean, Europe, or the Aegean they inevitably stumbled into situations with people they knew, which resulted in dinners, soirees, and even business discussions; so it was a priority to find a place where they could just vacation in peace. It was on their very first trip to the ranch that Bill caught Suzette's attention. Although he had no overt proof of a relationship between the two, Jack suspected that there had been at least one sexual encounter between them. Whenever Suzette "needed time alone" or began to mention a man casually in conversation it was a good bet that she was either sleeping with him or was planning to.

Bill was a bit different though. Jack came to like Bill and by their second trip had convinced him to invest in the Randolph Fund. At first it was a small investment of just over $100,000, which was the minimum entry-level investment which Jack would allow. Over time Pierce had place roughly $11,000,000 in the fund and was enjoying a healthy 15 percent return. Bill's money in the fund certainly helped Jack befriend a man he was sure was sleeping with his wife. The large returns from the fund allowed Bill to acquire a bit of fraternal affection for the man he hoped to replace as Suzette's husband one day. It

235

was an odd arrangement by most standards, but among people of high financial stature money always trumps romance. As much as money can develop friendship, it can also create catastrophic tensions, perhaps even deadly tensions, when the flow of money moves to the loss column.

The Randolph Fund had begun to spring leaks a number of years ago. Nothing drastic, but returns were falling, and there was even an occasional loss. Some of those losses seemed to have been at the expense of the Brandywine corporation. Bill had always been a risk taker, and with a lust for huge profits he had taken on some dubious investments with Jack. These investments had on a number of occasions cost him a good bit of money, enough money that he was feeling the pinch. Rather than stir up any undue interest from the Feds, Bill decided that he might just know a way to take Suzette and half of Jack's fortune from him. He was well aware that Suzette might not know much about investments, but she knew and helped charm investors. An estranged Suzette could easily strike a deal with Jack in which he would divorce her and give her half of his fortune in exchange for her silence about names and accounts.

Jack had suspected that Suzette had just such an idea in mind when she first asked for a divorce. His initial refusal had been met with veiled threats about the fund, but he also knew that a truly organized plan to blackmail him with the right detailed information seemed beyond Suzette. Knowing that his business relationship with Bill was very quickly cooling, while Suzette's sexual relationship with Pierce was heating up, made Jack fairly sure that Bill was the driving force behind those threats. Jack was just beginning to regain his confidence in his ability to squash Suzette's plan because of the murder of Bill Pierce, when she had hit him with the revelation that she knew about his affair with Evan. Jack thought to himself, *When am I going to catch a fucking break with this bitch!* as he began to reexamine the files which he was sure Suzette had copied and made off with. He knew that what she had copied was not as substantial as she thought, but at the same time he knew that a trained federal investigator might find connections and clues that could lead them to pay dirt, the kind of pay dirt that could ruin him, if not gain him a penitentiary visit.

Jack knew that the lion's share of his liquid assets was safely deposited in banks outside the reach of investigators. Business trips in private jets to the Cayman Islands had certainly paid off in the long run. The Caymans was the easy part. The accounts in Switzerland, Spain, and Argentina were much more difficult to pull off. When one has investors from around the world it is possible to transfer funds into American accounts and then to foreign accounts, but it is also a delicate process in which every detail must be done precisely and with as little identification as possible. Switzerland was the hardest place to bank these days, but it was also the safest. Although international rulings on Swiss bank account containing funds stashed from the Holocaust made the Swiss more open about secret accounts, that did not so readily apply to more recent deposits. Getting the money quietly into the Swiss accounts without arousing American suspicions was the difficult part, but once it was there it was safe. It had taken Jack a number of years to establish enough international connections to achieve that goal. He felt very confident knowing that at the very least the overseas accounts were there if he lost his American holdings.

Suzette had some knowledge about the overseas accounts, but no account numbers and no access. Jack doubted she had enough evidence to give the SEC to trip him up there, but she did know most of his overseas investors—where they lived and did business. Jack knew that people were beginning to suspect that he had something to do with Bill Pierce's death, but right at the moment he wished that it was Suzette's body which had been found in a car in Port Chester. At the present he considered that his "ace in the hole" was the fact that he had capitulated to Suzette and given her half his American funds. That should keep her happy and prevent any move to involve the Feds. Had Suzette any idea about the overseas money, she would keep her mouth shut in fear that she would end up like Ruth Madoff, stripped of the fortune she loved so dearly by the same officials who jailed her husband. Jack knew that in any game of extortion there were circles within circles. Some of those circles could be of use for his benefit and his protection.

Putting aside his review of his files, Jack poured himself a brandy and sat on the office sofa just to calm down and rest for a moment. The feel of the soft leather and the smell of the brandy brought back memories of times when he and Bill Pierce had sat discussing investments. Bill had begun to make trips to Greenwich just after the Randophs' second vacation at the Brandywine. The visits were to discuss money matters; but Jack was fully aware that such matters could be handled by conference calls, e-mails, and teleconferences. The business trips had been excuses to see Suzette, but back then a good investment was worth a cheating wife. Jack and Bill had dealings beyond just the Randolph Fund, some of them quite adventurous and daring. Jack smiled as he thought about the Bolivian gold mine in which he and Bill had

238

invested nearly two years ago. They had discussed the deal on that very sofa and agreed that they should visit the mine together before investing too heavily. The gold mine had sent a jet to pick them up at Kennedy; and together, dressed in khaki outfits, they had driven a jeep from the airport at the capital city of La Paz down to the mining operation in Tarija, near the southern border with Argentina.

It had been an adventure driving alone without government or company protection. It had been Bill's idea to put a Bolivian flag on the jeep in hopes that criminals would be afraid to attack government or army officials. The criminals did indeed leave them alone, but small rebel factions in the mountains had taken potshots at them on several occasions. Bill had a small scar on his leg from a flesh wound received during one such attack. The long arduous journey had paid off when the two discovered that the mine was a thriving and productive enterprise. After a two-day inspection they had decided to make a major dual investment. The grateful mining company then chartered a helicopter to return them safely to La Paz. Jack relished such memories and mumbled to himself, "If only he had not been screwing Suzette, he might be alive right now. But that is all water under the bridge."

It occurred to Jack that he was feeling some sentimentality about the past dealings with Bill, and it surprised him. He was not accustomed to being sentimental. God knew he could not recall being sentimental over Suzette or JR, maybe a bit over Suzy and a tad over Evan. So why would he feel that way about Bill? With a hard slap on the arm of the sofa Jack roared to the empty room.

"Goddamn it, he was actually my friend, a man whose company I actually enjoyed! No agenda and no ulterior

239

motives, I just liked him! Why did that son of a bitch have to be fucking Suzette!"

Jack could not recall having actually liked someone since childhood. He understood relationships as means to ends, not something one does for enjoyment, but he now realized that Bill had been a genuine friend. They had shared investments, yes, but they had shared much more. They had had good times together, and in Bolivia they had actually nearly died together. The thought of that seemed downright revolutionary to him at the moment. It also made him rue Bill's death in a personal way for the first time. The murder of Bill Pierce had been a thorn in his side, a huge inconvenience, and a danger to his good fortunes up until now. Suddenly he felt a real sense of loss, and that was something very new to him.

Rising from the sofa he grabbed the brandy decanter and took it to his desk. In a fit of remorse Jack downed several brandies in rapid succession. He was beginning to enter that state of mind between sobriety and inebriation, a place where one has fairly good control of facts and mental reasoning, but where emotions gain the upper hand and mix with logical thought. He slammed his fist onto the blotter of his desk and said out loud what he hardly ever dared to let himself think.

"Why did I have Bill killed? Why did I hire those thugs from Finelli and have Bill murdered? What the hell was I thinking? He could have been persuaded to keep his mouth shut, and I was never totally sure that Suzette had told him anything substantial anyway!"

Jack had never been a particularly religious man, and this was going to be about as close as he would ever get to confessing his crime, but for him this was a monumental step. For another type of man it might have led to repentance and redemption, but for Jack it was merely a mental exorcism to free his psyche and allow him to deal with what he had done. There was a good deal of regret in Jack. More over his mistake in having Bill killed than having actually taken a life. During a heated argument just after Bill's death Suzette had called Jack a "monster" over his indifference to the murder. Now, Jack realized that he might well be a monster, but what was done was done. The businessman clicked back on in his mind as he straightened his hair and jacket and went back to his files to continue his work.

Just when it appeared as if Jack Randolph had finally discovered his soul, he shook off his regret and remorse just as a dog shakes off cold rain water after a walk. He set his mind to covering his tracks on both the financial and criminal levels. If he had killed Bill Pierce, well, Stalin had killed Lenin and Hitler had killed Rohm when they got in the way; so it was just a trick of the trade for monsters. A man of substance needed to handle ugly details in whatever way he could. Bill had become an ugly detail, not so much because of his affair with Suzette but because he had endangered the Randolph empire! There was still a chance that Bill had not known anything about the fund, but that was a risk Jack could not tolerate, so Bill had had to die. Cold-blooded rationalism had replaced the sentimental stupor which the brandy had induced, and before long Jack was congratulating himself on having handled the matter as quickly and efficiently as he had.

Putting aside the files for a moment Jack ran down a mental checklist of who knew what about the fund and the Pierce murder. The fund might still have some loose ends to tie up, but the murder had been done by professionals, men who regarded murder as business and who knew how to keep their mouths shut. Jack had also taken care of the meddling comments of Ethan Rivers' nosy little Internet investigation. He marveled at how easily he had shut up the flamboyant realty man, but he had recently heard rumors about another nosy blogger who was dredging up dirt about the murder case. He had not paid much mind to the rumors he had heard, mostly overheard, at the club and on the golf course; but he did not care to have a loose end form a noose around his neck. He vaguely remembered the name of a blog, GreenwichSecrets.com, which he heard two club attendants talking about one afternoon. He typed the address into his computer and began to read Lizzy Dawson's information. He was not happy at what he was reading.

The name on the blog rang a bell, and he quickly found the same name on his Rolodex, Elizabeth Dawson Designs. Of course! It was that silly interior decorator that had done the house sometime back. *Aren't interior decorators supposed to be prissy middle-aged men who gush over material swatches and paint sample?* he thought to himself. *Why in the hell is this busybody so concerned about the Pierce case? Was she another of Bill's conquests?* The very idea that a woman was sticking her nose into affairs like these made him shake with rage. Couldn't this Dawson woman be content with buying furniture and arranging flowers? Why did she have to poke around in his business? He hoped that this blog might have a very limited audience made up of gossiping biddies who would spread their poison in a social circle that no one would take seriously. That had to be the case, but he decided to give it a read anyway just to make certain. He got comfortable and began to scroll down the pages.

If the thought of a blog researching the Pierce case had made Jack rage, what he was now reading nearly sent him into a seizure. His name and Suzette's were mentioned numerous times. Details he had paid to squash were there in plain sight on an Internet site open to the world. Jack's first thought was, *How did I not know about this all this time? Have I been blind to this viper's nest for months while thousands have had access to it all along?* Before he could bring himself to read any more of the stories which were posted, he began to search the names of people who had left comments after the articles. His heart sank as he saw names he recognized from town. Worst of all he realized that some of the names were those of judges, police officials, businesspeople, and even members of the press. Jack rubbed his neck to see if a noose was actually forming from this enormous loose end which he had just now become aware of. There was no physical noose, but he felt its grip nonetheless.

If William Pierce and Suzette Benoit Randolph had been ugly details, then this Dawson woman appeared to the ugliest of details and one which needed to be dealt with as soon as possible and as quietly as possible. Wars have been lost repeatedly when a leader allows himself to be engaged in combat on two fronts. Jack now found himself surrounded on three fronts. The Pierce murder investigation, Suzette and her knowledge of his financial dealings, and, now, Elizabeth Dawson and her meddling blog. Jack's face went black with rage as he lifted his laptop and threw it against the glass door of a bookcase across the room. He could always buy a new computer, and of course, the bookcase had been purchased through Elizabeth Dawson Designs.

Chapter Seven

The Evidence Considered

Have you ever put together a jigsaw puzzle? Depending on the number of pieces and the design of the illustration it can be anything from an easy experience to a daunting task. There are round-shaped puzzles which are entirely white with no corners or edges to give you a hint, nor are there any shapes in the picture to use to sort the pieces. No matter how difficult such a puzzle may be there comes a time eventually, when you know that you have mastered the thing and you can see the light at the end of the tunnel knowing that soon you will have the problem solved. Now imagine that same difficult puzzle's pieces mixed before you on a table, but you know that there are a dozen mixed pieces missing. You might just decide that the whole thing is not worth the effort. That is the way Lizzy was beginning to feel as she spread all the bits and pieces of information on the Case over the top of her shiny desktop.

There are dozens of legal pads and hundreds of notes piled one atop another, and sitting at the very apex of the pile like a cherry on the top of an ice cream sundae was the coroner's autopsy report. The multiple-page report, replete with measurements, details, and photos, shone in the glare of her desk lamp like a gem stone sitting on a heap of gravel. Lizzy knew that all the paperwork lying there was the foundation and walls of a case, but she also knew that the autopsy would be the keystone that held everything else together as a unified structure. The results of the autopsy would make or break all the clues and witness reports, all the rumors and facts that she had gathered over the past few months. If the autopsy proved, or at the very least strongly implied, that Bill Pierce had been murdered, then a case could be built to show who had been responsible. If that same autopsy report indicated that Bill had taken his own life, then everything else would amount to absolutely nothing.

From the early news stories Lizzy had a distinct sense that the confusion being reported was more than a matter of loose ends. Rather it was a deliberate effort to obscure an already-confusing mass of information and evidence. Someone was trying to make things appear disconnected and random, but she also knew that there were major pieces missing from the total picture. She had reached that point at which she needed to spread out all the pieces of the puzzle and decide if there was any use in taking a stab at organizing them; otherwise she would be better off just letting all her efforts go to pursue other interests. She had load of time, effort, and expense invested in this case. She also had a profound dedication to seeing justice triumph, but she was also tired of the endless runaround of pursuing leads only to have obstacles arise at every juncture. Furthermore, she was getting physically tired of the endless pursuit of information. Everyone has a breaking point, and in many ways she felt that she was quickly reaching hers. Rather than give up, Lizzy decided that it was time to call in the cavalry and ask for help.

Lizzy had pulled some strings with friends on the Westchester County Coroner's Office and managed to get a copy of the official autopsy report. What she read did not seem to add up, so she decided that it was time to call in a friend to help her with the details of the report. Bernice had suggested that she could rely on retired NYPD sergeant Abel Ramirez, formerly of a Washington Heights precinct and well-acquainted with murder investigations and autopsy reports. As Lizzy dialed the number of Abel Ramirez she felt a rush of confidence splash over her. The information which she had gathered contained vital material and details which she knew would add up to a case, but there had been scientific and police jargon which had stumped her to the point of desperate frustration, and now she stood at the threshold of a new and informed perspective. She would be dealing with a man who was well versed in the terminology of police work and in terms used in medical reports related to crime. If there were areas which he did not understand he also had the experience to track down the right person to assist them.

Abel had served a pretty roughneck area of the city. Even in the crime-dropping days of Mayor Rudy Giuliani the area of Manhattan known as Washington Heights was a dangerous high-crime area. One of Lizzy's clergy friends, Reverend Jeremy Collins, often told stories of his first day at a parish in what was commonly called "the Heights." He had arrived on a cold and windy day driving down from the George Washington Bridge to the church. Along Broadway he noticed police vans at every corner; their windows were ominously taped with exes of masking tape to prevent shattering. Apparently unbeknownst to Collins there were expectations of a riot in the Heights, and he had causally driven into the heart of the troubled area. Over the years the Heights had calmed down, but there was still an unhealthy amount of drug-related violent crime in the neighborhood. Sergeant Ramirez had been in the middle of it all for over twenty-five years, and he had seen some of the worst crimes committed in the history of New York City.

New York is a funny kinda place. A rich socialite on Park Avenue gets mugged and it's front-page news, but if an immigrant Dominican family gets slaughtered up on 175th and Broadway that gets mentioned on page 9 or 10 in the daily papers. The Heights was always a community of Hispanic immigrants from way back. Some of the first Puerto Ricans coming in the late 1940s and '50s settled in what had been a WASP and Jewish enclave north of Columbia University. Over the years the Dominicans followed and basically took over the entire northern 20 percent of Manhattan, of which the west side was the Heights. No one would say that any mayor or city council did not care about what went on in the Heights, but there always seemed to be some other priority which prevented them from taking serious action to improve the life up there. Abel never regretted spending his career in the Heights, but he always hoped that one day the area would rise above the poverty and violence it had become famous for over the years.

Life had been adventurous serving in such a combat zone of a precinct, but Abel was accustomed to having to do things the hard way. He had joined the army at age seventeen and spent his first year of enlistment serving in Korea as the war there was beginning to wind down. That year was a rough one, and a large number of his friends had been killed in the final battles of the conflict. In the next two years he had become one of the military police rising to the rank of staff sergeant and serving in Hawaii and other Pacific outposts. It was there that the police bug bit him even though it took him a decade of civilian life after the war to join the New York Police Department. Even in the NYPD life was not a piece of cake for him. New York City is known as a pretty open-minded and liberal city these days, but it has some dark spots in history that show that it was not always so accepting of all people. Although he was expertly qualified to become a police sergeant and had make excellent scores on the exam, a promotion was very slow in coming for Abel. On test after test he scored exceptionally well, but the newly minted sergeants always seemed to have last names like O'Malley, Fitzhugh, or Vitelli.

After being passed over for promotion three different times Abel read the handwriting on the wall and joined a group of nine other officers in a class action suit against the City of New York for racial and ethnic prejudice in their promotion practices. The group included seven African-American officers and three Hispanic officers, all of whom had excellent records as patrolmen and all had scored well on their sergeant's exam. The suit dragged on for three years before the superior court of New York State decided in favor of the complainants. The result was a promotion plus payment of back salary equal to what they should have earned as sergeants. There was an added bonus in that part of the settlement including the equivalent of two years' salary tax free in the way of damages done by the city's unfair practices. Abel was satisfied with the outcome, but he would have preferred a fair and equitable system which would have made the whole lawsuit unnecessary in the first place. For a rough-and-tumble street cop, Abel was and remained an idealist at heart.

When Lizzy caught up with Abel after several voice mail messages he seemed anxious to be become part of the action. Having been retired for almost three years Abel had not kept his fingers in police work like most retired cops. Abel had been married twice. His first wife left him for another cop; so the divorce was without financial consequences, no children needing child support, and no alimony. Luckily, it happened before his settlement with the city. His second marriage had ended with the death of Myrna, his beloved wife. She had been shopping near the home and collapsed inside a local grocery store. The hospital staff said it was a massive heart attack. So Abel had no family expenses to worry about, and he had wisely invested his settlement money, leaving him financially secure enough to live well from his pension and investments. Becoming a security guard or security consultant had no appeal. He had thought about moving to a community where he could serve on another police force, but he liked living in New York. He had no desire to start from the bottom rung of the ladder in another department. Still and all he missed being a cop, and this woman from Connecticut seemed to be offering him a chance to do some police work again.

When Lizzy spoke to Abel he immediately recognized her name from several conversations with Bernice. Lizzy did not take to him as quickly as she did to most people. There was a bossy and grating quality to his manner. It was obvious even from his tone of voice that he had spent years as a sergeant and was accustomed to giving orders and having them obeyed. They arranged to meet at a diner midway between Manhattan and Greenwich in New Rochelle, New York. Abel was interested in what Lizzy was offering, but not interested enough to drive all the way to Connecticut to size up the evidence that Lizzy had accumulated. Abel was born and raised in Spanish Harlem, of a Puerto Rican father and a Dominican mother. In all his years he had never lived more than six blocks from his family home. He liked his neighborhood and like many New Yorkers considered anything outside the five boroughs a considerable distance away. Connecticut was even another state.

The telephone conversations between Lizzy and Abel having gone extremely well, they were anxious to sit down together and begin work on organizing the evidence into a case. Abel knew practically nothing about the case which Lizzy had been so diligently been building, but from the brief phone conversations he knew that there were aspects of the situation which already smelled fishy to him.

He had a good sense about situations, almost an intuition about how things should play out, and he could usually identify any ways in which a situation deviated from seemed like its normal course. He had reviewed many coroners' reports and had, over the years, gained a passable knowledge of medical terminology which allowed him to understand clearly a doctor's message in what he called a "passive" autopsy report. Coroners are supposed to do the grunt work of cutting up and examining corpses; they are expected to present what Sergeant Joe Friday of *Dragnet* used to call "just the facts." But coroners are human beings, and they have opinions which they like to express and wish to have taken seriously. Unfortunately cops are a breed unto themselves, especially ones who hold high rank. They figure out for themselves what the results of an autopsy "should" show, and they don't like opinions which differ from their predetermined results. Being human, coroners want the truths they see accepted, so they flavor their reports in ways that other medical personnel can read, detecting discrepancies intentionally disregarded by the police.

Abel could sense from what Lizzy had already told him that this sort of interplay between police and coroner was going on in this situation. He had trouble falling asleep that night thinking about the details he would be reviewing the next morning when he drove out to New Rochelle to meet with Lizzy. He was also curious to see if he still had his keen ability to judge a person by their voice on the telephone. Had he lost his knack to imagine the height, weight, and general description by studying the voice and intonations? He imagined Lizzy as being in her late thirties, average height, and slim and brown hair. He would soon find out that he was right once again. He also was anxious to ask her what Caribbean island she was from since he noticed just a trace of accent in her voice. He was guessing Saint Vincent. Again, he would soon find out that his skills were very much intact. He did not need to use his skills or imagination to size up Bill Pierce, Jack Randolph, or Suzette Randolph since Lizzy had e-mailed him some basic information about them which included short biographies and photos. Abel noticed a resemblance between Jack and an old captain he served under in the Thirty-second Precinct, a captain he remembered with very hard feelings. *Rats always seem to look alike,* thought Abel as he closed the portfolio on Jack Randolph. That comment set the tone for how he would feel about Jack from then on.

After their initial meeting in the New Rochelle diner, Lizzy and Abel arranged for a sit-down at her home the next day. When Abel found the Dawson home he let out a long whistle of appreciation for the place. He liked things that showed class, and this house reeked of class. Lizzy did not hear him pull his car up to the house. The 1996

251

Toyota Camry looked like hell, but it was mechanically maintained as if it were a Rolls-Royce. Abel liked things that worked well but didn't give a damn about appearance, which might be the reason that his clothes were well tailored, clean, and well pressed but rarely contained two articles that matched in pattern or color. This day was like most others, and the sight of checkered patterned trousers with a striped shirt and wavy tie brought an amused smile to Lizzy's lips as she greeted the retired police sergeant at the door. Lizzy was no snob, but she could not help but recall the local joke about the severest crime in Greenwich, normally, being clashing clothing. Having had a second look at him she could sense that she might just grow to like this man. His light olive skin showed very few wrinkles, but that might have been in large part because of the pleasingly chubby shape of his face. He looked like someone's uncle and with his jovial smile appeared to be someone's beloved avuncular relative, despite his still somewhat gruff manner.

Abel wore a bright grin born of a sense of self-satisfaction knowing that Lizzy had been pretty much exactly how he had pictured her in his mind. Now the delight continued when he politely asked in what part of Saint Vincent she had been born, and she answered without thinking, "Kingstown, but grew up on Mustique." She giggled when she realized that there was no way he could have known that she was from Saint Vincent. Even Bernice did not know where she had been born. "Ah, you must have been a detective sergeant then?" she asked. "Nope. Just an old grunt sergeant, but you pick up talents of the detective kind over the years," he answered as they both let out a friendly laugh. It was already apparent that they were going to enjoy working together; but they did not yet realize how complementary their individual talents would be when used in concert to examine the clues, evidence, and details of the matter before them.

The small talk and coffee soon gave way to a sorting through of the evidence. The most important order of business was the reading of the autopsy report; but Abel, being a professional, decided that they must first sort the evidence into categories and address each one with the level of priorities to which it was assigned. The feat of sorting the piles of paper and notes took most of the morning and was followed by a very pleasant lunch at a local Chinese restaurant. Once again Abel felt like letting out a long low whistle when the two pulled up in front of the Hunan Garden in central Greenwich. Abel's idea of a Chinese eating establishment pretty much consisted of an open-view kitchen replete with open fires and safety valves above each stove on one side of the counter, a few grimy white tables, and several mismatched chairs around them on the other side. He was not expecting linen tablecloths and napkins set among huge fish tanks teeming with vividly colored tropical fish large enough to be stream trout. The meal was delicious, but after seeing the price and considering the size of the portions Abel decided that he would stick to the Great Wall take out over on Amsterdam Avenue.

Lunch was a time for the two of them to talk about themselves and give each other a perspective on where they were coming from in this whole matter. Abel had wondered why a bored rich lady would take up a criminal investigation as a hobby, but he came away from lunch with a respect for Lizzy's intelligence and her sense of justice. He could envision her as a district attorney or even a judge, but here she was in the role of private investigator crusading for justice against a well-heeled and powerful Brahmin who had every advantage in the game of murder.

253

Before lunch he had to wonder why anyone would care about a rich playboy being killed unless they themselves were somehow involved with him. After lunch he could see that Lizzy had an almost spiritual obligation to see that this man's death would not end up in a cold case file and as a long-forgotten story in the local newspaper archives.

Philosophers like to tell us that with the death of every single individual, humanity is made poorer. For Lizzy it seemed every unsolved murder cheated humanity out of its rightful claim on fairness and civility. Justice was bigger than any individual, but that was because it was composed of all individuals expecting to exist in order and peace. Bill Pierce's death had become a symbol of disorder and decay in society. If his death were swept under an expensive Persian carpet, why couldn't anyone else's also become so meaningless and invaluable? It was not a personal matter as much as it had become a principle to uphold. There was no hint of class warfare involved here. Lizzy may not have been as rich as Randolph, but she was certainly within his social strata, but still Lizzy resented the use of affluence to thwart justice and to exert power to distort reality to the point that even murder could be overlooked. Murder was not a faux pas, it was a crime and a most heinous one at that whether it was in her Greenwich backyard or on the streets of Abel's Washington Heights neighborhood.

The afternoon became a planning session instead of a return to sorting evidence. The ride from northern Manhattan to Greenwich took about forty minutes each way and, while that did not seem too bad a commute, would be nearly an hour and a half wasted each day. The solution was that Abel would could use one of the guest rooms several nights a week and, thereby, also share Lizzy's office. A private telephone line would be installed in the guest room and a second desk added to the office, set up face-to-face much like old-fashioned partners' desks from the nineteenth century. Unlike the nineteenth century, each desk would have its own laptop computer connected to a central printer. The prospect of living in someone else's home, even part-time, was not a welcome thought to Abel. He was a long-time-single man and had his set likes and dislikes, but the prospect of home cooking made the blow to his privacy much easier to take, as did the new plasma television installed in the guest room for his use. He also took a liking to Joe, as did Joe to him. There would be some masculine company to share sports and a cold beer with on occasion.

Decisions were being made quickly, and both Lizzy and Abel sat in near shock when they considered how far they had come in this situation after having met just a short time ago. Here they sat reading over the autopsy report, word by word, together at twin desks in their new joint office. Abel was enjoying the food, but he missed the strong black Dominican coffee back in the Heights. He had settled back into his shiny new leather chair and stopped short as Lizzy read aloud from the report. "Hang on a second," Abel requested as Lizzy neared the end of a paragraph related to the stab wounds found on Bill's body. Abel questioned the statement regarding the angle at which the wounds had entered the chest and throat. He seemed to have struck upon one of those areas where the coroner had presented an inconsistency without actually pointing it out. The autopsy report laid a very heavy emphasis on the power of the thrust with which the knife had entered the chest because the wounds had been deep and violent, and yet the report had described

255

the angle of the stabbing motion as having been shallow and awkward because of the angle at which the weapon had been held.

There was something very wrong here, but the coroner did not make the problem explicit. Either the depth and estimated thrust were incorrect or the angle and presumed manner in which the weapon was used were mistaken. Lizzy furrowed her brow as Abel identified the inconsistency.

"I am not getting your point here, Abel," she said as he stopped short and covered his mouth with his hand striking the pose of someone suddenly enrapt in thought. "Lizzy, don't you see that when you are striking out at a target you cannot gather momentum and power if you are striking from the side, you need to thrust down for full force or at the very least upward for a powerful blow," he explained. She still had a confused look on her face as he ended his sentence.

"Here, I'll show you," he said as he lifted his arm and made a violent downward motion to his chest. Then he made a similar motion from his side, and the movement seemed drastically less fluid and much slower.

"But, Abel, you started your side thrust at a much shorter distance than your first movement, so it had to be slower and less powerful. So what does that prove?" Lizzy asked.

"Ah, but you're forgetting that Bill was in a car at the time, on the driver's side. He was left-handed, so his arm would have been cramped between his body and the car door, not to mention the steering wheel. He would not have had the angle or the space to maneuver to derive the angle and thrust needed to inflict such wounds upon himself," was Abel's explanation.

256

Feeling quite pleased with himself he plopped himself back into the desk chair after having risen to add to the drama of his presentation. What Lizzy was about to say knocked him for a loop.

"I know and you know that Bill was left-handed, but didn't you notice that according to the police report the knife was found in Bill's right hand?"

Abel's jaw dropped as the realization hit him that nothing, absolutely nothing added up correctly in the autopsy report or the accompanying police report. It was as if the two were written about two very distinct and separate incidents. They could not have been describing the same act. No amount of incompetency could have allowed such glaring errors to remain in a finalized report, only a deliberate tampering with the facts could result in such a mishmash of facts. There was little doubt in Abel's mind now that what he was looking at was an autopsy of a murder victim which had been rewritten to make the murder appear to be a suicide. Lizzy had been right from the outset: somewhere someone was trying to cover up a cold-blooded murder.

The look of amazement on Abel's face surprised Lizzy. It had been a foregone conclusion to her for months now that Bill Pierce had been murdered. Even the police and press had quietly agreed that it was a murder. She stifled an urge to say, "Well, duh!" She considered that a professional would not see the humor in such playful derision. With that thought playing in her head she suddenly grasped the depth of what had just happened. An objective professional investigator with over twenty-five years of experience in such cases had just vindicated her conclusion. The conclusion had run so contrary to the police opinion for so long. Even now they only grudgingly conceded publicly that this "might" be a murder case. Here was an experienced cop who had been convinced of the facts that she had gathered and correctly deduced as a murder case.

Abel threw a bit of cold water on her joy when he told her that this was just the first baby step in what might be an endless and perhaps futile journey. Just because the two of them had convinced themselves of the crime made no headway in convincing anyone else. It certainly did nothing in the way of proving the hows, whys, and whos of the case. If Bill had definitely been murdered it still could have been a robbery gone bad, a gang initiation rite, or even the result of some bad trade prostitution. Celebrating at this point would be like toasting victory as the first shot of a war was being fired. There was a minor mountain of paper containing both pertinent and useless evidence spread across the office and in cabinets around the room. Now, the battle could be engaged. They could construct a case which could end up being an ironclad juggernaut of justice or a paper tiger of unfounded speculation which would blow to pieces the first time it was challenged. It was up to them and the quality of their work also which way the evidence would go in proving what they were already sure of as fact.

Lizzy had grown up in the West Indies but spent her teen years and adult life in the United States. As such, she was a product of American culture, and much of her outlook and expectations were also products of mass media. Thus, her understanding of life had a typically optimistic bias which assumes that good will always triumph over evil and every ending will be a happy one. Years of children's stories, cartoons, and movies had drilled into her, as they do with most Americans, that, to borrow from the old Superman television show, "truth, justice, and the American way" will always win out in the end. Even her deep abiding Christian faith told her that while evil might appear to win goodness would conquer eventually. The only event to rock that certainty of the triumph of truth was the presidential election of the year 2000. Somehow in that case the loser had defeated the winner, but surely that was an aberration from the norm, one which could happen only once in an eon!

It was with that mind-set that she had engaged this in matter which she now referred to as "the Case." If violence and evil had been done, and she was sure that it had been then justice would prevail even if she were the only means by which it could win. There was no doubt in her mind that somehow the facts would be uncovered and a case would be made to prove beyond a shadow of a doubt that Jack Randolph had killed Bill Pierce because of the romance which Bill had had with Suzette, causing the Randolph marriage to finally crumble apart. It had to have been a case of jealousy and loss which made a man's resentment and sense of loss turn into a murderous rage. The case fit so neatly into the scenario of almost any cinema thriller. Like those very same thrillers the killer would be brought in and the court system would do its duty to make that killer pay for his crime.

Abel on the other hand was the product of life on the mean streets of New York City. He had been an army man and a law enforcer in a family of criminals and draft evaders. His friends in the neighborhood despised the police and were often involved in drug trafficking or numbers running. The reality he witnessed every day of his life was that of pimps beating their whores and knifing Johns who failed to pay up. None of them seemed to be dealt any course of justice. Gangs roved his streets and robbed little old ladies and teenagers at will. When they were arrested they often jumped bail and disappeared for a few months before being back in the streets and up to their old tricks. He had no delusions about a scale of balance in the universe which assured that good was rewarded and evil punished. Life dealt you a hand and you made the best of it. Some people won and some lost while the majority just existed by breaking even.

His own life was a mixed bag of good and bad. He had always been treated as someone less than equal by being a Puerto Rican, even by the police department he served so well. And on the personal side of life the only thing he ever really valued in life was his Myrna, and she had died suddenly and way too young. Who was to say that things always work out for the best? He was a Catholic, but his faith never made much a difference to his everyday life. He guessed that in the end of things there would be a judgment and everything would be set right, but even that did not seem to him to be a sure thing. He saw too much bad happening and no one taking notice of it to believe that every crime would be punished. He had dedicated his life to making that happen in as many ways as he could as one single cop in a city of eight million. He did not believe in the court system, but he also did not believe in vigilante justice. He figured that even the most rotten systems could get it right once in a while, even if only by chance.

Between the two of them Lizzy and Abel struck a nice moderate balance. He did not rely on a mystic justice to cure all ills. She did not allow a sense of hopelessness to taint her efforts and drag her into a pit of desperation. They made a good team in the way that sweet and sour make for a tasty combination on the taste buds. The two extremes keep the course right down the middle.

He provided the scrutinizing eye, and she caught the subtleties of hue which might have gone unnoticed in the harsh glare of clinical examination. The fact that they liked each other helped the blending of their two outlooks and allowed for the growth of a certain kind of dependence upon each other which was new to each of them. Abel had had partners time and again in his career, and some had become close friends, but he and Lizzy began to build a dual intuition which allowed them to focus their expertise and feel comfortable in trusting the other to fill in the gaps which they might have missed.

Abel was like a bulldozer sorting through the piles of evidence. He strip-mined the piles and left the loose rubble for Lizzy to consider. He hit upon the big evidence and built the general framework of the case, but Lizzy provided the walls which made the framework into a cohesive structure. Together they were beginning to pull together a number of loose ends, and what was taking shape appeared to make a great deal of sense. It was all pointing very directly at two things: one was the undeniable fact that Bill Pierce was brutally murdered. The other was that a single person seemed to have all the reason and opportunity to commit the crime, and that was Jack Randolph. Again it was Abel who brought a heady Lizzy back to earth by reminding her that what seemed likely or even probable would not hold up in court where others would be allowed to contest and question its accuracy. They had built a house of straw within days of getting started together. After two weeks the house had now become one of wood, looking solid and indestructible. In court they would have to present a house of stone unshakable and unquestionable. In that endeavor their progress began to slow to a snail's pace.

Early one morning the phone beside Lizzy's bed rang, and the caller ID showed the name Ethan Rivers. Having not heard from Ethan for several weeks Lizzy hesitated in picking up the receiver. The last time they had spoken Ethan tried to convince Lizzy to give up her investigation warning her that she might be bringing herself and her family into a very dangerous situation. She did not feel like entertaining any more talk of threats and peril, so she almost ignored the call altogether but finally decided to answer it when she realized that for some reason the voice mail was not picking up the call. The voice on the other end was pleasant and lacked the usual eccentric intonations which were a trademark of Mr. Rivers. "Lizzy, it has been so long since we spoke that I have been wondering how you are," were Ethan's opening words. Lizzy greeted him in an equally friendly and cheerful way. Ethan apologized for the way in which their last conversation had gone. He had not meant to frighten her and had no intention of seeming the least bit threatening but had merely tried to express his sincere concern for her as a dear friend and fellow church member.

As the conversation continued Ethan asked if they could meet for brunch or lunch sometime very soon as he had an issue that he wanted to discuss with her face-to-face. He admitted that the issue was related to the Pierce case and that he wanted to give her some heartfelt opinions but had nothing to add to the substance of her investigation. Lizzy had a fondness for Ethan which overcame her weariness with his uninvited involvement in the Case and also allowed her to exercise her patience in accepting his invitation. She wanted this conversation out of the way as soon as possible, so she asked if they could meet for lunch that afternoon somewhere nearby in downtown Greenwich. He readily agreed, and they set a time for lunch at the quaint little diner at Salem Street off the Post Road. It was a quiet place and one in which the clientele tended to be the working-class residents of its Cos Cob neighborhood, people who would have long forgotten the small new item about the Pierce death months ago.

When Lizzy pulled into the tiny parking lot of the diner she noticed that Ethan's Land Rover was parked on the side street adjacent to the diner. Ethan was not known for his punctuality, so Lizzy surmised that whatever he had to say must have been very important to him. Ethan was seated in a corner booth by the window and was cheerfully dressed in clothing expressing none of his usual Edwardian tastes. He smiled pleasantly as he arose to greet her arrival; a handshake and a peck on the cheek seemed quite friendly and in earnest. A waiter took their drink order for a coffee and a Diet Coke as they settled down to some initial small talk. Ethan spoke about some of his recent business ventures and even mentioned that he had two potential clients who might be interested in Lizzy's interior design work. Between small talk they ordered lunch, Ethan asking for a gyro platter and Lizzy a cheeseburger on pita bread.

Something was very different about Ethan, and it had become more apparent as he ordered his meal. Ethan was a very odd duck in that he had always preferred the rather bland flavor of English food and in a situation such as this would fall back on a meat-and-potato diet of American cuisine. Lizzy had never imagined Ethan ordering such an ethnic meal as Greek gyros. Something had prompted a change in Ethan right down to his now quite normal attire.

Before even taking a bite of her burger Lizzy moved to get down to business by saying, "So, Ethan, what seems to be on your mind about this Pierce affair?"

Ethan looked a bit distressed at her directness but cleared his throat and said, "Lizzy, I honestly think that you are barking up the wrong tree and that what you are doing is causing a good bit of grief and pain to a very nice person. That just is not like you."

Now it was Lizzy's turn to display a look of distress and surprise on her face. Her mind raced as she questioned to whom Ethan could be referring in this matter as a "nice person."

Sensing Lizzy's question Ethan continued, "I am talking about Jack Randolph. I have had the chance to get to know him and have found that he is really a good and charming fellow, someone who could never do the ghastly things which you are accusing of him on your blog. As his friend and yours I really wish you would just stop!"

Lizzy smiled as she asked Ethan if he was now speaking of the same man about whom he had warned her just weeks ago, a man he had claimed made a veiled threat against his business and perhaps his life when he had discussed the same matter on his own blog. Ethan's reaction was sad and surprising as he sighed and expressed his sincere disappointment at her lack of being reasonable. Calmly Lizzy smiled and asked Ethan to answer her question unemotionally: was this the same man he had spoken of so badly just a short time ago? She was not asking for an explanation of his dramatic change of heart on the subject, she was simply asking him if he was indeed speaking of the same person. Her question was rhetorical and made simply for dramatic value, but she presented it as if it were a genuine request for a point of clarification on a delicate subject.

Ethan once again sighed and slumped in his seat in a sign of resignation and defeat. "You know who I am talking about, Lizzy, so why press the point?" was his only reply.

Lizzy looked Ethan directly in the face and quietly said, "Because I need to know if you are talking about someone else or whether you have lost your fucking mind. You seem to be defending someone who killed a man, threatened to do the same to you and maybe me." Ethan explained that he and Jack had become friends, and there were good and decent qualities which could be found in Jack if only a person tried to find them. He again pled his case for her to end her investigation and blog posting if for nothing else than the sake of their friendship. After pointing out that she thought that he was being played for a fool, Lizzy told Ethan that she would in no way end or even let up her investigation or her blog postings. She added that if her actions endangered their friendship then she must assume that it had never been an abiding relationship in the first place.

As she left the diner her meal hardly touched she shook her head and wiped a small tear from her eye and muttered the words "damned fool" to herself. She could understand Ethan wanting to back off the case because he felt threatened, but to have succumbed to the wily charms of Jack Randolph at this point in time seemed utterly ridiculous. Ethan knew how Jack operated. He knew that there was no moral or value that Jack would not hesitate to corrupt for the sake of profit. He also knew that Jack believed firmly in the principle that one could acquire as much or as little justice as he desired according to how much he was willing to spend on it. Now after the passing of a mere few months he was so enamored of this wretched man that he was trying to protect him from public scrutiny. Lizzy had always been fond of Ethan and even felt an amused tolerance for his many quaint eccentricities, though they could at time be trying. So it was hard for her to believe that Ethan not only was embracing Jack's innocence but also seemed to be adopting his casual but staid style. What in the hell had taken place to make such a sea change in Ethan?

What Lizzy was unaware of was the extent to which Jack had brought Ethan into the Randolph Fund. Over the years the two had done business, but after finding that Ethan could be cooperative when properly handled Jack decided that less stick and more carrot might turn him into a useful ally. With Ethan's blog out of the way there seemed to be only one thorn in Jack's side, and that was the continued digging and prying of Lizzy Dawson. Having seen that intimidation was useless against Lizzy, though he would never realize how much his threats had actually unnerved her, he devised a plan to use Ethan Rivers's friendship with Lizzy as a subtle way to encourage her to turn her invasive eyes elsewhere. What he had not counted on was the fact that Lizzy had burrowed much deeper than he ever imagined and that she had brought in assistance from other quarters which at this point would not agree to drop the matter. Jack had ensured that Ethan would remain an ally by investing him deeply into the hedge fund. Blood might be thicker than water, but money was thickest of all. By opening golden investment opportunities to Ethan he had managed to make Ethan dependent on the success or failure of the fund. The arrest and conviction of the fund's head would be disastrous for the fund and for Ethan's heavy investments.

Ethan may or may not have come to believe in Jack's innocence, but at his present rate of investment he was forced to make his appearance seem to be 100 percent and sincerely behind Jack's side of the case. Jack was like a many tentacled octopus, and he had several tentacles tightly wound around the life of Ethan Rivers. But for all his work on Ethan it bore no gain in his efforts to silence Lizzy, and that situation was beginning to frustrate him deeply. He had had some of the Dawson money in his fund, but because they were diversified there was never enough to use as leverage against them. He knew their friends, but none of them were very close to him, and he had no control over their business endeavors. Every way in which he turned in the hope of somehow manipulating Lizzy Dawson, he found nothing. She was like a rock which stood firmly in his path, and no matter how he tried to dislodge her, his efforts were useless.

Lizzy drove home rehashing her encounter with Ethan in her mind. None of it made sense. She made a quick call to Father Redanz at the church office and asked him if he had noticed anything peculiar about Ethan Rivers lately. She was shocked to learn that he had been absent from church services for several weeks now, and Father Redanz's efforts to contact him were to no avail. Although Lizzy was a regular attendee at Church of the Atonement she sat near the front of the church; and Ethan, who was chronically late, always sat near the door. He was also quick to beat a hasty retreated after the conclusion of the service, so she was not accustomed to seeing him on Sundays. To learn that he had not been attending at all surprised her. Perhaps the changes he was undergoing were more profound than she had supposed, but there was also the change that in his new persona Sunday morning tee times were taking precedence over worship.

When Abel returned to the house after spending a few days in his New York apartment Lizzy filled him in on the Ethan Rivers situation. She did not expect him to beam broadly as she spoke but was relieved to hear his take on the situation. It was obvious to him that Lizzy's work was hitting very close to home with Jack Randolph, and Jack was making his best effort to derail her in any way he could think of and implement. These were all excellent signs, and they indicated that the two of them were barking up the right tree. He reminded her of all those old Columbo movies in which the annoying invasions of Columbo's investigative interruptions unnerved the criminals and forced them to take actions without fully considering their consequences. That was exactly what they were doing to Jack Randolph. He was moving on reactions instead of logic and was beginning to foul up his own game plan. In effect he was beginning to do some of their work for them by uncovering his own motives and showing his hand on how he did business in these personal matters. It was a definite sign that they had him on the run, and if they increased the heat on him he might make some errors in their favor.

Getting back to the evidence Abel noted that there was more than one police report about the same incident. Usually an addendum would be placed on the tail of a report to correct some error or add further information. It was very unorthodox for multiple reports to be issued, and he wondered if the file at the station house would contain these several copies or if the latest of the reports would have supplanted the earlier editions. A quick and quiet visit to both the Port Chester and Greenwich courthouses would solve that mystery. Lizzy gave him the names of her contacts in both courthouses, and he took off for some snooping as she sat back on the office sofa to reread the multiple reports and define what changes had been made in the evolution of the forms. Her highlighter was in her hand as she spread herself comfortably across the cushions. There were many pages to consider, and she might as well make herself comfortable. The work promised to be boring, and she hoped that her comfort would not prompt her to take a little nap instead of doing her work.

Several hours later she had finished the correlation of the materials just as Abel came into the room. He had his now familiar grin on his face and plopped into a chair beside the sofa as he announced that all files had been sanitized and contained only the final copy of the reports. Someone at some point had correlated those forms and produced a final product which had eliminated all discrepancies and disagreements. He had even found an edited copy of the autopsy report in Port Chester which had eliminated the dichotomies which the coroner had placed in the original. Angles had been adjusted and depths of wounds changed, all being made to be consistent with a series of self-inflicted wounds, but still stating that the work had been done by a right-hand-held weapon. Someone had doctored the report but neglected to change that vital detail, knowing that such a change would negate all the other information in the report, thus hoping that the one glaring error would simply and conveniently be overlooked.

When Lizzy handed Abel her correlated copy of the several reports distilled into one he knew that it would read very much like the finalized copies in the courthouse records, except that Lizzy would have been consistent and thereby revealed the fatal flaw in all the condensation. Her distilled version would reveal that it was all impossible! Bill could not have inflicted such wounds upon himself with his weaker and less dexterous right hand with the force needed to make the wounds as deep and powerful as they were. One detail which they had overlooked in their initial review of materials was a reference to bruise marks on Bill's left wrist, small bruises consistent with those which would have resulted from someone holding his wrist while he struggled to break free. This reference had been found in the earliest report and was absent from subsequent reports. For the first time it seemed that there was not only evidence that Bill Pierce had been attacked, but it now appeared that there might have been more than one person involved in such an attack. One person held him while the other stabbed him repeatedly. The question now presented itself: did Jack Randolph murder Bill in a fit of rage, or did he plan and execute the murder with the assistance of someone else?

While such a revelation delighted Abel and the prospect of a multiple suspect case made him excited, it sent a cold shiver down Lizzy's spine. The idea of one person committing a murder was bad enough, but the idea of a well-devised and executed team murder horrified her. The concept of a man killing someone out of jealousy seemed logical—there was an emotional reason for the action. That did not excuse the crime, but it made it seem more human. A planned murder was so inhuman and calculated that it made the crime seem so much worse. It also made her endeavor seem much more dangerous since there were more people responsible and more minds plotting on how to protect themselves against her investigation. This revelation made her head whirl, and for a moment she felt as though she was about to swoon. Abel sensed that something was wrong with Lizzy, but he had no notion of the thoughts running through her head and the conclusions which those thoughts were leading her to, frightening conclusions.

A woman investigating a crime within a small sphere of people seemed almost like an extended and more serious bout of gossip, but now the full impact of the situation was hitting Lizzy. She asked Abel to sit back and hear her out. What she had to say did not so much surprise Abel as it made the distinctions between them more crystal clear in his mind. Things he took for granted were earth shaking to her, and everyday matters to him might be unique and awe inspiring to her. For the first time the murder of Bill Pierce sank into Lizzy's brain in its fullest sense of violence and brutality, things she was not accustomed to, but which Abel had seen almost every day for twenty-five years. He had seen this side of life in vivid color, spread across hospital operating tables and on Manhattan sidewalks. Now for the first time Lizzy's mind's eye saw them realistically and not as gory pictures or descriptions in a report or on a computer screen. This was for real, and Abel was going to have to help Lizzy get a grip on it. She was a strong and intelligent woman, and she would cope, but at least for the moment it was comforting to have an old veteran beside her to show her the ropes.

Even after all the time that he had spent reading and sorting material Abel was still not seeing the big picture. Lots of the printed material was enriched and fed by Lizzy's personal knowledge of this town, its history, and its people. She did not have the police know-how to make some of the connections that were there before her. Abel did not know the subtle interrelationships of situations which would have given him leads to follow. Together they were piecing it together, and now they were working on who might have been an accomplice to Jack Randolph in committing this crime. Abel could envision the "hired hand" aspect of a wealthy man looking for someone to do his dirty work. Lizzy began to consider the pool from which a man like Jack could seek such assistance. The name Finelli sprang into Lizzy's mind, and it struck an immediate cord with Abel as he recalled the Finelli family history back in Brooklyn prior to their move to Connecticut some twenty years ago. The name, the reputation, and the location seemed to fit. Now they needed to provide the provable links.

Besides the revelation that there might have been more than one killer there was now definite proof that evidence had been tampered with and altered. Lizzy made two calls the next morning, one to the justice department of the state of New York and one to the justice department of the state of Connecticut. Both departments seemed very interested in the evidence which Lizzy and Abel had uncovered. Each made appointments to meet with the investigative duo and accept copies of evidence of the improper handing of the Pierce case. This would become a civil matter for the moment, the investigation of the mishandling of a case, not an investigation of the murder case itself, but this was a most decided step forward. With the state breathing down the necks of each police department there would be renewed efforts in the case and perhaps even entirely new investigations.

While reviewing several witness interview reports, Abel noted the contention, ignored by the official reports, of Mrs. Rizzo of Port Chester, who claimed that the vehicle containing the body of William Pierce had been relocated from across the stream from her home. Across that twenty-foot-wide stream was another house-lined street, but it was in a different state. The stream was the border between New York and Connecticut. If a crime were committed involving two states it would be a matter for the Federal Bureau of Investigation. Able decided that it was time to call in the big boys, so he placed a discreet call to a friend of his at the Manhattan office of the FBI. Before long two special agents were quietly reinterviewing Mrs. Rizzo and other witnesses involved in the Pierce case. It seemed the FBI was, for the time being, looking into the criminal case and leaving the civil investigation to run its own course. There would be plenty of time for the tying up of loose ends when headway was made on each aspect of the situation.

Word was filtering back to Jack Randolph concerning the investigation being conducted by the states of New York and Connecticut, but those did not concern him all that much. Scandals in police departments were commonplace enough and usually resulted in the forced retirement of high-ranking members of the department, rarely in the arrest and conviction of lower-level officers. Either way the people he had paid off were paid well, and if they were forced into retirement he would adequately compensate them for the disgrace which they would endure. A dirty cop retiring in the same community in which he had served was a painful experience for the retiree, but a former small-town chief of police from New York living on a key in Florida was quite anonymous. If his residence was comfortable enough he might not even remember his disgrace for very long. It is easy to forget past problems when you are fishing for marlin in the Gulf of Mexico on your own forty-foot powerboat. If people needed to fall on their swords to protect Jack Randolph, then Jack Randolph would see to it that their "afterlife" was a posh and luxurious one.

What was sticking in Jack's craw were rumors that the FBI was nosing around in the now cold case of the

Bill Pierce murder. It was one thing to keep small-town police quiet and quite another thing to influence the FBI. It could be done but was extremely risky. Jack had contacts in Washington, and they were influential in the justice department, but they also had their limits as to how far they could cover anything up. He had donated millions to the Bushes and their cadre, but this was a whole new ball game. While he did not have much respect for the prowess of the new administration he knew that there were plenty of good people on the grassroots level who could find things and kick them up to higher levels. He would be sticking his neck out if he drew too much attention to himself right in the middle of all this heat. Besides, he knew that Washington was a small-enough place that word spilled from one agency to another quite readily. Even though his freedom might be on the line with the Pierce case, Jack was still most agitated by the prospect of the Securities and Exchange Commission nosing around too heavily in his funds. Another Jack, last name Benny, used to hesitate when made an offer of "your money or your life." But this Jack, last name Randolph, would have quickly taken chances with his life in order to protect his precious money. Some people believe in God. Jack believed in money, his money.

Lizzy was only taking all this in a bit at a time. Suddenly her small-time Internet investigation was becoming quite literally a federal case. Abel assured her that none of this meant that they could cease their own work. Too often he had seen the big guns sweep into a situation take a look around and just as quickly sweep out in retreat. Even worse there were more than a few times that he could remember where the Feds came charging in and fouled up major investigations in which the NYPD had invested years of work. The entire operation would implode under the weight of the federal investigation, the end result of which was that no one was convicted of anything, and after the fact, key witnesses in the failed cases either ran or disappeared. His contact at the Manhattan office of the FBI began to filter him information that the bureau was having second thoughts about the case. They were coming up with sketchy and circumstantial evidence, and there was pressure from Washington for them to expend more manpower on Homeland Security issues rather than interstate murder cases. He was trying to ease Lizzy into the idea that the entire federal side of the investigation might well leave them high and dry in the end. If the Feds were satisfied that there were insufficient grounds for a case they would hightail it out of town without a word overnight.

Things were looking up, but Abel was a firm believer in looking down and guarding each step that he took in an investigation. The small stuff on the ground could trip you up while the big stuff could evaporate in an instant. Lizzy took Abel's advice to heart and tried very hard to conduct herself in the same way that she had for all these months now, not a junior G-man but as an intelligent person unraveling a story which had piqued her curiosity and led her on this fascinating journey. She continued to make her calls to friends and people around town who might know somebody who knew somebody with a connection to the case. Her work was paying off, and little by little people were not only giving her details but also adding their conclusions to that part of events which they had experienced. Lizzy felt sure that within a few weeks they would have enough evidence to ask for the seating of a grand jury and have all their evidence considered with the result that Jack Randolph would be indicted for murder and be tried for a crime she was sure he had committed. In all this maelstrom of investigation and study she never ceased to take a moment each day to sit with her laptop and bring up her favorite picture of Bill Pierce. She looked at that picture in silence and promised herself that somehow she would make sure that his murder would be seen by the entire world for what it was, a senseless crime and not a personal act of despair. With the help of lots of other people it seemed as if that promise was beginning to reach the point of fruition.

Abel on the other hand was enjoying being back plying his trade. He too made sure to stop for a moment every day and look at a picture on his laptop. He looked at a picture of Jack Randolph and studied every line on his face and every reflection on his eyes and teeth. This was the face of a shark, and he could feel it deep down in his mind and heart. Abel did not believe in anyone being born evil, but he knew that power and money could breed a black-hearted bastard who knew no morals. He felt sure that somewhere along the line Jack had become such a fiend. It was no different from a drug lord who ruled over his own little kingdom of junkies, pushers, and crack whores. The limits and amounts were different, but the bottom line was power and money. Whoever could not be bought would be destroyed, and Abel felt certain that Bill Pierce had been someone Jack needed to buy. When he could not find Bill's price, he knew that he had to destroy him, and he did.

It was studying the photo of Jack that gave Abel a hunch, something which had no basis in fact whatsoever but seemed utterly logical. Abel decided that Jack was responsible for the death of Bill Pierce but that he himself did not commit the act of violence. Abel remembered reading criminal psychology as a young cop, and one story stuck in his mind: during all of history of the Third Reich, Adolf Hitler had never personally killed anyone. He had ordered millions of deaths, but he had never taken a gun or knife in hand and committed murder. It was said that when Hitler actually witnessed the shooting of his former friend Ernst Rohm he became violently ill, and it took him several days to recuperate. So how could such a disdainful and haughty man like Jack Randolph bring himself to commit murder by brutally stabbing someone to death? Had the mode of death been a single gunshot to the head it would have been more likely for a man like Randolph to execute, but even then Abel was not sure that such a person could bring himself to do it. Giving the order for a hit and paying for it seemed right up the alley of such a rich and powerful man like Randolph. A picture is worth a thousand words, and it seemed to Abel as if Jack's photo was singing to him every time he looked at it.

Cops will tell you that a good investigation is made up of three distinct parts. One is the hard work of gathering the evidence and talking to the witnesses. The next is trying to understand the circumstances of the crime and get into the mind of the criminal, and the third is a mixture of pure luck and intuition which the cops simply call a hunch. Abel had a hunch about Jack, and from everything that he was reading and hearing about him he was building a case for the validity of his hunch. Jack had a reputation and an observable demeanor that bespoke of a sense of self-importance without limit. Someone like that believes that he is the catalyst for actions and not the man on the ground who actually makes the things happen. From all that he heard Abel had pieced together a picture of the man, but there was no formal criminal profiling expertise in his repertoire. Abel needed to get an up-close view and see for himself what made this man tick. He drove over to the Bentley Cove Club and flashed his badge to get the attention of the general manager. They met in the manager's office, and Abel was blunt, but also bluffing when he convinced the manager to allow him to spend a week at the club as a bartender, a bartender who would give special attention and service to one regular member in particular. The bluff was a promise that the club would come under intense Health Department scrutiny if his request was turned down. With the deal done Abel headed to a local bookstore for a volume on mixing drinks, something he had done for years but was feeling a little rusty at just now.

The week that Abel spent at the Bentley Cove was not wasted. He managed to observe Jack quite often. Since the separation, Jack took many of his meals at the club and socialized by playing bridge and other games in the clubhouse as well as various sports such as sailing outside the environs of the nineteenth-century mansion which served as the clubhouse. Since Jack was a solid drinker, Abel made himself quite useful and avoided the interfering waiters by offering Jack advice on different brands and flavors of alcohol. Abel was no expert at liquors, but he knew enough about human nature and the mentality of this suspect to play a good game with him. Abel simply read up on all the most expensive brands and types of alcohol and recommended them to Jack, making sure to mention how exclusive and how much each cost. Soon Abel was regularly called to Jack's table to advise him on a drink choice. Abel was never allowed to sit down at the table, and the conversation was kept strictly on the subject of drinks, but the situation afforded Abel the opportunity to be privy to many of Jack's conversations with fellow club members.

Just prior to leaving the employ of the club Abel made a gambit which he would not have dared to before now. He brought up the subject of investments and asked Jack for advice. He knew that this foray into a somewhat personal subject with Jack would be considered an affront and end their conversations, but they were ending anyway. Jack's answer to his question might afford Abel an insight into the entire case. Abel excused his forwardness and told Jack that he had come into a small bit of money from an inheritance and wondered if Jack would be so kind as to give him advice on investing it, even suggesting that he would like to invest in the Randolph Fund. Jack's reaction to the question did not surprise Abel in the least. With much bluster Jack lectured Abel on the impropriety of a club servant asking financial advice from a member. After the show of indignation Jack gave an answer which shocked Abel and opened his eyes to a hunch which might blow the entire case sky-high.

Jack grumbled, "Abel, while I will not advise you in any way, shape, or form where to invest your recent windfall, I am grateful to you for some excellent assistance as a bartender, so I will tell you this in the strictest confidence: do not invest your money in my fund. Now let's let this distasteful subject drop from the conversation and from memory."

Jack Randolph. Chief executive of one the nation's largest hedge funds was giving out begrudging but nonetheless friendly advice to steer clear of investments in his own fund. Abel immediately realized that there must be levels to this situation which were far deeper than romantic jealousy and crimes of passion. Lizzy had told him that there had been rumors about the solvency of the Randolph Fund before, but Abel had spoken to several New York financial advisors, and they had all assured him that there are always negative rumors about any fund. Those rumors usually could be traced back to the owners of competing funds. But now there was a warning sign coming out of the mouth of the fund's owner himself. There must be severe problems ahead for the Randolph Fund. Once again Abel's police intuition was giving him a hunch that the death of Bill Pierce may have something to do with the monetary storm just breaching the horizon.

Things were beginning to add up in Abel's mind, and the totals that he was coming to were more complex and larger than he or Lizzy had assumed at the start of their investigative partnership. When the two sat on the sofa in the office recapping all that they had learned and deduced it was Lizzy's turn to let out a long low whistle. There were layers on top of layers going on here, and one of the things that now frightened her more than anything else was the renewed concern about the Dawson family investments which were heavily sunk into the Randolph Fund. If the entire case proved to be true and Jack Randolph was convicted of murder that was all well and good, but she hoped that in victory she would not find that she and her family would end up on the poor farm. She wanted to sit down with Joe and discuss the finances, but that was one additional complication which she just could not deal with at the moment. She was still very much concerned about the complications of the case and the fact that she was now possibly stepping on the toes of some very dangerous men.

Lizzy sat quietly alone in the office that evening. With the lights out she just let her mind wander. How had she gotten herself so deeply involved in a criminal investigation? Things had overtaken her, and she was still feeling as if she were in over her head. Abel's presence offered her a great deal of assurance. The support of Joe

280

and the boys gave her self-confidence a boost, but still she felt inadequate to the task. She had opened a can of worms which turned out to be a tidal wave of crime and deceit. In some ways she felt that her life and faith in humanity had been tarnished by the things that she had discovered. She had always known that human life was made up of the good and the bad, but now she had looked the bad, no, the intensely evil, right in the eyes, and what she saw demoralized her.

The time had come, she thought to herself, for the rubber to meet the road. She and Abel had put together the evidence, and it was substantial enough to take to the authorities. Abel agreed that they were on that threshold. She wondered how well she was personally prepared to face Jack Randolph in a court of law, a place where she would have to sit openly on the side of justice pointing an accusing finger at a very powerful man. She thought of herself as bouncing on a high diving board many feet above the water, looking down and hesitating to make that one great leap which would bring her crashing into the whole affair head on. No one was ever 100 percent certain of anything in life. Now seemed as good a time as any. Mentally, she made one final great bounce on that diving board and began her great leap.

Chapter Eight

The Puzzle Takes Form

So the march toward official action began. Lizzy and Abel felt confident that they had constructed a case worthy of being considered by a grand jury, but both knew full well that an indictment was just half of the objective. They needed a case which would withstand the attacks of a good legal defense and still bring about a conviction. Now the question at hand would be where the hearing would be held, which state would opt to hold a grand jury to decide on an indictment. The crime was reported as having been committed in the state of New York, but a great deal of doubt was being cast on that conclusion. In large part that doubt was being reconfirmed by the inclusion of the FBI in the investigation. Abel advised that he and Lizzy submit paperwork to both states and let them sort out the jurisdiction which would take the legal action.

Mrs. Rizzo of Port Chester, New York, had made a rather compelling statement to the FBI concerning the location of the car in which Bill's body had been found.

Earlier inconsistencies in her story were found to be some twisting of her story in the evolving reports which were now being examined by township and state officials. In the finalized FBI statement it was clear that she had seen the car cross a small bridge well in view of her home. It had been followed by a second car, and individuals had exchanged seats in the two cars before the second car drove off. She could not be specific, but she had the very strong impression that the second automobile had been an unmarked police car. She was quite positive that the license plates on the second car were from Connecticut. On that statement alone the FBI gave their opinion that the case should be handled by the Connecticut courts, that is if the federal authorities decided to pass on the case.

The expertise of the Lizzy and Abel team had reached its limits by now. It was without question time to call in a lawyer to review the situation. Lizzy made a call to Lucy Provence, her family attorney, for advice on how the structure of the case should be reviewed to test it for comprehensiveness and provability. Lucy was more than happy to assist Lizzy but quickly admitted that this sort of law was a bit out of her league. Years of practicing civil cases involving business ventures, accident lawsuits, and small business ventures left her devoid of the kind of legal expertise to judge the merits of a criminal case. Lizzy drove over to Lucy's office with a condensed version of all the materials she had collected over the months and had distilled with the help of Abel. Lucy quickly perused the files but once again reminded Lizzy that she did not feel competent to evaluate the evidence.

Lizzy was hoping that Lucy could act as her legal advisor and give her some idea of what would work in court and what would be easily counteracted by the defense. She spoke sincerely to Lucy when she admitted that she just could not afford to invest much more of her money to retain a lawyer and was hoping that Lucy would help in the best way she could with the legal knowledge which she possessed. Lucy was equally candid when she told Lizzy that it made very little sense to work with a lawyer who could very well miss major points of a criminal case. She also reminded her that the prosecution would certainly build their own case in both the grand jury hearing and the trial, if an indictment was handed down. Lizzy knew all that and desperately wanted to present a solid set of evidence to the prosecution so that they could finally determine if there was any merit to seeking an indictment. Lizzy would rather be shot down by her attorney than have the state officials reject the case she was building. Lucy asked Lizzy to give her a few days to think over what she might be able to do, and Lizzy agreed to meet her for lunch on Friday and discuss the situation again in light of Lucy's advice at that time.

Lizzy felt a bit crestfallen as she drove home from Lucy's office. She had really hoped that Lucy would be able to step in and help her and Abel judge whether or not to bring their case to the state, whichever state, decided it had jurisdiction over the case. When she arrived at home she found Abel in the office reading over several police reports he had collected from both the Port Chester and Greenwich police from the day of the murder and several days later. He was concentrating on a minor report filed a day after the murder in the neighborhood of Byram in western Greenwich. It seemed a home owner had heard some rustling in the area between his home and his neighbors. He thought he heard voices but had no desire to step out into the dark gangway between the houses. The following morning he examined the concrete sidewalk in the gangway and found stains of a rust color which he thought resembled dried blood. He called the police who came out and took samples of the stains and took a statement from the home owner. Abel could find no follow-up report on this incident, but he was preparing to drive over to the police headquarters to follow up on the matter.

Lizzy dropped herself heavily into an armchair and gave out a long frustrated sigh. Abel knew that could only mean that Lucy had balked at becoming part of the team. Lizzy sighed one more time as she poured out her frustration to Abel, hoping that he could give her some comfort and maybe an idea or two on how to proceed with her search for a legal consultant to assist them.

Abel answered, "Geez, Liz, all the lawyers I know are prosecutors, and they are gonna come at this thing in exactly the same way you and I would. They are gonna want to find it a solid case to drop a dirtbag with, but that kinda attitude leads them to be over confident. That is exactly what we wanna avoid."

He was not speaking the kind of words that Lizzy was desperate to hear at the moment; but she knew that, as usual, he was being blunt and he was being totally honest with her.

When the phone rang midmorning the next day and the caller ID showed it was from Lucy Provence Lizzy felt a rush of happiness. This had to be good news, and it was. Lucy still refused to join their work, but she gave Lizzy the name of a solid defense attorney from Bridgeport who was willing to assist them gratis. His name was David Cotter, and he had defended some of the roughest gang members in the tough city of Bridgeport. His record of acquittals was excellent. If anyone knew how to find the loopholes in a prosecution case it was Cotter. He had a very bad reputation among cops for his ability to get the bad guys out of jail, but that was exactly the talent and ability which Lizzy and Abel needed just now. They needed someone who would shoot holes in their case and then help them fix those holes. Cotter's aim would be to help them build a case that even he could not discredit.

While Cotter began to throw his best effort into reviewing and challenging the evidence of the case, Abel returned to his work of collecting reports and constantly reviewing the reports related to the murder itself. With every rereading of the reports he came upon new details and new angles with which to reexamine the details he had already noted. He also was asked by his friend in the FBI to meet with the field agents in Greenwich to try to give them a little of his insight into what they were reviewing and gathering for themselves. They were very interested in the evolution of the reports which Abel had uncovered and began to incorporate his ideas into their own developing report.

Several details of the police reports led the investigators to believe that the murder itself was not committed in the rent-a-car at all. There was far too little blood in the vehicle and the bloodstains which were in odd locations. One stain in particular troubled the police filing the initial report. There was a three-inch bloodstain on the driver's seat of the vehicle, which placed it beneath the victim's body. That bloodstain also was smeared from the leather seat to the victim's trouser leg and on to his jacket. Such a smear meant that the blood had been spilled onto the seat, and then the body had been placed on the seat in a slumped forward position thereby smearing on Bill's jacket. When the body was pulled to an upright seated position the blood then came into contact with the trousers. To add to the impossibility of the original scenario the stain was

286

static and did not increase in size from the seeping of an open wound. Added to that was the fact that none of Bill's wounds were located in any area close to where the stain was located. It was now obvious that Bill's body had been put in the car seat after having been repeatedly stabbed. In the process of placement blood from a chest or throat wound had spilled onto the seat.

The correlation of reports which Lizzy had done made the contradiction quite obvious. Abel wondered how any police officer could have overlooked the discrepancies or why they would intentionally doctor the reports to create the appearance that the death, be it suicide or murder, took place inside the rented vehicle. It did not make sense. He knew that cops were capable of changing evidence under many circumstances, some for their own benefit and sometimes to assure a conviction, but he could never bring himself to believe that any cop would cover up a murder. There had to be more to this story than even he and Lizzy had uncovered.

It did not make sense for criminals to kill a victim and go to so much trouble to relocate the body and then be so careless as to leave very definite signs of their actions. There seemed to be a professional hand involved in this murder, but there was also an amateurish quality which drove Abel to near distraction. The only solution which he could come up with was that the murder itself was done in a two-part action, one carried out by Group A and the second by Group B. That sounded too insane for Abel to give it very much credence. In the midst of all his conjecture Abel realized that he had let his intention to investigate the bloodstain report from Byram slip his mind. He made a call to his contact in the Greenwich Police Department and asked if he could examine any and all evidence regarding the Byram incident. His contact said that he was welcome to come in anytime. They would open that file for him without hesitation. An incident unrelated to the touchy Pierce case was no matter for secrecy. Abel arranged to visit the headquarters the very next morning.

When he arrived a small cardboard carton labeled with the case number of the Byram incident was ready and waiting. He drew up a chair and got comfortable, preparing for a leisurely and perhaps long read of the materials before him. His perusal time did not last much longer than five minutes. There on the very top of the material was a report sheet which stated that the blood was human and that the officers determined that it was the result of a possible gang initiation or a physical confrontation between teen rivals. With that summation the case had been labeled closed. Stapled on the back of the report was a small plastic bag containing several flakes of a dried brown material which Abel knew was blood.

Abel took the report and plastic bag with him as he marched to the reception room of the chief of police two floors above the office he was using. The chief agreed to see him immediately and heard him out about the possible importance of the blood sample he was holding in his hand. The chief placed a call to the Port Chester police headquarters and to the coroner's office in both Westchester County, New York, and Fairfield County, Connecticut. Before the day was done both counties would analyze the blood samples in the Byram case against blood samples from Bill Pierce. Abel knew that by this time tomorrow they would know if the blood samples matched. If they did, the location of the murder would be solidly place in the town of Greenwich. He put in a call to Lizzy and caught her in her car on the way to doing some grocery shopping. She was so stunned by the news that she had to pull over to the side of Putnam Avenue to calm herself down. The case was developing in ways and in depth which she had never imagined.

The next day the news came in the form of a telephone call from the chief of the Greenwich Police. The blood had matched. Bill Pierce had been killed in Byram, Connecticut, on a quiet street in the dark gangway between two middle-class Greenwich homes. The trial, if there was to be one, would be under the authority of and in the jurisdiction of the state of Connecticut. Now there was the matter of reinforcing the case to the point that the state attorney general would feel confident enough in it to seat a grand jury to determine whether or not Jack Randolph would stand trial for murder. Now was the time for David Cotter to delve intently into the many piles of material which Lizzy and Abel had sorted and organized. He was up to the task and began collecting materials from Lizzy's office to copy and take home for his examination. Everyone involved in the case was feeling happy, enjoying a renewed sense of confidence.

Some of the wind was knocked out of the sails of Lizzy and her team when they learned the next day that the FBI had decided not to pursue their case. They felt that there was insufficient evidence to pursue a case in the federal courts. They voiced the opinion that the changes in police reports and inconsistencies in evidence were due in large part to the inexperience of two small-town police departments in handling a complex murder case. A case in point was the handling of the autopsy and the initial determination of the Westchester County Coroner's Office that the death had been one of suicide rather than murder. The details in the autopsy report were so inconsistent and contrary that the FBI felt they were too blatant to be a willful attempt to tamper with evidence. Their final recommendation, as was often the case in such matters, was that both local departments invest in sending several of their senior officers to further training. Of course, the recommended retraining facility was their academy in Virginia.

Abel seemed the least surprised at the action of the FBI, but he explained to Lizzy and Cotter that over the years he had seen the Feds burst into a case with great fanfare waving their pretty little G-man badges around, only to decide a short time later that the case was not worth their time. Abel felt that having the Feds on your side was not a bad thing, but more often than not it also was not a very positive thing either. Now that the state of Connecticut had joined the act, he felt that there was a very good chance for a grand jury, an indictment, and, hopefully, a conviction. Now they needed to get down to the business of solidifying their evidence and having a case to present to the Connecticut people when they asked for their assistance. When the request for a grand jury was submitted the state did indeed make heavy use of the materials that Lizzy and Abel had given them.

The whole standing and function of a grand jury were a mystery to Lizzy, so Abel and David sat her down and gave her a tutorial in what was going on in this process. They also stressed that since the decision of a grand jury is not a conviction it would tend to be more open to indictment on evidence which would not necessarily hold up in a regular trial. A victory in the grand jury did not assure them of a conviction, so they needed to review and classify each bit of evidence and try to determine just how well it would stand up to any argument put up against it. It was in this area that David Cotter was now the backbone of their continued efforts. If he could find a weakness in any evidence or line of argument they would need to reinforce the item or classify it as something which might well be ruled inadmissible when challenged by the defense.

Dave Cotter was exceptionally talented when it came to finding weaknesses in prosecution evidence and became a local celebrity when he tripped up the former Fairfield County prosecutor nearly a decade ago. The prosecutor, Robert Finley, had made a name for himself as an organized crime buster, having managed to put away the heads of three of the four crime families in the western Connecticut area. But it was in his attempt to convict the fourth and final godfather that Dave Cotter threw a monkey wrench in his, up to then, promising legal and political career. Finley was an ambitious man but he had always also been a very careful man with regard to his legal career. He never bit off more than he could chew and hedged his bets by being very selective in the cases he decided to prosecute himself. His department had had its share of losses as well as victories, but it could be clearly seen that in every victory Finley himself had been at the helm of the prosecution, and that was no accident.

Finley had dreams of being governor, and he decided that being a Democrat he needed to have an angle, something which set him apart from other Democratic contenders for the governor's mansion. There were a few conservative Democrats around Connecticut, but generally the people of the state considered his party soft on crime. A hard-nosed "law and order" prosecutor would be a hard target for a primary opponent to hit and an even harder target for the Republican candidate to challenge in the general election. Finley thought he had written his own ticket to Hartford since he had convicted three of the state's top organized crime leaders, but being a careful man he decided he needed some insurance, the kind of electoral insurance which would come with a clean sweep of four convictions. For the first time in his career Finley had bitten off far more than he would ever be able to chew, and that oversize bit went by the name of David Cotter.

When the trial began Cotter let Finley bring out all his big gun witnesses and sat passively as each witness gave testimony against Mr. Grippa. The courtroom was abuzz with spectators, court officials, and the press wondering why Cotter seemed to be rolling over and giving up on the case. Even Grippa seemed to be agitated at the lack of fight in his attorney. This went on for days as one prosecution witness after the other spilled damning testimony into the court record. Cotter rarely objected to any of the actions or motions presented by Finley, and with each passing day Finley grew more confident and began to strut and preen like a peacock before the jam-packed courtroom.

After passing on cross-examining a major witness Cotter was asked by the judge, "Mr. Cotter, do you have any intention of participating in this case whatsoever?" Cotter simply replied, "When I believe the time is right, I will jump right in. Thank you for your concern, Your Honor."

Finley's onslaught finally came to an end, and Cotter took center stage. He began to call a series of witnesses which seemed fairly far flung from the case, so much so that Finley's objections were constant, but generally overruled by a judge who seemed keenly curious as to where Cotter was headed with his string of witnesses. After the third witness left the stand it was quite apparent what Cotter was doing; one by one he was introducing evidence which was in no way clearing his client of any blame but which was discrediting each and every witness and most of the evidence presented by the prosecution. Police witnesses were shown to have had dealings with Grippa's enemies or in one case not being able to prove that they had been physically present at the scene of an event which they were testifying about. One female officer had testified that she witnessed Grippa and his lieutenant escaping from the rear door of the warehouse which was being raided by police in northern Bridgeport, but a police dispatcher and radio transmission transcripts showed that she had been in a police car one block away from the front of the warehouse at the exact time she said that she had seen Grippa exit the building.

One by one the testimony of key prosecution witnesses came tumbling down. Then further witnesses damaged physical evidence by challenging the trail of how the evidence was gathered, recorded, and stored. Even expert witnesses in handwriting and voice analysis were challenged by other experts and, even more damning, by the presentation of records of their past testimonies which had been later overturned. Finley's case was beginning to resemble a house of cards, and layer by layer the cards were flying off in the breeze of Cotter's line of witnesses. By the end of the trial only one solid witness for the prosecution was left standing, and in his closing statement Cotter reminded the jury that this sole witness could not swear to being certain that the man he saw involved in a sting operation was in fact Grippa. The jury deliberated for fifteen days and on several occasions asked to examine testimony transcripts and review evidence. Finley sat and sweated while Cotter remained, as they used to say, calm, cool, and collected. When the jury returned, Grippa was acquitted on all counts with the jury foreman later telling news reporters that the jury was uniformly decided of Grippa's guilt, but definitely not beyond a shadow of a doubt.

That day Finley's aspirations for the office of governor were dashed forever on the rocks of defeat, and the legend of David Cotter rose up to the level of that of Johnnie Cochran and F. Lee Bailey. There were many attorneys who would claim that Cotter could not put together a defense case to save his mother's life, but he had the uncanny ability to dismantle and decimate a prosecution case with the ease of a child unwrapping a bar of candy. In this reputation among the jealous and disgruntled colleagues of David Cotter's lay the extraordinary value to Lizzy and the Pierce case. If he could find a way to counter all the flaws which he might find in their evidence then perhaps they could forge an airtight case to present to the state prosecutors for the trial they were sure would follow a speedy indictment.

Cotter, Abel, and Lizzy were found locked in Lizzy's study day and night for days during the weeks before the grand jury went into session. During the hearings all three would often be seen at the courthouse advising and assisting the prosecutor as the case was made for the indictment of Jack Randolph. Jack's attorneys tried repeatedly to paint the prosecution case as being a vendetta on the part of Lizzy due to her politics and social beliefs which ran so contrary to those of Jack. The subject of her decoration of the Randolph house in Southern plantation style was brought up as proof not only of her disdain for Jack but of her sheer contempt for him. Some of the statements made regarding Lizzy brought chuckles to the assembled attorneys and jurors. One statement concerning Lizzy did stick, however. When asked to relate how she had felt threatened by phone calls which she supposed were from Jack Randolph she could give no reasonable argument why she had immediately assumed that they were from him. Unfortunately, Lizzy stumbled on the question and began to speak about her feelings and intuition regarding the source of the threats. Such talk visibly troubled both the prosecution and the jurors.

Lizzy had always been a very spiritual person and someone who often felt that a divine providence was guiding her, which was all well and good in conversations at church or among like-minded friends, but in a hearing room of the Connecticut State Courthouse it sounded downright eccentric. The prosecutors made it very clear to her after the hearing that they felt that her answers may have damaged the attitude of the jurors toward evidence which they knew had come from her investigative work. They told her that grand juries were much trickier than regular trial juries; opinion and impression played a far greater role in these proceedings. Jurors were freer to give weight to feelings, and oftentimes a compelling testimony might well be one with very little legal substance. Talk of guidance and leadings were tantamount to talking about spells and witchcraft in the eyes of the state according to the chief prosecutor. He never seemed to catch the irony when Lizzy pointed out that each witness was promising the court that they would tell the truth in the name of God. Why was spiritual talk so alienating just moments after people had taken an oath with spiritual connotations?

Abel was called as an expert witness to explain many of the facets of the investigation and to outline the ways in which certain lines of reasoning evolved in the direction which they did in the case. One point at which the defense team hammered away was the implication of the Finellis and their associates in the murder case since there was no physical evidence to directly tie them into the case. Phone records showed that Jack had spoken to several of the Finelli associates in the weeks prior to the murder, but those calls abruptly stopped about two weeks prior to the crime. Abel pointed out that the calls did not really stop; only the traceable calls ceased, but a series of calls keeping in the pattern of the Finelli calls began the very next day following the last Finelli call. These calls were made between Jack's home phone and one or more untraceable cell phones. Abel was glad that the old-fashioned Randolph detested cellular phones and did all of his communications over a landline, thus making his calls a matter of record. The defense nearly screamed their objections to this line of reasoning since it was purely conjecture and had no relevance to fact.

Abel argued that the frequency and timing of the mystery calls were exactly the same as the earlier calls between Jack and the Finellis. He knew that while the odds of these calls being coincidentally identical to the earlier calls were phenomenally, if not astronomically, high, they proved nothing and simply made an implication of connection. Where the defense found themselves momentarily speechless was the introduction of a piece of evidence which Abel himself had discovered from his analysis of police reports on the condition of the vehicle in which Bill's body was found. The car had had a multiplicity of fingerprints in the interior and even some on the exterior which had survived exposure to the elements. Many were those of Bill Pierce, some were identified as those of the rental agent and of the porter who moved car around the lot of the rental agency, but there were a number of prints which were consider irrelevant since the car had, of course, been rented on many occasions prior to Bill's use of the vehicle. One thumbprint was found which was slightly smudged and had been written off, but Abel had taken the print to his friend in the FBI who then sent it off to Quantico for in-depth analysis and partial reconstruction. After it had been enhanced, it was run against the data banks of the federal fingerprint database, and it had come up as a nine-out-of-ten-point match with that of Joseph Finelli, one of the Finelli brothers and uncle to Matthew Finelli. Better known to the FBI as Joey "the Rat" Finelli he had a record of violent crimes and was known as the strong arm of the Finelli family. The defense was stunned and asked for a recess for the remainder of the day to react to the information which had been presented.

The next day the defense team deftly portrayed the fingerprint as incidental to the case since the car rental agency was owned and operated by close friends and business associates of the Finelli brothers. The defense assured the jury that Joseph had many opportunities to visit the rental agency and on occasion rent a car for personal and business use. Therefore, it was not impossible that he might have rented that very car at some point in the recent past. They failed to produce records showing that such a rental had taken place, but the prosecution let them slide on this matter for the moment. They knew that the damage had been done by Abel's testimony in the eyes of the jury. Such fantastic coincidences might be impossible to prove, but in a grand jury hearing impressions could be as damning as hard evidence. They knew that this point would be a very vulnerable spot in the defense case when they were arguing in an actual trial setting. Abel had insisted on including this matter in the hearing, but the prosecution regretted having allowed him to do so. They felt that such evidence should have been held back until the trial where it would seem like a bombshell. Abel was convinced that it was needed to secure the indictment. After all it would have been a moot point had the grand jury failed to indict Jack Randolph.

Another fingerprint, three actually, had proven to be disturbing to Abel when he reviewed the reports on the car. Two finger and one thumbprint from a left hand had been found on the interior door frame of the driver's side of the car. It appeared as if someone had grabbed the door frame from outside the vehicle while entering the car or in an attempt to steady themselves when tumbling inward into the driver's seat. The troubling part of the evidence was the fact that the prints were identified as those of a police officer, a police officer who had been working the night of the crime but who was off duty the day that the body was discovered and when the car had been brought into the lab for examination. One might have assumed that the prints were made by a sloppy and inefficient officer during the moving of the car or during the removal of evidence from the vehicle, but the lack of that officer's presence made such a scenario altogether impossible. One last fact which made the evidence explosive was the identity of the police officer. The car had been found in Port Chester, New York, examined, vouchered, and delivered to the crime lab in Westchester County, New York, by the Port Chester Police Department; but the fingerprints belonged to a member of the Greenwich Connecticut Police Force.

Abel knew the implications of this discovery, and he also knew that in court the argument could and would be made that both these fingerprints and the thumbprint of Joseph Finelli could not have been from earlier rentals since they would not have survived the throughout cleaning that the rental cars went through after being returned from the previous client. He decided to keep this information to himself for the moment, but he had knowledge to back up all these contentions since he had done his homework at the car rental agency. He had rented a car and returned it the next day, having put his fingerprints on both the interior and exterior of the automobile. He then returned the next morning and requested to rent the very same car, checking the registration and engine serial number to assure himself that it was the right car. Driving the car to Lizzy's home he wore leather gloves and then dusted the entire car for prints. He found nothing except prints from the porter at the agency. The fingerprints he had discovered from the police reports had definitely been made during the time in which Bill Pierce had rented the vehicle, of that he had no doubt.

Where such evidence would steer the case was anybody's guess, but Abel knew that it was too confusing to introduce to the grand jury. To ensure that it would not be included in the hearing, he kept these facts from the prosecutor's office until after the end of the proceedings. The prosecutor was furious, but Abel had seen far too many good cases ruined during his years as a cop by the inclusion of far too much information given to the grand jury. On one count it tended to distract the jurors and confuse the issue. In this case it would surely open a can of worms in the minds of the grand jury. Second, it might even raise doubts in their minds about Jack being the perpetrator of the crime. Providing a smorgasbord of suspects allowed the primary suspect to slip into obscurity and could make the evidence against him seem less concise and focused. The lawyers surely knew the law better than a retired cop, but Abel knew lawyers better than they knew themselves and would bet his last dollar that they could take a sure thing and foul it up, given enough evidence to play with. He was not going to hand them anything with which to blow this case.

The jury had heard the evidence, and the time had come to retire to their deliberations. Everyone gave a sigh of relief and congratulated themselves on having done the best possible job that they could have n the name of justice. Lizzy and Abel headed back to Greenwich for a short spell of rest and relaxation. They did not intend to return to the courthouse but would be content to have the decision telephoned to them at their homes. Abel drove back to Manhattan determined to visit some old haunts and get himself rip-roaringly drunk. He knew that after nursing a hangover he would start rereading and reanalyzing all the massive piles of paperwork he had spread across his dining room table, but for now he needed to enjoy himself and get drunk enough to have that hangover tomorrow.

Abel arrived at his apartment in the early evening. Driving back from Greenwich had been easy since he was driving against the rush hour juggernaut. New York and the surrounding area is a magnificent place to live. Culture and beauty can be found minutes away from wherever you may find yourself. Except in rush hour traffic, a ten-block drive can turn into an hour of parking lot conditions, and Abel was hoping that he would have a clear sail home. He had gotten too accustomed to the leisurely pace of traffic in and around Greenwich and found himself dreading the return to the hustle and bustle of the Heights. He parked his car in the parking space he rented in the driveway of a neighbor's house. It was cheaper than the monthly rental in a spot in his building's parking levels. He had money, but he also knew how to hang on to it.

After taking a quick shower and changing out of what he called his "monkey suit" he headed over to Lucky's Bar over on 186th Street. It was a Hispanic club with loud and frenzied music, and Abel was in the mood for a little bit of crazy fun. He might have a few years on his chassis, but his engine was purring just fine. He hopped on a barstool and ordered himself a Red Stripe Jamaican beer.

His friends often teased him about his choice in beer. After all being a Hispanic he was expected to like Corona or Heineken, but he had acquired a taste for Red Stripe when he had had a Jamaican partner for several years. In fact one of the reasons he especially liked Lucky's Bar was the fact that they served his favorite brew. He was just getting comfortable when a tap on the shoulder and a gentle tug pulled him off the barstool and over to the pulsating dance floor. He smiled as he saw the face of his other reason for liking Lucky's. Her name was Jessie.

Jessie was a beautiful African American woman in her late twenties or early thirties, and if there was any woman in the world that Abel might come to love after the death of his wife, it was Jessie. This was no Cinderella fairy tale relationship, however. Abel had met Jessie over ten years ago when she was barely legal. Whether or not her age was legal mattered very little because her profession was decidedly illegal. Jessie was a whore, to put it bluntly. In fact, that is often the way she described herself. She was not a serious drug user, nor did she sound crass and semiliterate like the prostitutes that you see on TV cop shows. She was soft-spoken and had a good command of the English language as well as a certain charm which made her seem like the kind of lady one might run into at a museum or maybe in church. Part of her popularity with clients was the fact that she seemed so out of place in her profession and at a place like Lucky's. No one knew her story, and in a town of people all too ready to sob on your shoulder and tell every detail of some hard-luck saga, she was unique in that she kept to herself and always seemed to be quite content with her lot in life.

Abel had met her by being the cop who busted her one warm summer evening. He was a fairly gruff man, and as a cop he could also be a bit rough, but when he cuffed her

301

and turned her around to take a look at her face he was moved by her beauty. Not just her physical looks but by an inner beauty that many men might not have seen, but which touched him. He had busted her a number of times before they actually began to get to know each other. He felt attracted to her, but it was as much personal as it was physical. At first he shied away from her because he felt ashamed of being attracted to such a young woman and, second, for being attracted to a prostitute. After a while he avoided situations in which he would be forced to arrest her and turned a blind eye to times when he ran into her plying her trade. Then they started to bump into each other at Lucky's, and suddenly Lucky's became Abel's regular bar.

For the first couple of years the memory of his wife and his feelings of guilt prevented him from acting on his feelings, but eventually hours of slow dancing and one too many Red Stripes made a sexual encounter inevitable. The night they first spent together was a drunken orgy of lust and orgasm, but it served to break the ice of the situation. They began to meet on occasion and have dinner, take a drive, or just watch a DVD together; and sex would follow. Abel still denied to himself that he loved her, but deep down he knew that he would like to spend the rest of his days with her. She, on the other hand, knew that she had somehow fallen in love with this chubby old cop who had put her to jail too many times for her to remember. She nicknamed him Sipowicz after the character on *NYPD Blue* and eventually shortened it to Sip. He just called her Jess.

That night after all the stress and strain of the grand jury hearing Abel had planned a quick drunken night and then a long deep sleep, but when he walked over to Lucky's he realized that he was hoping for something more. It bothered him to know that Jess was selling her body to other men, but he also knew that she was not about to give it up as her primary source of income. In the Big Apple there are all kinds of programs to help people find jobs. There is a lot of talk about educational and job opportunities, but when push comes to shove, being a whore pays a hell of a lot more money than flipping burgers at Wendy's. Abel was not ready to marry or even support Jess, so he really had nothing to complain about with the situation. Had he listed his situations on a Facebook account he would have definitely selected the option "too complicated to explain."

After three or four dances and as many Red Stripes, Abel took Jess to the Galicia café just down Broadway for a nice dinner of pernil, pork roasted Spanish style, as well as rice and beans. They strolled slowly back to Lucky's, but at the door Abel whispered to her, "Let's go home. Whadda ya say?" Without a word she took his hand and headed in the direction of his apartment.

They talked and laughed as they walked down the street until a teenage onlooker shouted, "Hey, Grandpa! Why don't you fuck somebody your daughter's age and leave your granddaughter to me?"

Within a second Abel's badge and service revolver were flashed, and the sound of the harassing teen's footsteps could be heard running in the opposite direction. Abel was not about to take any shit from a punk, especially in his own neighborhood.

Being a gentleman Abel opened his apartment door and let Jessie in ahead of him. As he entered the hallway he turned his back to her in order to lock the dead bolt and put in the security chain. When he turned to face her she leaped on to him, wrapping her arms around his neck and her legs around his waist.

They kissed furiously for long minutes until she broke off the kiss and moaned, "The way you handled that little fucker in the street made me wet my panties. Now it's time for Sip to show me what he is made of, and I am hoping it is gonna be pure steel."

Before he could speak one of her hands was grabbing his crotch, and finding what she was looking for she added, "Yep, tungsten steel to top it off."

Abel laughed and warned, "Well, *it* may be steel, but my spine is still just brittle old bone, and if I don't put you down soon, we are both gonna be on the floor."

He brought her over to the couch and gently laid her across the cushions; as he began to unbutton his shirt she already had his pants unzipped and was pulling both his trousers and shorts down to the floor. She had wiggled out of her jeans and top in what seemed like a split second. There he stood over her in a tee shirt, socks, and shoes and nothing else. She pushed herself back on the cushions and spread her legs wide to accommodate his bulky form. He leaned onto her and slipped himself into her as he locked his lips with hers. There was not going to be any fancy or kinky positions tonight, just straightforward and earnest sex. He was a man in love and making love to the woman he loved. No one in that moment was old. No one was flabby and no one was a whore. There were just two people who loved each other making love.

Abel lay awake next to Jessie long after they had finished their copulation, and he thought about the entire situation. Somehow he had to sort this all out and make it work. He was tired of being alone, and he was tired of seeing the woman he loved selling herself to men who only wanted her body. Life was complicated, but with some real effort there was always a solution out there.

He looked over at Jessie and decided that he would make that effort right after this whole case was finished. He was going to put the same kind of hard work into this relationship as he had into every case he ever worked on. Especially as hard as he was working on the Pierce case. With that thought his mind began to race, and the subject was not love anymore. His mind had returned to the case, and it had returned to it with a vengeance.

Back in Greenwich Lizzy decided to put everything on hold and take some time to let Joe, Troy, and Scott know that they had not lost their wife and mother. Joe and the boys had become so accustomed to Lizzy's devotion to the case that they were off in other parts of the house doing their own thing and giving her space to do what she had to do. Well, tonight things would be different. She made a quick call to Papa John's and ordered four pizzas. Each pie would have the favorite toppings of each member of the family. She made sure no one was in the family room and began to decorate the room as if it was a birthday party or holiday. Everything would be festive and all on paper plates and plastic cups to save them all from too much cleanup afterward. She also searched the wine cooler built into the kitchen cabinets and found a bottle of their favorite wine. Tonight was going to be family night, and everything would be just like the old days before she had gotten involved with the case.

She even programmed the cable box to the *On Demand* station and pushed the button to order the comedy *The Hangover,* something so farcical and funny that they would laugh away months of alienation and separation. She knew that none of her men begrudged her the work that meant so much to her, but she also knew that they had deeply felt her absence. She was going to make an effort to begin a healing process even though she knew

305

that there would be more work and separation in the foreseeable future. The case was now a very important part of her life, but it could never eclipse the importance of her beloved husband and wonderful sons. This was going to be their night, and she was going to make it as special as she could.

When the pizzas arrived she called out to the boys to get the door and hurriedly left two $20 bills on the table next to the door. Next she called up to the den and asked Joe to come down and help her find something in the family room. Her timing was good, and everyone converged on the family room together. They found her sitting with a broad grin on her face at a table set and decorated with festive tablecloth, napkins, and even a few streamers and balloons.

"So what's the holiday?" shouted Troy.

Lizzy threw him a kiss and said, "It's Welcome Home Mommy Day. Is that all right with you?" All three of the Dawson men said simultaneously, "That's great with us!" and took their seats around the pile of steaming pizzas.

Life had changed, Lizzy was well aware of that, but despite the changes she also knew life for the Dawson family was still good.

The family party was just like old times; and for a moment Lizzy, Joe, and the kids could pretend that the whole case and all the things they had been through had never happened. The phone rang while the family was eating their pizza. Joe walked over to the extension ready to pick it up. He took a glance over at Lizzy and the boys. Lizzy smiled and slightly shook her head no, so Joe removed his hand from the receiver, but when he saw the unhappy looks on Troy's and Scott's faces he bent over and unplugged the phone from the base unit, and the ringing went silent. The room had suddenly become very quiet, and the boys had put their slices of pizza down and looked over at their mom. Without a word Lizzy began to chuckle and then laugh. The whole family joined in, and when the laughter stopped and eyes were wiped dry, Troy blurted out, "Thank you, Mom," which caused one last tear to well up in Lizzy's eye. The roller coaster life of the past few months had taken its toll on everyone, but for the first time she realized just how much it had affected her beloved boys.

That night Joe stretched out on his side of the bed placing his hands behind his head in a truly relaxed posture. Lizzy smiled as she realized that she had not seen Joe looking so calm and relaxed in a very long time. More often than not, Lizzy would crawl into bed long after Joe had fallen asleep. The work of the case usually ran well into the late evening and night. In the morning an exhausted Lizzy would drag herself out of bed long enough to cook some breakfast for the family and give each one a peck on the cheek before crawling back into bed for a couple more hours of sleep. Her life as wife and mom had become robotic and prefunctionary. At this moment looking over at Joe stretched out peacefully on the bed she knew how much she had missed the routines that might normally have seemed humdrum but which now, in their absence, seemed precious and vital to her. Life had changed these past months, and many of the changes were wonderful. She was no longer a soccer mom sitting at home having pretty much ended her decorating business and not being able to invest on their house speculation business because of the mini-depression going on, so finding herself living vicariously through the business accomplishments of Joe and the boys' sports and academic achievements. She had found her place in

307

the world, and the place she was now occupying was a very impressive one.

The portion of her life that had been sacrificed to make room for her new achievements was without question her family life. She had always sensed that she was letting that aspect of her existence slip away bit by bit, but she promised herself that when this project was put to bed she would bring back some of the things which had been lost. Somehow she sensed that life had been changed, and once the toothpaste had been squeezed out of that tube there was no putting it back. Her plan was not to turn back the clock to the days before she had ever heard of William Pierce but rather to forge a new life that had balance and fulfillment not just for herself but for the entire family. As Joe lay there he looked over at Lizzy and saw the consternation on her face. Without a word he sat up, cradled her face in his hand, and gave her a sweet kiss on the cheek. Words did not need to be spoken. The two dimmed the lights and curled together on the bed holding each other and simply cherishing each other's presence. They woke the next morning exactly as they had fallen asleep in each other's arms and cheek pressed to cheek.

It was a Saturday, so they rose a little later than usual and found the boys lounging in the family room still dressed in their pajamas eating cereal and having tall glasses of orange juice.

Lizzy shook her head and asked, "Well, I suppose that since you fixed your own breakfast you have no interest in some eggs, bacon, and maybe a few mini waffles?"

She had not finished her words when both boys chimed in, "Heck, *no*! We always have room for one of your breakfasts, Mom."

It seemed to Lizzy as if time had really turned itself back to what she know thought of as "the good old days." As she opened the refrigerator she felt a sense of gratification. There on the shelf where she always kept the breakfast fixings was everything she needed to whip up a first-class hearty breakfast. Joe had done all the shopping lately, and every item was there just like normal; even the sizes and brands of the food were exactly the same as always. Joe had always been a supportive husband in all the things that Lizzy had done since they had married, but it was now apparent that he had been supportive as well in all the small special ways which make a couple and their kids a family.

Lizzy wanted this day to last forever, but she knew that she needed to see the case through to the end. She had too much invested in this thing to let go of it, even if it seemed as though the state was going to cut her out of the hands on side of the trial, if there was going to be a trial. She had felt confident when she left the courthouse yesterday, but doubts were beginning to creep into her mind. They had presented a lot of evidence, but she wondered just how solid that evidence would be when push came to shove. After having gotten to know Dave Cotter she could see that just about anything could have doubts cast on its veracity. She knew that several key pieces of the case were questionable; not that they were untrue, just that they could be interpreted in many different directions, some proving the case and others being totally irrelevant. Her newfound doubts managed to bring the case to the forefront of Lizzy's mind again, and she wondered if the call last evening was related to it.

When Lizzy examined the telephone base unit to retrieve yesterday's call she was shocked to realize that Joe had accidentally turned off the ringer on the entire base unit. None of the extensions had rung since yesterday evening, and there were now fifteen calls on the voice mail. She hit the caller ID button and began to examine who had been calling all evening yesterday and evidently for most of the morning. She was surprised to learn that fourteen of the calls had been from Dave Cotter and one from a neighbor. She hit the proper code into the phone, and the messages began to play. Dave sounded excited in the first few calls and simply asked that she call him as soon as possible. Then his tone took on an agitated tone, and finally, in this morning's messages he sounded almost desperate as he begged her to call because he needed to talk to her about details of the case. She called him back immediately and did not appreciate his scornful tone as he scolded her for not having picked up or called back until now.

In her mind she thought, *Brother, what is so frigging important at this point*. But she said instead, "Dave, we all deserve a day off, and yesterday was mine. Now what is so urgent at a time that we don't even know if there will be an indictment."

Dave mumbled that he had a source which was telling him that the indictment was forthcoming, and he took that source seriously, so seriously that he felt that they needed to jump back into their analysis of the evidence immediately. The same clandestine source had also told him that the state was planning to turn to Lizzy and Abel in a very big way to support their case against Randolph. Lizzy pressed for more information on this secret source and why Cotter found the information so unimpeachable. Cotter would give nothing except to say that she should trust his judgment and believe him when he said that the source was reliable. With not a little annoyance Lizzy shrugged her shoulders and agreed to call Abel and reconvene their sessions together that afternoon. So much for another family day.

Abel was not quite ready to give up his furlough from the case and protested vehemently when Lizzy and Dave called him on a conference call.

Abel responded, "Hey, even the department gives a guy a fucking day or two off every week. What is so fucking important that I gotta run out there again after one evening off?"

He was still enjoying the afterglow of a romantic evening with his Jessie and did not want to jump back into the case work without so much as a full day to relax and forget about evidence and judges and murders. Jessie had left earlier, but he really wanted to loll around the house and just think about his own situation and how he could make Jessie an "honest" woman and his housemate, if not his third wife. Just like Lizzy he knew that a day would come when the Pierce case was history and he could get on with his life, but he had hoped that he could take a little time off before the ordeal of a trial began.

Cotter laid it on the line by telling him that he had two reasons to demand that they get back to work on the case. One was his source's information. The second was something that struck very close to Abel's heart. Cotter told him that he had a hunch, a very strong hunch, that things were going to break soon; and they had to be prepared to strike while the iron was hot.

Abel's response was simple, "Fuck it! I'll be there in an hour."

Cotter agreed that they should all meet in one hour in Lizzy's office. Lizzy and Abel were sighing and rolling their eyes as they hung up their phones; it was only Cotter who was chafing at the bit to get back to work. Abel wondered as he drove up I95 what kind of source was so close to the case as to know the direction of how the grand jury debate was going and where the state prosecutors were heading in the preparation of their case against Jack Randolph.

Abel knew that there were only three sources who could know this kind of information: someone in the prosecutor's office, someone on the grand jury, and someone on the courthouse staff who would be privy to the goings-on in the grand jury deliberation room and the prosecutor's office. Only the last option seemed like a probable source, but even that troubled Abel. Anyone on the court staff would know who David Cotter was and his reputation as a defense attorney to the underworld, so why would any of them help him? True he was on the opposite side this time, actually trying to put a bad guy away, but would anyone in the courthouse really buy that hook, line and sinker? There was always the most obvious scenario, that Cotter had bribed someone for information. Then again, why would he spend his own money on a case which would bring him absolutely no profit? The source smelled rotten to Abel, but he had to admit to himself that he could be wrong. After all Cotter had a reputation for working miracles in the courtroom.

Lizzy's office no longer resembled a den in a private home. It looked more like the office of a junior partner in a law firm, the kind of junior partner who had to do all the leg work and dirty work for the showboating senior partners. The place was a mess, except for about six cardboard legal file boxes. These boxes were pristine; and the files inside them were orderly, neat, and in perfect sequence, something Lizzy and Cotter saw to themselves. Nothing was out of order in the files; but there were tons of additional materials all over the two desks, tables, and even the sofa which needed to be reviewed, categorized, and, finally, evaluated for relevance and legal strength by the entire team and then by Cotter. It was this pile of materials that was number one on Cotter's list of priorities.

Cotter spoke quietly and firmly as he told Lizzy and Abel that he felt that they had put together a great case for the grand jury and that it had been strong enough to ensure an indictment. But he felt that there were far too many sizable holes in the continuity of the evidence to prove a case against Randolph.

Cotter made his case, "For Christ's sake, we have never, I repeat *never* made any physical connection between Randolph and the murder. Nothing sez to me, 'Jack Randolph took a knife and stabbed this poor son-of-a-bitch Bill Pierce to death.' Nor do we have a stick of evidence, hard evidence without conjecture, hearsay, or circumstantial weight, to say that Jack Randolph hired anybody to kill Bill for him. Come on, people, we have to tear down this house of straw and start building something out of brick."

Both Lizzy and Abel were impressed by Cotter's determination to construct a case which would be able to withstand the grilling and objections of a top-notch defense team. Abel joked that it was to Jack Randolph's dismay that the great David Cotter was on the opposing side in this whole matter. He imagined aloud that Jack must be ruing the day that Dave had joined up with Lizzy Dawson. Dave laughed and added that there were cases where he knew what side he needed to be on. For the next few days Dave was like a possessed man, working on the file day and night. Reading papers while he ate and even spending the night on the office sofa more than a few days. Like an Olympic coach he spurred both Lizzy and Abel on to work harder and longer to make the case complete and solid before the trial might begin. Day after day they read materials and then round-tabled the value of what they could glean from them. Lizzy threw herself 100 percent into the effort, as did Abel, both of them dedicating themselves to seeing this thing not just through to the end but through to victory.

The news finally came one Tuesday morning that the grand jury had indicted Jack and a trial date was set. Lizzy went into the kitchen and retrieved a cold bottle of expensive champagne, popped the cork, and then poured each of them a glassful of the sparkling fluid. The glasses were her finest fluted crystal champagne glasses, nothing but the absolute best for this wonderful moment. A sense of fulfillment and accomplishment ran through Lizzy, and she could tell from the look on Abel's face that he too was absorbing the moment and cherishing the thrill of success. Dave on the other hand swigged down the champagne as he picked up yet another loose pile of papers to read and analyze. Lizzy found herself involuntarily rolling her eyes and thinking that Dave was beginning to get more than a bit annoying with his demands that they keep working on and on despite the need for just a little breather.

Dave asked Lizzy if she minded if he made copies of the content of every one of the cardboard filing boxes. He had copies of many of the papers which they contained, but he said that he needed to have copies of everything handy in case he was called upon to participate in the trial. Lizzy readily agreed and told him that she would help him cart the boxes over to the local Kinko Copy Shop to be reproduced. She looked over at Abel and found him looking a bit grim.

Later when Dave left the room to use the bathroom Lizzy confronted Abel about his sudden change in mood and demeanor. "Why the long face, Abel? You look as if we lost the grand jury hearing. I have never seen a man switch mood so quickly and drastically before. Have you got a little bipolar thing going here?" Abel told her that he did not suffer from bipolar disease, nor was he the kind of person who enjoyed the chase and then was crestfallen when the prize was won. No, there was something wrong here, and he could feel it but could not put his finger on it. It felt like an itch that could not be properly located to scratch.

Call it an old-fashioned police hunch, but he could sense that something was in play behind the scenes. He had felt a strange sensation in the back of his mind ever since Dave had told them about his top secret source which was sharing very sensitive inside information with him. He asked Lizzy not to allow Dave to copy all their hard work and carry it off to his own legal offices; that just did not sound kosher considering that they had all felt quite comfortable working together in the office all these months. Why the sudden need to have separate copies? There was something wrong here, and it was really getting under Abel's skin. Lizzy was beginning to think that Abel was suffering from a malady which she had seen in many detective films and read about in the same kind of novels. It was the tension and jealousy often felt between cops and lawyers. Cops tended not to trust lawyers totally and considered them the part of the law enforcement family that came from the wrong side of the tracks. She hoped that he would not allow these feelings to sour what had been a very amicable and productive working relationship between the three of them.

Abel had become a good friend, but Lizzy also knew that he still very much had a need to dominate and command the situation. She tried to prod Abel to either put a name and face on his suspicions or be willing to give them up for the sake of unity and accord in the group. Abel agreed to try and figure out why he felt the way he did and promised that if he could not identify his problem by next day he would drop the matter and continue to be a team player. That night Abel tossed and turned mulling over in his mind what the pieces in this situation were adding up to, the secret source who knew too much and now the sudden and unexpected need to have copies of all their work. He tossed and turned hour after hour, and just when he looked over at the clock and read that it was 3:36 a.m. he decided to give it up and admit defeat to Lizzy in the morning. He had just become more suspicious of everyone the older he got, that must be it. He rolled over and tried to get comfortable when he sprang up and said out loud, "A source who seemed to be inside the prosecutor's office. Yes! That's it! The source was Cotter himself! He has been working for the state all along! Well, at least he is still on our side."

The next morning Abel spilled his guts to Lizzy, and she began to see the clues which led Abel to that conclusion. Abel again asked that Lizzy not allow Cotter to copy all their files. She should let the prosecutor's office come to them and ask them for the assistance, not let it be hijacked by their erstwhile partner. Dave had been a late addition to their team, and both Lizzy and Abel knew that they could never have gotten the case as organized and fortified as they had without his help, but there had always been at least a little question about his motivation. Now it all made sense that Cotter was doing all this legal work not out of the goodness of his heart or some sense of commitment to justice that would have been quite new to him but because he was on the state payroll. Lizzy did not like the idea that she and Abel had been played for fools, but it made sense that the state had used a lot of the same evidence which she and Abel had gathered without ever having asked them for the material or their help.

Lizzy sighed one of her now-familiar sighs and turned to Abel with a weak smile saying, "Abel, I think you have hit the nail on the head, and we have been being played the fools, but consider this: it is all for the same cause, and we were never in this for our own credit or glory. I am going to let Dave have it all and just hope that the state puts it to good use." In all her life Lizzy Dawson had never made a more unwise choice or a bigger mistake than she had at that very moment.

The work was done and the indictment under their belts. Jack Randolph had been indicted by the grand jury on the charge of murder in the first degree. Even the prosecutors were surprised that the grand jury had indicted in the first degree since the evidence directly linking Jack to the act of murder was in their opinion shaky. They had hoped that the indictment would be for second-degree murder thereby allowing them to work toward proving that Jack had planned and paid for the killing but was not the physical murderer. There would be time for negotiating plea bargains and making deals in order to secure a conviction, so the state prosecutors hunkered down to their work. Lizzy, Abel, and Dave were a bit taken aback at the extent to which they were being excluded from the work of putting together the case for trial. Their evidence had been accumulated and taken by the state with many thanks, but their offer to assist and advise in the pending trial was politely and coolly refused. Lizzy wondered to herself if the prosecution did not consider her a detrimental witness after her meandering spiritual answer to questions posed to her in the grand jury hearing. Abel and Dave did not wonder about that question; they assumed that she had definitely spooked the prosecutor's office and made her participation in the trial a liability.

With the case being built by the state and their participation being generally declined Lizzy and Abel sat back and waited for the trial to begin. David Cotter thanked them for including him in their efforts and suddenly bid them farewell. They assumed that he was anxious to get back to his work for the prosecutor's office in Bridgeport. He had gathered what he needed to gather, and they had been as much use to him as they could be. They had enjoyed his company and greatly appreciated his hard work with the case. Their assumption was that despite defending criminals for a living he had made amends and decided to work on the side of law rather than on the criminal side of things. Maybe even in his own way he wanted to bring some justice to the Pierce case as some personal form of atonement for all the mobsters he had set free over the years. Having come to know and like him they wanted very much to find a reason to believe in him still and remember him fondly despite their suspicions that he had in some way betrayed them.

Just before the trial began the state prosecutor's office sent Lizzy and Abel court papers detailing the trial's participants including both legal teams. Lizzy glanced over the papers and put them aside still feeling stung by the aloof attitude of the state toward her participation in the upcoming trial. She thought that perhaps they might yet ask for her help beyond the testimony which she would be asked to make in court. It was Abel who took the paperwork home to Manhattan and tossed it on an end table to be read in the evening after a small gathering with friends being given to welcome him back home to the neighborhood. A few drinks and an excellent Spanish meal

318

gave Abel a warm and content feeling as he tossed off his shoes and propped himself up with a throw pillow to take a quick look over the pretrial paperwork. He read casually with half-closing eyes until he sprang up shouting, "That no good two-bit motherfucker!" He grabbed the phone and dialed Lizzy's number as he dropped the paperwork onto the floor. The page landed face up, exposing a list of advising attorneys for Jack Randolph. Halfway down that list was the name David Cotter, Esquire.

Chapter Nine

Rest in Peace

At last the day had come when a judge and jury would review the evidence and bring some justice to a very bad situation. It was a hot and muggy day as Lizzy climbed out of her car in the courthouse parking lot in Hartford. The air-conditioning had been on at full blast since she had pulled out of the driveway back in Greenwich, and the blast furnace effect of the weather hit her full force, making her stagger a bit as she left the car. It had been a quiet and pleasant drive across state to get here, and it had given her the chance to think over all the events which had led her to this point. She had been a far different person just under a year ago when she had first read about the Pierce case, a comfortable housewife and mother with the usual chores and concerns of a Greenwich citizen.

She had had her financial worries and her boredom with everyday life, but there had been no indication that life would bring her to this point, a place where she had become for all intents and purposes a detective, a journalist, and now an unofficial prosecutor. She knew the details of the case better than anyone who would be in Courtroom 7a of the Connecticut Criminal Court this morning. Because she sat above the case and oversaw the details of many different aspects she was aware of bits and pieces of evidence that blended together into a sprawling mosaic which none of the participants could see, while being parts of it. It was the old "not seeing the forest for the trees" logic in play. While all that she saw gave Lizzy a clear definition of what exactly had taken place, it also gave her a deep feeling of remorse being able to see death and self-destruction in so many lives. It was much like driving up on the scene of a grisly car accident which piques one's morbid curiosity at the same time evoking feelings of revulsion.

Lizzy's greatest hope was that bringing the situation to justice would bring closure to the living and restful peace to Bill Pierce. Her faith in God was deep rooted, and like many people it led her to believe in the need for departed souls to see the wrongs in their lives righted before they could truly rest in peace. She knew that no such idea was expressed in the Bible, and Father Redanz had told her many times that it was God and not circumstances which brought eternal peace. Yet deep inside Lizzy was certain that somewhere and somehow Bill needed closure as much as any of the living persons involved in the Case. It was her fondest wish that in a few weeks or perhaps months everyone concerned with Bill Pierce would be able to breathe a contented sigh of relief knowing that Bill's killer had been exposed and punished for his crimes. Reaching the huge bronze doors of the courthouse, Lizzy felt a wave of relief sweep over her. She and the Case had arrived at the final stage of events, and knowing what she did, there was no doubt in her mind that a sensible jury would find the evidence that Jack Randolph was guilty of murder and would send him off to the state prison for the rest of his life. She did not know the details of jurisprudence, but she knew that human intelligence could not possibly fail to see the guilt of such a blatant crime.

Her sense of justice and faith in human nature seemed to make Lizzy an ideal judge of events, justifying her predictions of a swift and thorough verdict in such an open-and-shut case. The ways of the legal system are often not as clear cut and evident as many people believe. A good attorney and a prosecution not convinced of the solidity of their case can greatly influence the path of a criminal case, not to mention the addition of some well-rehearsed dramatics in the defense's case. Lizzy, like many people, had already forgotten the "If the glove doesn't fit, you must acquit" defense masterfully used by Johnnie Cochran in the mid-1990s. Jack Randolph's legal team had not forgotten, and they had already devised some clever ploys which they hoped would greatly influence the jury into a favorable attitude toward their client. Lizzy was by no means a naïve woman; but she did possess a set of extremely high ideals which, at this moment, might be setting her up for a fall.

Everyone likes to think that there is an ideal by which all humanity rules itself and that that ideal within each human keeps our world in a balance of right always overcoming wrong. It was just this kind of philosophy which Lizzy brought with her into the courtroom, and it gave her a sense of triumph and satisfaction. Being more than an hour early for the opening of the trial Lizzy was able to secure a seat in the front row of the visitors' area directly behind the prosecutor's table. By the opening of the trial she was joined in that row by Pierce family members. She had saved the seat next to her for Tiffany, who had flown in from Wyoming two days ago and was now occupying one of the Dawsons' guest rooms. Tiffany had rented a car and decided to drive to Hartford on her own later in the morning. Bouts of morning sickness made any early morning activities very uncomfortable for her. She especially wanted to be in an undistracted state of mind for the trial proceedings. The schedule on the wall of the courthouse lobby stated that the trial of the *People v. J. R. Randolph* would commence in Courtroom 7a promptly at 10:00 a.m. It was now 10:37 a.m., and the judge had yet to arrive and open the trial.

Tiffany took her seat just as the bailiff intoned, "All rise, the Honorable Leonard Strauss, Superior Court of the State of Connecticut, presiding." It was an amazing thing that this case had even come to trial considering the fact that just a few months ago the death of William Pierce had been considered a dead issue by the district attorney of Fairfield County and nearly a year ago the coroner of Westchester County, New York, had initially declared that the death had been a suicide. It was the persistent work of Lizzy Dawson with help from her friends and associates which had persuaded a grand jury of the state of Connecticut to press charges against Jack. For all his influence and the calling in of many political favors, Jack could not make this matter go away. An equal effort had been made by the Finelli family to avoid the case from ever reaching trial status; but too many details had become public knowledge, through Lizzy's blog, for the district attorney to ignore the evidence. It was after all an election year, and there were many local voters reading Lizzy's blog with great anticipation to see where this would all lead.

As her eyes surveyed the assembled officials and spectators Lizzy could not help but notice that there seemed to be a clear divide among the people in the courtroom. The Randolph party and his "friends" were very clearly upper-class whites from the southern Connecticut shoreline. The Pierce family and friends were equally white, for the most part with a western flavor to their attire and even their accents. These two groups stood in stark contrast to the court officials and the jury. The judge was a prominent Jewish jurist with a record of supporting minority rights during his tenure on different levels of the Connecticut bench. The prosecutor was well-known as a rising star in local politics who came from a family of Italian masonry workers, who arrived on these shores only one generation ago. His assisting attorney was a young Hispanic woman who had for a time worked for Supreme Court Justice Santamayor during her time as a Connecticut federal judge. Lizzy hoped that the defense and the press would not paint the case as a harsh attempt by ordinary people to punish a rich WASP snob. Ignoring the truth of the matter, a case of a man who took another human life and needed to pay for that heinous act.

It was a certainty to Lizzy that Jack Randolph must have been very disapproving of the panel of jurors which sat for his trial. Jack had been disdainful of the common people of Greenwich during his single term as first selectman and chose not to run for reelection because he found governing the people a truly distasteful task. The members of the jury would never suit him as a gathering of his peers. The nine jurors and three alternates were composed of seven women and five men. All appeared to be from differing levels of the middle class, and their ethnic diversity was quite apparent. At least four of them were so diverse as to prevent anyone from accurately guessing what background they came from. These were the kind of people Jack might have referred to as "mutts" in the back rooms of one of his private clubs. Jack was definitely not a man of the people, but after all these years of snobbery and condescension he now found himself literally at the mercy of the very people he seemed to utterly despise. If nothing else were to come of this trial at the very least one might find some satisfaction at the comeuppance which had been dealt out in spades to this haughty denizen of mighty Greenwich.

Lizzy had no ax to grind toward Jack. She did regard him as an elitist, a sexist, and a racist; but those character flaws paled beside the fact that she knew him to be a cold-blooded murderer, who considered his social and financial well-being to be more valuable than someone's life. As she sat listening to the opening statements she considered herself nothing more than a concerned citizen and a spectator. There was no expectation of any role in either side of the case. She had presented all the evidence which she had gathered to the district attorney of Fairfield County nearly two months ago, and she had been interviewed and questioned by the DA and by the grand jury, so all there was for her to do now was to watch the trial run its course and update the blog each night to keep her loyal readers informed on the progress of the story. Those expectations were rudely shattered during the lunch recess of the trial that very first day when a court officer approached her to hand her a subpoena which stated that she would be required to testify at some future point in the trial. The real shocker for Lizzy was that the defense would be calling her as one of their witnesses.

The trial recessed for the day at 4:00 p.m., and Lizzy phoned Joe to inform him that she would be required to testify at some point in the hearing. She had decided to rent a room at the local Biltmore Residence Inn and asked him to drive up with several days' worth of clothing and personal items. Joe agreed to make the trip, which he did not mind; but he made it clear that he was not happy at the turn of events which would require her to spend several weeks, at the least, away from home. The boys were on summer vacation. He had hoped that they could all spend some quality time together after what had been a trying string of months in which Lizzy's attention had been shared with the ongoing investigations of the Case. He had been relieved when the threats and tensions eased after the initial indictment. No indicted person was stupid enough to threaten, let alone harm, a grand jury witness in this day and age. Joe knew that the real danger had passed and allowed his expectations to focus on a return to the "normal" life routines of the Dawson family at the pre-case levels. Now those hopes were dashed. He hoped that this too would pass, that normalcy was simply delayed and not vanquished forever.

Joe loved Lizzy. He was genuinely happy that she had found a fulfilling purpose for her life that had in so many ways improved their lives. He knew full well that some of the contacts which Lizzy made through her detective work had prospered their real estate ventures, making valuable business friends as well. He also rued the fact that he had lost a part of his domestic life which he had held dear. Being a bit of a sexist Joe had always taken pride in the fact that his wife had never had to work out of necessity. Now, although her work was unpaid and certainly not out of need, she placed an emphasis on her work which seemed to rival her role as his wife and the mother of his children. In some odd way he felt a jealousy of Lizzy's activities in much the same way another man would be jealous of a lover.

The prospect of having Lizzy living out of a hotel some seventy-odd miles away did not make Joe happy, but he did realize that the Case was an integral part of all their lives by this time. It needed to run its course before any of them could feel a sense of closure. Joe had never felt any sense of the need for Bill to acquire justice in order to rest in peace. He believed simply in the need for wrongs to be corrected and wrongdoers to pay a price for their misdeeds. He had an intellectual need to see this trial through and firm up his faith in our justice system. He, like Lizzy, believed in the justice system. Unlike his wife Joe had some doubts about the hard-and-fast rule that "good always triumphs in the end." He remembered too well the election of 2000 and how questionable the vote tallies from Florida were, but the political games were less upsetting to him than the mishandling of the court cases which followed the vote counting. If the Supreme Court could sanction the stealing of a presidential election, how could he ever fully believe in an impartial and impeccably honest justice system again? Maybe this case would heal part of that wound and restore some of his confidence.

The boys were disappointed that their mom would be in Hartford for what might be the entire summer. They knew she'd be home on weekends and they would drive up to see her every so often, but it would not be the same. For one thing, on a practical and everyday level they would be cooking, cleaning, and doing laundry, something they had not been expecting to do this summer. Dad would probably end up doing the lion's share of the domestic duties, but his cooking did not compare to Mom's. His idea of an ironed shirt was one that drip-dried on a hanger in the laundry room. Boys going out on dates are more concerned about pressed and starched clothing than most people would imagine. Troy and Scott were not completely mercenary. They would also miss their personal time with Lizzy. She was a ready shoulder to cry on and a fount of good advice when the boys found themselves in questionable situations. How many times had she given them expert and reasonable advice on their romantic lives? Too many times to count and certainly more times than either son cared to admit. The male trio in the Dawson house might not say it very openly or too often, but they all regarded Lizzy as the glue that kept them solidly together.

While Joe felt a peculiar jealousy of the case, the boys felt a more personal jealousy of the departed Bill Pierce. Bill was about the same age as their mother, but they saw him as occupying a place in her life which they felt should be reserved for them. Lizzy had taken a motherly interest in the Pierce murder and often spoke about Bill as a concerned mother might speak of her child who had come to a bad end. In their minds Bill had gotten a share of their mother's love and attention which a stranger was not entitled to in any way, shape, or form. In reality, Joe and the boys were overlooking the fact that any wife or mother working a full-time job had to devote part of her attention to her work without taking anything other than time away from her family. Lizzy had never lessened her love for any of them, but she had lessened her role as servant and washwoman. A father devoted to his job would be regarded as a person who expressed his love for his family by excelling as the breadwinner. A woman who pursued an interest of her own, commercial or otherwise, could easily be branded as a distant wife and mother. The attitudes in the Dawson household had not gotten that far, but this latest episode in Lizzy's devotion to the Case took them a step farther in that direction.

Lizzy's decision to stay in Hartford was a practical one. If she was going to be forced to play a role in the trial, then she had better remain there and be available to do her part. The sooner the arguments and statements were made, the sooner justice could be done, and she would be free of the whole matter. She looked forward to being home without a slate of daily appointments and phone calls. This entire matter had been great fun and exciting, but it had also taken a toll on Lizzy. She felt tired and listless which was not at all like her normal physical state. She had done so very much all on her own with increasing help along the way, but the bulk of the investigation had been squarely on her shoulders. When Joe had expressed his displeasure over her decision to stay in a hotel in Hartford, she had simply agreed with him and asked him to be understanding. She had been too physically and emotionally exhausted to engage in even a minor spat. She really could not comprehend how someone so close to her could not see that she too was worn thin by this experience. She was loath to spend so much more time away from her beloved family and the house she regarded as her haven and refuge.

She smiled to herself when she pondered why any person would want to engage themselves in any activity which tore them from their families. She wondered how a family man like President Obama dealt with the days and weeks of separation from his wife and daughters, whom he obviously loved so dearly. Lizzy had always admired Obama's devotion to his family, feeling that part of the burden of the presidency under which he labored was the sacrifice of family time he must make every day in the White House. She also understood that such a sacrifice could only be made if one had a cause in their heart which compelled them to see their task to the finish line.

A country did not depend on her, but a matter of justice did, and for her to see justice win the day was a vital goal in her life. She loved what she had been doing, and she cherished the accomplishments which were even now developing into the culmination of justice. It would all soon be over, and a little more sacrifice was worth the conclusion.

The second day of the trial seemed to have been a total waste of time for judge, jury, and spectators as the assembled teams of lawyers postured and argued over technicalities and procedures, much to the chagrin of the court and the boredom of the jury and gallery. One positive note for Lizzy was when the chief defense attorney stopped her in the hall outside the courtroom and informed her that he would likely call her as a witness on Thursday, two days hence. Lizzy decided to make a peace offering to her husband and children by taking off that afternoon, driving home to Greenwich and returning to Hartford on Thursday morning. For the next day and one half she would concentrate her attention on her family, forgetting the twists and turns which the trial promised to hold in the next few days. She felt confident that whatever the defense panel had in store for her would be easily deflected and that the preponderance of the evidence would overwhelm whatever tricks they might have up their sleeves for the immediate future.

Knowing that she would be tempted to delve into her blog and files of evidence during her time at home, she decided to leave her primary laptop in the hotel room, as well as taking her cardboard file boxes of material out of the car trunk, putting them into the closet of the room. She also approached Tiffany who had been driving each day to and from Greenwich, offering the use of the hotel room for two nights. Tiffany readily agreed to the arrangement.

She suggested that she too might rent a room and stay in Hartford until the conclusion of the trial. The snail's pace progress of the trial was beginning to wear very heavily on Tiffany's emotions. The long drives each day gave her too much downtime to rehash the day's events over and over again in her mind. Being a young woman and having had months to grieve over Bill, she also considered that a little nightlife in Hartford after each day's court session might ease her boredom and her frustration. She knew that it was apparent that she was pregnant. Enjoying some night life and the company of young men did not necessarily mean that she was going to have sex with anyone. She needed some release. Failure to blow off some steam soon would lead her to an emotional breakdown. Why not let her hair down and start to enjoy life again? Staying at the Dawsons had been a very good situation, but it was beginning to feel a little too much like home. It was not all that long ago that she had moved to Wyoming to get away from a homey atmosphere.

Lizzy's day and one half back home flew by much too quickly. The drive Thursday morning back to Hartford was a rough one. She had enjoyed the release time, but now she was beginning to feel the pressure of being called as a witness for the defense. They knew that she had gathered the bulk of evidence being used at the trial, so their intention must be either to discredit her or at the very least bring her role and motives in the investigation into question. During the day's proceedings Lizzy was puzzled at the tack which the defense was taking, wondering why they were failing to call her to the witness stand. By the middle of the afternoon session her nerves began to get rattled. Throughout the day she had been idly noting the objections being made by each side and the rulings handed down on each objection. By three in the afternoon she did a tally and was shaken to see that the majority of objections had been made by the prosecution, and nearly every one of them had been overruled by the judge. On the other hand the few offered by the defense had been unanimously sustained. Not being a lawyer herself, Lizzy wondered if this was a matter of bias or whether this bode ill for the case which the state had constructed against Jack Randolph.

Judges and even juries could be bought, but this judge had an impeccable reputation. Something seemed to be going wrong here, and although she could not identify what it was, she sensed that the prosecution was feeling it too. As witnesses had taken the stand the line of questioning from the defense team seemed to be leading the trial in a very odd direction. It almost seemed that they were building a case against Jack Randolph, not as a murderer but as a despicable, cruel, and bigoted elitist who deserved no mercy on any level. Even defense witnesses were asked what seemed like leading and irrelevant questions which were designed to make Jack seem like a modern-day monster. The prosecution cross-examinations merrily continued to heap scorn upon Jack as a poor excuse for a human being. Slowly but surely the defense was taking a two-pronged road in their argument. One was the foul nature of their client. At the same time they were attacking the credibility of the evidence against him, questioning the admissible status of each item of evidence.

No one seemed to understand the direction in which the defense was headed as that Thursday session drew to a close and Lizzy failed to be called as a witness. Everyone was surprised and dismayed when the judge adjourned the trial, announcing that the next session would not be until the following Tuesday. It was explained that Judge

Strauss had a long standing date set for an engagement at Stanford University Law School on the following Monday and needed to deal with some alumni business there over the weekend. The trial would have to wait. Lizzy's tension was accelerated as she wracked her brain to understand the defense's line of argument and how she could possibly fit into it. Now she found herself facing at least four more days in which she would stew in the limbo of uncertainty. She could sense a trap set in the offing, and she did not like waiting for it to be sprung. Where in the hell were they going with this two-pronged strategy? Anyone could see the attack on the credibility of the evidence, but why would they be casting their own client in such a horrible light? The attacks on the evidence were going along fairly well, but the character assassination was a smear campaign run amok. Feeling much like Alice stuck in an insane wonderland, Lizzy headed home for a long weekend. She prayed that she would be able to distract herself from the Case and enjoy another few days with her family.

Tiffany decided to stay in Hartford and rented a room at the downtown Hyatt instead of the Biltmore Residence Inn. She felt a distinct homelike quality in the Biltmore, and that was something she wished to avoid. No one could ever be sure if Tiffany was conscious of one fact about the Hartford Hyatt when she decided to check in there on that Thursday evening. It was the hotel in which the Randolph trial jury was sequestered for the duration of the trial. She would be living in the same hotel as the members of the jury which would be deciding the fate of a man suspected of killing her lover. Were this known it would cause quite a stir and could be cause for the declaration of a mistrial. Assuming that she did not know what the circumstance were, because she would never answer the question in the future, one could only guess that a combination of naiveté and youthful lust led her to spend that weekend in the way in which she did. During dinner at the hotel restaurant that Thursday evening she noticed a handsome tall young man sitting at the bar. She sent over a drink and an invitation to join her at her table. The man could not have been any older than twenty-two and was olive-skinned with light green eyes reminiscent of Alex Rodriguez of the New York Yankees, the kind of man that almost any woman would be attracted to.

His name was Caleb; and he was in fact twenty-two years old, born in Bridgeport, Connecticut, to an Ecuadorian father and a Costa Rican mother. Tiffany and Caleb hit it off immediately. To Tiffany's delight, he was a perfect gentleman with an accent that would have fit into any country club in Greenwich. He was a student at Yale having just finished an undergraduate degree at Columbia in January, entering graduate studies just two weeks after his graduation. He must have been quite a prospect for Yale to allow him to begin studies midyear, thought Tiffany. He also did not hesitate to come to the point as he asked her, "I can see that you are having a baby. So what does your husband think of you picking up men in hotels?" Tiffany liked his honesty and answered him equally bluntly, "The baby's father is not my husband, and at the moment I really don't care what he might think." There's no need to beat around the bush as Tiffany raised her martini to her lips with one hand, reaching into Caleb's lap with the other. What she found was a growing penis of considerable length and impressive girth. Her hand contributed to the growth that Caleb was experiencing, a fact that both of them relished there in the crowded but dimly lit corner of the restaurant. The evening was young, the dinner was growing cold, and the situation was gaining a sexual momentum which promised much more to come for the night and, perhaps, the remainder of the weekend.

The decision was made to retire to Tiffany's suite since hers was one of the larger rooms, provided with a sitting room which might offer more exciting areas for lovemaking than a simple bed. Caleb stood before the fully dressed Tiffany as she sat on the divan. He slowly removed his jacket and shirt to reveal a firm and hairless chest of a deep and creamy tan color, nipples of medium brown small and standing erect and hard as marble. His firm stomach showed the indentations of a fledgling six-pack with a tiny dusting of hair from his navel down into the yet-covered recess of his trousers. Tiffany remembered hearing such a growth of hair being referred to as a "treasure trail." As she considered where that line of hair was leading, she now fully understood the term and ached to acquire the treasure at the end of that hairy trail. When the moment came and Caleb released his now-unzipped pants she nearly gasped. With no underwear to hide his manhood Caleb revealed a luscious tan line outlining an expanse of lighter tan radiating from a nearly hairless crotch, from which rose a penis of at least nine inches standing at attention and pointing to the sky. What Tiffany felt within herself was far too exciting and sexual to be anything short of pure lust, so she rode the feeling and lay back to enjoy the ride.

As Caleb strode toward her Tiffany grabbed his arms and directed his body over her, bringing his midsection to her face. They would have all night to enjoy each other's bodies, but right now she desperately need to feel every inch of his penis in her mouth. She would not be denied that desire for a second longer. The moans streaming from Caleb's mouth were music to Tiffany's ears. Bill had been a wonderful lover, but as much as he gave her pleasure he never seemed able to show her that she was also bringing him to levels of sexual pleasure as well. Caleb was now quietly moaning out words of passion in both English and Spanish which excited Tiffany even more as she took inch after inch of his manhood into her mouth and throat applying as much suction as her lungs would allow. Caleb knew his limits of endurance and reluctantly withdrew himself from Tiffany's mouth, replacing his member with his lips. He passionately and deeply kissed her freshly fucked mouth. He kissed down her face to her neck and then to her breasts still covered by the flimsy silk blouse that she had worn that day.

To his surprise he suddenly felt her hands gently push him away from her body and saw that a concerned look had appeared across her beautiful face. "Have I done something wrong?" he asked plaintively. Tiffany struggled to tell him that he had done nothing wrong. She hesitated because she wondered how he felt about making love with a woman several months into a pregnancy. She was at that stage of pregnancy at which she was feeling ugly and bloated, while in reality she hardly showed evidence of her condition. Her face was as alluring and radiant as usual. Caleb assured her that had he had any reservation about such sexual activity he would not have allowed the situation to go any farther than their drinks in the restaurant. He sheepishly admitted that the prospect of making love to a pregnant woman was a kinky fantasy which he had entertained since seeing a pregnant woman in a porn magazine in his early teens. He hoped that this admission on his part did not repulse her and make her think badly of him. She laughed as she assured him that the present situation kind of pegged them both as kinky individuals. No judgments good or bad need be made and that they were now wasting time which could be better spent attending to each other's sexual organs. He readily agreed as he dove face-first into her lap.

Caleb had to admit around midnight that he was having the time of his life, but there were intricacies which he had not conceived of in making love to a pregnant woman. He did not let the odd positions prevent him from having a good time, but he wondered how his back and knees would feel come the morning. Tiffany agreed that their lovemaking was more inventive than any she had ever experienced before. This was her first sexual encounter since becoming obviously pregnant. Parts of her body were not as nimble and agile as they had been prior to her current state. She also commented that they were fortunate that Caleb's penis was so long since at certain angles excess length made penetration more feasible and pleasurable. Tiffany certainly enjoyed every inch of Caleb's manhood as he rode her from the side and from behind and she rode him as she sat atop his lankly frame.

Their lovemaking continued into the wee hours of the night. She was taken back a bit when he announced that he should be getting back to his room before the morning. Her face told him exactly what she was thinking. He preempted her questions by telling her that he had had a wonderful time with her. He had not used her for a one-night stand and a quick goodbye but that he would be expected back in his room in the morning when the bailiff and foreman did a morning head count prior to breakfast. She gave a small smile at his explanation and felt grateful that he was not simply running out on her after using her for sex. As Caleb tucked in his shirt and zipped his trousers the reality of what he had just told her sank in.

"Are you telling me that you are sequestered here at the Hyatt while you serve on a jury?" she asked.

"Well, yeah, I thought you were in the same circumstance and wondered how you had managed to get such a posh room," was his answer.

"Oh my god, please tell me that you are not on the Randolph trial," she pleaded with him.

With his face paling about three shades all he could say was "Jesus Christ, I thought you looked familiar. You are one of the people sitting just behind the prosecution desk, aren't you?"

"Are you a friend of one of the victim's family members or what?" Caleb blurted out.

"No, I am the victim's girlfriend. Please tell me that you are just an alternate juror, or else we may have just fucked up this case royally," responded Tiffany.

Both sat down on the divan and took a long deep breath as they began to devise a plan to keep this situation under wraps and the case from disintegrating into accusations of jury tampering. They decided that they must each forget what had just happened and relegate it to nonexistence in order to prevent the legal repercussions which could result from it. Tiffany knew that she could face charges if anyone informed the court of her seemingly convenient relocation to the Hyatt and accidental coupling with a member of the jury. This was a situation which she felt that she could not even share with Lizzy. It had to be buried. Caleb assured her that everything would be all right if they remained totally silent about this night, avoiding even eye contact in the courtroom. Unfortunately they must agree never to contact each other again. It was a seemingly perfect plan, one which could not have failed except for the fact that other jurors and the jury foreman had also dined in the same establishment that night. Their recognition of Tiffany Gould was more acute than that of Caleb. Their perfect plan was crumbling even before it had been devised. While they were enjoying each other's bodies on the twelfth floor of the Hartford Hyatt there were tongues wagging down on the fifth floor in several of the juror's rooms.

It seems that while several jurors had seen Caleb and Tiffany together one particularly inquisitive middle-aged man had been sitting at an angle which allowed him to see the discreet fondling which had gone on just prior to their departure to Tiffany's suite. Being a truly inquisitive character this particular juror followed them to the suite and took note of the room number before heading to the reception desk to inquire as to the name of the room's occupant. Suspicions and facts in hand he then called on the jury foreman to share his information. The two decided that they would not act immediately on the information. Each was rather enjoying the stay at the Hyatt and time away from their mundane professional lives. Why throw a monkey wrench into a good thing? They could milk this for a few more days of hotel living. Mr. Edward Janowski liked his room and the hotel food to begin with, and having the state pay for it made the deal even sweeter. Being a union electrician paid pretty well, but having an all-expense paid mini-vacation suited him just fine. The longer it lasted the better he liked it.

At age forty-seven Janowski also did not mind being away from Sylvia, his wife. After twenty-six years of marriage and three children raised and off on their own, his mind began to wander to thoughts of bedding down a fine young woman in her prime. It occurred to him that a beautiful young woman who had something to hide might be very grateful to someone who would keep her dirty little secret. Failing her gratitude, he could always make a case for sex in exchange for silence. The prospect of fucking a pregnant young woman did not totally appeal to him, but the young part of the equation definitely outweighed the less attractive aspects of her condition. He thought to himself that at forty-seven he still had a thirty-eight-inch waist and a muscular frame. Maybe his offer would appeal to her without too much pressure. He would approach her over the weekend and subtly try to bring up her indiscretion with young Caleb, and perhaps with a bit of finesse he could achieve his goal with something less-than-legal persuasion. He would try and corner Tiffany in the hotel restaurant on Saturday evening, starting with pleasant conversation before broaching the subject of sexual favors past and, perhaps, sexual favors in the future.

When one concocts a dubious plan they often manage to overlook some of the obvious flaws in it. Usually the enthusiasm they feel for the ultimate goal clouds their judgment, or they are seduced by what they regard as the sheer simplicity of it all. Major details can be ignored to the doom of the entire enterprise. Ed Janowski felt sure that he could charm and threaten his way into Tiffany's bed for at least one night of exciting forbidden sex. He seemed to forget that the scenario which he mapped out contained elements which had trapped Caleb and Tiffany in the first place. They, however, had acted innocently without realizing what role each was playing in the larger picture. Ed was a juror well aware of Tiffany's identity. He would be approaching her in public in the same venue that Caleb had. Furthermore he himself had tipped off the foreman to the situation. It was almost as if he had designed a plan meant to fail and to entrap him in a web of legal problems, not to mention the prospect of being accused of an attempted blackmail.

When Saturday evening arrived Tiffany was nowhere to be found. She had decided to have a quiet dinner at a nearby bistro called the Vault, a café and microbrewery located in a former bank building in the middle of downtown Hartford. She needed something quiet to allow herself to vegetate a bit and fortify herself with a few pints of quality beer. She sat on the balcony looking out the large windows at the lights of Hartford trying to forget at least for a few hours all the details of the past few months. The thought struck her that she should start her life over in a place like this, a city and yet a relatively small one where no one knew her and where her history could begin again with the past erased, for all intents and purposes. That thought appealed to her. Hartford itself seemed like a fair prospect until her eyes wandered over to some framed shots of local sites on the balcony wall, one of which was the bank façade covered in snow during a blizzard back in the 1930s. No, Hartford was not the place for her. Southern California might be a better choice.

Sunday found Tiffany in a much better mood sitting by the brightly lit windows of the Hyatt restaurant enjoying a delightful brunch. At the brunch buffet someone gently bumped into her and said hello adding that he loved buffets but found them less enjoyable while eating alone. Seeing no harm in it Tiffany invited him to join her at her table in the atrium. The gentleman introduced himself as Edward Janowski, a local tradesman taking a little in-town vacation. The two chatted for a few minutes about the beautiful weather, the good brunch offerings, and the quality of the service there at the Hyatt. Ed asked her how she liked her room and began to inquire about the quality of her mattress when the waiter stopped at their table and delivered two mimosas courtesy of a gentleman at the bar. Ed looked over in the direction of the bar to see the jury foreman smiling and lifting his glass in a mock toast to the two of them. Ed excused himself telling Tiffany that their benefactor was an old business associate he needed to greet and thank for his generosity. Ed left his food and strode over to the foreman. By the time Tiffany noticed that Ed was not coming back she could no longer see him or his friend at the bar. By mid afternoon she had totally forgotten ever having met him. That is, until she spotted him in the jury box the following Tuesday.

The four-day "weekend" seemed like weeks to Lizzy. She was enjoying her time with the family, but she was also constantly fighting with her mind trying not to drift off to thoughts of the Case and now also thoughts about the trial. More and more she felt sure that the defense team was building an elaborate trap into which they were leading the prosecution. Somehow she knew that she was the bait with which they were luring them. A night out on Saturday included a movie at the cineplex in Port Chester and dinner at the Copacabana Steak House down the street from the cinema. The presence of her husband and kids helped keep her mind off the trial. The three Brazilian cocktails did not hurt her state of mind either. Sunday was peaceful, and after church she invited Father Redanz over for an early afternoon barbeque in the backyard. Church matters and a little gossip were discussed, but everyone kept away from the subject of the Pierce case. Although nothing had been formally said everyone could see the stress beginning to take its toll on Lizzy. She looked a bit tired, but what was most notable was her seeming inability to remain on one subject for very long. It was as if her mind was struggling to return to a subject lying heavily upon.

The long weekend came and went. Before she really thought about it, she was once again sitting in the spectators seating directly behind the prosecution table, Tiffany sitting by her side. About ten minutes into the proceedings Lizzy felt the vibration of her cell phone going off in the pocket of her slacks. Silently signaling Tiffany that she needed to leave the courtroom, Lizzy slipped out the side aisle and went into the hallway to check her phone. The number was unidentified but did reveal it was from a New York cell phone. Answering the call she was more than a bit surprised to hear Bernice's voice greeting her.

After a quick hello Bernice cut to the chase, "Liz, I am on Interstate 91 just outside Hartford. I will be at the courthouse within twenty minutes. Meet me in the hall outside the hearing room."

Lizzy was stunned to realize that her old friend and NYPD chief was about to join her at the Hartford Courthouse.

Before she could ask any questions, Bernice cut her off, "I didn't have a chance to catch you before now, but I got subpoenaed on Friday to appear this morning in the Randolph case. I have no idea what the hell they want to talk to me about, but I guess we will soon find out."

Lizzy managed to eke out a quick three-word question, "Prosecution or defense?" Bernice grunted, "Defense," as she announced that she was pulling into the courthouse garage and would be seeing Lizzy in a matter of minutes.

Lizzy grabbed a nearby bench and cooled her heels waiting to see Bernice's tall and muscular form push open the hallway doors and join her. She did not have to wait long before Bernice was indeed walking through the doorway, but she was not alone. Lizzy assumed that she had dragged Mort along with her as company on the long ride from the city. Within seconds she realized to her shock that the accompanying figure with Bernice was not Mort but was Abel Ramirez, their mutual friend and retired NYPD detective.

All pleasantries were omitted as Lizzy greeted the two of them with "Just what the hell is going on here?"

Bernice explained that Abel too had been called upon to testify for the defense, and each was requested for that morning. The information which they received stated that they would be called to the witness stand sometime after 11:00 a.m. It was now ten thirty-five, so the mystery would soon be revealed.

Bernice, in her usual blunt way, told Lizzy, "You are the common denominator, Abel and I have no connection to this case except through you, so when they question us there should be at least some indication how they plan to tie you into all this."

Lizzy had to agree with that logic. She realized that it would not be long before the battle lines were drawn. Suddenly she felt the need to visit the ladies' room. Her nerves were now giving her that queasy feeling and were affecting her bladder. She used to have that same feeling as a girl when she was called in to speak to the school headmaster. Even when she knew that she had done nothing wrong, her mind still conjured up dire situations to agonize her. She had done nothing wrong here, and she knew that. In fact she compared herself to Dominic Dunne who instigated the Moxley/Skakle trial a number of years back. He had done the investigation but sat aloof from the proceedings, allowing his hired investigator, Mark Fuhrman, to take the questions and the heat. Why was she being dragged into the trial and, apparently, causing others to be involved as well? She apologized to Bernice and Abel for getting them involved, but they assured her that this was old hat for both of them.

It did not take long for the defense team to start the ball rolling as they called Bernice Kass to the stand. After swearing Bernice in the bailiff stepped away. The smiling face of the chief defense attorney appeared next to Bernice.

"Chief Kass, please state your name and your occupation for the court." Bernice gave her personal details for the assembled parties and waited for the real questioning to begin.

Defense Attorney William Crowley continued to smile as he asked, "Would you mind telling the court what your involvement is in this matter?"

Bernice gave a small smile of her own as she replied, "Actually that was a question which I was about to ask you, since I am a New York City police official with no jurisdiction in either Westchester County, New York, or Fairfield County, Connecticut."

The polite smile left Crowley's face as he returned her loaded question with one of his own. "Speaking of questions which need to be asked, I might venture to ask you why an NYPD chief had any dealings in a case well outside her jurisdiction and at a time when she was an active officer of the city police force?" *Touché*, thought Bernice as a tough grimace now came across her face.

Before she could reply to the comment Crowley continued, "While the defense would agree that you played a small role in this entire matter we contend that you actually did become involved at the request and to the assistance of one Elizabeth Dawson who was conducting her own investigation into the death of William Pierce. Is that not a correct contention on our part, Chief Kass?"

Bernice looked over at Lizzy and gave her a weak grin as she answered yes to the question. The entire line of questioning which followed lasted for just less than fifteen minutes and revolved entirely around what sort of assistance Bernice had provided to Lizzy over the past few months. She admitted that she had run a license plate number for her and that the plate was from the state of Connecticut, actions which would have caused her to be formally reprimanded by the NYPD were she still an active member of the force. None of the information which Bernice gave was particularly damning to anyone. It basically added up to a profile of Lizzy as a private citizen doing some junior detective work on a case which the authorities seemed to be neglecting. There was no crime in that, although most police departments frown on the practice. The worst thing that could be said was that Lizzy was a snoop and a police buff. There are millions of such people across the country.

One final question set the stage for the next phase of the defense tack.

"Chief Kass, at some point within the last four or so months, did you place Elizabeth Dawson in contact with a retired NYPD detective named Abel Ramirez?"

Bernice politely answered yes and was surprised to hear Crowley say, "The defense has no further questions at this time."

Instead of a cross-examination, the prosecutor raised an objection that this entire line of questioning was totally irrelevant to the case and asked that the exchange between Bernice and the defense be stricken from the record. The defense countered that this was just the first portion of a line of evidence which would become more apparent as the trial progressed. Once again a motion by the prosecution was overruled by Judge Strauss. He explained that if this was an argument being constructed from various angles, the defense had every right to proceed. If in the future it did not develop into something tangible, he reserved the right to strike it from the record when he saw fit.

After a short breather in which the judge called both legal teams to the bench for some private instructions, the trial continued with the statement "The defense calls Detective Abel Ramirez to the stand."

Once again the line of questioning took the witness through a series of relationships, most especially his working relationship with Lizzy, and his contacts with and questioning of various participants in the Pierce case. Much was made of his several conversations with Suzette and members of the Finelli family. Bernice had gotten off easy compared to Abel. By the time the defense ended their questions he had been on the stand for over two hours and the court's lunch break was well overdue. Judge Strauss adjourned the trial for a ninety-minute lunch break and asked that all participants return to the courtroom promptly as he expected an equally long cross-examination that afternoon.

Lunch was a miserable affair for Lizzy. She, Bernice, Abel, and Tiffany walked across the street to a quiet café called the Bench for a slow and relaxing lunch; but there was no part of Lizzy's mind which could be calmed or relaxed at the moment. She could now see that the defense was going to question her motivation and integrity regarding all the evidence which she had collected. Just before leaving for lunch the chief prosecutor had pulled her aside and informed her that the defense was planning to present a slide show in the coming days, a slide show of screen shots of her blog over an extended period of time. It was assumed that their plan was to call into question the relevance and accuracy of the materials which she had presented online to try to paint her activities as a vendetta against Jack Randolph, a vendetta which attempted to smear him socially, financially, and then finally criminally. The tack of their argument was becoming more apparent, and Lizzy began to have doubts about how she would look to the world when this was all over. The only thing that she still felt totally confident in was that the outcome would put Jack away for the murder of Bill Pierce.

When the trial reconvened Abel was cross-examined and began to delve into the many financial motivations which prompted Jack Randolph to eradicate anything which could expose his crumbling empire. At the first mention of the pending investigation by the Securities and Exchange Commission, a furious shout of "I object" was heard from the defense table.

"Your Honor, this supposed pending investigation by the SEC is at best nothing but hearsay and at worst a disreputable rumor. No such investigation has been identified by the SEC offices in New York City, nor has any confirmation of such an investigation been confirmed by the SEC headquarters in Washington. I would like to submit statements by the SEC refusing to confirm any activity on their behalf regarding my client. And I further object to the inclusion of this witness's statements on the grounds that, even if an investigation were under way, these matters are irrelevant to the case before us today."

Strauss thought for a moment and seemingly reluctant nodded yes as he intoned, "Objection sustained. Strike any reference to the SEC from the record. I would instruct the jury to ignore said reference and exclude it from their consideration of this case."

Lizzy's heart sank as she realized that the prime motive which she and Abel had identified, Jack killing Bill because he and Suzette threatened to turn over evidence to the SEC about the Randolph Fund, had just been permanently and finally tossed out of the trial. The bottom had just dropped out of their case. The only way it could be recovered was if Suzette would testify that she and Bill had made such a threat to Jack. Lizzy knew that such an admission would bring the house down on the heads of not only Jack but the Finelli family and Suzette herself. Were the Finellis implicated in this murder by Suzette she was sure that her life would be cut short regardless of her relationship with Matthew Finelli. When Suzette had refused to testify in the trial on either side, everyone realized that hard evidence would be hard to come by. The three people who knew the exact details of the situation were Bill, who was dead; Jack, who was the accused; and Suzette, who remained silent. For the first time Lizzy faced the fact that this might be one case in which justice would be thwarted, but she still held out hope even as its prospects dwindled before her eyes.

The lineup of witnesses which followed in the coming days included almost everyone Lizzy had ever talked to about the case. Even Ethan Rivers took the stand and confirmed that he felt that Lizzy had a predetermined verdict in her mind as she went about her investigation and asked questions which he felt were less than objective. He did redeem himself by relating the threat he had received when he began to look into the Pierce case and the cryptic comment which Jack had made to him shortly after the threatening telephone call.

Although his final comment was stricken from the court record after a defense objection, he said, "On a personal level I have no doubt that Lizzy was pursuing the right object, and I believe Jack Randolph had William Pierce murdered for any number of personal and professional reasons."

In spite of the objection which they made to that statement the defense team seemed to take it quite calmly. Even Jack himself appeared totally unaffected by such an inflammatory contention. As Ethan exited the witness stand Lizzy once again shuffled out of the courtroom toward the restroom. Her bladder and stomach were both feeling the effects of her jangled nerves.

Another week had come and gone. The parade of witnesses seemed to be overwhelmingly on the defense side of the trial. With each testimony the case against Jack Randolph seemed to lose more credibility although the picture of him as a person became more dark and sinister. People testified about his racism, his sexism, and his elitist disdain for people in general. Lizzy was surprised how utterly thorough the defense team had been in dredging up witness from the remote past. One of her furniture suppliers was called to the stand and testified that Lizzy had made numerous comments about Jack Randolph while decorating his house several years ago, comments about his racism and indications that she had selected a "Southern plantation" decor for his house as a subtle indictment of his racial attitudes.

Lizzy's friendship with Emily Engelby was brought up and related to Emily's continued legal situation with the Town of Greenwich over her racist expulsion from the beach at Todd's Point by the Randolph administration. Another friend who had a run-in with the Randolph administration was Greenwich Police officer Reggie Hayes, who had repeatedly been passed over for a promotion despite having scored a perfect grade on the sergeant's test. Officer Hayes being a Caribbean-American seemed to be his only failing in the eyes of the first selectman. The case was being powerfully made that Lizzy had consistently been on the side of many opposition causes to Jack Randolph's ruling philosophy during his four years at the helm of Greenwich government. At no point in the questioning was there any denial that Jack was in fact the bigoted and biased dictator which people regarded him as being. Not once did the defense argument make any effort to deny or excuse Jack's actions, attitude, or temperament.

Lizzy among others wondered why the defense continued their efforts to defame their client until one witness asked a question of the chief defense attorney. Police Officer Hayes was being asked about his relationship with Lizzy Dawson, how she had aided and assisted him in his legal case against the Town of Greenwich and First Selectman Randolph.

As the attorney basically agreed that Jack was quite capable of denying a man a promotion because of the color of his skin, Hayes blurted out, "If you full well know that he is a horrible human being, why in God's name are you defending the bastard?"

Crowley calmly stepped back and faced the jury as he very deliberately said, "Because a man is a seething racist, a rabid sexist, and an elitist beyond compare *does not*, I repeat, does not make him guilty of murder no matter how hard self-righteous individual may try and portray him as such."

The cat was out of the bag as the crowd reacted to the statement with a mixture of catcalls and applause. Judge Strauss sustained the objection of the prosecution as he banged his gavel to restore order in the courtroom. He would have liked to admonish Crowley for his dramatics, but he had to admit to himself that there was some validity to the point being made.

Leonard Strauss had never for a minute doubted that Jack Randolph was guilty of the murder of William Pierce, but he had always questioned whether there was ever enough hard evidence to indict, let alone convict him of the crime. At this moment he was torn. As a lawyer he concluded that the evidence was flimsy to begin with, and now there was ample reason to question its relevance due to the taint of what appeared to be a personal crusade on the part of at least one person with the help of a host of people with grudges against this despicable man. Were this a trial by judge, Strauss would entertain a motion for dismissal on the grounds of inadequate evidence because so much had now been relegated to circumstantial and hearsay status. Even if the guilt of a man were obvious to all present, it was the duty of the legal system to prove his guilt beyond a shadow of a doubt. The chances of anything in this case being beyond such a doubt were now gone Strauss simply longed to put this sad case out of its misery.

The day finally arrived, and Elizabeth Dawson raised her right hand and swore to tell the whole truth so help her God. The defense team was quite courteous to Lizzy. Their tone was gentle as they asked her questions about her involvement in past actions such as the Todd's Point case in which she had testified as a friend of the court on behalf of Emily Engelby and her support for Officer Hayes in making donations to his legal fees as well as holding several fund-raisers at her home for him. Then they began the slide show of screen shots of her blog, asking her about specific comments she had made over the course of the past few months. They asked what motivated her to become involved in the Pierce case. They asked why she had become so emotionally attached to the case that she had traveled to Wyoming and befriended Tiffany Gould, even housing Ms. Gould at her Greenwich home as well as sharing her rented room in Hartford at the Biltmore Residence Inn.

Lizzy answered all their questions honestly and thoroughly, sharing her contention that some sort of divine guidance had led her to certain avenues of investigation and surprise pieces of evidence. As she spoke she realized how insane some of this must sound to the purely secular ears of those assembled in that courtroom. She was a woman of faith and at that moment was feeling her belief system crashing down around her, but then she remembered something Father Redanz had said to her early on in her investigation: "Elizabeth, please remember that justice is always and finally in God's hands, put not your trust in princes . . ." Those words were being borne out by what was happening at that moment. The justice of human courts was failing to bring a cold-blooded murderer to justice. This was not the last word, and there would be another kind of justice later, a greater and more profound justice. Lizzy stopped herself from assuming the role of divine judge and calmly reconciled herself to the fact that it was not up to her to sit in judgment of even Jack Randolph. It was time to give up and let go. She had done her best to bring eternal peace to Bill Pierce, but she finally realized that bringing eternal peace to anyone was just not her job.

A peace flowed over Lizzy, and she quietly and honestly answered all the questions posed by the attorneys. Her stomach was settled and her bladder resting easy. When the prosecution passed on the cross-examination she knew that the trial was over. The judge asked the attorneys to present closing arguments and midmorning on the following day instructed the jury to retire to the jury room and begin deliberations on all that they had seen and heard. All present expected that the jury would be back in a very short time to deliver a verdict. That was not to be the case as the day passed, and so did two others without a verdict from the jury. The mood of the prosecutors seemed to lift a bit, and the faces of the defense team no longer seemed as steadily confident as they had up until now. Everyone wondered what could be happening

353

in the jury room. Why was there no consensus after what almost seemed like a surrender by the prosecution on the last day of the hearings?

Just before 4:00 p.m. on the third day of deliberations the bailiff intoned, "All rise. The Honorable Leonard Strauss presiding."

The judge instructed all present to be seated and asked the bailiff to escort the jury into the courtroom. When all had been assembled and seated an obviously angry Judge Strauss began.

"I have called you all into session to tell you that I have been informed of and investigated a serious charge of fraternization between persons involved in this case and members of the jury. I have found the charges to be substantiated and just cause for a ruling on these proceedings to be deemed a mistrial. I further instruct the court officers to detain the individuals whose names are contained in this document for further questioning regarding this matter. I also would add this judicial advisement to the office of the district attorney. I would find it unreasonable and unwarranted for your office to pursue this case any further, judging by the presentation I have witnessed these past weeks. The jury is hereby dismissed and this court stands adjourned. On behalf of myself and the state of Connecticut, I thank you all for your participation in this matter. Good day."

Lizzy slumped back in her chair with a deep sigh and reached out to comfort Tiffany just as a court officer politely asked her to accompany him into the judge's chambers for questioning. Lizzy's eyes widened as Tiffany left the courtroom with the uniformed officer. She had no idea what was going on, but she knew that at this point Tiffany was clearly on her own. The members of the district attorney's office filed out of the courtroom avoiding eye contact with Lizzy. She felt sure that they were blaming her for the disintegration of their case. She felt not the least bit of guilt concerning them or the failure of the case. They were the legal professionals who should have been able to tell if they had a reasonable chance of success with the evidence that they had gathered from her and other sources. She imagined that the blame game would begin as soon as the press began their coverage with the evening telecasts and late editions of the newspapers. It was just another sacrifice that Lizzy would have to make. Within a few days this would be all old news and life would return to normal. Lizzy now had to decide what to do about the blog. Would it be worth continuing it while concentrating on less controversial topics? One way or another, the whole experience of the past few months had been exciting and even fun. She could chalk it all up to a life-enriching experience.

As she strode serenely toward the glass doors of the courthouse façade she caught sight of literally hundreds of new reporters and people carrying placards. This too would be a momentary trial on the road to normalcy. She could endure the reporters and even the scorn of the public with a polite smile and some friendly words. She had meant no harm and would tell them just that. As she pushed open the door and stepped out of the building, she was shocked to be greeted by shouts of "It's her" followed by volleys of cheers. The reporters pushed hard against the police cordon keeping the crowds at bay. Each reporter shouted questions about how she felt after standing up to a complacent justice system and making such a poignant statement about justice being for sale to those who could afford it. Somehow Lizzy had become a hero to the average everyday citizen who felt that people like Jack Randolph could buy themselves out of justice. She tried to stop long enough to answer everyone's questions and greet all the people shouting to her from the sidewalk, but the police escort ushered her away from the crowds and into the courthouse garage where a police car was waiting to take her to her hotel.

She called Joe on the way to the Biltmore and could hear a crowd in her house cheering for her as the television in the background could be heard referring to her as Greenwich's own Joan of Arc. Joe told her that friends and neighbors had been coming over as soon as a news bulletin on channel 61 announced the verdict in the trial. He said it seemed to Joe that perhaps lost causes were more romantic to the average person than whirlwind victories, and judging by the neighborhood reaction they had heartily embraced Lizzy's efforts despite the failure to put Jack Randolph behind bars. It struck Lizzy that Jack's only vilification of himself had only contributed to her rising status. She had been the little person to stand up to the mighty ogre. Just the fact that she was still standing looked very much like a great triumph for virtue over power and money. Either way, or for whatever reason it was happening, Lizzy appreciated the adulation and the affirmation being expressed for what she had tried to do. She knew that somewhere Bill Pierce was resting in peace.

She and Joe decided that she should spend one more night in Hartford to rest up a bit and collect her thoughts before she returned to the tumultuous greetings she would find at home in Greenwich. As she entered the lobby of the Biltmore she was handed a fistful of messages divided into two piles. One pile contained messages from individuals wishing her well. The other contained offers from major news programs to be interviewed on television and radio programs over the next few days.

There were messages from *Good Morning America*, the *Today Show*, and every other New York and Connecticut news broadcast. There was even an invitation from Oprah Winfrey to fly to Chicago for an appearance on her show dealing with the empowerment of women in fields dominated by men.

What just hours ago Lizzy had accepted as a humbling defeat was turning out to be a new beginning, a chance to make a mark in the world for the cause of justice as an end in and of itself. Where this would all lead was anyone's guess, but she knew that she had made a statement about the value of a human life over and against the power of money and prestige. Just as she reached for the phone to order some food to be delivered, the motel operator told her that she had a call from Washington and she hoped that Lizzy was sitting down.

Another female voice told her, "Ms. Dawson, the president would like to speak to you for a moment."

In the next three minutes President Barack Obama told Lizzy that he was proud of her and that her actions helped all of us level the playing field for all Americans in the pursuit of justice.

He thanked her and added one bit of news before disconnecting, "Ms. Dawson, later this month the Securities and Exchange Commission will publicly announce that it has launched a full investigation into the practices and condition of the Randolph Fund. Please keep that between us until the formal announcement. Again, thank you and God bless you. Goodbye."

Lizzy called Joe and informed him of all that was happening. She was delighted to hear that he was in the car about a half hour outside Hartford and simply wanted to be with her in this magnificent moment in her life. Tiffany had arrived at the house and encouraged him to go and be with her, a suggestion which really had not needed to be made. Tomorrow Lizzy would belong to the world again, but for tonight they would simply belong to each other.

Chapter Ten

A Happy Ending for Some

The end of the trial had been a grave disappointment to Lizzy and everyone else involved in it. For a killer to be acquitted by a jury on the basis that the evidence left a reasonable doubt was anticlimactic, but in a small way it reassured Lizzy that the justice system was indeed a fair one. That knowledge did not lessen the sting of defeat one iota for Bill's friends and loved ones who had made Connecticut their temporary home during the weeks of the trial. They were all back home by now or were preparing to leave. Tiffany, who had occupied one of Lizzy's guest rooms, had left quietly while the family was out. They had all gone out for dinner to get their minds off the defeat, and when they arrived home, Tiffany and all her belongings were gone. All that was left was a short thank-you note for all the Dawsons had done for her. Lizzy was concerned that in Tiffany's state of advanced pregnancy she must have found it difficult to maneuver her bags into a taxi and handle all the travel that was ahead of her. *What was done was done,* Lizzy thought to herself and jotted down a note to call Tiffany in a day or so, just to see how she was doing.

It had been some time since Lizzy had devoted any time to the family real estate business, having allowed Joe to handle any deals that were pending. Her heart sank when Joe told her that the deal on the spec house over on Mountainview had fallen through. It seemed that the trust fund couple had every intention of purchasing the house at the agreed price but had presented Joe with a check drawn on a Madoff Fund account. The clueless couple had no idea whatsoever that the fund had collapsed and burned months ago. Apparently their minor expenses were paid through a much more modest trust fund which was still solvent, but the bulk of their money was gone. Joe broke the news to them gently: no house and no more large expenses, plus there might even be the requirement of a job or two in their future. Lizzy felt badly for the couple, but she felt even worse for herself and Joe. They had counted on this deal to set them on an even financial keel for the foreseeable future. Now that security was gone. They still had the house, but without a buyer it would drain even more of their assets.

Joe gave Ethan Rivers a quick call and asked him to list the property once again. Ethan had some good news which would cheer both Lizzy and Joe. A client had shown interest in the Mountainview house sometime ago and was disappointed to learn that it had been sold. That same client asked Ethan to keep an eye on the property and inform him if it returned to the market. There might not be any reason to list it, if the mystery client decided to make them an offer. Later that afternoon Ethan called and told Lizzy that a solid offer had been made for the property. This offer met their asking price which was $500,000 more than the deal which had been struck with the trust fund babies. Fortune seemed to be smiling on the Dawsons once again. Maybe this was a sign for Lizzy to stick to real estate instead of criminology. She thought not, but at the very least she could mix the two more evenly in the future.

The mystery buyer turned out to be none other than Lizzy's new old friend, Sanford Wainwright. Sandy had decided that he needed an additional house for a set of cousins who had had a reversal of fortunes and needed a boost financially to help them recover from major losses on the market. When he saw that the Mountainview property was up for sale and the sellers were Elizabeth and Joseph Dawson he decided to make an offer only to learn that someone else had agreed to purchase before him. Determined not to allow the chance at the house to slip away a second time he paid Ethan Rivers to keep watch on the deal and hoped that with some luck he might have another shot at it. When Rivers called him with the good news, he decided to meet the asking price. What was a few hundred thousand dollars among friends? Sandy was happy. The Dawsons let out a sigh of utter relief. In less than twenty-four hours they had gone from disappointment to elation with a deal that met all their monetary need plus more.

A few miles away at the Randolph estate the mood was far from happy. Jack had been acquitted on all charges by a jury of his peers, but the entire trail had brought his life and his finances under the microscope of public and governmental scrutiny. The results being the prospect of a future trial on criminal charges of fraud and embezzlement. With a good bit of help from Suzette the Feds had built an ironclad case against Jack, so ironclad that a grand jury indicted him after a one-day hearing and less than thirty minutes of deliberation. The vote had been unanimous to indict. Evidently Suzette had known and retained a lot more information than Jack had ever suspected. He ruefully wished that he had hired the Finellis to dispose of her as well as Bill Pierce. For his entire life Jack had underestimated women and their intellectual abilities. His worst injustice had been paid to his wife. Jack had written Suzette off as a mindless nymphomaniac who amounted to nothing more than one of his toys. She had always been a formidable woman—intelligent, cunning, and, when necessary, deceitful, not all that different from the man she married.

Jack sat and stewed in a morose and foul mood, teetering back and forth between regret and explosive anger. There was no self-pity in the man. It had been said in the past that pity of any kind was utterly foreign to Jack Randolph, and even in this sorry state of affairs Jack pondered missteps and faulty assumptions rather than bemoaning fate or luck. Through a series of mistakes, compounded by more follow-up mistakes, Jack had brought down his own empire. He had lost millions and destroyed any chance he might have had to rebuild after the Randolph Fund had come tumbling down. This murder nonsense had been so out of character for him, and now it was the foundation on which his enemies were building a case for his destruction. Never in any of his musings did Jack even once consider that his basic philosophy of life had contributed in his demise. The way he lived his life and interacted with others had doomed him to one day find himself in such a situation eventually. Although those circumstances would have been different, ruin was inevitable.

It was one thing for a man to face up to his misjudgments and quite another thing for him to take a stark and honest look at himself, admitting that what he had done was simply a natural result of what he was as a person. William Shakespeare places these words in Cassius's mouth, "The fault, dear Brutus, is not in our stars, but in ourselves . . . ," in the play *Julius Caesar*. A man like Jack would not seek fault in either the stars or himself, the fault was simply in making the wrong decision at the wrong time. Jack found no intrinsic problem with financial fraud or even murder, but his response to the circumstances which surrounded them was the problem. If only he had done this or that, all might still be well. Perhaps handling things differently, or even handling them in the same manner, but with a different time sequence the whole matter could have been avoided. One might judge Jack a callous and evil human being, but one could never accuse him of cowardice in facing the truth as he saw it. He would not blame an outside force acting upon him, such as fate. Nor would he blame some flaw of character over which he had no control. Instead he blamed himself and the decisions he had made with his sound and cunning mind. He had been wrong, and now he faced that fact unflinchingly.

Once again, Jack sat at his desk: the drawer open, the gun out, the safety undone, and the barrel resting on his right temple. He hesitated a moment to take a last mental inventory of exactly how bad the situation really was. He decided it was as bad as it could get. His funds had been confiscated by the federal government, including the offshore accounts which Suzette had known about. His family fortune was sure to be devoured by all the lawsuits from people he had bilked of their savings and investments. The alternative to a hot piece of lead to the brain was a life of poverty, even worse, a working-class existence, living and toiling with the people he detested the most, the middle class. His final thoughts were a dichotomy of love and hate. He cursed Suzette and wished her the worst that life could bring her. Then a fond thought of Evan and a hope that wherever he was, he was well and had found happiness. The single shot echoed through the lifeless rooms of the estate. Jackie Lewis found the body, falling to her knees and rocking back and forth quietly, sobbing out the words, "Mr. Jack. Poor Mr. Jack," over and over again. At least one person would mourn for the death of Jack Randolph.

Suzette Randolph, in an attempt to distance herself from the whole scandal, legally changed her name, returning to her maiden name of Benoit. She had proven to be a formidable opponent to her strong-willed husband, but her cunning intellect failed her miserably in the end. There is an old saying which states, "The devil is in the details." Suzette had overlooked one enormous detail. When she betrayed Jack's financial secrets she never considered that not only his ill-gotten gain would be confiscated, but her half of his money was equally tainted and had to be returned as well. The Feds had given Ruth Madoff a much sweeter deal, allowing her to keep 2.5 million dollars of her husband's money while stripping him of every cent. The SEC had felt that Mrs. Madoff had been at least somewhat unaware of the Ponzi scheme which her husband was working. It was obvious to the government that the information which Suzette had turned over to them showed that she was well-acquainted with every detail of the Randolph scam and was, therefore, as culpable as Jack himself. Their favor to Suzette was to give her immunity to prosecution, a favor for she was not particularly grateful when they took away her wealth. Serving a sentence, while knowing that millions waited for you at your release, would have been a much more tolerable situation for the fallen socialite.

Times were getting rather difficult for Suzette. Although she was always a survivor, she did not like the prospect of being devoid of the comfort and privilege which she so much enjoyed. Had she not jilted Bill Pierce over the Tiffany affair, she might have been the mistress of the Brandywine Ranch living in style and luxury out west. Then too, the chain of events which brought her to ruin would also have been altered. Bill would be alive, she would still have half of Jack's money, and Jack would live in constant fear of her wrath should he deny her anything in the future. The last part about threatening ruining Jack's life sounded the best to her as she thought over the lost opportunities. Her hope that Bill had left her something in his will was dashed when it was learned that he left the bulk of his estate, including the ranch, to his two brothers with generous endowments to close friends and relatives. Suzette cringed when she learned that Tiffany Gould had received a legacy of one million dollars. Bill had left Suzette nothing.

Having lived well and without any occupation other than grand dame did not read well on a resume. Suzette was having great difficulty finding a way to make a living. She might have ended up selling her body were it not for Matthew Finelli, who came to her rescue by arranging to hire her as the hostess at a very elegant restaurant, called Fiorello's, which was owned by one of his father's associates. It was not the same as living the carefree life of a Greenwich socialite, but the pay was adequate, and the place was crawling with handsome young waiters, which pleased Suzette greatly. She and Matthew were becoming a serious item, and some claimed that there was talk of an engagement in the offing. Suzette, in her forties and still beautiful, had no complaints at the prospect of landing the tall, lean, and handsome Finelli boy. He was slightly more than half her age and had been a devoted lover throughout the trials of the past few months. His background as the son of a leader of an organized crime family did not bother her in the least. Although she sometimes considered that this relationship may have contributed to the harsh treatment she had received from the federal government.

The government probably did not appreciate that she had gone from one corrupt and murderous husband to a potentially equally corrupt and murderous prospective husband. Contrary to the scenarios painted by television and the movies, sons of mobsters are not usually desperately trying to find a way out of organized crime. Matthew was not an emotionally torn young man trying to renounce the mob. Instead, he was an up-and-coming "made man," who was obediently and patiently awaiting the day when he would become the head of the Finelli family. Suzette sometimes wondered if Matthew had been part of the murder of Bill Pierce, but she drove that question out of her mind as quickly as possible. It was a thought which could complicate her current situation, and she did not care to have that happen. Matthew was taking care of her, and she did not want that to end, nor did she want to damage the magnificent sex she enjoyed with him. The thought of Matthew killing Bill would certainly be a huge turn off should it arise during sex, and for Suzette that would have been intolerable.

One prospect of being seriously involved with any mobbed-up man had not occurred to Suzette until a very unhappy incident took place at Fiorello's one night. A nineteen-year-old busboy named Nicky had shown undue attention to the lovely hostess. During a break period the two were found in the storeroom engaged in a fast and furious quickie. Before the evening had ended the news had traveled throughout the restaurant staff to the judgmental "tsks" of the female staff and the drooling delight of the male staffers. News travels quickly in a small setting; and eventually snickers and rumors were noticed by people in management, one of whom was Gennaro Finelli, one of Matthew's uncles who was partial owner of Fiorello's. No one likes to see a relative played for a fool, and that is especially true in a proud Italian family, so word was passed on to Matthew and his father.

By pure coincidence that night Nicky had been mugged on the way home when he had stopped for a soda at a local gas station. Such a crime was rare in Greenwich, but what made this situation even odder was the brutality with which Nicky had been robbed. The news report said that he had four cracked ribs, a pierced lung, and a fractured jaw. What had not been reported was the fact that he had been savagely and repeatedly kicked in the groin so hard that both his testicles had been ruptured beyond surgical repair. Equally odd was the fact that Nicky claimed to have no memory of the attack whatsoever when he had recovered enough to be interviewed by the police. The locals blamed the incidents on stray street toughs from Port Chester.

Life for Suzette was becoming that of a bird in a gilded cage. With Jack she had been free to mount any steed that happened to make himself available, with Jack pretending not to have noticed. With the Finellis everything was noticed, noted, and reported. It seemed as if she had found luxury once again, but at the price of serving a sentence of social and sexual confinement which she found more constraining than brick walls and iron bars. She knew that she loved Matthew, but she also knew that she loved other men, possibly her definition of "love" was not the normal one accepted by most people.

She also knew that she was not a person cut out for a life with restrictions like these. It would only be a matter of time until she had to escape this situation. The problem outside her own dissatisfaction was the question of how many young male bodies would lie broken and crushed on the pathway to her decision to leave. Nicky would simply be only the first.

In her darker moods Suzette compared herself to Adrianna, the character from *The Sopranos*, who deeply loved her Mafia boyfriend but also was entrapped by the FBI. She sometimes watched the episode where Adrianna packs a bag and drives away from the drama of her relationship with the mob. Suzette always turned off the DVD before the scene in which one of the mobsters puts a bullet into Adrianna's skull. That was a very possible reality which she did not even want to consider. She did need to accept two facts. The first fact was that given the choice between her and his business, Matthew would always select business (organized crime.) The second was that there might come a day when Matthew tired of her serial cheating and decided that it was time for her to be disposed of once and for all. She knew she had painted herself into a very deadly corner. Being a realist, she chose to take it as it came, at least for the time being.

The Feds had been generous with Suzy and JR; they each had a trust fund set up which took care of their tuition and other school expenses, as well as providing them with a stipend for living expenses. The money for the trust funds came out of Jack's assets, a tidy sum which had been seized but which was not the result of his illegal investments. Suzy had been admitted to Wake Forest, and JR entered his second year of studies at NYU. Both were happy to have the trial and scandal behind

them. Neither child missed Jack very much, although
Suzy had initially taken his death quite hard.

Suzy was now seeing a handsome fellow student who
was in the premed program at Wake Forest. They were
happy together, and as time passed their relationship grew
more serious. Stephen Chin was a gentle and caring young
man, so unlike Suzy's father. The prospects of a solid and
loving marriage appeared to be in the offing. Suzy followed
the example of her mother and had her name changed to
Benoit to distance herself from the whole sordid affair.
She found peace in her studies and her relationship. Her
grades were excellent, pointing to the prospect of success
in her chosen field of microbiology. She had actually met
Stephen in one of her classes, and the similarity of their
fields might lead to a joint career with him. Life looked
promising for her, and she was determined to keep it that
way. A good relationship with her mother was not yet a
reality, but that too was in her future plans. She would
rebuild her life, and she wanted her mother to be a part
of it.

Unlike her mother, Suzy was a chaste and modest
girl. During her four years at secondary school she had
dated several boys which had indicated to her mother that
Suzy was playing the field and enjoying the boys just as
a bee flits from flower to flower. The reality which eluded
Suzette was that her daughter was engaged in quite the
opposite. She would date a boy and try to build a loving
relationship with him only to break it off if he became
sexually aggressive or seemed obsessed with sex. Suzy
was saving herself for Mr. Right. She did not require that
her first sexual encounter be with her future husband
by any means, but she would give herself to a man with
whom she felt she had a loving and serious relationship.
She had no intention of giving herself to every pretty face,

muscular body, or large penis, but rather to a man who could be her friend and consider her an equal. The exact opposite of what her father and mother had in their years of unhappy marriage. She would not make the same mistakes which her parents had made.

Suzy's life was just beginning to recover from the horrors of the past year; she had a good relationship with JR and encouraged him to seek his own happiness with whomever he found suitable. Suzy had known about JR's homosexuality since they were children and felt comfortable with it. She had never been taught to judge other people's preferences, a lesson Jack had neglected to instill in her. Suzy hoped that one day in the future there would be holiday gatherings at which she and a man destined to be her husband and the father of her children would get to know JR and his lover. For all the wealth that Suzy had known during her short life, there had always been an emptiness in her life, a void which she now knew was the tight-knit relationship of family. Someday she knew she would reconcile with her mother. JR would always be her friend as well as her brother. There was something more she needed, something which she would build as the years progressed, something that she could only describe as "family."

Between Jack's two children he was missed less by JR. A life of being browbeaten and ignored had taken its toll on any positive emotional feelings JR might have ever had for Jack. JR had never hated his father. He disliked the way he was treated by him at times, but Jack had been civil to the boy, rather like a bank manager treats a lower-level client. There was never open animosity expressed from father to son, with the exception of the locker room incident. There had always, however, been that gap between them. The distance was made up of things which JR could not change, and Jack was too entrenched to accept. JR was a good son, but he simply could not fit into the mold which Jack expected from a son of his. Having a son who was contemplative rather than active was probably Jack's biggest disappointment with JR. It was one which drove them apart as each year passed. Jack expected JR to grow out of the traits which he held in contempt. When JR did not, the disdain grew. While Suzette was feeling the gilded cage surround her, her son was feeling like a bird set free to soar for the first time, and he appreciated the freedom as he stretched his wings and flew to the clouds.

JR had moved into campus housing at NYU and met someone. His name was Josh; and he, like JR, shared a love for the arts. Josh was a junior who lived off campus and worked at a nearby café, the same café where JR often sipped a latte and studied after class. A friendship developed and turned into a romance. At the end of the current semester they planned to move in together. They had no plans for the future but agreed to just enjoy life together and let things evolve between them. Everyone who knew them was sure that they would be together for the rest of their lives. JR had not changed his name but now referred to himself as Jon, his little way of distancing himself from the past. He had pushed the memory of his cold and sometimes cruel father out of his mind. He had also decided to distance himself from Suzette. She had been part of his old life, and now Jon had a new life, one with no room for Suzette.

Lizzy had taken some time off from all things related to the Case and was throwing herself back into family life. Scott and Troy were a handful as usual, and their increasing social life had warranted a family meeting to discuss condoms and safe sex; it had been an awkward discussion. Joe felt very ill at ease with it, but it had been a topic long overdue. With gritted teeth he and Lizzy had done their parental duty. Life was slowing down for the Dawson family, and Lizzy had to admit that the return to normalcy felt pretty good to her. Although the sale of the spec house to Sandy Wainwright had put the family on a solid financial base, she still wondered what would become of the large investments which they had made in the Randolph Fund. She asked Joe to sit down with her and finally review all their finances. Money coming in from one source did not mean that all they had built previously no longer mattered. She was ready to hear the bad news and begin planning for the future with whatever was left.

The worst of life was over. The death threats and the harassing phone calls were a thing of the past, and compared to those incidents some financial bad news would be a lot easier to take. Lizzy and Joe decided to sit out by the pond and talk over their fortunes. It was a warm sunny day, and the afternoon rays of the sun glittered off their matching laptops as they prepared to talk business. Joe could not understand the anxiety which was apparent on Lizzy's face every time finances came into the picture, so he was glad to have the opportunity to clear the air and find out what had been troubling his beloved wife so much in the past few months.

Lizzy came right to the point, "Joe, I know that we have been very fortunate with our realty deals lately, but I am not ready just to write off all the money we have lost in our investments. I know we must have taken a beating with the money we had tied up with Randolph. Please just tell me the truth. How bad is it?"

Joe's response stunned Lizzy as he laughingly tossed his laptop on the grass and came over to her and planted a huge kiss on her forehead.

"Baby, I love you, but you really need to start taking some herbal supplement to help you with your memory." He chuckled. His response had not put his wife's mind at ease judging from the furrowed brow which she was now displaying, so he continued, "Over two years ago when you were redecorating the Randolph house we agreed that we did not want our money managed by that creep, and together, you and I, liquidated our investments with the Randolph Fund. Does that ring a bell? And we divided up our money between the Vanguard Fund, Edward Jones, and Merrill Lynch, remember? Then you got so involved in the spec houses and your interior design work that you asked me to handle those investments. We took a beating in the downturn last year, but we have recouped 90 percent of our losses. Our money is doing fine."

Lizzy took a moment to recall the details of the situation, and as a single tear of happiness rolled down her cheek, it all came back to her. Her revulsion at Jack Randolph's comments and attitude toward minorities and women had enraged her so much that she had asked Joe to rearrange their investments. Her secret worry, tucked back in the recesses of her brain, had all been for nothing. Her own instincts had safeguarded their finances and had left them better off than they had ever been in their lives. Despite everyone's logical explanations for her good fortune in the Case and in her life, she knew that the universe or whatever you might call it had placed a watchful and protective hand on her shoulder. Some might call it the universe, fate, luck, or providence. Lizzy called it God, and at that moment in silence she said a heartfelt "Thank you!" to him.

Lizzy had plenty of loose ends to deal with, but at least now her finances were off the table. She decided that she should get around to giving Tiffany a call very soon. Her due date was somewhere during this week. Finding a few free minutes Lizzy plopped into her desk chair and dialed up the Brandywine Ranch to check on Tiffany. The receptionist told her that Tiffany was unavailable, which did not surprise Lizzy since it was likely that she was at the hospital either giving birth to Bill's child or recovering from the birth. She asked the receptionist if Tiffany was in the local hospital and was surprised to get the response, "I couldn't say, she is simply unavailable." Not to be deterred by an upstart receptionist Lizzy asked to speak to Nurse Regan. She was sure Judy would know what was going on. Judy warmly greeted Lizzy's call and explained that while Tiffany had been in Greenwich, she had made arrangements with movers to pack and relocate her belongings. She had also e-mailed a resignation to the acting general manager and a short goodbye to almost all the ranch's employees. Her note gave no details of her relocation or even a hint at the reason for her decision. No one at the ranch knew anything about her whereabouts, or at least no one was discussing the matter at all.

Judy reassured Lizzy that the note had been a pleasant one and seemed to indicate that Tiffany had made peace with her life but just needed to move on. There was a level of relief in Lizzy's mind as she hung with Nurse Regan, but she wondered why Tiffany had not contacted her with the same message. Lizzy would have to be contented with the short thank-you note which she had left when she departed from the house and Greenwich. She assumed that Tiffany would be a mystery, but as long as she was happy, it did not need to be solved. She could reappear by making a phone call or even with a comment on Lizzy's now-famous blog; either way it was up to her. Lizzy stopped and thought for a moment that she and the family could use another vacation. This time she would like Disney World or perhaps the Bahamas. Brandywine Ranch was far away from her plans. It was something not to forget, but it should be allowed to fade into memory where its more pleasant aspects would be best remembered. So much of the last few months needed to be sanitized by time; it had been an adventure, one she could never forget, but real life was upon her once again, and she would relish the mundane aspects of everyday life as she had never done before.

But how mundane could Lizzy's life ever be after her experiences with being an online detective? Early one morning before the breakfast dishes had been washed the phone rang, and Lizzy was happy to hear the voice of her friend Bernice on the other end. Caller ID showed that she was calling from the office of the chief of detectives at One Police Plaza in Manhattan. *A little cheeky of Bernice to be using her boss's line to make a private call,* thought Lizzy, but wherever she was calling from Lizzy was glad to have the chance to thank for hooking her up with retired detective sergeant Ramirez.

Before they began their conversation Bernice announced, "Lizzy, old girl, you are speaking to the newly appointed chief of detectives!" That came as very pleasant surprise to Lizzy. She knew Bernice was a top-notch cop and administrator, but she had no idea that such a dramatic promotion was in the works for her. It seemed an outgoing mayor rewarded his most loyal officials. As the top moves up, so do the underlings. Bernice was an underling no more. She had reached the corner office and was beginning to envision life after retirement, a retirement from the top tier.

Bernice had seen this promotion in the works for several weeks now and decided that she would keep this position until the new mayoral administration requested her resignation, as is customary when a new mayor takes office. That date was a few months away, and she doubted that the new mayor would keep her around. He was a different party than she and had promised to clean house in every city agency once sworn in. That did not bother Bernice. She was ready to retire, but now it would be at a super chief's salary, and that sounded very good to her. Being a city cop Bernice had acquired the common police attitude that no matter how high the salary or the pension, it would never be enough. She had spoken to Ramirez about his retirement and the consulting job he had taken for considerable compensation. The two had kicked around ideas, and a bright idea had hit them simultaneously. Their scheme was the reason for the call to Lizzy. It was a good thing that she had taken a seat when the idea was broached.

Bernice and Abel Ramirez had decided that there was excellent money in opening a detective agency. They had even agreed that Abel would scout out an office and retired cops to serve as their associate investigators. It was Ramirez who first mentioned that Lizzy's name was now almost a household name thanks to the Randolph case. Why not bring her into the deal and even name the enterprise the Dawson Agency to capitalize on all the media attention? Bernice jumped on the idea and agreed to contact Lizzy with the offer. Lizzy would be an equal partner with Bernice and Abel, but she would provide the star power, not that a retired police chief was anything to sneeze at. The retired cops would do the muscle work on each case. Eventually they would get Lizzy licensed, and they could rely on her to work the Internet as a tool of investigations. Two old cops who barely knew how to read their e-mails could use a savvy Web person to track down clues. They knew Lizzy had a natural talent for flushing out information from sources which most cops would consider dead ends.

Lizzy was floored by the offer and promised that she would not only consider it but would discuss with Joe and then the boys. As an equal partner she knew that money would come flowing in. Her part would never evolve into anything physically dangerous. The thought delighted her, but she wondered aloud to Bernice if she might be a "one-hit wonder." Maybe the Pierce case was all she had to give. Luck and persistence had played a good share in bringing the case together. Could she rely on luck on a case-by-case basis? Bernice laughed loudly and said, "Honey, 75 percent of the cases we solve in any given year get solved by a lot of hard work and a whole hell of a lot of luck. Maybe you are a cop and don't even know it. You got nothing to lose, kiddo, but we all have a lot to gain. Think it over and get back to me. No rush. Just think it all over." Joe would be an interesting sounding board on this, and so would the boys. First Lizzy had to decide if she herself was really interested in making this part of her life.

Things had been blowing into Lizzy's life like a hurricane lately, but she had to admit that this one took the cake. Elizabeth Dawson, interior designer, could now begin a new career as a detective. The prospect boggled her mind, but she noticed that the longer she thought about it, the more she liked the idea of it. Lizzy put the matter out of her mind long enough to start the grill and prepare for a nice barbeque. As she prepared the sauce and unpacked the ribs and chicken she stopped a moment to consider where her life was headed. Very soon she would no longer have the role as Mommy: Scott was about to start college in the fall, and Troy would follow a year later. The birds were leaving the nest, and their absence would leave a gap in her life. It would be a bittersweet gap, knowing that her boys were becoming men and starting to build their own lives, but she would miss the daily love and care she gave them as boys. Maybe this new career was something which she had secretly hoped for when she first picked up on the Bill Pierce story.

When dinner was ready, both boys devoured their food and asked to be excused to meet with dates at the library. With the boys out Lizzy found the perfect opportunity to tell Joe about Bernice's stunning offer. Joe snapped his fingers as he remembered to tell Lizzy about a call for her last evening.

He quickly reported, "Last night a guy named Phillip Galinowski called for you. He said he was from Caudwell Publishing in Cleveland. Something about your blog and the Pierce story. I wrote it down, but I lost the note."

Lizzy had no idea who this man was or what he wanted from her, but that had to wait as she blurted out Bernice's conversation with her earlier in the day. Joe looked like he had been doused with ice-cold Gatorade as she finished her recap of the conversation.

His reaction came as a pleasant surprised "Holy Moses, Lizzy! You could be a partner in a multimillion-dollar agency! Those agencies usually develop into security firms as well as investigative services. You could be making hundreds of thousands of dollars on each assignment. I hope you are seriously considering the offer."

Lizzy smiled as Joe added that his expectations were for her to remain safely in the office while the associates worked the streets. Joe always thought of her first, and she knew that he would utterly reject the idea if he thought she would be in the slightest bit of danger. Over dessert they agreed that this was the opportunity of a lifetime and that Lizzy would take the offer. Even if it ended up that she was detective in name only, she would still become wealthier than she had imagined from the profits of using her name to lure in clients. Now it was a matter of talking the deal over with the boys. She and Joe could not see any objections which they might have. In fact, they were willing to bet that they would think the idea was "totally cool," as they might say. Later that night when they returned home that is exactly what the brothers did say. In their minds this was one cool family, and Lizzy was the coolest mom they could have imagined.

The prospect of a very large and stable income appealed to Lizzy. The real estate speculation market was a profitable one, but one never knew when and how much income would come in. There was always budgeting and keeping money aside in case of a long dry period. That would all be history now. Both she and Joe had agreed sometime ago that if they were to find themselves with a large surplus of cash they would reach out to Lizzy's sister Suzanne and her husband, Scott. The downfall of the Madoff Fund and then the Randolph Fund had devastated their fortune. Scott had suffered a nervous breakdown when the Madoff Fund turned out to be a scam. The second huge loss drove him into a mental rehab center for several weeks. When he got out of rehab he returned to his movie deals only to be forced out of several contracts because of his erratic and explosive behavior on the set. As their fortunes began to decline severely Scott came to the startling conclusion that the only way out was to sell the house, the cars, and the other luxuries which he and Suzanne had collected during their brief time at the top of the heap.

A man without a head for money often overlooks some of the basics of finance. When one has a huge mortgage on a $17,000,000 house and sells it, the mortgage company takes the lion's share of the sale price. Scott had not counted on that. The same is true on the most expensive of cars. They are only worth anything after their notes are paid off, so the sale of so much of their prize possessions added up to a very meager sum of just over $100,000. That sum might be fantastic to an average man or woman, but in the face of financial ruin it might be gone in a matter of days. The realization of how far they had fallen caused reactions in Suzanne and Scott which surprised even them. Scott had taken a nasty cocaine habit. Suzanne had begun a secret career of selling her body to fans that were anxious to sleep with Scott Delaney's wife. It was tawdry and unsavory, but such a steamy practice was actually paying most of the bills and keeping the two in rented lodgings at the moment.

Lizzy did not know the half of the predicament that the Delaneys were in, but she had her suspicions. However badly the couple had fallen, Lizzy felt sure that in a very short time she would be at a place where she could play the big sister riding to the rescue. She was unaware not only the depth of their losses but also that fortunes had improved a bit for them. One of Suzanne's paid customers was a die-hard fan of Scott's and used his considerable holdings to produce a new action-adventure movie, in which he insisted Scott Delaney should star. Scott had thus far been able to hold on to himself and put in a decent performance. He still had his coke habit, but so does half of Hollywood. He marshaled himself and managed to come through for the producer and for Suzanne. If the movie had a fair audience they would be back on their feet to a certain degree. If it were a hit, they would back on their way to a lifestyle which they had cherished so dearly. Suzanne made Scott promise that any new wealth would be spent responsibly and carefully, no more high-risk investments and no more Rolls-Royces.

Lizzy phoned Suzanne at the Milford Plaza Hotel in New York, the residence where the production company had put them up during location filming in the city. After making several attempts at reaching her sister, Lizzy decided simply to leave her a message and give her the time and space to contact her when she felt up to it. Lizzy was a concerned and caring sister, but she also knew when to leave a person be, giving the breathing room that they might be needed while at the same time leaving the door open if help was needed. She did not realize it, but Suzanne and Scott were very grateful to know that Lizzy and Joe were there. Right now they needed to try to work things out as best they could on their own. The day would come, hopefully soon, when they would feel confident and comfortable enough to reenter the family; but the time had not yet come.

It had been two days since Joe had mentioned the call from Caudwell Publishing. He had cleared the caller ID on the phone, and he had never found the note he had written with the call's details. Lizzy decided to look up Caudwell Publishing online and find their number before she totally forgot about the message. Phillip Galinowski sounded like a kindly old gentleman as he introduced himself to Lizzy when she was connected to his office. He explained that he was one of the senior vice presidents of Caudwell Publishing and that his call was representing the editorial board of the firm. The Pierce case had made national news. Everyone was well aware of it, but several people at Caudwell had dug deeper and researched the extent to which Lizzy and GreenwichSecrets blog had played the central role in bringing the case to court. The research material had reached the office of the president.

381

She had found the material exciting and appealing, exciting in the way that keeps a person riveted to a story and appealing in the way that sells books, lots of books.

Mrs. Caudwell had called the senior editorial board into a meeting to discuss the possibility of approaching Lizzy to offer her a contract for the rights to her story. Wanting to express their seriousness in making the offer the board had asked Galinowski to do the honors of reaching out to Lizzy. Having been an avid advocate of the idea Phillip jumped at the chance. Secretly, Phillip hoped that if a bargain could be struck he would be allowed to edit the book and maybe even assign himself the task of coauthoring the book with Lizzy. At the age of sixty-two Phillip was an enthusiastic supporter of the Internet and promoted its almost limitless applications in any way he could, despite the fact that he knew that the evolution of the Internet would eventually doom the future of the ink and paper book. Literature would survive, but it would be found on disks and monitors instead of the dried pulp of trees one day soon. Phillip cared more about the words and ideas than the means of their transmittal. He wanted to be a part of the book's future. This was his opportunity.

Lizzy was stunned by the interest being expressed by the Caudwell Company. It had occurred to her often along the way that the Case might one day be the grist for a TV movie, but she never imagined that anyone would be willing to spend long hours reading a step-by-step account of her actions in investigating the Pierce murder. Galinowski assured her that there were many inquisitive minds that would like nothing better than to live vicariously the thrills which she had experienced in her months of playing amateur sleuth. Knowing his business exceptionally well, Phillip warned her that the window of opportunity was not unlimited. If they waited too long the media buzz and public interest in this case would wane. Once that happened such a book would be sent directly to the wholesalers and end up in the $5 book bin at the local Walmart. One must strike while the iron was hot, and he convinced Lizzy that the time was now.

Lizzy made a quick call to Lucy Provence for advice on legal representation with the book deal. Lucy explained that being a specialty lawyer she had very limited knowledge on such matters, but she came up with three names of lawyers who represented literary figures and advised Lizzy to speak to all three. She felt sure that any one of the three would be helpful. It was always better when a lawyer and client clicked, so she should meet and get to know all three before making her selection. It also would not hurt if each of three knew about the other two; a little competition might make a final deal a bit sweeter for Lizzy. Lucy also added that she should try to strike a bargain in which her lawyer would settle for a percentage of the book deal. If the book took off he would be well compensated, but on the outside chance that the book tanked Lizzy would not be socked with outrageous fees that could easily eat up any profit she might gain. Lucy was a clever attorney, and she was also a good friend. Lizzy knew she could trust her advice and knew that she would follow it.

Arrangements were made for a face-to-face meeting between Galinowski and Lizzy for the following Tuesday. The vice president, a company lawyer, and one of the editors would be flying into Westchester Airport at 9:30 a.m. and would rent a car there. They estimated that they would reach the Dawson home at about eleven. That would give them time for introductions, lunch at a restaurant of Lizzy's choosing, and then three or four hours to discuss the contract before they would fly back to Cleveland. Joe, who had been informed of the deal from the very first day, could not contain his excitement at the thought of his wife being the key figure in a murder mystery and asked if he could take a day off and join the meeting with the publishers.

Lizzy kissed him on the cheek as she told him, "Darling, why do you even need to ask? This is our story, and you are as much a part of it as I am."

Joe expected such an answer while admitting to himself that no one was as big a part of this story as his Lizzy. This was her story, and he was happy to be even a small part of it.

Within two days Lizzy had met with all the lawyers recommended by Lucy. She decided that any one of them would be a pleasure to work with, but she found that there was a certain chemistry between Jessica Dillion and herself, so Dillion it would be. The Tuesday meeting went off without a hitch. Lizzy realized that there was a familiar air to Phillip Galinowski which she found very appealing.

It was only after the meeting when Joe made a comment, "That Galinowski fellow reminds me a lot of Sandy Wainwright, paternal, but not the least bit condescending."

That was why she liked him from the first handshake. He did indeed remind her of their now good friend Sanford Wainwright. In her heart she knew that she could trust this total stranger. The sense of familiarity and the fact that he obviously admired her and the work she had done with the Case gave her a reassuring feeling about this. Here she was fresh from signing a book deal and she already had a new friend, a coauthor, and her first fan.

Sunday found the entire Dawson clan in their usual pews at the Anglican Church of the Atonement. Nothing in the world would stop them from church that morning. Each of the Dawsons felt the need to go into God's house and express their thanks to the one who had inspired, protected, and prospered them, individually and as a family. Lizzy pulled Father Redanz aside during the coffee hour, which she had hosted that morning, and told him that the parish could expect a generous gift when the money started to come in from both the Dawson Detective Agency and the forthcoming book sales. Redanz, ever the gentleman, thanked Lizzy with a heartfelt gratitude which brought tears to her eyes. He leaned in toward Lizzy's ear and whispered, "Forget about Freud and Jung, my dear. There is no doubt in my mind that the Lord has shined his light down upon you." He could not have uttered more welcome words to her.

Before they parted Lizzy asked Father Redanz what had been done in the way of a funeral for Jack Randolph. Looking a bit surprised at Lizzy's concern for the departed villain of Randolph Hill, he recounted what he had heard. Jackie Lewis had handled the arrangements when Suzette declined to deal with them. A funeral had been held at Saint Saviour Episcopal Church, modest but elegant, and the attending congregation had been comprised of Jackie and most of household staff, with the addition of a handful of friends and business associates. No family member had attended Jack's funeral service or the committal ceremony at the Randolph family plot. It might be noted that there had been a spray of gladiolas which bore a ribbon containing a single word, "Dad." It had been a sad end to a man who once might have had the entire town mourn him. Lizzy knew that Jack had been an evil man and that one might even say that he had been more evil than good, but still in all, he was a child of the same god who smiled on her, and she felt a deep sadness for him which belied the fact that he had once threatened her life. That was just the kind of soul Lizzy had. She felt pity for a man who had destroyed his own life. A few days later a funerary wreath of delicate lilies appeared on Jack's grave with a sash that simply read, "May God rest your soul."

Being the inquisitive woman that she was, a trait inherited from Great-Aunt Joan, who still enjoyed her feisty life to the fullest, Lizzy decided that she needed to know what had become of Tiffany and the baby. She contacted Emily Engleby and got Harold Gould's home number, which she had misplaced sometime ago. Harold was very happy to hear from Lizzy and immediately asked her if she had heard from Tiffany since the end of the Randolph trial. Lizzy hated to disappoint Mr. Gould but admitted that she was about to ask him the very same question. Gould had not seen or talked to his niece since the trial, and although he was sure that she was more than capable of taking care of herself, he still worried about her and wanted to know how she was faring in her post-Brandywine Ranch life. Lizzy too felt sure that the capable young woman was building a good life for herself in some undisclosed location. She did wonder if she was happy and how she was dealing with the difficult task of being a single mother. A million dollars could certainly give her the security she needed, but even a billion dollars would not buy the happiness that the poor girl desired after the complicated mess her life had been since Bill's death. All Lizzy and Harold could do was hope for the best and wait for a word from Tiffany.

Relaxing one evening Lizzy decided to take a quick look at the comments on her last blog entry made just after the end of the Randolph trial. She was not at all surprised by the hundreds of comments on her posting, but one caught her notice which sparked her interest and gave her a chuckle. It seemed that a local witness from Port Chester had seen a curious scene play out on the street in front of her house the night before Bill Pierce's body had been found nearby. Mrs. Sylvia Rizzo was having a bout of insomnia that fateful night and had noticed two cars pull up several yards from her home. She would not have thought much of it except that one of the cars was a Greenwich Police cruiser. She watched from behind her sheer curtains as someone exited the civilian car, stopping to pull the passenger-side occupant into the driver's seat. The figure then climbed into the backseat of the police car just as it pulled away and headed up the street toward the border.

A series of follow-up comments either elaborated or questioned Mrs. Rizzo's comment. The suggestion made in one of them implied that the Greenwich Police, ever mindful of the safe reputation of their town, had found the car and body of Bill Pierce just inside the Greenwich town line. The responding officers had been ordered to get the car and body out of town. One anonymous tip claiming to be a police officer reported that a watch commander had decided that such a crime had probably been committed in the New York town anyway, so they needed to return the evidence quietly to the likely scene of the crime. Lizzy decided to leave this issue alone, but her curiosity demanded that she would at the very least put in a call to a friend on the Port Chester Police and find out what had actually happened. Her friend told her that the details were sketchy, but he did know that a meeting between their police chief and his counterpart in Greenwich had ended in a screaming match and an office door slammed so hard that it cracked the window pane in the door. Nothing more had been said or done since the incident, and it seemed as if everyone had agreed that what was done was done and should be left alone. The phone call ended with a desperate plea from the office asking Lizzy to just let this lie. With a smile Lizzy assured him that she had no interest in making an issue out of the story. Her future investigations would be the kind you get paid for, and those would be handled by her new agency.

Lizzy wondered if taking on cases not of her choosing would be as interesting and as enjoyable as the work she had done on the Case. Happening upon Suzette and Matthew Finelli in the McDonald's parking lot had been a stroke of luck. She had enjoyed the thrill of following them and eventually finding them at Todd's Point. She feared that when her exciting hobby would become an actual job the adventure of it all would be gone. As she furrowed her brow in consternation over the future the thought occurred to her that her life had rapidly gone from quite ordinary to incredible. She really had no reason to have any disappointments real or imaginary. If the Pierce case were her one and only investigation she would have memories to last a lifetime. Should the future hold only a mundane existence she could always reflect back on the heyday of her first experience of a criminal investigation. As the reality of the good fortune which she had enjoyed sank in, she also knew full well that she would interject the same enthusiasm and adventurous spirit into every case which she undertook. Life was only as good as you make it, and Lizzy knew how to make hers exceptionally good.

Within a week of her meeting with Phillip Galinowski the two of them were sharing daily calls, three- to four-hour calls, calls in which every detail and step of

Lizzy's investigation was discussed, reviewed, and turned into text. Jessica Dillion had worked out a very solid deal with the publishing house. Since they were anxious to get the book written and distributed they had been generous in their negotiations, giving Lizzy a large share of profits from the book as well as provisions to develop the book into a major motion picture or even a television series. As the book took shape Galinowski began to make weekly visits to Greenwich for roundtable discussions with Lizzy and her circle of friends who had in some way participated in the investigation.

At one of these discussions the topic of a possible series or miniseries was on the table when Joe threw out an idea for a series title. It had been meant as a joke, but he offered the title *Murder, She Blogged*, which raised a chorus of laughter among the assembled participants. Everyone had a good laugh, enjoying the pun on the Angela Lansbury series *Murder, She Wrote*.

Phillip laughed as long and as hard as everyone else but then added with a serious note, "I know you were just joking, Joe, but that may be an excellent idea and one which just might catch the attention of a television producer. In the end the name probably would not fly for copyright infringement reasons, but it could do the trick in getting the project notice."

He also mentioned that he and the Caudwell Company had business dealings with HBO and ShowTime, and he would be able to float the idea by some of their executives after the book itself was completed.

"When a project like a book on a current topic gets rolling there is no limit to what can develop. In this case, the 'everyman,' or, should we say, 'everywoman,' nature of the story will have a great mass appeal," explained Phillip.

Did you ever have one of those days? You know the type. A day when you wake up praying for some kind of distraction or diversion from the bullshit which life throws at you. Well, that is exactly the opposite kind of day to those which Lizzy Dawson had been experiencing the past couple of weeks. Life was tossing rose petals in her pathway, and just about every aspect of her life was turning to the positive. Her immediate family, always tight and emotionally healthy, was now also financially sound for the rest of their lives. Troy and Scott were off at school, doing well and dating lovely young ladies who were keeping their boyfriends on the straight and narrow. Lizzy and Joe were as much in love with each other as they had ever been as they tried to settle into a new domestic routine. With the boys off at school they had expected to have more free time and a slower pace to their lives, but things had not worked out that way at all. Their days were now filled with managing an ever-increasing realty business, although these days the repair work on spec houses was being done by hired workmen, instead of the two of them. New constructions had crept into the business as things expanded. The Dawson Detective Agency was building a client base which included some heavy-hitting cases. Even better, they included some heavy-paying cases as well. And the book was coming along so nicely that Caudwell Publishing was seriously considering a series of Lizzy Dawson mysteries.

Lizzy's thoughts went back to the trial and how gravely disappointed she had been at the acquittal of Jack Randolph. At the time it had seemed like the worst case of injustice that she had personally been part of ever in her life. She remembered back in the year 2000 how troubled she had been by the stolen election in the state of Florida and the rage she had felt at the fact that people were complacent to the events even while most recognized the injustice. For a moment she contemplated trying to dig up enough evidence to prove beyond a shadow of a doubt that Jack Randolph was guilty of every accusation lodged against him just for the sake of justice. Then Lizzy considered the way things had turned out in the end. Jack had tragically come to a bad and self-inflicted end. His wife had been humbled. His children had been liberated. Others who had suffered were relieved. Those who were wronged found satisfaction. Things had worked themselves out; and maybe God, the universe, or fate had devised the most just conclusions of all. Lizzy decided she could be happy with that kind of conclusion.

Despite all the business demands on the two of them, Joe and Lizzy still found time for an occasional evening in the chaises beside the pond, listening to the frogs croak, the geese landing in the still waters, and buzz of beautiful dragonflies around them. At moments like these there was little use for words. Hands held and eyes half closed to the setting sun had meaning enough not to be clouded by verbal exchanges. Lizzy could honestly say that life was wonderful. As pleased as she was with the way her life was going, she would honestly tell herself that she was no happier than she was when she and Joe married and struggled to build a life together or when the boys were born or any one of a million blessings which she had had before this entire episode of her life began. If she was happier about any aspect of the present circumstances it had to be about the contentment which her baby sister, Suzanne, and her husband, Scott, were feeling in their new and rehabilitated lives and the fact that, in some small way, justice had been done in giving Bill Pierce the eternal rest which he deserved. Lizzy thought to herself,

God is in his heaven and all is right with the world. So it was for her and those she loved.

Meanwhile across the country in a San Diego hospital, Tiffany Gould was in labor. With the mandatory amount of pushes and deep breaths she was birthing a healthy baby boy. As the head of her son breached the birth canal, the attending physician smiled broadly. The beautiful bald head was now clearly visible, his skin a beautiful creamy tan. "Well, Tiffany, you are the proud mother of a beautiful baby boy. He's got all the right amount of fingers and toes and is one of the most adorable babies I have ever seen! Have you decided on a name for him yet?" asked the doctor.

With a smile tempered by a long and trying labor she informed him, "Yes, I have. He is going to be named after his father and great-grandfather, Evan Lewis III."

A beaming Evan stepped away from his new son cradled in the doctor's arms and went over to Tiffany. Without a word he kissed his wife again and again.

He broke his silence to tell her, "Tiffany, we did good. We did real good."

Evan had taken Jack's money and used as little as possible to get himself moved to San Diego months ago. With the funds he had purchased a share in a swimming pool company, staying in a field he knew well, which had done very well despite the economic hard times. His short affair with Tiffany during one of the Randolphs' visits to the Brandywine Ranch had blossomed into a deep and abiding love between them, so much so that before her stay with Lizzy in Greenwich she had flown to California, and the two were married at a small wedding chapel in Carmel, up the coast from San Diego. With his business flourishing and Tiffany's inheritance from Bill, the new family had purchased a modest house furnished with a brand-new nursery prophetically done in robin's egg blue. All was right with the world for the Lewis family, and for them all the drama had led them to a most happy ending.

The End